'This is the city of R'Frow. You wish to enter. Only one human can enter at this gate at this time. You will be tested. If you succeed, you will enter R'Frow. If you enter R'Frow, you will stay one year. In R'Frow you will be given gems, new weapons, and new teachings. This is the city of R'Frow.'

The Breel shrieked, 'Two hundred six!' and held a stone above her head. It was Ayrys's number.

'Please!' the man begged. 'Sell me your lot! Please!'

Ayrys ducked into the inn for her pack. When she came out, he ran alongside her, so close she felt his breath, fetid, on her cheek. 'Please, artisan, please sell me your lot' Thirty habrins! Forty!'

When Ayrys didn't answer, his tone changed suddenly from a whine to a vicious hiss. 'You don't know what you're risking. You'll never come out alive – never, never! They'll roast you on a spit, they'll drink your blood like warrior-priests, they'll rape you blind, you whore! You'll never come out again. You don't know what you're risking!'

Nancy Kress

AN ALIEN LIGHT

A Legend book
Published by Arrow Books Limited
62–65 Chandos Place, London WC2N 4NW

An imprint of Century Hutchinson Limited

London Melbourne Sydney Auckland
Johannesburg and agencies throughout
the world

First published in legend in 1989 by Century Hutchinson Ltd

This Legend edition 1989

© 1988 Nancy Kress

Phototypeset by Input Typesetting Ltd, London

Printed and bound in Great Britain by
Courier International Ltd, Tiptree, Essex

ISBN 0 09 961990 3

For Jeff Duntemann,
who brought me into the twentieth century,
and for Mary Stanton,
writer, boss, friend

CONTENTS

I
THE CENTRAL PARADOX

All cities are founded on fear
—John Anthony

1

'One,' the Ged said. 'From the third gate.'

'What does it do?'

'It beats on the wall to escape.'

'Already,' the second Ged said, in the grammatical configurations of an observed fact. The two gazed at the wall screen, which showed a small, brightly lit, windowless gray room with a human pounding on the wall. The Ged closed all but his central eye, so high on his forehead that its field of vision extended to the zenith, against the hurtful brightness. His pheromones took on a faint tinge of discomfort, and the first Ged moved closer to him, his own pheromones smelling of sympathy.

'How many now have come inside the perimeter?'

'Five hundred seventy. We will admit thirty more,' the second said, although of course the other already knew it; that was why he had asked. Both voices were low, vaguely growly, almost entirely uninflected. For a moment the first Ged let his pheromones smell of weariness, and the sympathy smell of the other grew stronger.

'This one?'

'Probably not. If he conquers this violent fear and returns to his mind, perhaps. But he has not even taken the gem. His very desire seems to be lost to his violence.'

The human, who wore the drab tebl of a Jelite citizen, sank to the floor and curled into a tight, trembling ball. The Ged watched, each holding back the strong pheromones of distaste out of courtesy to the other. The room

where they stood, inside the double perimeter wall enclos-
ing the empty and waiting 'city,' was lit with the dim,
orangey glow of the Ged sun; it smelled of the good,
methane-based air of Ged; it was a suitable temperature
for the seriousness of this Ged project. But it was not
Ged, and both of them were homesick. They would have
preferred to be on Ged, or else with the Fleet, were they
not needed here. Each smelled the other's homesickness,
one strain of pheromones among all the others, but they
did not speak of it. There was no need. All eighteen Ged
within the perimeter smelled the same.

The first Ged blanked the wall screen, returning the
room to normal light, and the two opened their high
central eyes. Although it had evolved to sight formidable
dominant predators extinct for thousands of millennia and
so was now mostly useless, there was still a feeling of
discomfort when the central eye was closed. The Ged faces
– bilaterally symmetrical, hairless, humanoid except for
the three eyes and a lack of subcutaneous muscle – showed
no expression. That had been one of the hardest things
to grasp during the year spent observing humans outside
the perimeter wall: that the grotesque distortions of the
human facial muscles carried information. It had been
hard for even the Library-Mind, which had taken much
longer to find that pattern than the patterns of the language. The Ged had not expected the sophistication of pheromones, but neither had they expected muscle spasms.
No other sentient race, anywhere, conveyed information
by muscle spasms.

One more bewildering difference.

'Significant data,' the Library-Mind growled softly.
Both Ged turned to listen. 'Significant data, Level Three.
Biology confirms that all humans are indeed of the same
species. Central paradox is not resolved by multispecies
explanation.' The Library-Mind offered the last two
words in the configurations of an explanation discovered
to be contrary to fact.

The first Ged hummed softly in exasperation. The other courteously stroked his companion's back and legs, radiating the pheromones of comfort.

'It would have at least explained their violence to each other!' the first Ged said.

'Yes. Harmony sings with us.'

'Harmony sings with us.'

'May it always sing.'

'It will always sing. We are no closer to an answer than we were, Grax.'

'No. Perhaps when the humans come inside.'

The first Ged glanced at the darkened wall screen. The other did the same. In both minds ran the same thoughts – not because they shared mind, as some species did, but because the thoughts were the ones that all Ged, genetically similar and so capable of intelligent civilization, would have in this situation. They smelled each other's pheromones and they thought of Ged, they thought of defending their home, they thought of the Fleet, they thought of the importance of resolving the Central Paradox.

They thought of time running out.

2

Between its banks the river was rising, a dark rush of water moving in two directions at once. A Firstnight breeze carried the scent of mountain water to Ayrys, motionless beside her fire. Built on a wide, bare shelf of rock between the river and the upland veld, the fire could easily be spotted from the surrounding hills, a beacon in the deepening gloom. Such a fire for a lone, inept traveler was stupidity, or defiance, or both. Ayrys no longer cared.

A knife, which she did not know how to use, lay on the rock beside her, along with a lumpy bottle of blue glass. Small Moon had risen, veiling the veld in cold white light. The vast stirrings of the veld as threenight began, which a few hours ago had sent her scurrying wide-eyed for the safety of the barren rock ledge, seemed to have finally ended. What next? Town-bred, she didn't know. Dusk had been bizarre enough.

Just beyond the rock ledge, a huge kemburi plant, which had sprawled quietly soaking up sunshine all three-day, had snaked vast spongy tendrils into a dense ball against the coming cold One tendril had curled around some small, ragged-eared animal Ayrys could not identify, a small pocket of moving heat, and drawn it inward; the animal had screamed only once.

Beyond the kemburi, spikebushes had fired sudden, sharp, spore-carrying thorns onto the scrubby grass. Small, hectic wildflowers, having grown feverishly in the glare from Firstmorning to Lastlight, just as quickly

folded bright petals under spiny outer leaves. Something
unseen sprayed pungent moldy scent onto the wind, and
something else unseen had responded with quick crackling
of twigs. The whole veld had folded in on itself against
the night, a dull green spiny skin crawling over the rock
beneath, and once those heaving vegetable hours had
begun, no animal howled or moved.

They were moving again now.

Wearily, Ayrys moved from the fire to the riverbank,
knelt, and thrust her hand downward to grope for the
blobs of clay she had stuck under the overhand of rock.
Both blobs were still there; the river, then, was not rising
as fast as she had feared. It would not flood – at least, not
this portion of it – until the threenight had passed. She
could wait here, if she chose, until Firstmorning.

Why should she wait? In a few more hours, Big Moon
would rise, providing enough light to walk; there was no
reason to wait. There was no reason not to wait.

Embry . . .

Eyes squeezed shut, hand still cleaving the cold water,
Ayrys waited out this fresh rush of pain. It would pass –
that she had already learned in her three days of exile. It
always passed. She dug the nails of one hand into the
wrist of the other and waited.

The fire had burned low. Ayrys rebuilt it, skillfully
feeding in bits of grass and twig, making the most of each
scrap and conserving the rest. A pile of woody scrub lay
beside another pile of the long, fork-tipped grass that
inexplicably grew in some places on the veld and not in
others. A good fire builder, she thought derisively – all
glassblowers were good fire builders. It was the first thing
she had done well in her stumbling exile from Delysia.

When the fire again blazed brightly, Ayrys squatted on
her haunches and stared into it. Firelight slid over the
curves of the blue bottle. On the dark veld the grass
rustled, smelling of thornbush and some sharp, thin reek
Ayrys couldn't identify. Beyond the veld stretched more

veld, always sloping downward, till somewhere three days behind her lay the wide valley sloping to the sea. And Delysia. And Jela. And ahead, higher in the mountains . . .

Something with four wings and a huge, bobbing head flew an arm's length above her head. In the distance a kreedog, night-prowling and vicious, howled at the cold moon.

A sound like jaws snapping, and then a scream.

Ayrys rolled from her blanket and scrambled to her feet. For a sickening moment, not fully awake, she didn't know where she was, or why. The scream rose again, something flashed white in the gloom just beyond the rocky ledge, and Ayrys sprinted forward. Halfway to the kemburi, her mind, coming from farther away, caught up to her muscles. The scream hadn't sounded the high pitch of fear; it was something else.

The kemburi, hidden in waist-high grass, had sensed heat and opened its ropy vines. Encircled by gray-green coils near the rock ledge, a woman fought.

She slashed at the plant with her knife and screamed again, a cry high enough to hurt eardrums and with enough relish in it to stop Ayrys short, disbelieving: The woman was *enjoying* her battle with the kemburi! Two thick, spongy vines held her left leg, while more of the coils crept toward her. Slowed by the night cold, the bulk of the kemburi moved slowly as it shifted toward the warmth of the woman's body. It would not shift in time; already the prey had severed one coil and begun on the other with a warrior's practiced blows.

Warrior – she was a Jelite sister-warrior.

Ayrys tightened her grip on the knife that she had snatched up, without looking, in her half-sleep. But her grogginess had betrayed her; she held in her hand not the knife but the blue glass bottle.

A fierce slash severed the second vine. The Jelite's crossbow lay strapped uselessly to her back, but she didn't need the crossbow to win this battle. With the same motion that cut her free of the second vine, the woman turned toward Ayrys, swinging her face into the moonlight. She was Jelite and she was smiling, a smile of bared, bone-white teeth. She stepped forward.

'Delysian,' she said softly. 'Now you, Delysian. Now you.'

Something in Ayrys snapped. *Delysian* – she was going to die for being Delysian, just after Delysia had disowned her, torn her from her daughter, banished her to die on the veld. It was too much, too balanced; the last three days had been too much as balance teetered wildly and everything she thought she knew about the city that bred her had blown itself into fragments. Heretic, traitor, threat to the minds of Delysian children, including her own – and now she was going to die for being a *Delysian*. She! Reason collapsed and Ayrys covered her face with her hands and laughed, great howling sobs of laughter tearing up from belly and throat in shrieks and yowls, whooping and choking on shards of laughter. '*Now you, Delysian.*' Delysian!

The Jelite woman frowned, hesitated – this was clearly not the reaction she had expected. In the moment of hesitation, the second kemburi struck. It lay upriver from the first, hidden in the grass; the Jelite's fighting had moved her warm body toward it. Two coils as thick as wrists closed around her thigh, then another, and another. The woman faced Ayrys, not the kemburi, and she was both caught off guard and positioned badly to fight. But her reflexes were superb. In a moment she had twisted and begun to slash, warding off coils that reached for her knife arm, shrieking her battle yell as if it, too, were a weapon.

Ayrys, as repelled by her own savage laughter – *if I go on like this, I will go mad* – as by the fighting, shrank back onto the safety of the rocky ledge.

The Jelite slashed and yelled. She struck two ropes from her right leg while another snaked around her left ankle. To sever that one, she would have to bend, which would bring her striking arm too close to the coils that writhed in the grass. Instead she threw all her strength into straining backward, stretching the vine to weaken its grip, trying to edge off the veld and onto the ledge. But she had miscalculated. While her attention had been on Ayrys, the first kemburi, further aroused by the body warmth, had shifted toward her, and her straining backward once more brought her within its reach. A massive coil, gray hairs abruptly silver in the moonlight, wrapped itself around her hips.

The Jelite stopped fighting. Her face, tipped to the light, was etched in white shock, each line as pure and hard as glass. Only a moment, and then she was battling again, evading more coils, slashing with power and precision, her superb reflexes keeping both striking arm and face protected from the coils that sought their heat. Only a moment, but Ayrys had recognized that moment's glass shock – *this cannot come to me* – in her own belly and spine. Nausea, cold, the quick black sweep of faintness – but, no, that had been *her* moment three days ago; this was the other's. But by the time her dazed mind separated the two moments, her arm had swung, as it had not dared swing three days ago, to hurl her knife at her attackers.

Blue glass spun from her arm toward the kemburi.

The bottle, slim at the stopper and wide at the base, arced erratically, struck a rock, and exploded into blue shards and clear liquid. The sharp odor of acid filled the air. The kemburi screamed, a single unanimal note of gases hissing outward to blow off the burning acid, and released the Jelite. She sprang onto the rocky ledge, caught Ayrys around the waist, and rolled with her toward the river, out of range, as the kemburi in its agony sent coils thrashing and writhing in all directions. The kemburi screamed again and then, having blown off as much of the acid as it could, drew its shuddering and burned vines into its central mass. Within moments it had vanished into the grass.

A bottleneck of blue glass rolled out onto the rocky ledge.

Ayrys lay dazed. The Jelite sprang away. When Ayrys finally sat, staring at the shadowy line where veld met rock, the Jelite stood on the other side of the fire, Ayrys's knife in her hand. She stared at the knife incredulously; when she raised her eyes to Ayrys, the incredulity still shone in them, and Ayrys suddenly saw how young she was.

'This is a *carving* knife!'

Ayrys said nothing.

'A *carving* knife, Delysian. What did you hope to do with a carving knife?'

The howling, horrifying laughter, sour as bile, licked again at Ayrys's mind.

'I asked you what you hoped to do with a carving knife!'

'Carve,' Ayrys said, and pushed away the awful laughter, and resisted the impulse to put her hands to her ears. The bottle had been fired only a tencycle ago: Embry's small hand excitedly pulling at the cooling tray, tracing the curve of rough blue glass with one satisfied dirty finger, showing off the childish design to the other women in the glassyard. And she, Ayrys, had smashed Embry's bottle. In stupid panic, and to the benefit of a Jelite sister-warrior who, Ayrys now saw, was mistaking Ayrys's bitter self-mockery for bravery.

Across the fire, the two women studied each other.

The Jelite was much younger – was in fact little more than a girl; her skills as a warrior must be formidable for her to already wear the embroidered tebl. She was beautiful. Smooth black braids coiled into a warrior's knot at the back of her head; long slim neck; dark Jelite eyes; and the effortless vitality of a superb athlete superbly trained.

'What did you throw at the kemburi?' she demanded.

Ayrys looked toward the veld. The blue bottleneck, still stoppered, lay at the edge of the stone. She inched toward it, picked it up, and turned it over and over in her hands. A few drops of acid burned her fingers.

'I asked you what the bottle held!'

'Acid. To mix with copper paint,' Ayrys said; she scarcely heard herself. 'It gives the paint a better flow, and a better bite on the glass. . . .'

'You are a maker of glass?'

'I was.' At the contempt in the Jelite's voice, Ayrys looked up. 'Fortunately for you. The acid burns plants as well as fingers.'

The girl flushed irritably and moved closer to Ayrys, who stood, tightened her grip on the bottleneck, and said, 'Be careful. Now I am armed.'

'With that? Against *me?*' the Jelite said, outraged. 'Sit down!'

Ayrys sat. The girl squatted nearby, poised lightly on both heels, intensity radiating from her like heat from a kiln.

'Delysian. Why did you save my life?'

Ayrys. Why do you endanger your child's life? The tone was the same: the circle of accusing men, city fathers of Delysia standing in the brilliant multicolored light from the council windows of Ayrys's own mother had once painted, and the Jelite sister-warrior, squatting in the chill gloom on bare rock. The same tone. The mirthless laughter pushed up against her yet again, and Ayrys almost opened herself to it, gave in, let her reason go – and with it, most probably, her life. Did it matter if she died at the hand of this girl, or from cold and exposure on the veld? Let the laughter come.

But, bleakly, it didn't. Apparently she was choosing to live. 'Does it matter why I saved your life? I did.'

The girl's black eyes glittered, waiting.

'I saved your life. Now we stand on the same blade of honor.'

The girl sputtered at what must, to a Jelite, seem blasphemy. How did she, Ayrys, get so skilled at blasphemy? She?

The Jelite said, 'The warriors' code does not extend to Delysians!'

'Doesn't it? Then it isn't a code of true honor.'

'A Delysian talks of honor?' The girl spat dramatically – and a little ridiculously – into the fire. An ember smoked.

'Our cities are not at war. At this moment. Therefore, we stand on the same blade. What is freely given must be freely returned.'

The Jelite studied her narrowly. Ayrys made herself see with the girl's eyes: a Delysian citizen, not even a soldier; dirty despite the cold river; Delysia and Jela at war three years ago, uneasy allies this year, war already again in the wind for next year. And against that, only the girl's youthful trust in the exaggerated simplicities of a warrior's honor. She would not do it. She would find it easier to kill Ayrys and be done with her.

Ayrys's fingers tightened on the neck of Embry's bottle.

The girl swore, a vivid flow of warrior's curses, and then spoke as if the words were carrion in her mouth. 'You claim the blade of honor?'

'I have saved your life.'

'You haven't said why!'

'Honor does not require that I say why.'

'You know too much about warriors, Delysian!'

She was going to do it; she was going to acknowledge the claim of honor. Not until Ayrys became sure did she feel her own fear, and then it was a crawling thing, slimy at the back of her throat. Had she not thrown the bottle, had her glassyard not traded enough with Jela to learn its warriors' convoluted ideas of honor, had the Jelite been older, or been male . . .

' "We stand on the same blade," ' the girl snarled,

hatred in every word of the formal oath, ' "bound in–"
Stand up, Delysian whore! "We stand on the same blade,
bound in the honor of life itself. What is freely given must
be freely returned. None but children may accept as a
right the strength of others without return, lest it weaken
their own strength and they become cripples in life. None
may choose to offer their own strength in bargain, lest
they put life at the service of clay. What is freely given
must be freely returned." '

'Now name your return, you shit-licking kreedog!'

Ayrys thought swiftly. 'Your protection for one cycle
of traveling. This threenight and next threeday. Then the
claim of honor will have been met.'

The Jelite scowled. She was free to refuse the offer; the
oath bound her only to save Ayrys's life once, as Ayrys
had saved hers. But that would mean she would stand on
the blade of honor with Ayrys until such an occasion
arose, and plainly she hated the idea. Ayrys had learned
from the furtive inter-city trading, which nothing short of
actual war seemed to stop, of warriors' alternate offers of
settlement for claims of honor. Without them, the cross-
ings and recrossings of loyalties for various claims of honor
would have become a web too dense to unravel. She had
never heard of a Jelite warrior who had not fulfilled a
claim of honor. They died first – or perhaps they were
killed by their own fierce, unbending kind. If so, not even
their own citizens, considered not good enough for any
warrior to even bed, ever heard of it. *'Jela for loyalty,
Delysia for treachery'* ran a Jelite proverb quoted even in
Delysia itself. Ayrys thought of the city council, and her
mouth twisted.

'I accept your return,' the girl said sourly. 'Where do
you travel?'

'To the Gray Wall.'

The Jelite's chin jerked upward. 'Why?'

'I don't choose to tell you that.'

The girl scowled. 'As you choose. But you don't think they'll take *you* behind the Gray Wall?'

Ayrys stared at her. Slowly she said, 'You're going there, too. To the Wall.'

'They accept only warriors and soldiers, Delysian.'

Ayrys had not heard that. Rumor, counterrumor, denial – Delysia boiled with conflicting stories about the Gray Wall, mixed and heated with conflicting stories of another war with Jela. Delysians did not like to leave the city to verify the rumors; better use of them could be made unverified. But she had not heard that only warriors and soldiers were admitted behind the Gray Wall. If it was true . . .

If it was true, she would have no place at all left to go.

'I don't care where you choose to be denied,' the Jelite said. 'The return has been accepted. My protection until we reach the Gray Wall. It won't take a whole cycle – only a flabby Delysian citizen would think so. We sleep now and travel through Darkday, or as much of it as you can stand up for, and reach the Wall by the end of Firstmorning. Or during Lightsleep at the latest. But I don't rest by fires that attract any scum on the veld, and I don't make camp with whores. I'll protect you, Delysian, but you sleep and walk alone. If you need me, call.'

'Wait – what do I call? What's your name?'

'Jehane. What other weapons do you carry in your pack?'

'None.'

Jehane snorted. 'Unarmed and alone on the veld?'

'Yes!'

'Then why so loud a denial? I need a better knife than this one.'

She reached for Ayrys's pack. There was nothing Ayrys could do. She couldn't get to the pack first, couldn't . . . what? Throw it into the river before the sister-warrior opened it? Helplessly she watched while Jehane searched for the weapon that was not there, and watched while

Jehane's hand closed and drew an object into the moon-light. The Jelite gasped.

It was a sculpture of glass, a double helix half-blue and half-red, the two spirals joined by a curving ladder whose rungs, spaced not evenly but with some pattern by their own, shaded from blue to indigo through purple to magenta to red. Moonlight gleamed dully on the heavy glass. Against that watery light, the helix shone in balanced precision, curves balanced by straight lines, the lure to the cradling hand subtly balanced by some mysterious pull on the mind, as of a pattern glimpsed but not understood. The glass was without flaw, but some markings or light shifted between the walls of both spirals and made them seem more than glass, as if they curved of themselves and the breath that had blown them was their own and not the glassmaker's.

Jehane stared, stupefied, across the fire at Ayrys. 'You dared to make . . . *you* . . .'

The city council had asked her the same question, and with the same outrage. 'Yes,' Ayrys said.

'You – a *Delysian?*'

Ayrys closed her eyes. 'Yes.'

'*Why?*'

'Because it is beautiful.'

'Beautiful! It's the emblem of rank of a Jelite warrior-priest. Did you know that when you cast it? Did you?'

'It is not cast. The glass is blown.'

'Blown! You put your mouth . . .'

So had the council looked. Stupid, they were all stupid. How could people be so stupid?

That stupidity had lost her Embry.

'You dared to–' Jehane said, and stopped, stifled by her own outrage. She had tightened her grip on Ayrys's carving knife. Ayrys saw the girl's murderous face reflected over and over again in the curved sections of glass, distortion upon distortion.

'Delysia and Jela are not at war. What does it matter what emblems artisans make?'

'We will be at war again. As soon as your city breaks the alliance!'

It was probably true. It had always been true before. The fertile land along the coast shared by both cities was not quite enough to support them both, and growing crops on the higher ground of the veld was more trouble than arranging for Jela to have fewer mouths to grow crops for. Crops, game, fish, timber – *Jela for loyalty, Delysia for treachery. . . .*

'I made the helix,' Ayrys said deliberately, 'because it is beautiful. And because I knew how to make it. And because if the legend your priests tell should happen to be true–'

'How do you know what legend our priests tell!'

'–should happen to be true, and both Jela and Delysia were built by people who escaped in the same boat from the Island of the Dead, then your daughter and my daughter share motherlines. And because even if they do not, and even if the cities are enemies until the end of time itself, no city can own a shape made of matter and air. It is a *shape*, Jehane – look at it. A shape of glass. Not the object of fear and respect you make of it, just a shape–'

'No more!' the girl yelled. With all her strength she threw the double helix to the ground and brought her boot heel, metal sheathed with leather, down hard on the fragments. The glass first shattered and then crunched. Jehane did not stop grinding her heel until the sculpture was a smear of powder on the stone.

'I sleep within call,' Jehane said. 'Don't try to sneak up to me, Delysian, I sleep light.' Without glancing down, she stalked into the darkness.

Ayrys sank to her knees and touched the powdered glass with one finger. A few grains stuck. Closing her eyes, Ayrys dragged her finger across the stone, pressing down as hard as she could. When she opened her eyes, blood smeared the rock and her finger was embedded with ground glass. Viciously she dragged another finger across the glass, and then a third.

When she forced the heel of her thumb across the glass, a sharper pain leaped the whole length of her arm, so that for a moment she could not even see.

For a long moment Ayrys crouched on the rock, head bent, blinded by pain. When it had subsided a little, she rose and thrust the hand into the river, holding it there until the cold had numbed it completely, and then a long time afterward.

With her left hand she built up the fire and pulled her burnous around herself. Her right hand lost the cold of the water and began to hurt agonizingly. Ayrys laid it outside her bedroll, on the hard stone. With the pain of the mind thus dwarfed by the pain of the flesh, and for the first time since she had been pushed, hooded and booted and without Embry, through the east gate of Delysia, she was able to sleep without dreams.

3

The Delysian woman slept through all of Firstnight. She didn't wake to tend her fire, she didn't wake to as much as sniff the *air*, Jehane thought with disgust. From the moment the slug rolled in her blanket until the moment Jehane kicked her awake, she lay like a stone, blind as a stone to the kreedog that had slavered near, or to the new height of the river rising.

Were they all like that, the Delysians? Couldn't be, Jehane argued with herself, or in the last war – in which Jehane had been too young to fight – Jela would not have been forced into alliance instead of victory. *Some* Delysians must be skilled fighters. But of course this one was scum, blasphemy, a citizen outcast by even her own people. A Jelite warrior, in such an unthinkable position, would have killed herself. Pride – the Delysians had no pride. And such a thing she, Jehane, had bound herself to protect! An exile, a glassblower, a free-rutting bladder-muscled slug who snored on the open veld from Firstnight to Darkday, and would have gone right on snoring through Darkday if Jehane hadn't woken her.

Jehane had spent the long hours of Firstnight in four light sleeps. Between them she had driven off the kreedog, kept sentry net over a large semicircle backed by the river, retrieved her knife from beside the kemburi, now tightly sealed by its own warmth-preserving juices and so harmless. She had tested her weapons – knife and crossbow – and pitted her muscles against each other in a warrior's

motionless exercises. The periodic activity kept her body
supple against the creeping cold as Qom made its slow
turn away from the sun. With a warrior's disciplined
timing, she rose from her last short sleep just as the
bright twin stars of the Marker rose above the horizon and
signaled the start of Darkday. Jehane splashed her face
and arms in the icy river, scattered all signs of her camp,
and went to wake the Delysian slug.

Fauggh, but it smelled! Jehane couldn't remember
hearing that Delysian women didn't bathe, but apparently
this one had not for several days. She lay heavily asleep,
her scent enough to attract every kreedog on the veld. If
Jehane hadn't thought the thing would drown, she would
have thrown it in the river before breakfast.

'Delysian. Wake up. It's Darkday.'

No response. An enemy could have cut off this woman's
legs before she knew they were missing.

'Get up!' Jehane kicked her, not gently.

The woman moaned softly, sat up, and blinked, as if
the light from the stars and the two moons were bright
day. Her face was white, her movements stiff. Jehane had
been right: a slug, with a slug's stupidity. Jehane had had
hours to think over last night; it was possible that the
Delysian's saving of Jehane's life had been not battle but
stupidity. Why else would she destroy the bottle of acid
she needed to make her miserable citizen's living? Stupidity. And she smelled.

Then she threw off her blanket, and Jehane saw her
palm.

'What happened to your hand?'

'I cut it,' the woman said levelly.

'*Cut* it? Across all five fingers like that? It looks like
ground meat!'

The slug said nothing. Jehane said, 'You did it yourself.
You ruined your right hand. The thumb—'

'Does that concern you?'

'Ruin what you want,' Jehane said contemptuously.

Crazy – the woman was not only stupid but crazy. Jehane stood on the blade of honor with a stupid, helpless, crazy woman who didn't even have an animal's respect for its own body, and Jehane had bound herself to protect this kreedung all the way to the Gray Wall on what was supposed to be her, Jehane's, First Proving. The taste of it was bitter.

'Eat and be ready to march.'

The Delysian unwrapped food from her pack. Apparently she was not going to wash before breakfast. Cold air, the particularly cold air of a cloudless Darkday, stirred her hair. The woman shivered violently. In her matted hair was some sort of dust, some powder probably used in her glassmaking. She stared at her food.

'I can't eat it. Do you want some?'

Surprised, Jehane glanced at the stores. Graincake, fresh dahafruit, salted fish – ridiculously bulky foods for a veld journey; but then, the Delysian was too stupid to have thought of that. Jehane carried only dried fruit and meat. The graincake was laced with red; sometimes Delysians put sugar in their graincakes. Jehane's mouth filled with sweet liquid.

'You might as well take it. I can't eat.'

'That's stupid. You'll have even less strength to march than you do now.'

'I will manage.'

'We march all of Darkday. No sleeping like a stone.'

'I said I will manage. And the Gray Wall isn't moving anywhere. It's been there for nearly a year, it will still be there if we arrive one day later.'

Jehane's lip curled. *Sluggish*. Shivering, wounded, and her white face set in that closed, strained look – she would never last through Darkday.

'Take some graincake, Jehane.'

'I want none of your food, Delysian. And if you collapse on yourself while we march, I'll leave you. Not even the blade of honor demands that I protect you from yourself.'

'I'm not going to collapse on myself,' the woman said, and smiled so mockingly that Jehane was startled. What was there in the warning to make the slug look like that? No one could understand the mind of a Delysian; they were too devious. At least she, Jehane, would not have to walk near enough to smell her. Fauggh!

Nor did she. The two women kept to the river, cutting across sections of veld only when the banks became too steep or overgrown for travel, or when Jehane decided on a more direct route than following a great loop in the river. In the cold night the veld lay both still and alive, thornbushes and kemburi and the lush, spiny daha all motionless dark shapes outlined with starlight. The animal life stayed mostly unseen except for a quick rustling of grasses, a distinct cry. Once they came upon a katl, that strange, symmetrical mass of hard green that grew in straight lines of crystalline rock but drank in water and light, and which not even the warrior-priests could name either plant or mineral. Jehane gave it wide berth.

Ahead, dark mountains sliced across the starry half of the sky, blotting out part of the Scimitar, the edge of the Sign Wave. Kufa shone dull red, nearly alone in its part of the sky. Between its banks the black water of the river rushed and murmured, until in one quiet, unexpected pool it shone like dark glass reflecting the twin silver lights of the Marker.

Jehane kept no fixed position. She traveled sometimes ahead of Ayrys, sometimes behind, sometimes alongside, with Ayrys between her and the river. Once she materialized at Ayrys's side and loosed her crossbow. A solid thump, a howl of pain, and something ran yelping through the grass.

Jehane smiled. 'Kreedog.'

The Delysian only stared at her with big, exhausted eyes.

She was as bad as Jehane had feared. She crashed

through immature kif and released their noxious smell, plodded with her head down along level stone, stumbled over air. She never even glimpsed the kreedog set to attack her until after Jehane had shot it.

That was a saving of the slug's life; *that* would have released her from the blade of honor, had she not sworn to protect the bladder-muscled carrion all the way to the Gray Wall. Fauggh!

When the Marker stood nearly halfway up the sky, Jehane again materialized beside Ayrys. 'We rest now.'

'Now?' Ayrys spoke dully, swaying with exhaustion.

'Now. If you need to sleep again, do it now while your muscles are warm – or as warm as yours are likely to get. If you sleep later, you'll freeze. And eat something.'

The Delysian did not move. Jehane saw that her words meant nothing; the slug was too worn out with simple walking to understand. Cursing, she built a fire – she had hoped to avoid a fire – thrust the Delysian before it, and yanked open her pack. 'That graincake – eat it all!'

Ayrys ate. Before she had finished, she was asleep. Jehane wrapped the Delysian's burnous around her – she, Jehane, could have survived without one, if she had to. That, the training masters taught, was the mark of a warrior: how much was not needed to survive. Not that the slug could have understood that.

Jehane finished her food and sat with her back to a tree to keep watch. This was Qom's darkest hour, halfway through Darkday, but not its coldest. The masters had tried to teach Jehane, who had not been a quick pupil, how all of Qom turned around on itself. Laboriously, and only because she would be beaten otherwise, she had mastered the strange idea of Qom rotating and the sun staying still. Then the Masters told her the even stranger idea that this turning produced one cycle: sixteen hours for Firstmorning, four for Lightsleep, sixteen for Last-

light, and then ten hours for Firstnight, sixteen for Darkday, ten for Thirdnight.

But that knowledge – essentially useless; cycles passed
whether you understood them or not, so it didn't matter
why – had not been enough to answer the one original
question she had ever asked. If the cold comes because
Qom faces away from the sun, demanded the child Jehane,
and if Darkday faces away the most, then why is Thirdnight and not Darkday the coldest? The masters had not
known. That, they said, was just the way it was. Such
words had been exactly Jehane's feeling about the matter
of rotation, and thereafter she stopped struggling with
the masters' useless explanations and took their beating
instead.

The welts still lay on the backs of her legs, accepted
without resentment but with a certain contempt. The
masters who taught weapons she obeyed scrupulously;
that could save your life in battle. But to waste all your
life after your Cadre Leaving with this bloodless stuff!
Better, even, to mate with a brother-warrior and become
a mother to warriors, or to become a designer of weapons
that could, unlike this drivel about rotation, at least be
touched.

Jelite scouts had said that the Gray Wall could not be
touched.

Jehane scowled into the darkness. That had to be non-
sense – how could a wall not be touched? A wall was a
wall, solid, or it would keep nothing out, or nothing in.
But Jelite scouts were not Delysians; they did not lie.

That question led to all the others about the Wall, all
the guesses and conjectures, based on the scouts' scanty
reports. What if the conjectures were true? It didn't
matter if they were true; all that mattered was that there
were new weapons there, weapons that would arm Jela as
she had never been armed before. Weapons, and danger.
On that, all the reports agreed.

Jehane pushed away the confusion about the Wall.

Better to think first about reaching it. The Delysian could not be allowed to sleep much longer – only a slug would need to sleep in the middle of Darkday, after sleeping ten hours in Firstnight – or she would freeze. The Marker climbed up the glittering sky. Still, better she should sleep now than in the deeper cold of Thirdnight.

The last time Jehane had passed a cycle on the veld, she had been in training, and her sisters not on the sentry net had slept close to her for warmth. Now Jamisu had been picked by a cadre, and what were Nahid and Aisha doing? Pretty Aisha . . .

That confusion, too, Jehane pushed aside. Her task was to reach the Gray Wall and enter it. That was the way it was.

By Thirdnight, the cold penetrated to their bones. Clouds blew in from the lowlands. Clouds earlier, at Lastlight, would have warmed the threenight, but clouds now only obscured the stars. The land became wilder, shot with ravines and outcroppings of rock, as the veld rose toward the inland mountains. Cold and darkness and the terrain made travel impossible.

'We'll make a fire,' Jehane said.

Ayrys said nothing; beneath the hood of her burnous, her teeth chattered too violently for words.

Jehane would not let them sleep. She heated water on the fire, river water that burned their hand with cold when they dipped it and their throats with heat when they forced themselves to drink it. The water made them urinate, an agonizing exposure to the cold. Periodically Jehane hauled Ayrys roughly to her feet and made her run in place. Ayrys winded easily; the great gasps of air she took in made her lungs ache and her bones rattle.

Kreedogs howled nearer. Jehane built up the fire with one hand on her crossbow. When Jehane made them eat, Ayrys silently pushed graincake toward her, Jehane ignored it.

'P-p-payment,' Ayrys said. 'C-consider it p-p-payment.'

Jehane grimaced in contempt. 'Payment is for b-b-buyers and sellers.'

'What else are w-w-we?'

Jehane's hand tightened on her crossbow. 'Say that again, D-delysian, and I will k-k-kill you. A warrior's p-protection is not b-bought. Except perhaps in Delysia, w-w-where everything is for sale!'

'N-n-not q-q-quite everything,' Ayrys got out. She covered her face with her hands and shook with what looked to Jehane like more of that weird howling laughter.

Crazy. The slug was crazy.

Despite the running in place, Jehane could no longer feel her feet in their leather boots. Now the western sky had cleared. The Markers had passed the zenith long ago, what seemed like days ago. But still the Marker was not far enough down the sky for Firstmorning. She had never seen them set; Firstmorning always washed them out. 'Can one see the Marker set?' was a proverb for uselessness in Jela – and, she had once heard, in Delysia as well. How could that be, a Jelite proverb in Delysia? Probably they stole it.

She did not want to freeze to death beside a Delysian.

The kreedogs would not care from which city came their carrion.

'W-w-wake up!' Jehane said, and kicked Ayrys. Ayrys stirred and moaned, shuddering violently. Jehane stood to haul her to her feet, and felt the air stir against her cheek. Through her own shivering and teeth-chattering, hope pierced her. The winds were starting.

They would be severe; they always were when the night had been still. But Jehane would welcome their rawness, for when the winds began it was almost dawn. She had deliberately built their fire on the leeward side of the boulder. The wind was the last test, the final quarrel the veld could loose at the jelly-armed dung that was Jehane's responsibility.

'W-w-wake up!'

Finally, clouds lightened in the east. The Marker paled, then disappeared.

Exultation filled Jehane. *She had done it.* She had survived on the veld without her training sisters, she had not lost the Delysian slug to its own weakness, she had kept upright on the blade of honor.

And when the sun rose, its light glinted off the Gray Wall.

It stood a few hours' march from them, yet clearly visible as a huge shining rectangle set high on a hill. *Wanting to be seen.* Jehane thought approvingly. And why not? A battlefield challenge always showed itself.

'Look at the breadth of it,' the Delysian said. 'Even from this distance.'

'Natural rock,' Jehane said, before she knew she had spoken aloud.

'No. It's not.'

Jehane said scornfully. 'What else could it be but rock?'

'Look how much light it reflects, and how evenly. That's not rock.'

'Afraid, Delysian?'

'Yes. Of course.'

The quietness of the answer caught Jehane off guard. She frowned, squinting at the distant fortress. Her midriff tightened, a quick pull of muscles and flesh. So did the old stories say the Island of the Dead looked – a gray, dissolving pile of shining death. . . .

'If you talked with your own scouts,' the Delysian went on, 'you must have known it's not rock. Even in Delysia rumor says–'

'Shut up. See that hill, where the Gray Wall stands? At the base of it, my protection of you ends. The blade of honor finishes. At the base of the hill, I'm done with you, and what happens to you after that doesn't concern me.'

The Delysian didn't answer. She stood, filthy and shivering, her hand raised to shade her eyes from the rising sun, studying the rocky land between the slight rise where they stood and the Wall. Jehane had started down the rise before she heard the woman say quietly, 'Nor me, either,' but that was too stupid. She must have heard wrong. Even a Delysian – even as stupid and bladder-brained a Delysian as this one – must care what happened to herself. They could not have *that* little loyalty to themselves.

No matter how they stank.

4

The Gray Wall was farther away than it looked. Four hours into Firstmorning, the women had not yet reached it. Ayrys's muscles ached from the unaccustomed exercise, although the steadily increasing warmth of the sun soothed them slightly. Around her, kemburi plants uncurled and sent vines creeping across the veld, soaking up sunshine, as harmless now to walk on as grass. Wildflowers unfolded for their three-day bloom and turned blind centers toward the sun. Dahafruit glistened purple, ripening fast. The river sparkled in the light.

'Wait,' Ayrys said.

'You can eat after I'm rid of you. Move.'

'I don't want to eat, I want to bathe. We leave the river soon. There's a calm pool over there by those trees, and I want to wash before we go on.'

The Jelite was staring at her in surprise – why? Was bathing such an outrageous idea? Only if I don't drown, Ayrys thought. She pulled off her clothing and dived off one of the great outcroppings of rock along the riverbank. The water was icy and she came up gasping and blue-lipped. She scrubbed with soap from her pack – laundry soap, the first thing snatched up in the frantic packing permitted her by the council – and dragged herself back onto the bank.

The Jelite stood with her back to the river, spine stiff. Ayrys had heard – who in Delysia had not? – sniggering jokes about sister-warriors, but surely lovers of women shouldn't be so modest about nakedness before other women . . . Shrugging, Ayrys picked up her leggings and tebl. They stank. She leaned over the bank, scrubbed them with the harsh soap, and pulled them on to sun-dry as she walked.

The soap, lye-based, made an agony of her lacerated hand. Ayrys stared at her swollen fingertips and the deeper, rawer cuts at the base of her thumb. They were an angry purple; it was possible there were still shards of Embry's glass embedded under the skin.

Firstmorning – where was Embry now? Not in the glassyard, smashed into rubble by council soldiers. She had left Embry with Najli, the sister of Ayrys's dead mother. Whatever Najli felt about the disgrace of the motherline, she would see that Embry was physically cared for. But what would Najli do with Embry's bewilderment at the mother who had left her, or with Embry's shame? Embry, who wouldn't even permit herself to cry because eleven was too old for tears . . .

'Let's walk,' Ayrys said harshly to Jehane, but Jehane was no longer there. They had not yet reached the place where Jehane said her protection would end, but she had melted into the rough country. Ayrys shaded her eyes and squinted toward the Wall, but she didn't see the Jelite. She pulled on her boots, picked up her pack, and began walking alone.

After a few steps, she heard voices moving toward her.

Men's voices, ahead of her. Ayrys glanced around, but the voices must have been closer than she thought and traveling fast. She stood in an open place by the riverbank; before she could find a place to hide, the men emerged from the trees ahead. There were two of them, their tebls Delysian, though both were nearly as swarthy as Jelite. When they saw Ayrys, both stopped.

'Look,' one said. He had several days' growth of beard and small, sharp eyes in a fleshy face. 'You alone?'

'Not likely,' the other said. He was smaller, with hands

that twitched at his sides and a nose that had once been broken.

'My lover hunts nearby,' Ayrys said. She tried to walk easily around them, hugging her pack in front of her.

'Come on, Ralshen,' the small man said. He glanced fearfully across the veld.

'Not yet. You're very wet, pretty one. Wasn't the water cold on that pretty skin?'

The other said sourly, 'Proving the Wall didn't unman you, Ralshen?'

'Shut up.' He smiled at Ayrys, the mocking smile of a man relishing his greater strength, his greater speed.

Ayrys said carefully, 'I am a Delysian.'

Ralshen laughed. 'And traveling to the Wall. I do you a favor if I delay you from that.'

'My lover will return soon from hunting our meal.'

He said softly, 'Then we'll need to hurry, won't we?' and lunged forward. Ayrys threw her pack at him and dodged sideways, but she was not quick enough. Ralshen caught her arm and yanked her toward him. At the same moment she kicked him as hard as she could, and they both crashed to the ground. Then he was on top of her, her mouth full of his beard so that she choked and flailed uselessly against him. Her right hand struck his jawbone and the lacerated thumb exploded into pain. Ralshen crouched astride her, one hand pinning both of hers to the ground above her head, the other tearing her wet tebl from neck to belt in one vicious motion that yanked the cloth against the back of her neck hard enough to make her cry out. With his free hand Ralshen struck her in the mouth, and then closed the hand on one breast.

The next moment his entire body shuddered violently, his head jerked back, and his mouth opened in a scream that came out a bloody gurgle. He slumped sideways across Ayrys, Jehane's quarrel in the side of his neck.

'Don't move,' she said to the other man, who stood

staring at her crossbow, pointed at him and already fitted
with another quarrel.

'*No*,' he said. And then, 'I wasn't going to touch her!
Only he was!'

'Who else is with you?'

'Nobody! Just Ralshen and me! And I wasn't going to
touch her – you must have heard me say to him to come
on! I did!'

'Where were you going?'

'Delysia.'

'Where were you coming from?'

'The Gray Wall.'

'You? Why?'

Ayrys shoved Ralshen's body off her own, staggered to
her feet, and wrapped her arms around herself. Jehane
ignored her.

'I asked you why you left the Gray Wall!'

The small man hesitated. His eyes flickered in cringing
puzzlement from the Jelite sister-warrior to the Delysian
Ayrys, clutching her torn tebl across her breasts. Sweat
and oil filmed his face. Finally he said, 'We were afraid
of what the Wall said.'

'What it *said*?'

The man nodded, licked his lips, and tried to smile at
Jehane, a horrible twisting of lips like a whipped kreedog.
Jehane grimaced in disgust and drew back her crossbow.
The man whimpered. Jehane set her jaw and fired. The
quarrel pierced the man's throat; Ayrys cried out and
turned her back, to not see the rest.

'A Delysian,' Jehane said from behind her. 'From your
own city. You are less than animals.'

Ayrys fought down nausea. She heard her own voice
quaver and break: 'And in Jela rape . . . rape never
happens.'

'Not by brother-warriors to Jelite citizens. For that we
have whores.'

'Who were once Delysian captives,' Ayrys said. She

scarcely knew what she said; her voice had steadied, but now her knees felt watery, wavering and fluid as the river. She stumbled to a tree and leaned against it, closing her eyes, both hands holding together the torn front of her tebl.

'I have needle and thread,' Jehane said calmly.

'I have them in my pack!' Ayrys said. Did she have them? Or had Jehane smashed them? No, it was the double helix that Jehane had smashed, blue and red glass in the moonlight, blood on the dark stone, and rolling from the veld the other blue glass of Embry's smashed bottle. . . .

'Jehane,' she said slowly, closing her eyes against the dark rush in her head, 'what if they had been Jelite? Would your blade of honor have protected me then?'

There was no answer. Ayrys opened her eyes. Jehane stood over Ralshen's body, wiping a quarrel free of blood.

'Jelite citizens, Jehane. Would you have killed *them* to honor your oath?'

'Cover yourself properly!' Jehane snapped, and stalked, spine stiff, to the small man's body lying faceup on the riverbank. With one violent motion she ripped her quarrel from his neck; instantly the body was covered with blood. An insect crawling over the broken nose became mired in the gushing red.

Ayrys fumbled in her pack for thread and needle, pulled the torn tebl over her head, and began to stitch. The repetitive motion calmed her a little; when she pulled the tebl back over her head, her fingers no longer trembled and her knees held. Jehane stood with her back to Ayrys, scanning the veld.

Ayrys picked up her pack, keeping her eyes from the corpses lying in the sunlight.

'Jehane. Thank you.'

'I don't want your gratitude, Delysian. It soils me.'

Ayrys found nothing to say to that. The two women

turned from the river and toward the hill crowned with
the Gray Wall.

Away from the river the land began to slope upward,
and after a while it took all her effort to climb, panting,
after Jehane. The Jelite moved lightly, not even breathing
hard.

Once Jehane stopped, shaded her eyes, and squinted at
the sun; Ayrys guessed that Jehane was judging whether
Firstmorning had ended and Lightsleep begun. Ayrys
could not tell. A town woman, she had timed her days by
the bells in Delysia's towers. She was not sleepy, although
she thought grimly that she ought to be.

The sun grew hotter. The tenderest of the wildflowers
that had opened at dawn closed against the harsh direct
light of Qom's approaching noon. Other plants, which
Ayrys had never seen before, opened wide: great yawning
green holes drinking in sunlight like water. One had a
central orifice surrounded by a thick, waxy rim set in
layers of spiny leaves. As Ayrys watched, the rim rose
and fell in some unheard rhythm, as if sunshine were
music. She looked away.

Twice others had passed Ayrys and Jehane, one group
traveling toward the Wall and one away from it, and both
times Jehane had taken elaborate care to avoid getting
close enough to identify either group by speech or dress,
or to be identified by them. She had doubled back on
their trail, circled off the direct routes, adding hours to
their travel time. Ayrys had not protested. Sweating and
exhausted, she kept up as best she could. Jehane's face
looked hard and dry as the baking ground, and her black
eyes ceaselessly raked the landscape, missing nothing.

At the foot of the hill on which the Gray Wall stood
was a well-worn path, but when the two women reached
its base, no one else was in sight. Jehane's doing. The
path was steep, snaking from the veld up over the unseen
rim of the flat-topped hill. From below, the highest edge
of the Gray Wall was just visible, a straight line of shining

gray. Jehane stared at it a long moment, and then turned formally to Ayrys.

'We have stood on the same blade, bound in the honor of life itself. What was freely given has been freely returned; strength has been honored with strength; the named return of my protection is dissolved. Agreed, Delysian?'

'Agreed. My name is Ayrys.'

'I never asked it,' Jehane spat, and was gone, bounding lightly up the trail and disappearing over the rim.

Ayrys followed more slowly, leaning forward into the steep climb, pushing her pack over the rim and then pulling herself after it. When she stood on level ground, there was no sight of Jehane.

The plateau extended much farther than she had imagined, and was absolutely level. The grasses had a low, young look, and no other plants were visible at all – as if, Ayrys thought dazedly, the wildest of the rumors were true and the evenness of the very ground, as well as the evenness of the Wall itself, were a *made* thing and the plants had had less than a year to flourish on new, empty ground. The Gray Wall stretched in both directions, and from where Ayrys stood she could see one corner, sharp and precise as sheared glass. Was the Wall a square? A cube?

A figure, too distant to identify, rounded the corner in her direction, stopped, shrank back, disappeared again around the corner.

Afraid, Ayrys thought. *Of me*. She put her hands over her face and laughed shakily. Then she picked up her pack and walked to the Wall.

It towered ten times her height, and shimmered faintly. The material looked like some sort of lustrous metal, but Ayrys found that she could not touch it. Her fingers were stopped, within the span of an infant's thumbnail, by some invisible material smooth as glass but with a faint tingle to it, like the fizz of certain drinks. How could that

be? Palms flat on the surface, Ayrys leaned close to the
Wall and sniffed. No smell. Only that sheath of something
unseen, and that faint tingle in her palms.

The Wall spoke.

'This is the city of R'Frow. You wish to enter. The
gates are in the eastern wall. Go to the eastern wall to be
tested for entry.'

Ayrys jumped back and looked wildly around. There
was no one in sight. She stood alone, heart thumping in
her chest, in the bright sunlight. Finally she reached out
her left hand and pressed the palm to the Wall.

'This is the city of R'Frow. You wish to enter. The
gates are in the eastern wall. Go to the eastern wall to be
tested for entry.'

We are afraid of what it said, Ralshen's companion had
stammered.

Again Ayrys pressed her palm to the Wall. It repeated
its message a third time in the same voice, flat and a little
fuzzy, like a growl deep in the throat but with none of
the warming of a growl. She had never heard such a voice.

I am afraid, Ayrys thought clearly. At the same moment
she again stepped forward to study the material of the
wall. What could it be made of? Whatever it was, the
Wall seemed to be made of it uniformly, without flaw or
variation, not even streaked by the weather.

She trudged along the Wall, rounded the corner, and
stopped dead, staggered by the length of the southern
wall. It stretched at least four or five times the length of
the huge western exposure; if the city inside were a long
rectangle, its walls could encircle all of Delysia, all of the
fields and vineyards that surrounded her gates, and part
of the coastal forest. The southern wall took full sun, and
it glittered like water, an upright sheet of untouchable
gray water too vast to be real.

In Delysia, rumor had said that the Wall, discovered
standing here where less than a year ago had stood
nothing, must have been built by spirits from the Island

of the Dead. No one but children was supposed to believe
in spirits; Delysia was too practical, too interested in metal
and glass and cloth, to believe in spirits. But there were
those who in the middle of Darkday would draw their
burnouses close around them and mutter into glass cups
of kaf that once people had come from the Island of the
Dead – how else had Qom's two cities begun? There must
always be a beginning. And not even the most skilled
fishers had ever found the island, nor any island at all in
the vast empty sea, so obviously it must be very far away.
Spirits could fly across the sea, spirits could build this
mysterious wall. . . .

Ayrys did not believe in spirits. But who had built it?
Not Delysia – there were no artisans capable of even this
material, let alone this scale. And certainly not Jela, that
city of passionate battle and dark healing, that made well
only weapons. So who? No one in the world.

Dizzy, Ayrys closed her eyes and pressed her palm to
the Wall.

'This is the city of R'Frow. You wish to enter. The
gates are in the eastern wall. Go to the eastern wall to be
tested.'

Far ahead, two figures moved along the wall – away
from Ayrys, toward the east.

Who?

Her throat tightened. She began to walk along the talking Wall, over the young grasses on the flat plateau, which
should have been covered with kemburi and thornbush,
silverbell and nameless waxy vegetable mouths.

When, finally, she reached the edge of the southern wall
and turned the corner, she stopped and stared.

A ramshackle village – no, two villages – stood parching
in the harsh sun. First came the eastern wall, made of the
same material as the others but broken by three equally
spaced gates, each twice as high as a man, framed in black
and closed. Opposite the northern and southern gates

stood a cluster of buildings. The cluster closest to Ayrys – the other was too far away to see clearly – consisted of lean-to's, badly patched tents, and rough stone-and-mud hovels, none of them even whitewashed. Between the Wall and the nearest tent was a wide empty stretch, as if no one wished to come too close to the Wall.

From between two buildings a Delysian soldier, armed and unsmiling, walked toward Ayrys. Dirty brown hair fell to his shoulders.

'Just come from Delysia?'

She nodded numbly.

'You're in the right camp. Your good fortune you didn't come around the other corner.' He said it with a somber intensity, as if her good fortune were personal to him. Ayrys glanced at him, but he was not looking at her. He gazed with hatred at the other cluster of buildings.

'Jelite,' she guessed wearily.

The soldier nodded, his head still turned.

'The Wall said . . .' She heard herself, and a reckless bubble of despairing laughter rose with the words. 'The Wall said I should go here to be tested. For entry.'

Get a lot from the Breel. That place there.' He motioned with his thumb toward the nearest building; it faced away from Ayrys, but the back was a squat, windowless rectangle of mud bricks. 'You can get a bed at her inn till your lot is drawn, if you have any money. If you don't, you set up in that grove of trees. Don't leave the southern side of the Wall if you want Delysian protection. The sentry net doesn't patrol any farther than that. There aren't enough of us left.' He turned to go.

'Wait!' Ayrys said.

The soldier did not slow down. 'Get a lot from the Breel.'

Ayrys walked into the camp. She saw few people; most were probably taking Lightsleep. In the grassless central square stood empty bazaar booths, each no more than a cloth or woven-branch shade on sagging poles, hot in the

sun. Two men cast gambling stones in front of a torn
tent. From the mud-brick building came a snatch of song
in a woman's high, drunken voice, abruptly cut off. The
building had no door, but Ayrys could see nothing in the
unlit gloom within.

A second soldier, cleaner but just as grim, stared at her
hard. Perhaps he thought she would steal one of the
shades. Reassured that anyone in this butt end of the
world would still consider theft a crime, Ayrys walked
over to him. Unlike the first soldier, he wore no formal
emblem of rank; without it, his left shoulder looked strangely naked. His coloring was light even for a Delysian.
One strand of sandy hair, the same color as the stubble
on his chin, fell across his cheek. Against his soldier's
deep sunburn, his eyes showed startlingly light, a pale,
filmy blue like watered glass.

'Where is the Breel?'

His stare hardened even more. 'What for?'

'I need a lot. And a bed.'

'You going to whore for her?'

Ayrys jerked her chin upward. The soldier's stare softened slightly. 'If you're not, you don't want to bed there.'

'I was told it was an inn.'

'That's a word for it. But there's another inn, where a
woman can choose her bed partners for herself. There,
that building on the end.'

'Thank you.'

'Who told you to go to the Breel's?'

'Another soldier.'

His mouth tightened, and Ayrys saw that she didn't
need the emblem to know his rank; he was used to coerc-
ing men but not to leading them. 'Whoring is for the
Jelite. We should leave it to them.'

'The soldier said I needed a lot from the Breel.'

'You do. To be tested.'

'Are . . . are all these people here to be tested by the
Wall?'

'No. Most come for that, then change their minds. Some come to sell the camp supplies – mostly grain, from an outland settlement over there somewhere. Some just come. A few get cast out by the Wall, and you want to stay away from them. They're angry.'

Ayrys heard a Delysian voice saying sourly, *'Proving the Wall didn't unman you, Ralshen?'* She set her jaw and dug the nails of one hand into the wrist of the other.

The soldier was watching her intently. 'What artisan were you?'

She noticed that he used the past. 'A glassblower.'

He nodded respectfully; glassblowers held position and rank in Delysia. His glance was curious, but he asked no questions, and this courtesy suddenly made tears prick her eyes. Courtesy – how could she forget in just one cycle what it felt like? *Stupid*, she told herself, even as she felt exhaustion, shock, hunger, all held back in her wonder over the Wall, rush in on her again.

The soldier touched her arm. 'Sit here and I'll get your lot from the Breel. A glassblower doesn't have to deal with her kind. Sit under here, out of the sun.'

Ayrys sat, bending her head against the sudden rush of stupid faintness. The soldier walked to the mud-brick hovel and pounded on it near the doorless opening. A woman appeared and he seized her by the arm and dragged her out. She was large and draggled, blinking with paint-smeared eyes against the sunlight. The soldier and she argued in low, passionate voices. Ayrys saw the bright glint of metal leave the soldier's hand, and then he came toward her carrying a stone painted with a blue number: 206.

'How much did it cost you?' Ayrys said. Her stupid tears were done; there was no place, in this place, for tears.

'Six habrins.'

Ayrys gave him six habrins. He frowned, and she had the brief impression he had thought her without money, and would have preferred it that way. But he took the coins.

'Stay near the southern end of the Wall. The sentry net can't protect farther than that – too many soldiers have already been taken by the Wall. Stay at the inn or the bazaar and you'll be safe. Don't go onto the veld.' His face softened slightly, a somber softening that did not reach his pale eyes. 'Keep well, glassblower.'

'You too.'

The 'inn' was one big windowless room, its back half divided by splintery partitions into private cells, its front half a featureless common area filled with sleepers. Under the low roof the air was close, hot, and stinking. For a few coins a man let Ayrys unroll her burnous on the dirt floor of a partitioned corner, which she reached by stumbling over bodies scattered in the gloom. Beyond her partition a sleeper groaned heavily. Despite her exhaustion, it was a long time before Ayrys could sleep. She lay staring into the darkness, telling herself that for the first time since leaving Delysia she was safe – except when her tired mind thought of the future, or the past.

Lastlight, and the shoddy camp swarmed with movement. Hunters bartered game from the veld and strange, small, freshwater fish caught in a tributary of the river. Women sold simple graincakes baked on hot stones, or dahafruit gathered on the veld. At the Breel's hovel, kaf flowed. The hot air thickened with smells of food and bodies and a sewer ditch, with curses over gaming and women, with the sullen bustle of Lastlight before the cold and dark closed in for another thirty-six hours.

Ayrys woke ravenous. She bought a bowl of stew, surprisingly good, from a woman with a rough, open face who stirred it over a fire in the bazaar. The woman smiled when Ayrys praised the stew, and this led Ayrys to say abruptly, 'Why are they all here? What brought *you* to the Wall?'

The woman stiffened. 'What's it to you?'

'Nothing. I don't mean to offend you.'

The woman stared at her, then shrugged. 'Can you see the Marker set? I come with *him*.' She pointed her ladle at one of a motionless group of men who sat talking in low tones, none of their eyes leaving the portal of R'Frow.

'Why did he come?'

'The gems, of course. You know where else you get free gems like that? But now,' she said, her face sagging with resentment, 'he won't go in. Like all that bunch, he just sits and watches. Lost his courage, along with his manhood. He's no use to me or any other woman. But here I am.'

'You could go back to Delysia.'

The woman shrugged. 'Oh, it isn't so bad here. No tax collectors, no council. Plenty of room.'

'You could go into the Wall yourself.'

'No! Not for a cookpot of gems! Cities that talk aren't for me.'

'Who are they for?' Ayrys said intently. 'Who do you think built—'

'Quiet! It's opening!'

The camp fell silent. People crowded at the edge nearest the Wall, streaming from hovels to watch, all their faces drawn taut. Only the cracklings of cookfires broke the hush.

Into that silence the Gray Wall spoke. 'This is the city of R'Frow. You wish to enter. Only one human can enter at this gate at this time. You will be tested. If you succeed, you will enter R'Frow. If you enter R'Frow, you will stay one year. No one who enters will leave before one year. In R'Frow you will be given gems, new weapons, and new teaching. This is the city of R'Frow.'

In the hot sunlight, Ayrys felt chilled. *No one who enters will leave before one year.*

The Wall repeated its message. As it began, the framed gate dissolved. There was no other word for it — one moment the gate was there, and the next it was not. Ayrys strained to see a short corridor that turned at a right angle, leaving only blank gray wall in view.

'One hundred fourteen!' screeched the Breel, waving a painted stone above her head. 'Lot one hundred fourteen!'

A man stepped forward into the clear strip between the camp and the Wall; it was the man whom the cook woman had pointed out with her ladle. Ayrys heard her draw a sharp breath. The man picked up a ragged pack and began to move toward the Wall. Every eye followed him: voracious and fearful, pitying and jealous, calculating and contemptuous. The Wall began its message a third time. The man moved slowly forward.

'Faster!' Someone yelled.

Halfway to the gate, the man broke. He ran back to the camp with a curious stooped run, his face already melting from fear to defeat.

The cook woman let out her breath in a long curse. The camp broke into sound and movement. From the Breel came a single bark of laughter. The man collapsed where he had sat before, his face in his hands.

Ayrys stared at the Wall. The gate had not closed, but it *was* closed, the gray material forming as abruptly as it had dissolved. She fought off a sharp sense of dizziness and turned on the cook woman. 'How does the gate close? How–'

But the woman, churning with her own disappointments, waved Ayrys away with one short chopping motion.

Ayrys's hand tightened around the stone that held her lot. The edges of the stone were sharp, and the pain brought her control of the fear.

Spirits from the Island of the Dead. No. But who?

'How many people have already gone into the Wall?' Ayrys demanded. But the woman stirred her stew angrily, and would not answer.

5

The gate in the Wall opened nine times more during Lastlight. Each time Ayrys watched. Four times lots were called and no one entered. Three times Delysians entered and, an hour later, emerged: two carrying gems that would buy a house in the best quarter of Delysia, one empty-handed and babbling. And twice Delysians entered and did not emerge at all.

One of them was the light-eyed soldier who had bought her the lot from the Breel.

Ayrys asked questions of whomever would answer. She learned that the Wall had begun to talk and to open only three tencycles ago, although the camp had existed beside it much longer, and the Wall itself longer still. She learned that the Wall could not be burned, nor dented, nor dissolved by acid – all had been tried. She learned that some Delysians were amassing incredible riches by repeated trips into the Wall; that the Jelite received richer gems; that the Jelite received no gems at all but rather weapons of magical power and speed; that the Jelite received nothing at all. That the 'test' did not exist, or was a test for fools who would pass up the chance to receive gems, or killed everyone who never emerged from the gate because monsters inside wanted to eat them, or was a spirit bridge to the Island of the Dead.

Ayrys began to think that the best of the Delysians who tried the gate – those with sense and courage, given neither to panic nor thievery – must have been the ones who were taken inside the gate. Taken for what? Why? And then she would be told of some man or woman, silly or murderous, who had nonetheless disappeared into R'Frow, and of some other, steady and brave, who had not. There was no reason to it, and no sense.

'Buy that lot from you,' a man said. He was old and stooped, and looked at Ayrys from sly, desperate eyes. Earlier his lot had been called, and he had not gone.

'No.'

'Ten habrins.'

'No.'

'Twenty.'

'No!'

The man stared hard at her, and then began to cry. He cried soundlessly, without motion of face or body, the tears sliding through the dust on his face. Sickened, Ayrys turned away. With her pity came a touch of contempt; she had not cried even for Embry.

Embry . . .

Ayrys forced herself to walk: across the bazaar, through the camp. It was long moments before she realized the man was following her.

Fright quickened her step. She hurried back into the bazaar just as the gate dissolved.

'This is the city of R'Frow. You wish to enter. Only one human can enter at this gate at this time. You will be tested. If you succeed, you will enter R'Frow. If you enter R'Frow, you will stay one year. No one who enters will leave before one year. In R'Frow you will be given gems, new weapons, and new teachings. This is the city of R'Frow.'

The Breel shrieked, 'Two hundred six!' and held a stone above her head. It was Ayrys's number.

'Please!' the man begged. 'Sell me your lot! Please!'

Ayrys ducked into the inn for her pack. When she came out, he ran alongside her, so close she felt his breath, fetid, on her cheek. 'Please, artisan, please sell me your lot! Thirty habrins! Forty!'

When Ayrys didn't answer, his tone changed suddenly from a whine to a vicious hiss. 'You don't know what you're risking. You'll never come out alive – never, never! They'll roast you on a spit, they'll drink your blood like warrior-priests, they'll rape you blind, you whore! You'll never come out again. You don't know what you're risking!'

Ayrys stopped dead, thrust the palm of her empty hand at his chest, and pushed hard. He fell into the dust, his seamed face astonished.

'I risk nothing,' Ayrys said coldly. 'I have nothing left to risk.'

A woman snickered.

The old man lay blinking on the ground. But at the snicker he suddenly yelped in fury, scrambled to his feet, and ran after Ayrys. She had already reached the empty strip of grass beyond the camp, and he stopped, unwilling to follow. He picked up a stone and threw it at her.

It caught Ayrys on the side of the head. She staggered, dazed.

'This is the city of R'Frow. . . .'

Another stone flew past her from another direction, followed by a shout of protest from somewhere else. For a second she couldn't see – from the blow, from anger, from the gloom of approaching Firstnight? The Wall yawned ahead.

Scuffling sounded behind her. The gate began to shimmer faintly, as if to close. Ayrys bit her lip hard and let the pain clear her head.

No one who enters will leave before one year. . . . Embry . . . *roast you on a spit . . .'*

Ayrys ran inside the Wall.

A few steps and she had reached the right angle of the corridor. To the left lay another corridor, another right angle. Ayrys glanced over her shoulder. The Wall had stopped repeating its message the instant she stepped through it; at the same instant, it had soundlessly closed. But the *light* . . . With the gate closed, there should have been no light – there was neither lamp nor fire – yet the corridors glowed with an even, dim light that came from everywhere and nowhere.

She felt the tremor of fear, different from her fear in the camp; that had been only danger.

The second right angle led to a small room of the same gray metal. Ayrys stepped into it, and the wall closed behind her. Fighting down panic, she stared straight ahead: the only break in the bare metal was a shelf jutting seamlessly from the opposite wall, on which lay a cut gem.

Ayrys picked it up. It was a krigass, rare and cherished. In the inexplicable light it flashed blue and violet, cut into a long oval that felt cool and heavy in her hand. In Delysia it would be worth a small fortune.

Enough of a fortune to bribe the city council?

Her hand tightened convulsively on the stone. But the krigass was too small, or the council too large. Still, for a moment she thought her feet had begun to run – toward the gate, toward Embry – until she looked down and saw that they had not. She looked up again, and saw that there were two indentations in the wall above the shelf, and that the left one was oval and the size of the krigass.

She held the gem against the wall. Its cut facets matched exactly the planes inside the oval indentation. After a moment's hesitation, Ayrys placed the krigass on the wall. The bottom of the indentation opened, the gem dropped inside, and the left indentation disappeared entirely.

Ayrys groped at the wall. That section was as flat and featureless as if the indentation had never existed. Like the outer Gray Wall, this could not be touched directly, but seemed to be overlaid with a clear layer than tingled slightly. Ayrys thrust her fingers into the other indentation, a faceted square; it did not give. She stepped back and watched the wall intently. It did nothing.

Minutes passed. The small room was absolutely silent. Nothing happened. Finally Ayrys sat, bewildered, on the floor.

Had that been the test? And had she passed or failed? Those who kept the gem and carried it out into the camp – they must not have passed or they would have stayed inside the Wall. But had she passed? How?

She wanted the krigass back. It was not enough to buy back her exile, but riches, riches . . . she had been a fool. The krigass had felt so heavy and cool in her hand, as heavy and cool as the double helix, red and blue glass smashed in the moonlight–

'Again,' the Wall growled quietly.

Ayrys jumped to her feet. On the metal shelf lay a square-cut firestone, red as blood, with orange and yellow flames at its heart. Its shining facets matched the planes in the square indentation on the wall.

Another chance. They were giving her another chance to decide. Keep the gem, or put it into the slot, lose it, and perhaps gain entry to the Wall. How much did she want to enter R'Frow? Did she want it more than the firestone?

Delysians had come in, clutched the first gem, and sat waiting for the gate to open again. Did whoever waited within R'Frow know that? They must have; gems were taken, and Delysians walked back through the gate. How could they have so many gems? Rich, powerful, mysterious, able to make such a thing as the Wall – and willing to give her, Ayrys, a choice. Ayrys's mouth twisted. A choice – that was more than the city council had been willing to give.

She pushed the firestone into the second indentation.

Immediately it dropped through the bottom. The indentation disappeared, and the shelf silently drew inward and stretched outward so that it became the blank wall, like cloth smoothed by an invisible hand. Clattering sounded behind her, and Ayrys whirled around.

A low slot had opened on an adjacent wall, and objects poured toward her. Ayrys cried out and jumped backward, but almost immediately the rush of things stopped, the slot disappeared, and the rolling objects came to a natural halt. Heart pounding, Ayrys stared at them, not daring to back into any wall. But the walls stayed motionless, and eventually she knelt for a closer look at what they had vomited forth.

There was a knife made of the same gray material as the walls. But, no, it was not the same – squinting at it sideways, Ayrys could see that the tingling clear layer was missing. She could touch the metal of the dagger itself. It was cool, smooth, and honed to battle sharpness.

You will be given new weapons. . . .

There were two cylindrical bars of a darker metal, almost black, and ten or twelve other substances. Puzzled, Ayrys stared at the bars. What was she supposed to do with them?

One by one, she picked them up. One of wood, one of stone, one of some chalky substance that left powder on her hands. One bar was glass, and that one Ayrys examined minutely, amazed at the unvarying evenness the unknown glassmaker had achieved. She knew of no method – not blowing nor lost-wax nor core molding – that could produce such precision. One bar was a strange, slippery substance of pure white, like nothing Ayrys had ever seen. The other seven were of various metals, some of which Ayrys did not think were forged in Delysia.

What was she to do with them?

If she did nothing, if she merely sat and waited for the wall to dissolve and let her out . . .

Ayrys moaned softly. If she merely sat and waited, she would have the camp, the Breel, and the man who had whined for her lot, over and over again. The habrins she had been permitted to take from Delysia would not last long. What then? No one in that butt end of the world would buy glass, even if she could build a kiln and find

what else she needed. What then? Become a cook, become
a beggar, become a whore, existing day to day in hope of
obtaining from the Wall gems she could not return to
Delysia to sell.

She tried the dagger on each of the cylindrical bars.
The ones she would have expected to cut – wood and
chalk – cut. The ones she expected to scratch – stone and
some of the metals – scratched. The others did nothing.
She felt like a child, like Embry, squatting on the floor of
the glassyard, combining mud and sticks with a child's
aimlessness.

Embry . . .

She held the glass bar to her cheek, considering. It was
a lovely color, pale blue, like linwood drawn only once
through the dye vat. She had once made Embry a tebl of
that color, when Embry had been little more than an
infant. A soft color, a safe color, as if she had been stupid
enough to think that beauty could keep her daughter
safe . . .

Color.

Ayrys looked at the bars scattered over the floor. All
different colors except for two, the dark bars that were
also the only two made of the same substance. The two
bars had rolled to opposite ends of the tiny room. Ayrys
retrieved them and brought them, one in each hand, close
to her face for a better look.

The two bars pushed apart.

Startled, Ayrys dropped them. They had felt as if they
were trying to *escape* her. But they hadn't felt like that
when she picked each one up before to try the knife on
it, and they had not tried to escape the blade. Cautiously
she retrieved both bars.

One of them had fastened onto a different metallic bar.
When Ayrys picked up the dark bar, the other came as
well, until after a moment it broke loose and clattered to
the floor. She picked it up and brought it back to the dark
bar; the two leaped together like lovers.

Fear shivered over Ayrys, a long frisson thàt began at her neck and snaked slowly down her spine. The dark bar *wanted* the metallic bar and fled from its brother dark bar. Was it then *alive?* And the walls that shivered and grew and closed up, like a huge kemburi, a living mindless mouth that had swallowed her whole . . .

For a moment she crouched, mind blind and howling, while the world became a living devourer and no footing held. Then reason fought clear. The bar was not alive, it was a metal strange and wondrous but a metal nonetheless, and the only thing alive in the room was her own heart, pounding against the wall of her chest, and her own mind. Metals did not flee, and a maker of glass knew that ores could change form and qualities.

Ayrys brought the two dark bars together, one in each hand. This time they rushed together. A little manipulating showed her that two combinations of ends would attach themselves to each other; two combinations would push each other away. Fascinated, she next touched each dark bar to every other bar. Six metallic bars attached themselves to either dark bar, but the bars of wood, stone, chalk, glass, one unknown metal, and the unknown slippery substance would not. Neither would the knife.

One metallic bar that had fastened itself to the dark bar would not, after she happened to rub it against the dark bar, come near the dark bar's opposite end. This startled her so much – it had not behaved like that before – that she dropped the bar on the floor. When she picked it up again, it did not leap away from the dark bar.

Why not?

A faint odor rose on the air. Ayrys wrinkled her nose. Before she had time to identify the smell, the bars she held in either hand slipped to the floor, and the gas took her.

Her body slumped against the wall. After a while, when her breathing had sufficiently slowed, the floor tilted slightly. The cylindrical bars rolled back down the incline to the slot that opened to receive them. The gray knife and Ayrys's pack stayed on the floor as it rose to lift her body.

The ceiling dissolved. The floor carried Ayrys up and then sideways, through a lengthy and mechanical process of decontamination that would have shamed her, even with the lightness of Delysian modesty, had she been aware of it. A long time later it brought her, dreaming strangely, to a tiny rectangular cubicle within the eastern perimeter of the Wall, and deposited her there.

The floor-conveyor moved back, the cubicle sealed, and she lay paused between one breath and the next in the timeless frozen dream of stasis.

6

'Five hundred eighty-four,' the Library-Mind said aloud.

The three Ged gazing at the wall screen did not answer. On the screen a huge figure stood in the testing room of the central portal of R'Frow, where neither 'Jelite' nor 'Delysian' had ever entered. The human stood as tall as the portal, or half again as tall as other humans and twice the height of a Ged; in the tiny room he had to bend his head to avoid the ceiling. He was dead white. Skin without color, not even burned by the sun; hair white as frost, tied in ten braids that fell past his enormous shoulders; cloth covering bleached white and without ornament. His eyes, too, were without human color, and so faintly pink from the blood vessels within them. He had come to the portal in darkness. He made no sound.

'A related species?' a Ged asked. He spoke in the configurations of a wildly speculative explanation. None of them had seen anything like this.

'Perhaps. Harmony sings with us.'

'Harmony sings with us.'

'May it always sing.'

'It will always sing.'

The three Ged moved closer together, hands resting on each other's back, neck, legs. Their pheromones smelled of uncertainty.

The white giant pressed the firestone into the square indentation. Cylindrical bars clattered onto the floor.

'Should it be admitted, or should we should send it directly to Biology? I am not sure.'

'Harmony sings with us,' the other two murmured.

The Library-Mind growled softly, 'Admit it to R'Frow, although there will be insufficient sample for language analysis. Communications with it will be primitive. What effect it might have on the Central Paradox is unknown.'

The answer came as a surprise to none of them; each already thought the same. The Library-Mind had been created and patterned by Ged.

The huge albino had ignored the cylindrical bars and picked up the knife. He tested it on one finger. A single drop of blood stood red against the calloused white.

The three Ged watched without expression.

7

As soon as she awoke, Jehane's hand groped at her belt. The superb foreign knife was still there, as well as her own knife and the stubby dark club. Perhaps she should not have taken the club; it was too short to be effective, despite its good balance, and there was no hand grip. The master warriors of R'Frow – could they be very small, that their clubs were so short? But the knife had not been small, and the idea of master warriors who were very short was stupid. No leverage. But then, it had been a stupid test – anyone could have picked out the best weapons, one for each hand, from that sorry bunch. Stupid!

All this Jehane remembered, thought, felt, in a single moment, as she opened her eyes to see where she lay.

On a narrow shelf, open along one side. She scanned the room beyond, swung her long legs through the opening, and dropped lightly to the floor, her knife drawn. The light was very dim. But the people climbing from other shelves all seemed to be Jelite. Jehane looked them over and felt a brief shock: *not all warriors.*

But how could that be? Master warriors never bothered with citizens, and some of these citizens hardly looked worth even protecting. There stood a potter, from his tebl not even craftsman to a cadre; there stood a spindly-shanked boy with the shoulders of a broom doll; there stood . . .

A whore. Behind the Gray Wall – a whore! That couldn't be!

Unless she, Jehane, was not behind the Wall.

A spasm of fear shot through her, of the only sort she ever felt: of falling short, not being able to prove herself, not measuring up to the Marker. *She* – not taken by the Wall . . .

But the room around her was gray Wall metal, a bare and windowless rectangle of it. And of the Jelite coming down from the shelves where they had slept – why? how? – at least half were warriors. Of course she was behind the Wall.

'All Jelite,' a voice rasped beside her. A sister-warrior with gray-streaked hair, weather-battered skin, and three suns sewed onto her left shoulder.

Jehane flicked her left wrist in salute. 'Yes, Commander.'

'But not all human,' the warrior said. She stared at the whore, who immediately bent her head and looked respectfully at her feet. The commander looked contemptuously away. Jehane did the same – on second thought, if there were brother-warriors, there would have to be whores for them – but not before she had caught the girl's movement from the corner of her eye. As soon as the commander had turned her head, the whore had looked up, glanced around the foreign gray metal that surrounded them, and brought her gaze full and level with the commander's face. The girl's eyes, deep black and still rimmed with traces of garish paint, looked defiant and scared, but there was no doubt that the insult was deliberate. Jehane, outraged, tightened her grip on her knife and strode forward.

The commander's movement stopped her. The older warrior drew her knife, and Jehane glanced up to see why. Three figures had appeared at one end of the room, on a platform that a moment ago had not existed, standing motionless in a sourceless glow of orangey light.

The warriors sprang into a protective cordon. No command had been given; none was necessary. Jehane stood where her rank placed her, in the rear guard at its left flank. The formation was headed by the woman with the gray-streaked hair; holding the highest rank present, she was automatically high commander. Over the herd of citizens crouching in the center, Jehane could see the crown of her head, almost as tall as the brother-warriors on either side; and above those three, the three figures on the platform.

They were *metal*. No, not metal, but dressed in some light metallic armor that covered them from neck to feet, and shimmered faintly. The shimmer seemed to surround even their heads. They were small, too small for warriors, with hairless heads, with flat ugly gray faces, with . . .

With three eyes.

All the childhood stories of the Island of the Dead rushed in on Jehane. Then a citizen cried out in fear and Jehane was all right, turning the point of her knife toward the man and making sure he saw it. The commander had signaled for silence, and silence was what she would get – a bunch of screaming citizens would only make battle with the monsters harder, if the commander signaled battle.

The citizen met Jehane's eyes, dropped his own, and clamped his lips tightly over his teeth.

'We are Ged,' the figure on the left said. 'We built R'Frow.' He stopped and waited. *Measuring us*, Jehane thought. *Watching our strengths*. That was what master warriors would do. And the monster looked strong, despite his shortness: broad chest, barrel legs. His voice sounded like the Wall, low and growling, and his weird face showed no reaction to being so outnumbered. That, too, was how a warrior should behave.

'You chose to enter R'Frow. You chose what R'Frow can give you instead of choosing gems. You have come to learn, to gain riches, to gain weapons. We will teach you. We will give you riches and weapons. R'Frow is our city,

the city of the Ged. While you remain in our city, you
will do as we say.'

Jehane listened intently. A claim of honor – the monsters were saying the Jelite stood with them on the blade
of honor. They had been freely given the new weapons,
and now were being asked for the return of a year's obedience to Ged laws. A hard claim – the superb knife and
that club, no matter how well balanced, were hardly worth
the relinquishing of command!

Unless . . . unless the monsters meant that there would
be more, better weapons given later on. But that began
to smack of a bargain, not of a return of strength freely
given. . . . On the other hand, if the weapons were truly
wondrous – and these weird monsters had after all built
the Wall – it might be only prudent to give them out
slowly, as weapons masters did, when the necessary body
training made their use effective. . . . Jehane scowled
fiercely. Less than an hour into the Wall, and all these
stupid word battles! But fortunately she did not have to
fight them. That was what the commander was for. Jehane
looked at the older woman's straight back and wondered
what the sister-warrior would do.

'You will live in R'Frow as you choose, by your own
usual ways of limiting action.' It took Jehane a moment
to realize that the monster meant laws. 'Except for two
actions. One – all humans will spend six hours each day
in the Hall of Teaching, where Ged will teach you many
things. Two – no human may kill or seriously injure
another human. All must remain alive for the teachings.'

Murmurs came from the citizens. Jehane was stunned.
'All humans will spend six hours in the Hall of Teaching'
– were these Geds going to teach weapons to nonwarriors?
That was blasphemy, as well as stupidity. Warriors were
warriors, and bladder-muscled citizens, however necessary, were something else. And no killing – did that include
even in discipline? No master warrior would be so soft!

The whore was looking directly at her.

Jehane's eyes glittered dangerously. The girl's insolence reminded her of the Delysian slug she had dragged with her across the veld. But this was worse, a greater insult – the Delysian had been foreign and crazy as well, but this one was Jelite and knew her betters. Jehane tightened her grip on her knife and met the whore's eyes, and after a moment the girl dropped her gaze. She stepped forward and Jehane saw that she had been standing on a large pack to see over the crowd; standing on the floor she was astonishingly tiny, reaching no higher than Jehane's breastbone. But the curves of her body were not the curves of a child.

Under the savagery of Jehane's glare, the whore bent her head and stared at her feet. *Not good enough*, Jehane thought, *not good enough at all*.

The Ged, after another of its long pauses, spoke. 'We have much to teach the humans of Qom. But you must agree to those two limits of action. As you pass through this portal into R'Frow, each of you will speak your agreement.'

Outrage filled Jehane. To ask for an oath of honor from citizens – from *whores* –

'I speak for Jela,' the commander said loudly. She vaulted onto the platform and sheathed her knife courteously. Jehane approved. Even that close to the monsters, the commander showed neither fear nor submission. The Ged, Jehane noticed, did not have the sense to shrink back from *her*. They looked at her calmly, and finally one – she couldn't tell which one, they all looked alike – said, 'You speak in harmony for these humans?'

It was a deadly insult: doubt of a high commander's authority. Jehane felt her midriff tighten. Would the commander demand apology? She gave no sign of being insulted, but Jehane knew better. Even though this commander had vanished into the Wall before Jehane reached the camp outside, warriors in the camp had told how she had killed a cook who had presumed that because he was

no longer in Jela, Jelite discipline no longer held. He had
laid a hand on the breast of a sister-warrior. His body had
been dragged to a ravine beyond the camp, to await the
kreedogs at Firstnight.

The commander said coldly, 'I speak for all Jela.'

The Ged turned to each other. The movement made
the orangey light glint off their helmets, clear helmets
made of glass. Who would wear helmets made of glass?
One good blow would shatter them. And now the third
Ged was speaking – there was no way even to tell which
one commanded. Stupid!

'Your speaking is accepted. You will – '

'Not yet,' the commander said, not gently. Formally
she drew her knife. 'We stand on the same blade, bound
in the honor of life itself. What is freely given must be
freely returned. None but children may accept as a right
the strength of others without return, lest it weaken their
own strength and they become cripples in life. None may
choose to offer their own strength in bargain, lest they
put life in the service of clay. What is freely given must
be freely returned.'

'Harmony sings with us,' one Ged said.

'May it always sing with us.'

'It will always sing with us.'

What the darkcold were they saying? It made no sense
to Jehane. But at least the commander had been clear
enough. Warriors stood on the blade of honor with the
Ged. If the commander said the claim was honorable, then
it was.

'Now you will enter R'Frow,' one of them said. 'After
you enter, the perimeter will be closed to you. All your
body needs will be provided in R'Frow. The light has
been altered to match the patterns of your body, sixteen
hours of light followed by eight hours of darkness. At the
start of each teaching, the grauf will sound' – a deafening
rasp sounded, like metal on stone, and just as abruptly
stopped – 'and you will come to the Hall of Teaching, in

the center of R'Frow, along with the humans from the other two portals. Now enter R'Frow.'

Along with the humans from . . . There would be Delysians in R'Frow. *Delysians.*

She had no time for outrage. The wall behind the Ged dissolved, they walked through it, and it closed seamlessly behind them. The wall across the room dissolved to form an arch, through which trees could be seen. For a frozen moment, no one moved. Walls that opened and closed, a city they could not leave for a year, monsters with three eyes . . . The commander turned and signaled to her warriors, and the bad moment passed.

Sudden exhilaration filled Jehane. She was going to receive weapons no Jelite warrior had ever wielded. A year's claim of honor, and then she would be one of a cadre of sister-warriors such as the world had never seen. She had measured up to the Marker, and in future days the measure of the Marker would be set by the Jelite cadres armed in R'Frow. Her heart swelled.

In formation with the warriors of Jela, she marched through the arch into R'Frow.

8

'Another contradiction,' the Library-Mind said. Eighteen Ged, the full planetary number of the project, turned from watching the wall screens to listen as one. 'Sunside: Most cooperation was shown by the subgroup "Jelite." One human sang harmony for all, as if they were Ged. Unlike the other subgroup, they entered R'Frow with order and peace, and chose sleeping rooms with only a few words of discussion. There was no division about which humans would inhabit which halls, nor which humans would perform which functions. All proceeded with mutual aid.

'Darkside: In both speech and actions of the humans outside R'Frow, the subgroup "Jelite" had the highest content of violence.

'How this relates to the Central Paradox is unknown.'

The room filled with the pheromones of frustration. Nothing fit. Not the behavior of the two groups of humans, not the data gathered during the Library-Mind's year-long observation of the humans beyond the project, not the startling results of the biological examination of the giant albino human while it lay in stasis.

The Ged moved closer together, stroking backs and legs and necks. Someone turned the temperature of the room down three full units, and the others growled harmony. The irrationality of the human data justified the cold.

Irrational, immoral, uncivilized humans – who should not have existed.

'News from the Fleet,' a Ged said, and all moved closer

yet, radiating the pheromones of despair in order to trigger the ones of sympathy, and so smell what comfort could be had in a situation that should not have existed in the galaxy, could not exist in the galaxy – and did exist.

Of all the myriad forms life could take, of all the species on all the inhabited worlds, there existed only three types. There were those species of little or no mathematical intelligence and wide variance among their genes. They evolved, rapidly, by survival of the strongest. Some practiced intraspecies violence, some did not, but none ever reached significant technology. To the Ged they were animals, to be used if they were useful.

There were those species of mathematical intelligence and wide variance among their genes. They evolved, rapidly, by survival of the strongest, including intraspecies violence. Eventually they reached the technology of the atom. The Ged left them alone, not even spending much time in studying them. There was no point. Before they could reach beyond their own solar systems, they blew up their own planets. Always.

There were those species of mathematical intelligence and little variance among their genes, like the Ged themselves. They evolved, very slowly, on old planets of ancient stars. Advances came from the millennia-long accretions of tiny changes, in civilizations where none was sacrificed to others. Intraspecies violence was not genetically possible. Because there existed only one route to a star-drive technology, through mathematics, their minds did not seem that much different from the Ged's. Body uses followed mind, and so space-faring species in the galaxy tended to resemble each other. It was a galaxy of mental cousins.

The Ged tried always to arrange treaties with such species, although when their species territoriality proved as strong as the Ged's, this sometimes proved impossible and war became necessary. The Ged always regretted it, and their pheromones smelled of lament for the Oneness of the lost species.

There had *never* been a species that practiced intraspecies violence and still survived to reach star-drive technology.

Until the humans.

They had created chaos, ramming into space with a technology they should not have and a territoriality as strong as the Ged's own. A brash, young race preferring unaesthetic yellow stars, breathing oxygen, changing so fast they could not be predicted in battle, fighting as much among themselves as with the Fleet. That was what appalled the Ged the most – *they fought among themselves, with the technology of the star drive.* They should not exist; they should have blown themselves up on their home worlds and the survivors been reduced to barbarism.

Sometimes they did. But not often enough, and there was no understanding that. It was not genetically possible. Yet it existed, and the humans existed, and the destroyed human and Ged ships existed – bright, frozen radioactive tombs drifting through the void. Tombs that could answer nothing.

The news from the Fleet smelled of despair: another battle lost to the humans, whose strategy today could not be predicted from their strategy yesterday.

'The Central Paradox,' growled the Library-Mind. 'Sunside: The humans are violent among themselves. Past a primitive level of evolution, intraspecies violence is not species-beneficial: It destroys resources and drains energy. In a species of wide genetic variation, it may destroy those minds most capable of new ideas that could compensate for lack of species cooperation.

'Darkside: The humans have reached star-drive technology. Therefore, they must use number-rational mathematics. They are winning territorial battles. They still exist.

'We must understand why. We must resolve the Central Paradox.'

The Library-Mind changed grammatical configurations, to a grammar rarely used. The configurations denoted a tentative explanation that seemed supported by facts but also seemed logically absurd. 'In this species, the intra-species violence and the development of star drive are positively linked. Equations follow. . . .

'How this happens is unknown. How this happens is what we must discover.'

The Library-Mind had been created by the Ged. Partly organic and partly not, it embodied the patterns of count-less Ged minds. After a moment, it growled, 'Harmony sings with us.'

'Harmony sings with us,' one Ged answered. Her name was Krak'gar, and she was a poet.

'May it always sing with us,' said young R'gref, barely past cub. This experiment was his first away from his homeworld.

'It will always sing with us,' said Grax. He had sung harmony with the human female who spoke for her sub-group. He was a teacher of cubs, in the same way the poet was a poet – from courteous choice, and with pleasure in filling a Ged need. He could have been a poet; the language would not have differed that much. But he liked being a teacher. The design of the Hall of Teaching, worked out in apprehension and hope, was his.

On the wall screens in this main room, dozens of humans moved through the hall of R'Frow. The Ged watched a little longer, then switched off the screens. None of them could pay attention. Their pheromones smelled of grief, of loss that must have the only comfort possible, mourning for those killed in the battle. The eighteen left the room, hands stroking backs and legs and arms, to mate all together. They would mate in cold temperatures, in the pheromones of lamentation, in the knowledge that the vial of mingled seed would not be drunk but burned. They would mate for the dead.

'Harmony sings with us.'

'Harmony sings with us.'

'May it always sing.'

'It will always sing.'

The Library-Mind remained, watching and listening, sorting through billions of molecules and bits of new data from the human city, looking for answers.

'. . . Human intraspecies violence and the development of star-drive are positively linked. . . .

'How this happens is unknown.'

II
WALLS

He who has a thousand friends has not a friend to spare,
And he who has one enemy will meet him everywhere.
— Ali ibn-Abi-Talib

9

They had moved the sun.

Ayrys stood in R'Frow and stared upward. Around her Delysians streamed through the arch from the perimeter into the city, the first time any of them had glimpsed R'Frow. They pushed and stumbled and cried out, but Ayrys stood still and heard none of it, caught in fearful wonder that grabbed at her mind in spasms. *They had moved the sun.*

It had been the start of Firstnight when she ran into the Wall from the Delysian camp. She didn't know how long she had slept in that box she didn't remember entering, but while the Ged had spoken to the awakened sleepers, Ayrys had caught sight of the pale-eyed Delysian soldier who had bought her the lot from the Breel. Then he had had a light stubble of beard, perhaps a day's growth; he had it still. The stubble had not lengthened. Therefore it must still be Firstnight, or at most, Darkday. Yet the sky above R'Frow was the sky of threeday, too heavily overcast to locate the sun, but definitely day. And the air was *warm*, the mild, even warmth of early Firstmorning.

'*The light has been altered to match the patterns of your body, sixteen hours of light followed by eight hours of darkness.*' That was what the three-eyed men, the Ged, had told them. Three-eyed. And they had moved the sun.

No. That was not possible. The Ged must have done

something else. But what? How could they have created a new sky? They had forged wondrous walls – but *sky?*

Ayrys lowered her head; her neck ached from craning backward. Emotions moved in her like slow currents: awe, fear – and something else, smaller and retaliatory. Delysia had exiled her, had torn her from Embry, had used its force in the service of panic to crush her life. But the force of R'Frow dwarfed that of Delysia, and made the city of her birth look like a dung heap. Delysia created exiles – but R'Frow created sky.

R'Frow did not look like a city, as she understood the word. No whitewashed domed buildings bright under glaring sun. No tall, slender Delysian minarets. No gardens or bazaar or walled glassyard, forge, leather shop, drill ground. Instead, she might almost have thought herself back on the veld – but a veld mapped and tamed and enclosed.

R'Frow was wilderness. The Gray Wall enclosed mostly trees and plants, jumbled densely together, crossed by streams and great outcroppings of rock. From her place by the east wall, Ayrys saw groves of mature trees that could only have grown where they stood over long years. Between the dense trees were patches of thick brush, clearings with waist-high grasses, stretches of scrub. But it did not look like the veld. She saw thornbush but no kemburi; wildflowers but no poison-spine; trees with long, feathery branches that trailed to the ground but nothing with a thick, waxy rim that rose and fell around a central orifice. The stream to her right was swift and clear: too swift for the level ground, too clear for the clay upstream.

A breeze stirred; the air smelled as sweet and fresh as if it, too, had just woken from the same strange sleep as Ayrys. Rainwashed forest filled the entire enclosure that was R'Frow, surging to the walls themselves with jumbled green life. And not just green: Ayrys saw the grass ripple as something, startled by the Delysians pushing past, scurried toward thick thornbushes. But the vegetation did not heave and crawl as it should have in preparation for Firstnight – if this *was* Firstnight. And all across the exuberant green life, as bizarre as living insects in rigid glass, sliced paths of gray metal.

The paths, precise-edged, wound in all directions. Above the tops of the trees to her left, Ayrys saw more metal, the flat roofs of huge cubic buildings built close to the southern wall.

Green wilderness, gray metal. Behind her, the arch had closed in the now-featureless eastern wall: an opening there might never have existed. Ayrys squatted to lay both palms flat on the metal path. Faintly, her palms tingled.

'Are you hurt?'

'Ayrys looked up: the grim-faced soldier from the camp outside the Wall.

'No, I . . . What have they done to the light?'

He glanced up indifferently. 'What about it?'

'It couldn't be Firstmorning yet – not enough time has passed. In the camp you had that same stubble, not yet a beard. . . .'

He touched his chin, and looked at her more intently. 'The others have gone to the halls. You shouldn't be back here alone. The Jelite halls are over there, along the north wall. Are you hurt in some way?'

Ayrys straightened. 'No.'

'Then go to one of the halls, glassblower. There isn't a sentry net set up yet. Here, I'll take you.'

'I can go myself,' Ayrys said, but the soldier ignored her. He held her arm firmly and started along the south wall.

'I am Kelovar.' He offered no motherline name.

'Ayrys.'

She did not ask him why he had come to R'Frow; in her brief stay in the camp, she had already learned that no one asked, or answered, that question. As they walked, he glanced appraisingly at the inside of the south wall, at the trees and undergrowth and astonishing, impossible metallic cliff.

Ayrys said quietly, 'A year. We cannot leave for a year.'

'Can't we? What is that wall, ten times a man's height? And the trees grow close to the base. We can leave if we want to.'

'Do you want to?'

'Why? They promised us weapons for a year's service. I can serve a year. Watch out for that branch.'

Ayrys had already seen it. Kelovar did not loosen his hold on her arm.

They came to the first of the halls; others were visible beyond. Each was a gray metal cube, windowless, with a single arch on each side. The arches were doorless and large, Ayrys wondered how the buildings were supposed to hold heat at night.

'Hard to defend,' Kelovar said. The line of his jaw tightened, and for a moment there flickered something in his eyes that made Ayrys glance away, chilled.

The ground floor was one huge room, lit mostly by the arches. There was a single glowing orange circle on one wall, but it gave little actual light. After the squat and plain exterior, the inside surprised; it was filled with floor cushions of bright colors and intricate, strange designs that caught and held the eye, sweeping it along lines it had never before traveled. The artist in Ayrys dropped to her knees to trace the odd, beautiful swirls with one finger.

'Get up,' Kelovar said. 'The rooms are upstairs.'

Except for the cushions, the only other furnishings in the room were small, round, immovable tables scattered wherever the floor suddenly rose to form them, like frozen bubbles on a metal pool. Ayrys touched one; her finger tingled faintly.

'This way,' Kelovar said.

He led her to a ladder ascending to a second story. Here were corridors of windowless gray, lined with doors.

Delysians stood in some of the open doorways. At the top
of the ladder, three men blocked the corridor.

'Twenty habrins for a room, soldier.'

'What?'

'You two want a room, it costs you. Nothing's free.
Twenty habrins, or my partners and me stick our thumbs
in all the doors left and you sleep free only if we decide
not to enter that night. Cheaper to buy it now, and then
the door's yours alone.'

Kelovar paled; a scar Ayrys had not noticed suddenly
stood out on the side of his neck. Within seconds he was
not the same man – a little too brusque, a little too protective – who had walked her to the hall. He drew both
knives, the Ged and the Delysian, and his face went still
and gray, stone in which his light eyes glittered like jagged
glass.

'Get out of my way.'

The man who had spoken, heavy-jowled and squat,
eyed Kelovar coldly. His two huge partners had drawn
their knives. 'You don't want to do that, soldier. You
swore to the Ged not to kill or maim. You want to lose
your chance in R'Frow?'

'Do *you*?' Ayrys demanded.

The squat man grinned at her. He had the odds on his
side, both in numbers and in nerve. Ayrys saw that he
knew few would risk Ged vengeance for a broken bargain
the first day in R'Frow, before any chance to assess what
that vengeance might be; better to pay and wait. Such
reasoning was what the three counted on – and they were
justified. Along the corridors behind him, doors closed.
No one else wanted to know what happened.

Angrily Ayrys reached into her tebl for her coin purse.
'Here! Forty habrins!'

'If you need two rooms . . .' the man said, still
grinning.

'*No*,' Kelovar said. He crouched and began to circle for
position. There was something mad in his pale eyes, some

refusal to see anything but the two armed men blocking
his way; Ayrys thought confusedly that it was not the
same as Jehane's soldierly training but was something
different, more deadly. One of the other men seemed to
sense the danger in such rigid intensity. He glanced uneas-
ily at the squat men, who did not glance back. The other
smiled and also began to circle.

*Two bodies bloody beside the river, quarrels in their
necks . . .*

'No,' Ayrys said, and threw the coin purse at the squat
man. He caught it deftly in midair. 'Take forty habrins,
and call off your kreedogs!'

'Thank you, pretty love. Beshir, that's all. She paid for
both of them. Let him pass.'

Beshir stepped well aside, knives still drawn. Kelovar
stayed as he was. When Ayrys touched his arm, it felt
like wood: He turned and stared at her as if he didn't
remember her. She felt frightened, but when she tugged
at his sleeve, he followed her, and around the turn of the
corridor his face became his own.

'You would have killed him – or been killed. I thought
you wanted to serve your year in R'Frow!'

He didn't answer, but he looked down at her from his
greater height with so much sudden pain that again she
wondered why he had come to R'Frow, and sympathy
stirred in her. *The sympathy of the maimed for each other*,
she thought bitterly, and hated the bitterness as much as
the truth.

He said, 'Don't cry.'

She hadn't been near crying; he had misread her. But
she had the brief impression that he would have wished
her to cry, and suddenly she remembered the moment in
the Delysian camp when she had thought that he would
have preferred her to be without coins to pay for her lot,
and his care in guiding her over the path where no guid-
ance was needed. But his face over the two knives . . .

The Wall behind her growled softly.

'Place your thumb in the door. If you are the first person to place your thumb in a door, it will open. From then on, it will open only for your thumbblock. If you wish to permit the door to open for other humans, press your thumb and another thumb in the thumbblock together. From then on, it will open for each of you. Place your thumb in the door. If you are the first person . . .'

The message repeated three times. 'They always do that,' Ayrys whispered. Kelovar did not answer; he pressed his thumb into the door. It swung open.

Inside was a square, windowless room all of gray metal, bare except for three of the bright cushions, these longer and thinner than the ones below. To the right of the door, on the otherwise featureless wall, a flat orange circle glowed faintly, not nearly bright enough to light the room. With the door closed, it would be in darkness. The room was a dark bare box, meant only to lie down in. Like a burial box. Ayrys shivered.

She felt Kelovar watching her, turned, and caught his look before he could mask it. A look easy to recognize, but nothing stirred in her – no answering desire, no interest, not even vanity.

'If you're afraid, alone in this place . . .'

'I saw a door still closed in the next corridor,' Ayrys said, as gently as she could. 'I'm going there.'

She pressed her thumb to the door's lock. The room was identical to Kelovar's. On impulse, she pressed the orange circle. Light sprang into the room, light from everywhere and nowhere, light faintly orange. It was so sudden that Ayrys cried out. She pressed the circle again; the light vanished. A lamp – it was a lamp.

On her knees, she examined the strange lamp. The circle was flush with the wall, seamless. It did not become warm. But what was the fuel? Where was the flame? She sat for a long time, bewildered and fascinated and afraid. When someone knocked on the door, at first she didn't even hear it.

Kelovar stood in the corridor, his arms heaped with bright cushions.

'These are yours.'

'Mine?'

'From the hall below. They are buying and selling them. I took these for you. There are no burnous, no cloth merchants – the whole city is just wilderness and paths, probably clear to the north wall. You can cut off these cushion covers for cloth. A tailor in the corridor is setting prices for tebls.'

He looked at her breast; for the first time Ayrys remembered her tebl, torn by the Delysian on the veld, clumsily mended. Kelovar did not drop his eyes. Ayrys took the cushions from him and turned away to set them on the floor.

'How did your tebl get torn?'

'It just did.'

'Ayrys – ' he began, but she had no time to do more than raise her hand against the note in his voice before a woman's scream sliced the air. Shouts and cries arose from the room below. Kelovar whirled and raced for the ladder; after a second's hesitation, Ayrys pushed her door closed and went after him. At the bottom of the ladder, she stopped to stare.

Each of the floor tables bore four steaming bowls – no more, no less, precisely arranged in the exact center. A woman beside Ayrys caught her expression.

'The tops of the tables dissolved,' she said in a voice so shaky that Ayrys had to lean closer to hear her. 'The same as the arch in the Wall did before. One minute the metal was solid, then there was a sort of . . . of shimmer and it wasn't there at all. This other metal rose from underneath, with the bowls on it.'

'A scream – '

'That woman over there was startled – the fat woman. I think the bowls hold food.' Her soft voice rippled with

an undercurrent, like a quiet pool over rocks. 'Look –
Khalid T'Alira is tasting it.'

Across the room a tall soldier with a shock of curly hair
and the rank of captain scooped something from one of
the bowls and put it to his mouth. He chewed thoughtfully
and nodded at a group of soldiers beside him. Suddenly
the fat woman shrieked, 'It could be poisoned!' Once
started, she seemed unable to stop: 'It could be poisoned,
it could be poisoned, it could – '

The tall soldier reached her in two strides and put his
hand over her mouth. He was not rough, but he gazed
directly into the woman's face and said something Ayrys
could not hear. The woman quieted, but now angry or
fearful voices began to buzz around the room. Khalid
T'Alira turned to face them.

'Delysians! This woman is merely frightened. Think –
if the Ged wished to kill us, did they have to wait until
now? The bowls merely hold food. I have tasted it – it's
not vile. Are you still frightened? Then wait and watch
me, and you can see what the effects of the food are. Are
you hungry? Then carry the food to your rooms and wait
there. Are you bewildered? See, the Ged wait on us, like
the servants we left behind!'

'Or feed us slops, like animals in a pen,' Kelovar said.
He scowled beside Ayrys, but his gaze rested on Khalid
with a wariness she did not understand. 'Don't eat it,
Ayrys.'

She said, a little tartly, 'What else would we eat?'

'Hunt game.'

'But, Kelovar, even if R'Frow holds game, it wouldn't
last a year.'

He would not be argued with. 'Sentry net first. Then
hunting. Don't eat the slops.'

Ayrys bent down to the closest table, gingerly fished a
chunk of something from the bowl, and held it close to
her nose to sniff. It was brown and unidentifiable, dripping with brown sauce, also unidentifiable. None of it had

much odor. She put it in her mouth; neither did it have much taste. But at the first touch of it on her tongue, her mouth filled with saliva and suddenly she was ravenous. She ate the chunk and reached for another, not looking up when Kelovar's boots strode by with the quick pace of anger and vanished through the archway.

The woman with the soft voice knelt next to her. 'Is it good?'

'It's food,' Ayrys said, more harshly than she had intended. 'Who is Khalid T'Alira? His is the first mother-line name I've heard here.'

The woman ignored the comment on motherlines. 'He's a captain – he was captain to the city council guard in Delysia.'

Ayrys stopped chewing.

'I don't know why he left the city. But he must rank here; I heard someone say he is setting up the sentry net. I am Creejin, gemcutter.'

'Ayrys Glassblower.' She did not offer her motherline; Creejin did not ask.

'Does it taste – '

A man suddenly appeared in the archway, his eyes wild. 'Firstnight is falling!'

Silence. A long moment of it, like glass poised to shatter. Ayrys found herself squeezing her eyes shut. *No more. No more wonders. No more.*' The moment she opened her eyes, the glass shattered, and panic – the panic Khalid T'Alira had averted over the floor tables – burst forth and would not be dammed.

Babbling, shoving, crying, they pushed through the archway to gaze at the sky. It was darkening rapidly. Firstnight without the rest of Firstmorning, without Darkday, without Lastlight. Impossible, mad, in a long strain of impossible madnesses, and people began to cry that this was a city of death, that they all would die, that they were already dead. Someone began screaming and

would not stop, and a man began to beat his head against
a tree, over and over.

In the midst of the pandemonium, Khalid T'Alira suddenly appeared above them, leaping onto a huge streaked
boulder. 'Delysians!' he shouted, and somehow was
heard. Ayrys, trying to force her way back inside, turned
her head; this man had the authoritative voice that com-
mands respect. His eyes swept the panicked crowd without wavering.

'Delysians!' He made quick chopping motions with his
left hand toward a soldier standing near the fat woman; a
moment later the shrill screaming stopped.

'Delysians!'

Gradually they quieted, enough of them for him to
make himself heard.

'So the sun sets – haven't we seen the sun set before?
Perhaps this is Lastlight, and perhaps it is not. Perhaps
we don't know what it is. But the Ged have promised to
meet with us in their Hall of Teaching when morning
comes again, and we can last until then. Is the nightfall
hurting you? Are you suffering? You are not. Go inside,
before the soldiers must force you to go, and take your
courage from them!'

The soldiers, who had not looked particularly cour-
ageous a moment ago, straightened. The few people still
trembling and pointing at the sky were quieted by others.
Khalid spoke on, at first demanding, then cajoling, gradually lowering his voice to a calm tone full of that utter
conviction that reassures no matter what actual words are
spoken. Eventually the Delysians were nodding, and then
they began to move inside the hall.

Khalid jumped lightly from his rock and spoke in low
tones to a soldier, who set off at a dead run for the next
of the Delysian halls.

Ayrys looked for Creejin, who had been separated from
her in the push of bodies. She saw her in a corner, clinging
to the hand of a small Delysian man who wore the tebl

of a trader. With the fall of night, some unseen light source bathed the room in an orangey glow, much dimmer than in the sleeping rooms above.

The bowls of food had disappeared.

Ayrys slumped against a wall. Too much – too much panic, too much change, too much hunger and anger and fear, and even too many abrupt endings to each of them. She thought of glass brought too fast from the kiln to the cooler air of the glassyard – it cracked inside, and sometimes not even the master glassmaker would know. Wearily, she climbed the ladder and locked herself safe in her own room.

She lay on one cushion, drew another over her, then shoved it away; the room was warm. Her belly rumbled with hunger. For this she had struggled across the veld to reach R'Frow – for this empty weariness in a windowless coffin.

Embry . . .

Ayrys dug the nails of her good hand into the injured thumb of the other. Pain tore through the lacerated thumb, but this time bodily pain failed her: It could not blot out the pain of the mind. She pressed the orange circle, and the room light vanished, although the circle itself continued to glow.

She never knew how long she lay there in the darkness. It was worse than the council exile, when she had had rage to sustain her; worse than the veld, when she had had danger. Here was nothing, a dim orange nothing, and she lay alone with the alien nothing until a knock sounded on the door.

Kelovar held two small lori, already cleaned and roasted, the smell of the woodsmoked meat strong in the corridor. He did not speak, merely held out the savory lori in a Ged food bowl. The other hand dangled loose at his side, and his eyes were frank with need. Ayrys saw in the loose lines of his long body, humble before her despite his greater strength, the undefended openness offered as bodily plea, the uncertainty offered as appeal for warmth. It was not a style of bedding, even in a lover for a night, that she had ever much liked.

But she didn't think of style now. The smell of the food filled her mouth with saliva, and Kelovar bulked large against the light behind him in the corridor. He, too, exuded a smell, of fresh night air and clean male sweat. He was a living body in the gray metal room. He was human, with only two eyes, the known among the unknown, the solid in the formless nothing. The alien coffin had leached out the last of her strength, and for this night she could not face any more nothing.

Ayrys pressed the lamp and drew Kelovar in.

The circle on the wall continued to glow, a watching orange eye in the eventual darkness.

10

Across R'Frow, in the Jelite corridor set aside for her kind, the whore sat on a cushion with her spine against the metal wall. She was alone, her black hair streaming unbound over her small shoulders and tiny breasts. When she leaned forward as far as she could, the hair fell in a black river over the floor.

SuSu spread her legs wide, held apart the soft folds of her loins with her fingers, and looked. But no matter how hard she looked, she could see no sores. They were still gone. They had been gone when she awoke on the shelf inside the Wall. The sores were gone.

But they could not be gone.

But they were gone.

SuSu whimpered softly. Her mother had been a whore; she had grown up in the alley behind a brother-warriors' hall in Jela; she knew that the sores of whore's rot did not go away. They thickened and spread, as they had spread in her mother, so that in one threeday her mother had been turned out of the alley, in two more she stank of rotting flesh and babbled in pain, and on the fourth threeday she had been dead. SuSu had taken the body herself to the funeral kiln, wrapping her mother in a burnous and dragging it along the street because her tiny body could not lift even her mother's shrunken weight, the burnous scraping away on the stone so that her mother had gone to the Island of the Dead with her buttocks scraped raw and bleeding, stinking of oozing putrefaction.

SuSu knew, as all whores knew. The sores of whore's rot did not go away.

Her sores were gone.

She sniffed herself. The seed of the last brother-warrior, her own juices – and that was all. No rot. No smell of rot since she had awoken in this hard metal place, where she had fled because if she must die her mother's death, she would not do it scraped raw by the streets walked by brother-warriors. Better the streets of a City of Death.

But the sores were gone.

Blows fell on the door. The whore raised her head and looked at the door, her black eyes opaque as dark glass, without expression. The blows continued to sound, louder now. She put her hands over her ears and pressed hard, but despite the violent gesture her eyes remained expressionless, without fear or anger, giving away nothing.

11

From the Library-Mind, given in the configurations first of observed fact and then in the configurations of hypothesis for which there exist some supporting facts:

'Biological examination shows that the generative cells of the human giant without pigmentation are genetically deformed; sexual reproduction is not possible. His vocal tissues are deformed; speech is not possible. His blood and internal organs are contaminated with radiation, types eleven to sixteen, Level Three.

'The human giant's tissue damage and radiation scan sing in harmony with the radiation detected on the planet's one other landmass, the island eighty orfs from this inhabited continent. It is probable that he came from the island.

'Darkside: Even a human must need a reason to sail in a water-risk boat away from his mating group over such a large distance, alone. Both "Delysian" and "Jelite" outside the project walls seek the company of other humans of their subgroup.

'Darkside: No human speech has ever mentioned other humans living on any island, or any boat within their technological grasp that has sailed so far.

'Sunside: The humans speak of the "Island of the Dead." Most references seem to correlate to the equivalent of some configuration for poetry or unsubstantiated wild hypothesis, if the human grammar were advanced enough to sing in harmony with grammatical configurations. But the overall human instance of fact expressed as poetry varies wildly (Levels Four to Twenty-eight).

'The radiation from the island matches that of human ships whose star drive has been destroyed by the Fleet, adjusted for decay over time (2164 freg, nonrelativistic).

'It seems likely that humans first came to the planet on a ship partially disabled by Ged near the beginning of the war, landed on the island, and later came to this landmass. Bringing humans over the sea would have required either "boats" beyond what the "Delysians" and "Jelite" can build now, or shuttle technology. If this happened, the organic components of both ship and shuttle would have decayed human generations ago. If the human information system were like our information system, the radiation would have destroyed the molecular matrix.

'If the damaged giant did come from the island, there may be other humans there. No Ged should approach the island. Monitoring probes, basic designs with no molecular components, should be sent to watch.

'Leaving some humans on the island generations ago and bringing the rest here makes sense only if some humans were so badly damaged by radiation that they were a danger to the others. But such badly damaged humans could not breed over the generations, and the human giant would not exist.

'The human giant does exist.

'There exists no number-rational solidarity to the humans on the planet having made themselves into three subgroups instead of two.

'There exists no number-rational solidarity to the humans on the planet having made themselves into two subgroups instead of one.

'There exists no number-rational solidarity to this speculative history of the humans on the planet.

'There does exist solidarity to the humans' own poetry-configured explanation of their history on the planet. They say they were brought all together at one time from the

Island of the Dead by ((untranslatable concept: beings who have no being)). But it is not number-rational solidarity.

'None of the speculation explains why the humans do not speak of any history before coming to the planet.

'Scans of the giant, alone among the humans in the project, show severe radioactive contamination throughout all sections of the brain.

'His pheromones do not differ from those of the other humans. Nor does he show any greater capability to respond to pheromones than do the other humans.

'None of them shows any capability.

'The human giant is dying.'

12

It was beyond belief. It was not to be borne. These Ged, whatever else they were, were fools.

Jehane stood scowling on the gray metal walk before the Hall of Teaching, a bright red circle on her outstretched palm where one of the Ged had just placed it. The monster wore some sort of armor, all of one piece, that shone like metal but moved like cloth. Could it actually protect him? The clear helmet covered his whole head – what could it be made of? Not glass after all; glass made no sense. Whatever weird material it was somehow let his words come through unmuffled by anything but his own growly speech. Still, Jehane had understood him. He said the red circle meant she belonged to a cadre, the Red Cadre, and would train with them. Jehane could understand that much – obviously there were too many Jelite to train all together. Sense would break them into sister cadres, brother cadres, and – stupid as their presence was – the nonwarriors that the Ged thought they could train, perhaps as some sort of inferior support forces. So much was reasonable.

But Jehane had seen the Ged hand a red circle to a *Delysian*.

'I do not train with scum.'

The Ged took a long time to answer; it looked to Jehane almost as if he had to figure out what the words meant. Was he then stupid?

'You will go to the room with the red circle over the door.'

'Not if there are Delysians in that cadre! I am a Jelite sister-warrior! I do not train with those who shit on honor!'

Again that pause, this time even longer. Jehane eyed the monster coldly – no way to tell how good the armor was, but he carried no weapons – at the same time that she tried to keep her temper. It was, after all, possible these foreigners didn't *know* what Delysians were. If they didn't know that the scum not only bargained over life but then didn't keep their own filthy bargains; if they didn't know about the truce that had ended the last war – until the Delysians broke it; if they didn't know about the sneak raids run not for honorable battle with warriors but for enslavement of citizens, including children, Jehane would explain. It might, after all, be an honest mistake. She was prepared to be fair.

But the Ged did not ask for an explanation. He just repeated, 'You will go to the room with the red circle over the door.'

'*No.*'

'You have agreed to come each day to the Hall of Teaching. The woman sang in harmony for you.'

'The high commander ordered me to come, and I did. But no Jelite warrior trains with scum!'

Two other Ged had walked to stand beside their brother-warrior as soon as Jehane raised her voice. But they did not form a phalanx with the first one, or draw any weapons – they just watched. Jehane couldn't even tell which one held rank. These were master warriors? Even citizens would have done better. Disappointment added itself to contempt, and Jehane drew her knife.

'Give me a circle for a cadre of sister-warriors.'

Others milling before the Hall of Teaching, Jelite and Delysian both, paused where they stood, watched.

The Ged hesitated for the longest time yet. The humans

glanced at each other: sideways, surreptitious glances. All three Ged gazed at Jehane in silence. Yet she had the mad thought that they heard each other.

The Ged said, 'You will go to the room with the red circle over the door. This group of humans will be both "Jelite" and "Delysian." All are the same in R'Frow.'

The *same* – he had as good as called her a Delysian, a citizen, a whore! And the insult was made *worse* by the Ged's calm. He did not even give her the courtesy of violent expression. Calm said she was not enough of a challenge to even become angry over, and among warriors not under the same command, no insolence was greater. Jehane flushed; her eyes glittered; she tensed into the crouch of hand-to-hand knife combat.

The Ged remained upright, and he drew no hidden weapons. After another of his pauses, he repeated, 'All are the same in R'Frow.' Jehane sprang.

The circle of humans gasped. Jehane's knife struck the Ged at the throat, where metallic armor cloth met glass helmet. The blow should have pierced the cloth, shattered the glass, or found the weak point where the two were joined. But instead she felt the knife strike rock and break, and her shoulder wrenched with the unexpected shock. The Ged did not even stagger; it was like hitting a cliff. It was not possible. *It was not possible.*

The Ged said – calmly – 'You will go to the room with the red circle over the door.'

Jehane felt her legs tremble. She drew her other knife, the gray Ged dagger, and tensed to spring again.

'Jehane!'

The high commander, Belazir herself. Jehane straightened and flicked both wrists. Her muscles still trembled in disbelief.

'He insulted Jela, Commander. He said warriors are the . . . the same as Delysians, and will train in the same cadres with them!'

'We will train as we are ordered.'

Jehane went cold inside. The older warrior continued in the same harsh voice. 'We have bound ourselves in honor to the Ged command while we remain in this city. The greater dishonor would be in not standing on that blade.'

Jehane's eyes met Belazir's. Jehane saw the implacable hardness of a warrior cleaving to a hated oath. The sight was bleakly reassuring. Molag didn't like this either, but she had said it was honorable. And if that were so . . .

'Then I have attacked one to whom I am bound. My warrior's life is yours.' The inner cold crept along belly and bone; the words were ritual, but the punishment need not be.

But Belazir only set her jaw more firmly, and then hesitated. In the hesitation Jehane saw uncertainty, even vulnerability, and a shock tore through her that had nothing to do with her wrenched shoulder. *A high commander – uncertain.*

'I return your warrior's life,' Belazir said. 'In their own training hall, you will obey the Ged completely.'

'Yes, High Commander.' *Uncertain . . .*

Belazir flicked her hand in dismissal, and Jehane walked into the Hall of Teaching. She had dropped the red circle, but now she saw that the color had dyed itself onto her palm. It would not rub off.

Marked. Like some child's game, like some illusion by a street juggler in an outland bazaar. Tricks and illusions, no sense anywhere, stupid as a bucket of hair . . .

What had she struck with her knife?

The Hall of Teaching, like R'Frow itself, was a windowless hollow wall around an empty rectangle, which Jehane assumed was the training yard. Four archways, one per side, led directly to this yard. Within the wall a corridor circled the perimeter, broken by doorless archways that led into small rooms, each with a colored circle above its arch. Under the red circle Jehane paused.

Floor tables. Cushions. The glowing orange circle on

the wall. In the center of the room, a Ged sitting
expressionless. Around him, nineteen humans: nine Delysian, nine Jelite, and a creature such as Jehane had never
imagined – a huge mountain of a man, with a young face
but hair white as frost, cascades of hair from head and
neck and massive forearms, and all of it, even on the
forearms, braided in tens of tiny, intricate braids tied with
white cord. Even his tebl was white, and big enough to
make a tent. The pale giant sat alone, in the center of the
room, staring straight ahead from eyes the color of a
skinned animal.

Along the far wall were the Jelite – warriors standing
grimly with their backs to the wall, citizens sitting farther
away from the Ged. Two sister-warriors, two brother-
warriors, and Belazir's first lieutenant, Dahar, whom already Jehane had heard about. A male citizen in the garb
of a stonemason, a female common laborer – and the little
whore from inside the Wall.

Against the same wall as the doorway stood four Delysian soldiers. They stared hard at Jehane. Sitting beyond
them were five Delysian citizens, one of them the slug of
a glassblower Jehane had brought across the veld. The
glassblower was stupid enough to glance at Jehane with
recognition; on the Jelite side, the whore knew better.

Jehane stalked to her position with the warriors. They
outnumbered the Delysians, but the scum held the side
of the room with the door. How the shit had the lieutenant
allowed that to happen?

She studied him covertly. Not tall, but massive in the
chest and shoulders – he would be strong. Ugly – Dahar
looked like a laborer, not a soldier. Dark even for a Jelite,
coarse black hair, coarse features. Hadn't she heard that
he wasn't even from Jela, but from some outland town?
And he was a warrior-priest, neither blade nor bowel, the
double helix woven across the two suns on his left
shoulder. Jehane didn't know one of them could rise that
high, and she didn't like it. She didn't like any of it.

'First,' said the Ged, 'will be the teaching of things known. After, there will be time for the other teachings: for the testing of things known, for the creation of things, and for the teaching of weapons.'

The Ged paused. No one else spoke. Jehane waited, her gaze divided between the Delysian enemy and any possible signal from Dahar, but they, too, remained still.

Minutes dragged by.

The silence stretched tighter and tighter, until tension prickled over the room like heat. And *still* the Ged, monstrous face impassive, said nothing. This was 'teaching'? This was training? This was shit.

No one spoke.

Without shifting her position of attention, Jehane just caught the gaze of the sister-warrior on her right, a tall, bony girl with hair a startling shade of red. Red hair was usually Delysian, but the girl's stance and body proclaimed her a warrior. She and Jehane exchanged furtive glances of bewilderment, and the girl turned her thumb very slightly inward: the sister cadres' traditional, always secret signal for official stupidity. Jehane did the same and returned eyes front, slightly reassured. Not every one in R'Frow was crazy.

No one spoke.

Just when she thought she could no longer stand it, Dahar demanded of the Ged, 'If this is the time for the teaching of things known, what things known will you tell us?'

The Ged said promptly, 'The answers to whatever questions you ask.'

'We are permitted to ask questions?'

'Yes.' The Ged studied the Jelite lieutenant. Whenever one of them stares, Jehane thought resentfully, they never give the courtesy of showing any expression. They were going to have to be pretty shit-fine warriors to balance that much bad manners.

A spasm went through her shoulder where she had wrenched it striking the Ged.

The lieutenant, on the other hand, was giving full courtesy to the monster. A warrior-priest – they had their uses, of course, on the battlefield, healing wounded warriors, but to command . . . Still, despite his coarseness, Dahar looked like a fighter, not just a driveling healer. His black eyes burned, a hot fire from hard wood. But then, a lot of the warrior-priests were like that – intense even when not in a challenge, asking questions about things, *thinking* about things that didn't need thinking about. Too often the hard wood was in their heads.

Dahar said, 'I am Dahar of Anla, warrior-priest and first lieutenant to the high commander of R'Frow.' He paused, waiting, but the Ged did the unthinkable – *he did not freely return his own name.*

Both Jelite and Delysians understood the insult; the slugs looked openly amused, even the soldiers – fauggh! What they called discipline! Jehane's eyes narrowed. Beside her, the red-haired sister-warrior curled her fingers into a fist.

Dahar forced it. 'Give me your name.'

The monster answered. 'I am Grax of the Ged, from a world circling another star.'

Silence crashed onto the room. Jehane snorted inwardly – she'd see the Marker set before she believed that dung. But Dahar leaned forward a little, and the intensity in his voice pierced like a hot spear.

'Why do you come to Qom? Why have you built R'Frow?'

'To teach humans.'

'Why?'

'Because we choose to teach.'

'Are you a master warrior? Is this a priesthood?'

A pause; it looked to Jehane like the pauses of the monster who had provoked her attack: as if the Ged were *listening*. To what?

'We are not a priesthood. We come to Qom to teach because we wish to learn how humans think.'

'Why?' shot out another voice: one of the Delysian soldiers. He had spoken before his commander did; Jehane could hardly believe it. The soldier's tone was surly. 'What do you gain?'

'Things known that we did not know before. Do you not want to know things you did not know before, for the pure knowing?'

'No,' the Delysian said, surliness bordering on insolence. 'What I want is the gems you promised. When do we get them?'

'All who stay the year in R'Frow will be given rich gems.'

Dahar said, 'How can we do anything else but stay when the walls are sealed and the sky is a wall?'

Jehane jerked her head to stare at him. The sky a wall! Murmurs broke out on both sides of the room, fearful or scoffing or bewildered. Only the strange white giant looked unperturbed. Was he deaf?

The Ged said to Dahar, 'How do you know this?'

'I climbed a tree in the wilderness. Close to the Wall. And I touched a sky of glass.'

The murmurs rose. The Ged sat silent – listening again! – while across the room a Delysian citizen suddenly jerked forward and covered her face with her hands. A Delysian soldier drew her knife, and beside Jehane the red-haired warrior drew hers. Citizens and soldiers smelled of panic, except for the tiny whore and the glassblower scum, who was staring at Dahar as if she saw his words in the air before him. A direct stare at a first lieutenant! She, Jehane, should have let her and her insolence freeze on the veld.

Dahar pressed on. 'The glass curves upward over all of R'Frow. Another wall.'

Finally the Ged answered. 'Yes. There is a dome, although not of glass, over R'Frow.'

Another wall . . . and her knife had struck some sort of wall around the Ged. . . .

Dahar said, 'You have imprisoned us.'

'No. The dome was not built to imprison humans. It was built to imprison the air.'

The air! Imprison the air – the monster was mocking them! A Delysian soldier took a step forward, muttering curses. Murmurs spilled into panic; voices shouted and more knives were drawn. The whore clasped her hands together hard enough to whiten her knuckles. Some woman cried out.

Then across the noise Dahar's voice whipped a command. 'Silence!'

Instantly half the room froze. No Jelite, warrior nor citizen, moved. The Delysians, caught by surprise, eyed the Jelite obedience. Jehane saw their commander scowl, and felt a flash of grim amusement – the dung could not get the same discipline, and he knew it. He barked a string of orders to his soldiers, who in turn snarled at each citizen individually. One had the insolence to speak back – in Jela, he would have known what to expect for that! They were a pack of kreedogs, kept in line only by filthy bargaining, undisciplined as beasts.

Slowly the Delysian half of the room quieted. The Ged watched it all, and his expression never varied.

Dahar demanded, 'Why is the air imprisoned?'

To Jehane the very question seemed ridiculous. But the Ged answered.

'The air is imprisoned so it can be kept heated, just as your buildings enclose air to heat it with a fire or cool it with shade. The warmth you feel now is the way the air will stay for the year you remain in R'Frow. The air will not become colder or warmer.'

Jehane started. No freezing cold, no burning heat . . . but fighting in heat or cold was part of a warrior's strength! A citizen did not have the toughening to do that. A warrior *did*. Were the Ged going to wipe out all distinctions between citizen and warrior?

The Delysian glassblower leaned forward – the first time she had moved. 'That isn't the sky we see either, is it? The dome is smoky glass, not clear. That is how you altered the light. It's not sunlight at all, it's . . . *made* light, created light under the glass dome, like the created light in the halls?'

'Yes.'

A Delysian citizen shouted, 'But I saw clouds!'

'You see a picture of clouds, moving within the clear material of the dome.'

'Pictures don't move!'

A babble of voices, all Delysian, all angry with the anger of people who suspect they are being made fools. Only the glassblower pressed on, her voice cutting across the din with a force that surprised Jehane. 'Shadow pictures move! It's like shadow pictures, isn't it, looking like the sky but not the sky, and the real sky is still out there beyond R'Frow?'

'Yes.'

'Why?' She had to shout now, to be heard above her own people. The Jelite, held by Dahar's order, made no sound.

'Things known need quiet to be heard,' the Ged said.

Again the Delysian commander quieted his soldiers and citizens – without meting out any punishments, Jehane noted with contempt. Ayrys repeated her question.

'Why have you altered the light?'

'Is it better to have sixteen hours of dark and eight of light, or to have thirty-six hours of dark followed by thirty-six hours of light?'

Against her will, Jehane thought suddenly of the dragging tiredness of Lastlight after the brief rest of Lightsleep, and of the frozen dark hours at the end of Thirdnight, when everyone had slept enough but morning had not yet dawned. Citizens shivered restlessly and cursed

the dark, the sick grew sicker, and children born then
to mother-warriors often came hard. 'Dying Time,' the
warriors-priests called it.

A Delysian woman, fleshy and broken-nosed, called out
angrily, 'The sun is the sun! All this talk of altering the
light – dung! Threedays are threedays! And your dome
could not be glass – glass could not be molded to cover a
whole city!'

'It is not glass.'

The Ged touched something half-hidden in his hand.
The tops of the floor tables dissolved, and other tops rose
from beneath. On each top lay not food bowls but a square
of gray, metallic-looking cloth. The Ged picked up the
square on the table before him; it draped over his hand
in soft gray folds.

'Touch it,' he said to the room.

No one moved.

'From this material is made everything in R'Frow,
except the cushions. Walls, tables, dome, food bowls,
paths are all of this. You can call it "wrof." '

The Delysian citizen snorted. 'That cloth? The Wall is
hard!'

The Ged held out his hand. On it lay a small black box.
His fingers moved over the box – and suddenly the soft
drapes of cloth were a rigid square in the Ged's hand.
Rigid, hard, with a faint shimmer around it . . . Jehane
stared. The Ged held a piece of the Wall.

He moved his fingers over the box, and he held a piece
of gray cloth.

Coldness crawled through Jehane's stomach. To change
cloth to metal, metal to cloth . . . The child's fear of
magic touched her with icy fingers – *run, hide, spirits from
the Island of the Dead will get you in the night* – to be
replaced a moment later with the adult fear of power.
*Power – no one had realized just how much power the Ged
really had.* . . .

A woman suddenly screamed. Then the fleshy Delysian

leaped at the Ged. Her face was frozen in surprise, the look of an untrained fighter who attacks not from calculation but from sudden, uncontrollable fear, to squash the unthinkable before it can spread. The woman hit the Ged and bounced back, just as Jehane had. She fell heavily to the floor, eyes wild and face twisted with the pain of hitting a solid wall. She writhed between two floor tables.

'It is around you,' Dahar said, his voice so toneless that Jehane wrenched her eyes from the writhing Delysian and looked sharply at her commander. 'The same clear rigid . . . wrof' – he stumbled over the nonword – 'that makes the dome. It's around you, so we cannot touch you. The same wrof I felt when I touched the sky.'

'Yes. It imprisons air for me to breathe, a different kind of air from yours.'

The Delysian stumbled to her feet, clutching her right arm, glancing helplessly around. When neither the Ged nor the Delysian soldiers told her what to do, she shambled to the farthest corner of the room and crouched there, squeezing her eyes shut against what could not exist.

'What is it made of?' Dahar said, still in that toneless voice – courtesy forgotten, Jehane thought. Or else Dahar did not trust his voice. She found her knees were trembling, and she locked them before anyone could notice.

'It is made of a small amount of matter and a large amount of force and energy,' the Ged said.

Jehane scowled. What the dung – 'force' was making citizens do what they were supposed to do; 'energy' was being able to train for hours without feeling tired.

Dahar said, 'Tell us what–' He broke off, began once more. 'Tell us what that means.'

The Ged studied him for a long time without answering. He looked carefully at Dahar's face, then at the Delysian glassblower, then around the entire room. The Delysian in the corner had curled into a tight ball, arms around her knees, eyes still squeezed closed. Others stared fearfully at the Ged, except where fear was already giving way to the resentment of the powerless. The huge white barbarian sat perfectly still and perfectly expressionless; he might have been carved of ice. The Ged looked back at Dahar.

Then he began to speak of force and energy; of air and no air; of things in the air that no one was supposed to be able to see, but which made different kinds of breathing air for different suns; of Ged air and human air and trapping Ged air inside wrof. Dahar listened with an almost violent attention, his ugly face as alert as a kree-dog's in firelight, his powerful shoulders straining forward. Jehane's opinion of him rose. He was giving the monster a commander's courtesy, even when the Ged droned on and on.

And *on*.

Was this going to happen every day? Human air, Ged air – air was *air*. This was as bad as the masters had ever been with their bloodless drivel. Still, it would have to get better eventually – the Ged had mentioned the teaching of weapons. Until then . . .

Beside her, Jehane sensed the tension leave the sister-warrior's lanky body, replaced by bored slackness. She warmed to the red-haired sister. All over the room, humans had sheathed weapons and began to slump against walls. Only Dahar, bound by his rank, showed any interest. Dahar – and the Delysian glassblower. She sat with her eyes wide, and a small muscle beat fiercely at her temple, under the skin. Jehane frowned briefly, and then shrugged. She already knew the glassblower was crazy.

Jehane fixed her eyes on the three-eyed monster from a world circling another star, let its words slide over and past her mind, and prepared to be bored.

13

Ayrys knelt by the glowing orange circle in her sleeping room, a cylinder of glass in one hand and a square of white cloth in the other. Across the small room Kelovar sprawled on the floor cushions. His naked body still glistened with water from the bathhouse behind the hall. He watched her from narrowed eyes. They had been in R'Frow for five of the cycles that were not cycles but only onedays.

'Come lie down, Ayrys. It's late.'

'Soon.'

'You've done that four times already.'

'I know. I . . .' She didn't finish. A deep line stretched across her forehead, and her eyes were wide and liquid. She rubbed the glass hard with the silk and then moved it toward the floor. The bits of dry leaves lying there leaped up to the bar and clung. Ayrys laughed shakily.

'Ayrys . . .'

'Wrof,' she said, and laughed again, a strangled, hushed laugh that ended in a whimper. 'From that – to wrof. The same "force." The same.'

'Will you come to bed?' Kelovar said harshly. Ayrys heard the harshness and looked up. 'Tricks. Tricks and toys.'

'No. No, Kelovar, don't you see – they can show us how–'

'Tricks and toys. It doesn't mean we should trust them.

A day's worth of talk and toys, and one new weapon we could have thought of ourselves.'

Ayrys glanced at the threeball in the corner. She said softly, 'But we didn't, did we? Nobody on Kendast thought of a threeball.'

Kelovar made a gesture of dismissal, a downward chopping motion with his powerful arm. 'They're not our kind, Ayrys. Remember that – they're no more our kind than the Jelite are.' His voice softened, turned indulgent. 'Of course you're interested in all this talk of the "teaching of making" – that's natural. You're a glassblower, not a soldier. Just don't trust them.'

Ayrys said carefully, 'Delysia is not enemy to the Ged.'

Kelovar snapped, 'I did not mention enmity.'

'No. But, Kelovar . . .' She crossed the room and dropped to her knees beside him, her words coming in a rush. 'What the Ged said, about the whole world being made up of tiny whirling bits combining and recombining, of matter and force – the *whole world*, Kelovar . . .'

His irritation vanished; he smiled at her. 'It impresses you, such talk.'

Ayrys stared at him. Kelovar reached for her hand and began tracing slow circles on the tender underside of her wrist with his thumb.

'Kelovar, don't you think it's true? Are you saying that the Ged talk of matter and force – all of it is lies, none of it truth?'

'No. I don't say it's lies.'

'What then?'

'It may be truth, it may not. It doesn't matter.'

'Doesn't matter? It is the whole planet they're explaining, how everything in it is *made*.'

He put her wrist to his mouth and bit gently, as he had done the night before when they bedded. 'If the Ged tricks and the Ged toys amuse you, then I'm glad. I want you to be amused. But the first task you and I face is carrying you past the idea that there is any value in tricks and toys.'

Ayrys yanked her hand from his. Kelovar looked surprised. In the orangey light she searched his face; the surprise was genuine. He did not see the offense in the idea that she needed to be carried past any idea in the carrier of his amusement. But beneath the amusement Ayrys had sensed something else: some furtive fear in the depths of the pale eyes, something that made him suddenly scowl at her. On the palm she had just shoved away was a circle of green.

'Kelovar, you weren't in the same group at the Hall of Teaching that I was. Didn't your group talk about matter and force, about what the Ged say Qom is made of?'

He was still scowling. 'They talked about that.'

'Tell me what they said.'

'Why?'

'Because I asked you to. Whatever they said. Please.'

'It was only talk. It doesn't matter. Only the weapons matter.'

'Please tell me.'

'No.'

'Please.'

Kelovar stood and pulled on his tebl and leggings with short, angry jerks. When he was dressed, he strode toward the door. Ayrys remained kneeling by the bright Ged cushions, her head a little bent.

He didn't know. He didn't tell her what the Ged had said to his group because he could not, because he had not understood it enough to be able to repeat it.

With his hand on the door, Kelovar paused. 'Ayrys . . .'

She looked up at him. He stood as he had when he came to her room the night before: hands dangling empty at his sides, face unshielded and humble in desire.

'Ayrys – I don't want to go.'

She said nothing.

'I want to stay here with you. If you'll let me,' he said in a voice of soft pleading that suddenly made the muscles tense on her neck. The voice was false, somehow, wrong – but yet it was not. Confused, she said nothing. When she did not object, Kelovar pressed the orange circle. In the sudden darkness she felt his arms go around her and his face bury itself in the heavy skeins of her unbound hair. 'Will you let me stay, Little Sun?'

'Yes,' Ayrys said tonelessly. With one swift motion he pulled her tebl over her head, and then reached for her leggings. He smelled of clean water from the baths. She thought briefly of telling him that she didn't like bedding names, but pushed the thought away as petty. In the darkness she heard their two breathings, his growing heavier and faster, hers calm and unaffected.

The orange light from the glowing circle was too dim to make out anything but rough shapes. As Kelovar lay on top of her, she looked for but could not distinguish the ceiling, made of tiny whirling bits of matter held in place by Ged mastery of the force of which the world was made.

In the sister-warriors' hall, Jehane lay with one arm flung across the back of the tall cadre sister, Talot. The orange circle in Talot's room yielded barely enough light for Jehane to see Talot's bony shoulder blade, a sharp ridge softened by a tress of long red hair. Jehane toyed with the tress, and then put it to her lips and began to chew absently.

'When do you go on sentry net, Talot?'

'Second watch. You?'

'Third. We should sleep now. You felt good, Talot.'

'You did too. Why are you chewing on my hair?'

Jehane smiled in the darkness, and stretched luxuriantly. She felt warm and languorous all over. Talot had indeed felt good. 'I don't know. Bad habit.'

'You always chew on your lovers' hair after sex?'

'Usually on my own. Yours is pretty, Talot. Unusual.'

'You mean the color,' Talot said. Her voice had changed; there was a wary note under the pleasure. Red hair was more Delysian than Jelite. Jelite hair was black. But there was nothing Delysian about Talot. She had outrun Jehane in the training exercises that the commander had already set up, she knew what was interesting and what was drivel, and she was the best bed partner Jehane had ever had – although Jehane was not ready to tell her *that*. Still, Talot was the best thing she had seen about R'Frow, a sister-warrior through and through. Who cared if her hair had been green?

'I like the color,' Jehane said. 'I *like* it.' She tightened her arm around Talot. But to her surprise, Talot's wary tenseness only increased.

'I like you,' Jehane said. There was no answer. 'Talot – do you already have a lover?'

'No.' The word was barely audible, low with strain. Jehane frowned in bewilderment. But she wasn't going to stop now.

'I would like to share the thumblock to my room with you. So both of us could come and go here, and be together when we're off sentry net.'

Talot rolled over, far enough away that Jehane's arm slid off her back. She lay rigid, staring upward; Jehane could see the plane of her cheek dim in the orangey light.

'You don't want to,' Jehane said flatly. 'Fine. All you had to do was say so.'

'I do want to. I like you more than any sister I've ever been with, Jehane.'

'Then what the shit–'

'I have to tell you something first.'

Talot stopped; Jehane waited in bewilderment already sliding toward anger. What in the darkcold . . .

Talot rolled over yet again, lying on her stomach just beyond Jehane's reach. Her words came with painful slowness.

'I want to tell you something first because you might want to choose a different sister-warrior to . . . to share your thumblock with. After you hear it. If so, I will still ask your silence. As the courtesy due a sister-warrior. Do you agree?'

Jehane said grimly, 'I agree.'

'I am not . . . not chaste, Jehane. I have had sex with a man. It was before I was chosen for a cadre, I was still only with the masters, but still . . . I did it.'

'You took a chance like that with your whole life as a sister-warrior?'

'Yes.' After a moment Talot added fiercely, 'There was no baby!'

'But there could have been!' Revulsion swept through Jehane. 'And then you could never have been a fighter, you would have to become a mother-warrior who didn't even have *any* battle experience – a freak! How could you have so little discipline?'

Talot was silent a long time. When she finally spoke, the fierceness had left her voice, and it quavered slightly. 'I know what I did. I don't spare myself. I chose sex with him over standing on the blade of honor of a sister-warrior. Do you want to leave my room?'

Jehane sat up, hugging her naked knees, careful to move no closer to Talot. Talot's confession shocked her; it showed an irresponsibility, a lightness toward the blade of honor, that deserved contempt. You were a sister-warrior and chaste, or a mother-warrior who chose babies over fighting. But mother-warriors were old – maybe even thirty. They had slowed down. It was all right for them to choose babies – that was all they could do, probably. But Talot was *young*. Talot had showed a lack of discipline, a softness, a stupidity . . . Talot deserved contempt.

But Jehane liked her. How could that be, if Talot deserved contempt? Jehane scowled into the darkness. She felt confused, and confusion always made her angry.

'Did your training master know?'

'I told her. Afterward.'

'So you showed that much honor at least.'

'Yes.'

'What did she do? Didn't she burn you from training?'

'*No.*'

'Was he at least a brother-warrior? Or do you have sex with citizens in your cadre?'

Talot rose angrily to her knees. In the dim light the two women faced each other an arm's length apart, bristling.

Talot said, 'He was a brother-warrior.'

'But not an honorable one. You must have had a kreedog training group. In my group, any sister-warrior who broke her honor like that would have been burned forever.'

'Wonderful for you. I'll match my training with yours anytime.'

'Is that a challenge?'

'If you want it to be!'

'Careful, Talot. I have no dents at all in *my* blade of honor.'

Talot sprang. Jehane closed with her and the two wrestled in darkness, rolling off the Ged cushions and onto the hard floor, silent and deadly. Talot, taller, had the advantage of leverage, but Jehane was more muscular. Both were hampered by the long, unbound hair. Silence gave way to pants and grunts. Both superbly trained, it took a long time before Jehane was able to pin Talot, sitting astride Talot's back and wrenching her right arm upward just short of the force needed to break it. Sweat poured off both their naked bodies.

Jehane gasped, 'Do you yield!'

'Y-yes.'

Jehane let her go. Talot stumbled to her feet, putting one hand against the wall for support. Her voice trembled. 'You win. So now you can leave my room.'

But Jehane found she did not want to leave. The hard

fighting, satisfying by itself, had dissipated her anger. Talot had been a tough opponent, worthy of respect. And that little tremble in her voice . . . Jehane rose to her feet, panting heavily, and eyed Talot. She said slowly, 'The masters still let you become a sister-warrior.'

'Yes.'

'What was your punishment?'

A wary hope crept into Talot's voice. 'This. Here. The training master sent me to R'Frow, to bring back the new weapons to the cadre. To make up for . . . for what I did.'

'What happened to the brother-warrior? Was he disciplined for using you instead of a whore?'

'Yes.'

'What discipline?'

He was sent on a First Proving. Even though he'd been picked by a cadre for over a year.'

'And you had let him–'

'Yes!'

'Why? Why in shit did you want to, with a man?'

'I suppose you never wanted to!'

'No! Why, Talot?'

'I don't know,' Talot said. After a while, in which neither moved in the orangey darkness, she said, 'He could outwrestle any brother-warrior in his cadre. He was as good as the lieutenant was in the practice yard this afternoon.'

Despite herself, Jehane was impressed. Dahar had been incredible.

Talot said, with dignity but that slight tremble still in her voice, 'I'll understand if you leave my room, Jehane. But I ask your silence. As the courtesy due a sister-warrior.'

Jehane heard the quaver. Talot's scent came to her in the darkness, sweet and warm. She could just make out a tress of the beautiful hair, falling forward over one small breast.

'Talot. If you give me the thumblock to your room, I'll give you the thumblock to mine.'

Talot drew a long breath. 'After what I . . . did?'

'Over with. In the past. Only one man?'

'Only – of course only one!'

'Over is over. What the darkcold does it matter now? You're standing on the blade of honor in bringing back the weapons, and you won't have sex again with a man until you're a mother-warrior.'

'No!'

Jehane pressed the orange circle. Light flooded into the room. She grinned at Talot. 'You're a good fighter.'

Talot grinned back and moved closer. 'Not as good as you. You wrenched my shoulder nearly out of its socket.'

'Should I get a warrior-priest?'

'No. It's not so bad that I want one of them here.'

They smiled at each other with shy respect. Jehane put her arm around Talot and drew her toward the cushions on the floor. 'We should sleep, if you've got second sentry net and I've got third.'

'I'll wake you. Curse this light – in Jela I would wake myself up minutes before my watch.'

'Of course.'

'Jehane, did you understand all those things the Ged said about the light and the air and the forcing?'

Jehane shrugged. 'Dung. As long as they go on giving us more new weapons, let them talk.'

They pressed the orange circle and lay down on the cushions, Talot wincing a little when her weight rested on her right shoulder. She had a warrior's gift for instant sleep; her breathing had already slowed when Jehane, staring open-eyed at the ceiling, spoke softly.

'Talot?'

Talot shifted her weight slightly.

'Talot – how did it feel? With a man?'

But Talot was already asleep. A little ashamed of herself, Jehane closed her eyes. It was done; more questioning

would only be a discourtesy to Talot. She was not a citizen
or a whore. She was a sister-warrior; her training masters
had not burned her from the ranks, and they knew best.
That was why they were training masters. They did not
make mistakes.

Jehane closed her eyes and slept.

The Jelite whore SuSu rose gracefully to her feet in the
darkness. The brother-warrior did not move; sated, he
lay full length on the bright cushions. She could not tell
if she had pleased him or not, and that frightened her.
The high commander's lieutenant . . . the weight of his
chest had pressed down on her cheek, his male smell had
filled her nostrils, his powerful body had pumped into her
with that hard thrusting that even now, even after all this
time, still hurt. Yet throughout, SuSu could not push
aside the thought that the lieutenant was not really there.
He had hardly looked at her, and he had not spoken. If
she displeased the high commander's lieutenant . . .

Suddenly she had to know. Fear coiled through her,
the soft, misty dread that never really left, that she lived
with as other whores lived with bad skin, or a weak back.
With only a slight hesitation at the strange orange circle,
SuSu pressed it and light sprang into the room.

The lieutenant flung one arm over his eyes. 'Why did
you do that?'

Relief touched her; he did not look angry. But he still
had that absent look, as if he were not really in the same
room with her – or as if she did not exist. The dread
returned, twining around her in cold wisps. She forced
herself to a bright, horrible laugh.

'To see you better.'

'Don't lie to me,' he said sharply.

The fear suddenly blew full strength, a white cold fog.
If she displeased the high commander's lieutenant . . .

And then the other thing began again, the thing that
had started when she found her whore's rot mysteriously

gone, the thing that was so much worse than the fear: the dark furry voice that came out of the white fog and would not leave her alone.

What? What if you did displease him? the voice said. *What if you did displease the high commander's lieutenant? There are four whores in this city, and there are doors. There are locks on the doors. What if you displease him, what if you refuse him, what if you refuse them all? Here you can still eat.*

SuSu clapped her hands over her ears. STOP, STOP, she shrieked silently at the dark furry voices. Stop I cannot do that I am a whore STOP . . .

He stood beside her, pulling her hands from her ears. 'What is it? Are you in pain?'

SuSu looked up at him, unable to remember for a moment who he was, where she was. R'Frow, the whores' corridor . . . the high commander's lieutenant. Yes.

The dark furry voice receded.

'Are you in pain?' the lieutenant demanded again, and SuSu remembered that he was a warrior-priest, a healer to his caste. She shook her head.

He dropped her hands. He said flatly, 'I did not mean to frighten you. I told you not to lie to me because of the way you sounded when you did it.'

'How did I sound?' SuSu said, and laughed again, and this time she heard it herself.

'Like that.' His voice had something in it. Disgust? Contempt? She had not been very skillful, and he had been big enough to really hurt her and that had made her tense up. . . . Anger? She didn't dare look at his face to see. If she looked at his face, the voice would start again.

When he silently paid her the full amount and left, SuSu was so grateful she nearly cried out.

She shut the door on him and leaned her naked buttocks against it, body bent forward, fingers pressed to her temples. Let the furry voice not start again, let it *not start*. . . .

It did not. Gradually her panic ebbed. It was hours into the third sentry net; probably there would be no more brother-warriors tonight. She could sleep.

She could not sleep.

Bending forward as far as she could, she spread the folds of her genitals with one hand. But no matter how hard she looked, she could find no sores. They were still gone.

Because you are in R'Frow, the dark voice said suddenly inside her head. *R'Frow is different from Jela, the three-eyed monsters who command are different from brother-warriors, you do not have to whore to eat, you could lock–*

'Stop!' SuSu shrieked aloud. 'Stop! I cannot! I cannot!'

No one heard her. The strange metal walls blocked out sound between sleeping rooms. And the dark furry voice did not answer.

14

Inside the perimeter, the Library-Mind growled softly in the configurations of observed fact.

'Any human participation at all, even one question, in the Teaching of Knowledge: one hundred twenty-one humans. Participation in the Teaching of Testing of Knowledge: seventy-two humans. Any participation in the Teaching of Making: thirty-nine humans. Any participation in the Teaching of Weapons: five hundred thirty-four humans. Any questions or words in any way suggesting a need for the Teaching of Oneness: zero humans.'

The room already smelled of confusion and strain. All eighteen Ged, gathered as close together as they could, had considered the bewildering report from the monitor sent to the other landmass. A band of humans lived there, at least half of them genetically damaged. Cubs without arms, adults without sight, one slobbering thing without age or mind which no one had even returned to a mating for the dead. Humans – but too few to have survived in this mutated state over this many generations. Far too few to comprise a gene pool, pathetically scrambling away from the monitor, and then . . .

. . . and then nothing. For 'days', nothing, the last transmitted image frozen in the Library-Mind until a short while ago, when it had suddenly began to transmit again. Moving meters above the ground, it showed the ruined hulk of the smashed human ship, much of its inside components already decayed but the star drive still intermittently spewing waves of radiation and stasis around the Island of the Dead.

'How long?' Kagar had said, reeking of disbelief for all of them. 'How long does each period of stasis last?'

But there was no way to know. The monitor had transmitted a short while longer and then frozen again and remained frozen, sending a single image caught in time:

An ancient human, face of craters and ravines between gray hair and grizzled beard. A torn uniform with symbols the Ged recognized from the memory of the Library-Mind. The symbols had been glimpsed on the hulls of some human ships in that brief span between the moment a Ged ship emerged into space-time and the moment it fired: crescent moon with stars, above a double helix. The human glared directly at the monitor probe. His wizened hands, caught in stasis, were suspended fiercely in front of a small screen lighted with more frozen symbols.

'How long?' Grax had repeated. 'The unpigmented giant must have grown from cub to adult in the spaces between stasis – but through how many generations of humans here?'

There had been no answers.

And now the Library-Mind growled again, with observed facts of a different configuration:

'Two hundred sixty-seven humans remained alone in their sleeping rooms. Three hundred and thirty-four spent at least part of the period of darkness with another human. Two hundred eighty of these involved mating behaviors – two hundred sixteen a male with a female, two a male with a male, sixty-two a female with a female.

'There were no humans mating in groups, and hence no variant form of Oneness.'

The Ged looked at each other. Their pheromones smelled of both surprise and disgust. Number-rational intelligence – and no group matings. No drawing together for strength and comfort and solidarity against an environment the humans must find new and disturbing. Pairs only.

'Words classified as violent, Levels One and Two and Three, were spoken by forty-one of the mating pairs. Actions classified as violent occurred in six pairs. Analysis follows. . . .'

The smell in the room changed to amazement, and then to horror. The Library-Mind had recorded nothing like that in the number-rational universe, not anywhere. *Violence in the act of mating . . .*

One of the Ged was sick.

It was R'gref, the cub. He went into biological shock: His spine muscles buckled, his three eyes rolled in his head, and he lost control of his pheromones. Smells spewed forth into the room. The others nearest to him instantly climbed onto his back, wrapped their arms and legs around the stricken Ged's body, and began stroking him on belly and legs, arms and head. All seventeen murmured in the configurations of Oneness, despite not being in trance. Genetic shock was not something to take lightly. It persisted from the dim primitive time when solidarity was still becoming genetic, and survival advantage went to those groups whose members did not turn on each other – because it brought about the condition R'gref writhed under now. The seventeen breathed shallowly against the reek of uncontrolled phermones.

'Harmony sings in us, R'gref.'

'Harmony sings with us.'

'May it always sing.'

'It will always sing, fragrant R'gref. . . .'

'Warm smelling R'gref . . .'

'Harmony . . .'

All else was forgotten. Comfort, solidarity, the restoration of health.

Someone spoke to the Library-Mind, and it blanked the wall screens. The images of Ayrys and Kelovar, Dahar and SuSu, Jehane and Talot vanished to all but the

Library-Mind itself, which went on ceaselessly watching, analyzing, learning.

III
KREEDOGS

If you must punish, punish only in the measure
you were punished.
But it is better to endure patiently.

—The Koran

15

'Ayrys! Are you all right?' Ondur, a woman who slept in the room next to Ayrys's, hurried toward her along the wrof path. Ondur's round, pretty face creased with worry, and her hands were clasped tightly in front of her. Ayrys stopped in surprise. She had been scooping up clay along the stream that ran through the woods between two of the Delysian halls; her feet were grimy, and gobs of slippery clay filled both hands.

'Why wouldn't I be all right? I was inside the sentry net.'

'Then you haven't heard.'

'Heard what? I went after clay for—'

'Don't stay out here! Come on!' Ondur glanced fearfully around, grabbed Ayrys by the sleeves of her tebl, and hurried her along the wrof path and through the archway into the hall.

She stepped into a scene of furious activity.

In the tencycles since they had entered R'Frow, the Delysians had transformed their halls. Except when everyone was required to be in the Hall of Teaching, the halls were as much like a Delysian bazaar as people who had left Delysia behind could make them. Tailors with new tebls made from Ged cushions taken apart and resewn. Cobblers with soft sandals of animal hide bound with the thin copper wire taken from the Ged demonstrations in the Hall of Teaching. Traders with every Ged object available within R'Frow: food bowls, wire, magnetic bars,

cushions, wrof containers, threeballs. Human objects
made from materials within the city or brought from Delysia: knives, cups, soap, razors, glass, nets, belts, even
face paints and earrings. Food gathered or hunted in the
wilderness of R'Frow's western end, varying the diet
offered four times a day by the floor tables. The services
of musicians with wooden flutes, of jewellers with glitter
fashioned from stolen Ged wire, of knife sharpeners and
bodyguards and gambling dens and healers and whores
and laundresses and midwives who concocted foul-smell-
ing herbs for pregnancy, miscarriage, and sex play.

When Delysians went to the Hall of Teaching, much
of the bazaar went with them. It had very quickly been
discovered that the Ged required only each human's presence, plus reasonable quiet to talk their irrelevant talk.
At the Delysian side of each teaching group, it all continued at a lower pitch: gambling and bargaining; stitching
and sleeping; threatening and carving; and over all, the
hard faces of soldiers, watching the Jelite warriors and
not the Ged, hands close to the weapons at their waists.

But the noise that struck Ayrys when Ondur pulled her
into the hall was not the din of trading.

'What is it? What's happened?' Ayrys demanded.
Ondur pointed to the center of the room, but Ayrys could
see nothing but angry backs.

'Don't do that again, Ayrys. Don't go out after your
toys again!' Kelovar. His pale eyes glittered at her. Ayrys
pulled away from his grasp on her arm. She disliked it
when he ordered her.

'The slime killed him over an awl,' Ondur said bitterly.
'An *awl*.'

The crowd parted briefly. A body lay between two floor
tables. Fleshy, unwashed, with blood dried over a face
gone slack and blue. The cobbler.

'He was in your teaching room, wasn't he?' Ondur said.
'He was a Red. They got him with a quarrel in the neck.
A favorite Jelite trick.'

A quarrel in the neck, and the heavy body clawing at her torn tebl and slipping sideways . . . Ayrys looked away.

'He was down by the stream,' Ondur continued angrily. 'Inside the sentry net. Somehow the bastards slipped through. He was looking for a jonkil for the leather, because he had a good offer on a pair of sandals. See that girl over there, crying? She told me. They shared thumblocks.'

The girl stood with her hands over her face, flanked by an older woman and a hard-faced soldier. The soldier was trying to question her, but the girl merely shook her head from side to side, fingers spread over her eyes, her thin shoulders trembling. She was very young. The older woman said something sharp to the soldier, who moved off, scowling.

'She's little more than a child,' Ondur said. 'They'll pay.'

Ayrys said stupidly, 'Jela.'

'Jela,' Kelovar agreed softly, and Ayrys turned to look at him. His face held anger, and hatred – and something else, a strange and terrifying triumph half-ashamed of itself. But only half.

Was it so strange that a soldier should welcome a chance to fight? No. But even as the thought formed, Ayrys knew it was more than that.

'There's Khalid,' Kelovar said. 'Don't leave the hall, Ayrys – not for any reason, not to barter or walk or even go to the baths. Stay here. I'll return when I can.'

Ondur watched with grim satisfaction as Kelovar left with Khalid. 'They'll pay it back. When the firing time actually comes, Delysians always crowd into the same kiln.'

'To burn together?' Ayrys said. She scarcely knew where the words came from; they were out before she knew it. But Ondur did not notice the heresy, if heresy it was.

'Maybe to burn together, but I don't think so. Our

soldiers may not jump to silence like Jelite warriors, but
we won the last war, didn't we? They won't go unpunished for this! And over an awl!'

'An awl–'

'He made an awl out of one of the cylinders the Ged
have – you know, that they think are so important. This
cylinder was hard enough to pierce leather for sandals,
but soft enough to sharpen, and he made an awl out of it
for his work. I suppose he didn't have one from Delysia.
The Jelite took it – must have thought it was a weapon.
Or maybe they just wanted to kill. Can one see the Marker
set?'

Ayrys said slowly, 'The Ged have forbidden killing in
R'Frow . . . on threat of . . . exile . . .'

Another woman had moved closer to hear, a low-rank-
ing soldier with eyes like knives. Delysia had fewer female
soldiers than Jela had sister-warriors, and Ayrys had
observed that when Delysian women did become soldiers,
they often looked like this one: as if they drank bile. The
soldier said, 'Should be exile for only the Jelite. *They* did
the killing. The Ged should exile all of them – and without
any of the riches.'

'But if we strike back–'

'We won't be killing! We'll only be defending Delysians. Only defending our own.' Suddenly she looked hard
at Ayrys. 'Nothing wrong with defending our own, is
there, glassblower?'

'No. Defend your own,' Ayrys said, and turned her
back on both the soldier and Ondur to climb the ladder
to her room.

She shut her door on the tumult below and pressed the
orange circle. On the floor was a tangle of cylindrical bars,
copper wires, food bowls, and metal plates. She saw none
of it.

How would the Ged react to the killing of the cobbler?
They seemed to make no distinction between Delysian
and Jelite – would they exile all the humans from R'Frow?

She had nowhere else to go.

For tencycles she had been fighting off the crippling desire for Embry. Now it flooded over her. She could not go to Embry, she could not survive on the veld – what would she do if her exile from Delysia were followed by her exile from R'Frow? She could stay with Kelovar – but probably not if Kelovar discovered she was an outcast from the city he was so glad to fight for.

And she didn't want to stay with Kelovar.

The metal door felt hard to her hand. Yet she had seen such metal dissolve in a moment, vanish as if it had never been, when Grax decided in his alien mind to do so. Could the Ged dissolve all of R'Frow?

The thought made her gasp. But she understood, after cycles of the Hall of Teaching, the extent if not the workings of the forces involved. They could do it.

If they chose.

Jehane whistled happily as she walked from the practice yard – the large treeless space between the sister-warriors' hall and the looming gray cliff of the Wall – toward the baths. She was satisfactorily hot and dirty, and all her muscles throbbed with the pleasant warmth of a really good workout. She had been the best warrior on the field with the new weapon. She had drawn praise from Belazir herself, before the high commander had been suddenly summoned from the yard. And she wasn't even good with the threeball yet – not good like she was going to be, anyway. She was going to be the best. She and Talot – she would work with Talot, until Talot was as good as she was herself. Give them a tencycle more and not even Dahar would be able to outthrow them.

The three-eyed monsters had actually proved honorable after all. Three-eyed, threeball . . . she could just picture a hairless, grayish Ged with three balls. Jehane smiled. She would have to remember to tell that to Talot when Talot got off the net.

No one else was in the baths. Jehane stripped and settled into the artificial pool, lined with wrof and fed continuously by some warm underground river. Or maybe the Ged had created the river. Jehane didn't care which. The baths were a handy thing, and this crazy R'Frow was turning out better than she had expected. Fondly she eyed the threeball on the rim of the pool.

Why hadn't Jela thought of it long ago? Unlike most Ged devices, it wasn't stupidly complicated. Three balls of some heavy metal, one lighter than the other two, were fastened together with leather thongs of what the Ged said were carefully measured lengths. It didn't have the power of a crossbow, of course, but it let you take game without spoiling the hide. The first time Jehane had taken it in her hand, the threeball had felt like a part of her. She threw with more accuracy than anyone but Dahar, and she planned on bettering him because she practiced more.

Dahar . . . he puzzled her. Day after day he kept up full courtesy to the Ged monster, listening to its drivel and even manipulating all the weird objects that kept rising from the floor tables. The courtesy was right, was good – that was his duty as ranking warrior in the room, as well as the high commander's first lieutenant. But how could he keep up that intent watching, just as if he were really interested, and still be alert enough to the slime across the room? Once or twice it had seemed to her that he had almost forgotten there were any Delysian soldiers there at all . . . No, not that, of course not that. He was the high commander's lieutenant. But, still, he played with the Ged toys and his eyes looked . . . looked . . . shit, she didn't know how they looked. He was the first lieutenant, he knew that was right, he could best any warrior on the practice field, and had. And she wasn't going to let any stupid thoughts spoil her good mood.

She stretched luxuriously in the warm water – really, some Ged things were sun-warm nice – and then smiled in pleasure as Talot, just off sentry net, walked into the baths.

But Talot was not smiling.

'The cobbler is dead.'

'Cobbler? What cobbler?'

'In our training cadre. Delysian. Fleshy, stupid, broken nose – you remember. He was flashing that sharpened Ged cylinder at the teaching.'

'I saw it.' It was one of the things she had thought that Dahar missed. 'A possible weapon.'

'Yes. The Delysians found his body. Quarrel in the neck.'

'Ours?'

'The quarrel had been pulled out.'

Jehane thought briefly of the Delysian she had killed on the veld, the dung who had tried to rape the glass-blower. A quarrel in the neck wasn't easy to dislodge without leaving a piece inside. You had to know just how to twist it.

'It wasn't broken off,' Talot said. 'Someone was at least skilled. The Delysians will claim the kreedog was killed by a warrior.'

'Maybe he was,' Jehane said coolly.

'No. Belazir bound us to the two Ged laws. A warrior wouldn't break oath.'

Jehane looked away. Talot flushed suddenly scarlet, and also looked away. There was a painful silence. Finally Jehane said, 'This is different from your . . . it's a *battle* oath, almost. Probably the cobbler was killed by a Delysian soldier. They don't defend their citizens, they bleed them. Whores and cowards.'

'It might have been a Delysian. Yard talk is that the cobbler was found inside their own sentry net.'

Jehane grinned. 'That doesn't prove anything. How hard is it to get through *their* net?'

Talot said seriously, 'I don't know. I've never done it.'

Actually, Jehane hadn't either. But everybody knew the

Delysian net was rotten with holes. Yard talk was that soldiers could *pay* each other to stand their net duty. Fauggh!

She swung herself out of the baths. 'I'm going to eat. You?'

'No, you're not. Dehar wants to see all off-net warriors in ten minutes. He's been shut up with Belazir since she got word of the killing.'

So that was why Belazir had been called off the practice field. Probably the net would have to be doubled, in case the Delysians decided in their slimy minds to thrust this killing on Jela instead of on one of their own. Because of course now that she thought about it, Talot was right: it couldn't have been a warrior. Belazir had bound them all to the Ged law against killing while in R'Frow.

Jehane's blood quickened a little. If the Delysians attacked . . . neither she nor Talot had been old enough to be picked for cadres at the time of the last battles with Delysia.

Jehane swung herself out of the water, reaching simultaneously for her tebl and her threeball. She smiled at Talot and began again to whistle.

Dahar watched Belazir flex the muscles in her shoulders: a quick hunch forward, a roll back. He saw the moment she caught him watching. The troughs from her nose to mouth deepened; he thought that it would be hard for her to admit to weariness. To admit to anything. Dahar stood straighter, shoulders squared.

'No unusual approaches, Commander. No additional information on the Delysian's death. One brother-warrior did not take his place on the sentry net, second watch.'

'Have you dealt with him?'

'Substitutions on the net have been arranged. The warrior will not stand sentry for a tencycle. He will not be able to stand at all for a threeday.'

'Name?'

'Fastoud. Hall Three.'

'I know him. A slug. In Jela he would never have been selected by a cadre. He may even have been burned from one. In this place there's no means to be certain.'

'No, Commander,' Dahar said. Belazir interested him. She was too old to be commanding a sister cadre; in Jela she would already have become a mother-warrior, before she also became too old for that. He guessed that she hated the idea, from a dislike of inaction or a dislike of pregnancy, and that this was why she had come to R'Frow, where she found herself high commander.

Shrewd, fair, reticent – she had proved an excellent commander. No detail of sentry-net placement or cadre training was too small for her to consider over and over. This would have exasperated most lieutenants; Dahar liked it.

He sometimes thought that when Belazir looked at the double helix on his shoulder, she glimpsed, more than most, why he wore it, and at what cost. But perhaps not. Outside, in the darkened corridor, the sister-warrior who was Belazir's lover waited patiently. Dahar had caught the look she had tried hard to hide as he passed. Belazir, too? Probably.

She said, 'Fastoud is worse than most. But too many of these warriors are not cadre material. Too young, or too undisciplined, or badly trained. Not Jela-trained. Outlanders.'

Dahar said quietly, 'Perhaps the commander is not aware that I am also an outlander.'

'You?'

'From Anla.'

Belazir studied him frankly. 'I didn't know. I would have taken you for a Jela cadre leader.'

Dahar waited; when she didn't say it, he did. 'And not for a mining-camp Blue and Red.'

Belazir glanced at his shoulder. Watching her closely, Dahar caught the flicker of distaste, and the courtesy of

hiding it. The distaste was familiar, the courtesy rare –
especially among the warriors in R'Frow. They didn't like
having a first lieutenant who wore the double helix. None
dared say so. None had to. From long years of practice,
Dahar kept his face impassive. Belazir wasn't done yet.

'Born to it, Lieutenant?'

'No. My mother was an outlander cadre leader.'

But Belazir's reticence held; she asked none of the usual
questions: *Then why does a warrior of your strength and
skills make himself shunned as a Blue and Red? Do you really
dissect the bodies of those warriors you cannot heal, and then
bury them dishonorably mutilated? Are your healing brews
cold magic? Does the priesthood drink human blood?*

When she didn't speak, Dahar's respect for her grew.
She did not ask him for the explanations she would then
fail to understand. She did not demand of him the personal reasons he would have refused to give. And she did
not thrust at him the childish argument of most warriors,
the jeers he had heard since his tenth year: *Of course only
those who themselves fight can have the right to touch the
bodies of wounded warriors. No citizen must do it. But no
warrior who ministers to pain and sickness, no warrior who
has vowed to ease pain, can have the same fighting edge as
one who only inflicts pain. Somewhere there will be a softness,
a pulpy, decayed weakness – and that weakness could kill me
in battle. I don't want to fight under a warrior-priest. I avoid
them.*

From avoiding to despising was a short distance, no
longer than the thrust of a warrior-priest's knife the first
time a wounded brother had to be cut. And died anyway.

Childish. Painful. Blind – with the blindness of a hunter
who does not see that the kreedog cast out from his own
pack is made more dangerous, not less. But there was
something deeper, some wordless repugnance for the warrior who groped with trained fingers through the broken
and helpless bodies of his own kind . . .

Belazir rubbed her hands over her face. The skin under

her eyes stretched taut, the color of old jonkil leather. 'It would be a mistake to underestimate the Delysians. Their soldiers are dishonorable and treacherous and every one of them would sell their own lovers, but they can make ferocious fighters if they think there's a chance for looting or rape. And their ranks in R'Frow may be made up of too many uncontrollable outcasts.'

Like ours, Dahar thought, but did not say so. 'You still do not expect a direct attack.'

'No. if they haven't done it yet, they won't. Delysians either attack immediately or seethe, getting angrier. No discipline. It's their weakness, but it can be a strength if a commander is smart enough to twist the anger where he wants it. Khalid may be. I hear from sister-warriors in his Ged Teaching that Khalid can talk well. Talk can twist anger. But I don't think they'll attack directly.'

'A retaliatory killing of a Jelite warrior.'

'Yes. I think so. If they can get at one. We've made that difficult.'

Dahar said, 'I asked a Ged today what is the penalty for breaking the law against killing.'

Belazir took her hands from her face. Her eyes narrowed. 'That is a defense measure. You should have asked permission.'

'I'm sorry, Commander. I didn't see it as a defense measure. I asked him during the Teaching of Knowledge. He answered, "All number-rational principles hold over time." '

Belazir considered, her eyes thoughtful. 'Not very clear.'

'No. But he had been talking of magnetism; I couldn't tell whether he intended some subtlety about the laws of force and the laws of Ged.' Dahar watched Belazir; he saw that she did not understand what he had said. The word *magnetism* tasted odd in his mouth, in this room, before this person.

'Why do you think the Ged didn't immediately punish the killing? They will lose discipline doing that.'

'I think they are waiting.'

'For what?'

'I don't know. Perhaps they want to see what happens next. They have said they are studying us.'

'When they decide to punish, what do you think they will do, Lieutenant?'

He was silent. Then slowly, keeping his face rigid, he said, 'They might choose to exile all humans from R'Frow.'

Belazir said sharply, 'Is that what you think?'

'No.'

'Why not?'

'I don't have a reason to give.'

'It's a strange use of the word *exile*, Lieutenant. R'Frow is not Jela.'

'The commander forgets that I am not from Jela.'

'I forget nothing,' Belazir said, and looking at him directly, her black eyes measuring . 'I am told that during the teaching you display a great interest in the Ged toys, Dahar.'

So it was to be the distrust after all, merely arrived at by another route. Dahar felt a stab of disappointment, followed by the bitter smile he did not let reach his mouth.

'Displaying interest in courtesy due the Ged.'

'Yes. Apart from courtesy, do the toys themselves interest you?'

'Yes, Commander.'

'Why? Do you see them as more than toys?'

The perceptiveness of the question surprised him. 'Yes. In time. The Ged have much knowledge that could be of use to us.'

'I think,' Belazir said shrewdly, 'that you would be interested even if the toys had no use. You want to know because you want to know.'

Dahar did not answer.

'Take care, Lieutenant. your first loyalty belongs to Jela, outlander or not.'

Anger flared a second before he saw that the half-insult was deliberate – a knife probe to test the thickness of the scar tissue, to discover if loyalty to Jela still underlay the double helix on his shoulder.

'My loyalty has always belonged to Jela, Commander,' Dahar said stiffly, and saw Belazir smile. She rubbed her fingers across her eyes.

'I am satisfied of that, Lieutenant. You may go.'

Dahar flicked both wrists in salute. The sister-warrior still waited in the corridor. She saluted respectfully, but he caught the tightening around her mouth and the quick, furtive look at the emblem on his shoulder.

He left the hall and slipped quietly through the darkness, to make sure yet again that the sentry net was secure.

But when he was satisfied of the net, he still didn't turn toward the brother-warriors hall. He wasn't sleepy. Restlessness seized him. He stood indecisively on the wrof path, the smells of thornbush and silver-bell thick around him in the darkness.

The dome above never darkened completely. Without moons, without stars, it nonetheless glowed faintly even during the 'night'; branches swayed against the dome, moving gray shadows tapering down into visible black trunks. The only true darkness lay within the sleeping chambers.

Dahar half-turned toward the hall where the whores had their corridor. A whore would give a few moments of physical relief. But afterward the restlessness would still be with him, and he knew from experience that it would be worse. A blank-eyed smile, a face barely hiding eagerness for him to leave, a laugh as stupid and shrill as that last unskilled whore, the tiny doll-like one, pretty, but only what they all were. Until his body again drove him to it, he didn't want a whore. Tonight he didn't want a whore.

What did he want? The restlessness grew worse – the old seeking for something that couldn't be named, welling up from a depth within himself that neither mockery nor contempt had ever been able to still. He wanted, without knowing what he wanted. Next to his restless wanting, which took him in black moods, the distrust shown him by his warriors and even by his commander was only an irritation. The closest he had ever been able to come to satisfying the want had come with the Masters of the Double Helix, learning from them the arts of healing, turning the dubious and fragmented bits of knowledge over and over as if they had been stones in his hand. And even that had not stilled the nameless seeking very much. More – somewhere there must be more.

The sentry net was secure, but not so secure that Dahar himself could not slip through it if he chose. He dropped to the ground and began moving through the net, toward the Hall of Teaching.

16

She could not believe the softness of the silence.

The pounding on the door had finally stopped. Lying on her cushions, fists clenched at her sides, SuSu had listened to them pound on her door over and over, for minutes at a time. First the steady knocks. One fist, two. Then harder, blows muffled by the thick Ged door but still separate and clear, each one. The blows became a cadre marching song. They were playing. Then, when no other warrior came irately to kick open the door and say she was taken, a brief pause. And then the serious pounding, kicks as well as fists. There were at least two brother-warriors. At each kick she had winced, as if at thrusts from their hard maleness already in her. She had not gone to the door.

And then, this silence.

She waited for the dark furry voice to jab and taunt her – *you don't have to in R'Frow, you don't have to here in R'Frow* – but now that she did not open the door, it did not come.

Instead was only dark furry silence.

When had she ever heard silence like this? She had never heard silence like this. Awakening cold and shivering late in Thirdnight in the Whores' Alley in Jela, already old enough to know she must not try to crawl to her mother's bed for warmth, the child SuSu had listened in fear to a silence laced with sound: a dreaming groan from another child, footsteps staggering by in the alley, from her mother a muffled laugh that had sounded to her worse than a cry. She had thought that the silence was like her dread, trying to hold still, trying not to be found. But the sounds found it anyway. Sound was the hunter, and silence more awful and desperate than sound.

But this silence was soft, dark, furry. The furry voice had somehow become the furry silence, and SuSu was not afraid of it.

She lay for a long time, thinking about that. R'Frow had cured her whore's rot, and R'Frow had somehow cured the tormenting voice as well, giving her this soft silence. Or maybe the silence had cured them both, disease and voices.

The pounding on the door had gone away. The brother-warriors had gone away. No one but Falonal, one of the other whores, shared her thumblock. No one could come through the door.

No one could come through the door.

She turned on her side to stare at the closed door. The air was warm enough for her to lie naked, but she had kept on her tebl and had even added a blanket made from a cushion cover on top of that. She flung out one arm, and the space across empty cushions was hers. And all around her the warm, furry, dark, sweet silence cradled her until she slept.

'You didn't open up last night,' Falonal accused, coming alongside SuSu as she walked along the wrof path to the Hall of Teaching. The day, like all days, was warm and cloudy.

'No.'

'Were you bearing blood?'

'No,' SuSu said softly. She walked with her head bent down a little. Beneath her bare feet the path lay clean and gray.

'Then don't do that. Jamila and I can't slit all the warriors alone.'

'You will have to slit them all,' SuSu said even more softly. 'I am not a whore any longer.'

Falonal gaped at her. 'What do you mean you're not a whore?'

'I stopped.'

'*Stopped*?'

'I was stopped,' SuSu said, and waited for the dark furry voice. It didn't come.

'Stopped by *who*?'

'I was stopped,' SuSu repeated, and smiled slightly, her gaze slanting upward at Falonal from her bent head. Falonal's eyes, dark and a little sunken, narrowed to gashes. She had leathery skin, despite almost never having seen the sun, and a round bony chin like a buried stone.

'You can't stop whoring.'

SuSu said nothing.

'You can't stop whoring, because you're a whore,' Falonal said. She scowled, laughed harshly, then scowled again. 'I suppose you think it's that easy.'

Almost inaudibly SuSu said, 'We're fed here, Falonal. Fed and warm. I . . . stopped.'

'They won't let you,' Falonal said angrily. 'What would the warriors do if whores stopped? They won't let you!'

'The silence let me.'

Falonal put both hands on her hips and studied SuSu. Her mouth jerked downward, hardening her chin even more. 'You think you're better than Jamila and me.'

'No. You could stop, too.'

Falonal gasped. 'You're crazy, SuSu!'

Her raised voice had drawn Jamila, a little way behind them on the path. 'Why are you shouting?'

Falonal said, 'SuSu says she's no longer a whore. She says she stopped.'

Jamila, rounded and pretty, with blue gems in her delicate ears, gaped at SuSu. 'Why?'

SuSu shrugged, a tiny rise and fall of thin shoulders.

'Why would you want to stop?' Jamila said, genuinely

bewildered. 'The brother-warriors here pay better than in
Jela. And there's fewer of us – I can have as much trade
as I can handle. Twelve last night.'

Falonal said, 'They won't let you stop.'

Jamila said, 'Why would you *want* to?'

SuSu answered neither of them. She walked down the
path. With startling suddenness Falonal hissed after her,
'You're a whore, SuSu – a *whore*. You're no better than
Jamila and me. Don't try to strut around like some clean-
slitted sister-warrior – I know what you are!'

SuSu didn't answer. She walked into the Hall of Teaching, entered the room with the red circle over the arch,
and sat, as always, in the farthest corner, folded as small
as she could, head bent a little down. If anyone glanced
at her, she would not see it. She listened to nothing that
was said. She sat apart on a safe island, and the silence –
furry, dark – lapped gently at the shores.

Today, no gambling with jonkil bones. No trading, no
whispering, no negligent leaning against the walls. Warriors and soldiers both stood straight, grim, and through
their belts glittered Jelite knives, Delysian two-pronged
gouges, Ged knives of dull wrof. Citizens stayed at the
rear of the room, silent. Only the huge white barbarian,
impassive and uncomprehending, sat as usual at the central floor table, his pink eyes blinking at the Ged. Ayrys
wondered if he knew about the cobbler, if he was capable
of knowing. She slipped into her place, on the Delysian
side of the room but close to the Ged, the first floor table
in front of Grax, the one at which he would touch and
explain the alien materials. It was the best place to see,
to question, to miss nothing. It was also closer to the
Jelite than any other Delysian . . . she pushed the thought
away.

The floor table where the cobbler had sat seemed glar-
ingly empty.

Ayrys kept her eyes on Grax. Her throat tightened. *If humans were exiled from R'Frow . . .*

Grax moved his hand, and the top of the floor table dissolved and was replaced by another, bearing the now familiar materials. Grax did not look at the objects. He scanned the human faces, and when he opened his mouth to speak, there was a sudden tightening of the air, and somewhere behind her Ayrys heard indrawn breath hiss between clenched teeth. Would the Ged talk of the killing? What would he say?

'This wire is not copper,' Grax said. 'The electron river will flow along it harder and faster than along copper.'

He was not going to talk about the killing! Ayrys found that her legs beneath her felt watery. She glanced to her left; the Delysian commander's face had darkened in rage.

'The wire does not come from one ore,' said Grax. 'It is a mixture fused by great heat.' He said no more; the Ged way was never to direct what was done with the materials they provided. They would state facts and answer questions, no more.

No one moved. The silence lengthened. None of the new wire, nor the other objects, disappeared into Jelite or Delysian tebls.

Grax waited. Ayrys thought again that the waiting made him far stranger than the three eyes did; Ged could sit waiting for hours, for a whole day in the Hall of Teaching, and neither speak nor move till some human did something. In the beginning, Grax sometimes had. But now he must feel the difference, must know it was the humans who waited for whatever form Ged justice would take. The Ged had given laws; the presence of law implied punishment. Although, Ayrys thought bitterly, the opposite was not necessarily true.

When the silence had become unbearable, the Delysian commander suddenly spoke harshly. 'A Delysian has been killed by Jelite scum.'

Knives slid from belts.

Grax turned his head to regard the commander – a rare event. Ordinarily he looked directly only at those concerned with the Ged science. He said calmly, as he had on the first day, 'This is the Teaching of Knowledge.'

The commander scowled savagely and stepped forward, knife drawn. Ayrys felt, rather than saw, the tensing of the Jelite warriors to her right. But the soldier was looking not at the Jelite but at the Ged, and suddenly Ayrys was aware all over again of the invisible armor that wrapped the Ged. Grax did not move. The commander hesitated.

'This is the Teaching of Knowledge,' Grax repeated, and his gaze returned to the floor table in front of him.

For a second the commander remained undecided. Ayrys saw in his angry face the moment when he gave in, both to the impossibility of attacking Grax and to the stupidity of attacking Jelite here, in this closed room where warriors outnumbered soldiers. He stepped back to the wall, and Ayrys unclenched the hands in her lap and laid them on the floor table. Under the nails were drops of blood.

The wire before her was silvery gray. She focused on it and looked to neither side. Seconds passed, then minutes, and no armed bodies hurled past her from the right or the left. Finally she heard a slight motion to the left and behind, and turned to look.

A Delysian citizen was scooping the new wire off a floor table and into his tebl.

All over the room, objects began to disappear from floor tables, as if this morning were like any other. Ayrys reached out and put her hand on her own pile of wire so no one would take it. After a moment, she picked it up.

'The Teaching of Knowledge,' the Ged had said. They must not care what humans did, so long as humans came to the Teaching of Knowledge and learned. But then why the vows of obedience?

A Delysian, misled by Ayrys's motionlessness, reached for a wrof bowl on her floor table. Ayrys covered it with her hand and the interloper returned to his place somewhere behind her.

There were two bowls, filled with an acid Ayrys knew from glassmaking. She inserted the four plates of metal into the bowls; now she had two cells. Could she have a third? No, she hadn't been quick enough; all the Delysian floor tables were stripped. There were plates and bowls only in front of the white giant, who would not touch them; neither did anyone else dare get close enough to him to try.

She connected the new wire to both cells and nearly cried out in pain.

Finger in her mouth, she studied the wire. How could the shock be so much greater than with the copper? How could she handle it?

The same way she handled acid in glassmaking, of course – with something else. Cautiously Ayrys took a chip of wood from her tebl and used it to edge the wire toward the second cell. Connected, the wire did not glow, but when she brought her finger slowly toward it, she felt the heat radiating outward and was startled by its strength. Fire – it felt like a fire, which no one had needed since coming to R'Frow.

The possibilities began to absorb her. She tried one thing and then another as they occurred to her, and the room around her gradually faded. Her fingers, used to glassmaking, were deft and sure, and her breath came a little faster as ideas came to her one by one.

What if the wire became hot enough to warm a hunter on the veld in Thirdnight? Or a sick child? Some way would be necessary to increase the heat, to keep the wire from burning skin, to contain the wire in a compressed space. What if she added a third cell? She could not enclose the whole in wrof; there were no food bowls large enough. And the whole would have to contain more wire than cells if it were going to give heat. . . .

She caught a slight movement to her right. The Jelite

was watching her cells. He, too, had two of them; he connected them in the same way she had, felt the wire, jerked his hand back, and frowned. He bent over the floor table; when he straightened, Ayrys saw that he had bent his wire into coil after coil and pushed them close together, like the heavy coiled bracelets Jelite citizens sometimes wore on their upper arms. He hooked this to both cells and held his hand over it.

Would coiling make any difference? Ayrys bent her wire the same way. It became hot, and the heat was more contained, but the shock was still there as well as the heat; some more reliable way would have to be found to connect and disconnect the wire and keep it in contact without constant hand pressure through the wood chip. . . .

Suddenly she realized whom she had copied.

She jerked her head upward and met Dahar's eyes. The Jelite first lieutenant stared at her hard for a long moment, identical coils and cells – identical alien objects – in front of them both. The blue and red double helix shone on his shoulder. His dark Jelite face was impassive. Ayrys felt something turn over in her stomach: fear, but not all fear. Her eyes flicked away from his, back to the coil of Ged wire, with its rising heat.

A second later she glanced around the room to see who had observed the making of the two coils.

No one watched except the Ged.

17

'This is a new weapon,' the Ged said.

SuSu stood by herself to one side of the central court in the Hall of Teaching, which was always used for the Teaching of Weapons, and watched without curiosity while the Ged held up a palm-size piece of bright red cloth. SuSu had been given a threeball a tencycle ago, but of course had not thrown it. No sister-warrior would have permitted that. Probably the brother-warriors would not have stopped her. SuSu, like other whores, had had her share of clumsily mishandling brother-warriors' weapons, sometimes after slitting but more usually before. Some of them liked that. But from the sister-warriors, punishment would have been swift. SuSu had left her threeball in the courtyard, and some warrior must have carried it off. She would do the same with this red cloth.

A Delysian soldier said in a tight voice, 'A new weapon? Now?'

'Yes,' the Ged said. The high commander's lieutenant (*He used you once*, something said inside SuSu, but it was not the terrifying dark voice so she didn't care) looked hard at the Ged, and then at the Delysian who had objected.

'On my world it is used to capture wild animals without killing them. It does not cause pain. It is not like the threeball. You will not be able to make it yourself, not yet, but you can learn how later. The strip acts on the things inside the body that control the body. One human will come to me so I can show you how it works.'

No one moved. SuSu stared dreamily at the ground; this had nothing to do with her.

Dahar strode forward. 'Show how it works with me.'

Jelite warriors glanced sideways at each other. SuSu saw Jehane flush high on her cheekbones. The Delysians muttered among themselves.

'Yes,' the Ged said. 'Take off your tebl. The strip is pushed anywhere along here.' With one finger the Ged traced the first lieutenant's spine, from the base of his neck down to the small of his back. SuSu had never seen a Ged touch a human before. Dahar stood rigid, a head taller than the Ged, although Dahar was not especially tall. His muscles shifted in a hard mass beneath his naked shoulders and tapering back. SuSu watched unmoved, but the sister-warriors stared fiercely at the ground, their faces red and angry.

The Ged pressed the red strip to Dahar's spine. Instantly the powerful muscles went loose and slack, and Dahar collapsed into a heap at the Ged's feet.

The Jelite warriors sprang forward, although none touched the Ged, nor seemed to know what to do once they had sprung. A brother-warrior hesitated, dropped to his knees, and turned Dahar over. The sister-warriors kept knives and eyes trained on the alien, and did not look at Dahar's sprawling, half-naked body. His eyes remained open, staring sightlessly. As the brother-warrior turned him, his eyes rolled in his head.

The Delysian commander started forward for a closer look. Jehane turned toward him, deliberately blocking his view, and the Delysian halted.

'He breathes,' the brother-warrior said.

'Wait,' said the Ged.

They all waited. On all four sides the wrof walls gleamed, clean and blank around the yard worn dusty by human feet.

Dahar's eyes focused. he stirred, shook his head, rose to his feet. The red strip stuck to his spine, red as blood.

'What happened?'

'You were as dead,' the brother-warrior said. He had gone a little pale.

'How long?' Dahar said, with so much intensity that the brother-warrior stepped back a pace before answering.

'A few minutes.' His voice grew thoughtful. 'Long enough to capture and bind.'

Dahar faced the Ged. 'And you use this to make animals as dead. Why?'

'To make them quiet enough to untangle from a three-ball and set free.'

There was a dangerous edge in Dahar's voice. 'You don't use the threeball on your world. Not with the kinds of forces you command.'

Grax regarded him calmly. 'Our children do.'

'Children,' Dahar said. 'Children and animals,' and at the sound in his voice SuSu suddenly wrapped her arms around herself and returned to staring at her feet.

'Adult Ged use it to capture wildlife for study,' the Ged said. There was an ugly silence.

Dahar said, 'But you give it to us as a weapon.'

'Weapons are what you asked for.'

Dahar said nothing. SuSu saw that the other warriors were looking hard at him, even the sister-warriors, though he had not yet put on his tebl.

The lieutenant didn't like the new weapon, and the others did. Why? SuSu didn't try for understanding. It – none of it, nothing any warrior thought – had anything to do with her again. She was free of them.

'Do you want this weapon?' the Ged asked.

'*Yes*,' Dahar said, and the warriors looked confused. 'I want to know how it works. *How inside the body does it work?*'

Jehane glanced at Dahar's tebl, lying in the dust. The double helix was half-visible. The Delysian commander,

whose view of the fallen first lieutenant had been blocked
by Jehane, glanced at the helix as well, and Jehane scowled
savagely.

'How it works is for the Teaching of Knowledge. Now
is for the Teaching of Weapons. You will try this strip in
twos. Each pair of humans will try the strip on one of the
pair.'

SuSu's breath stopped. Like the others, she counted
rapidly, the counting so inevitable it was not even
necessary.

Jehane and Talot. Two brother-warriors with each
other. The other sister-warrior with the female citizen,
already cowering and sweating. The stonemason left to
Dahar, who would now be the one in the pair to inflict
the weapon. Even the eight Delysians, now that the cobbler was dead, had paired, one sister-soldier with a brother-soldier. SuSu had heard that Delysian women, even
the soldiers, were all whores *how could that be the warriors
had said so, their weight crushing her and they sniggering to
her what they would do if they caught a female Delysian
soldier at battle, and could SuSu . . .*

There was no one left but the white barbarian giant.

The Ged gave to each human one red strip. Each pair
decided who would have the strip pressed to the spine,
who would do the pressing. Soldiers and warriors wanted
to get the feel of the new weapon, to adjust their responses
to it. They talked in low voices, and then moved the
vulnerable partner away from the enemy. Some pulled off
their tebls, some felt above the back of the collar for the
vulnerable part of the neck.

SuSu stood with her small fists clenched at her sides
and her eyes on the dust. Fear kept her rigid. The barbarian giant had moved to her side; she could feel the
huge male presence of him, smelling his strong sweat. She
barely came up to his waist. He would strip off her tebl,
put the thing on her, and she would fall as the first lieutenant had fallen, to the ground and farther than the ground,

to that dark unknown place where the dark furry voice had gone and now waited to torment her there. The whore's rot – it must be there, too; it had gone before the voice came, and if the voice and the rot found her once more, this time they would never let her go . . . never. . . .

There was a movement at the very edge of her vision and a body tumbled to the ground: Jehane. Talot stood fierce guard over her. Jehane lay helpless, not an honorably wounded warrior but a sprawling slackness, sent down after the dark furry voice, gone. SuSu squeezed her fists tighter. *He would do that to her.* Somewhere on the Delysian side of the yard, another body fell. The white giant made a movement beside her. She could not look up, she bit back her whimper, heard herself whimper and the dark furry voice growled somewhere deep and . . .

A face loomed up at her from the ground. *Up.*

The barbarian giant had knelt and twisted his face sideways to look up into hers without touching her. Even kneeling, he had to duck his head to bring it lower than hers. SuSu looked down into eyes of no color, white on white, the white turning a filmy pink around the pupil. Tens of silky white braids stuck out around a male face quizzical with unspoken questions. On one huge palm lay the red strip, dwarfed by the white hand that held it, and the giant was holding it out to SuSu.

He wanted *her* to put it on *him.*

Numbly, SuSu took the red strip. The giant rose, pulled off his tebl, and turned his back to her. The base of his spine was level with her eyes.

Around the yard, Jelite and Delysians both glanced surreptitiously from their fallen partners to the naked torso of the barbarian monster. The masses of muscle made even Dahar look puny. The skin in front of SuSu was dead white, hard and taut but clear as SuSu's own, with neither hairs nor shading, less like a man's body than like some huge outcropping of white rock.

She pressed the red strip to his spine, rising a little on tiptoe to reach. Instantly the rock melted, nearly engulfing her. SuSu jumped sideways, and the man-mountain lay at her feet, as helpless before her as if she – she, *SuSu* – were a warrior and he a hunted animal.

Or a whore.

A strange thrill shot through her, flashing from neck down her own spine, dark and furry as the dark voice itself. She looked down at him from black eyes wide with the first power of life.

Moments passed. Around the courtyard, bodies began to rise to their feet. Still the barbarian giant lay sprawled below her. Finally he twitched, sat up, and stood to tower at twice her height.

SuSu would have turned away, but his gaze caught and trapped her. Dirt smeared one cheek where he had fallen. He said nothing, but he stared down at her from his immense height and smiled faintly, very gently, the first smile anyone had seen him give in R'Frow. His lips were very pale, colorless as silent clouds.

18

'A few have wondered about the giving of a new weapon just after the first act of violence,' said one of the Ged. The others turned to her to consider this, although all of them and the Library-Mind had considered it before. Otherwise, she could hardly have voiced it.

They were all eighteen together, for nearly the first time since the first frantic days in R'Frow. It was good to sit and consider in the dim orangey light like the light of home. It was good to stroke very slowly, share pheromones, say aloud the obvious over and over in different voices that were reassuringly the same voice. It was good to be civilized again. Someone, acknowledging the occasion, had turned the temperature up two units.

Complex smells washed through the room. R'gref, the young Ged who had lost control of his pheromones at the last full gathering, smelled faintly of shame, and a persistent undersmell of reassurance streamed toward him from the others. Mating pheromones wafted freely, preparing for the Oneness that would eventually happen, in good time. Although worry over the Fleet was never absent, it had become an undertheme, faint in the dominant smell of pleasure: pleasure at being all together again; pleasure at the sharing of mating fluids yet to come; pleasure in the rich, slow smells enclosed where the raw and troubling humans might be talked of but where they would never come.

The Ged stretched luxuriously, sniffed deeply, moved

closer together. Each voice wove another calm strand into the design each already knew, before any voice began. Oh Ged, where communal weaving was the prime art and tapestries were treated to retain the pheromones of all the artists, they would have sat in silence. Here the rasping of humans had left them all with the longing for verbal and pheromonal tapestry.

'The ones who wondered about the stun strip are the same ones who show the most intelligence in the Teaching of Knowledge,' offered R'gref, and the pheromones of reassurance increased and took on tinges of pleasure at his participation.

'Harmony sings with us.'

'Harmony sings with us.'

'May it always sing.'

'It will always sing.'

'That they could be so different from each other in intelligence,' one said. Astonishment, old but still strange, weaved through the air. The differences among the human minds had been expected in a genetic-divergent species; the size of those differences was still a shock.

'Perhaps we should have waited with the stun strip.'

'Perhaps we should have. Harmony sings with us.'

'May it always sing.'

'It will always sing.'

'We can balance any drawing back on the part of the ones who wonder by giving them new knowledge.'

'That's what we agree to do.'

'We all agree to do that. Harmony sings with us.'

'Harmony sings with us. We are in agreement.'

'May it always sing.'

'Which of the humans most need to be kept from drawing away? Which seem the most promising?'

'Harmony will always sing.'

'Dahar. Grax's group.'

'Yes. Dahar. We are agreed.'

'Harmony sings with us. Dahar.'

'Harmony sings with us.'

'In Wraggaf's group, the human Creejin.'

'Yes, Creejin. We are agreed . . .'

And so for hours, savoring the pace and the sweetness, moving closer to the greatest sweetness of a Oneness mating, circling and skirting.

Hours of talk, and the eighteen decided to do what they had known, before they began, they would do. They would follow the Library-Mind's recommendation. They would give to the humans some of the knowledge of their own bodies that the Library-Mind had learned from Dissection and Decontamination. The presence of the double helix should make such knowledge interesting to the most intelligent among the humans. The presence of pregnant females in R'Frow, which there now were, should make the promise of health for their children interesting to the rest. What species did not value the health of their own cubs? Knowledge, healing, weapons – whatever kept the humans cooperative until the Central Paradox was resolved.

The room smelled suddenly, after hours of rich solidarity, of anxiety. But no Ged mentioned aloud the Central Paradox. The one wall screen awake showed the unchanged image from the monitor probe:

Bearded ancient human in a torn uniform with crescent moon, stars, double helix. Glaring from the ruined ship, the uncontrolled stasis, the lost history.

Three voices growled softly, simultaneously, at the Library-Mind. The image disappeared. To mate in Oneness was sweet, and they would not permit it to be spoiled.

The fluid vessel was brought out, the temperature turned up the full fifteen units, the trance began.

And the mating smelled sweeter than any of them could remember.

19

'Rain,' Talot said. 'It smells of rain.'

'It doesn't rain in R'Frow,' Jehane said, but she squinted upward and frowned.

'Wait a minute, my sandal's loose.' Talot bent and Jehane instinctively kept watch, even though they were back within the sentry net. Jehane held a dead lorus in one hand; another hung at Talot's belt. The hunting in the wilderness end of R'Frow had been good, despite the heavy air pressing down from the sky that was not a sky. Sweat and dirt smeared them both.

'The baths for me,' Talot said.

'*Listen.*'

Talot froze, tensed to fight. But what Jehane had heard was the patter of water on trees, almost forgotten, a gentle drumming that sounded distant right up to the moment that drops of rain spattered on their shoulders and upturned faces.

'To wash the trees,' Talot said, with pleasure. 'The Ged did it to wash the trees. There's more dust on them than rot on a whore. Look at that – rain!'

'I wish there were thunder,' Jehane said suddenly. 'I like thunder.'

Talot laughed. 'I would have guessed you like thunder.'

Jehane grinned at her. 'How would you guess that, Sweeting?'

'I just would.'

Jehane cuffed her playfully. Talot grabbed Jehane's

hand and they moved toward the sister-warriors' baths. SuSu, sitting hidden in a thicket, heard their voices grow fainter and disappear.

She had been bathing in one of the streams that welled from the ground all over R'Frow, ran for lengths or tens of lengths, and vanished underground. She knew better than to try to use the baths behind the citizens' hall. When she heard Jehane and Talot, she had just emerged from the hidden crook of the stream and put on her tebl, still wet from scrubbing.

After the sister-warriors had gone, SuSu waited until she was sure no one else lurked in the space between the thicket and the hall. Moving quickly through the light rain, choosing the most unobtrusive route at the edge of overhanging trees, she slipped into the hall. Two female citizens, chattering to each other, climbed the ladder. SuSu followed close behind. Rain dropped off the hems of their tebls onto her head, but neither acknowledged her presence. Turning into the corridor set aside for Falonal and Jamila and her, SuSu darted down it before any door could open, thrust her thumb into the lock, and closed the door behind her.

Safe.

The silence greeted her, lapping around her in little waves, warm and dark. She didn't turn on the light. Instead she sat in the dark silence, glorying in the quiet. Once she stood and walked around the perimeter of the entire room, from the glowing orange circle back around to it again, her small hands rubbing each handspan of the metal wrof: palms flat, delicate fingers splayed to cover as much area as possible. There was no window. There would never be a window to let faces peer in, to let sounds ooze through to tear at her. R'Frow had no windows, and her door was locked.

SuSu smiled to herself. She dried her long black hair, combed it, took off her wet clothes, and spread them on the floor to dry. Then she sat once more against the wall.

The room contained no amusements, no Ged objects taken from the Hall of Teaching, nothing but her cushions. She needed nothing. She had the silence.

When she grew tired, she curled up on the cushions and fell asleep.

A long time later, the door flew open.

SuSu sat up and cried out as light sprang into the room. *The door* . . . the door could not open . . .

'Close that door,' a man hissed. 'Kick it!'

SuSu had a brief glimpse of Falonal's face, triumphant and ashamed, before the door was kicked closed and the corridor vanished. Another kick, and pain exploded in her chest.

'Shut me out, will you,' the brother-warrior grunted through closed teeth. SuSu clutched her rib cage and screamed. Light flooded the room and his face swam above her in waves of pain, one ear half-gone and hideously scarred.

'Don't hit her again!' a man hissed. 'Shit, we haven't even used her yet!'

The half-eared warrior hit her again, in the face. Blood filled her mouth. 'Just so you open up next time, Sweeting.'

SuSu tried to scream again and could not, choked on blood and began to gasp. Flailing wildly, she rolled off the cushions and onto the floor, where hands seized her hard.

'Naked already – she was waiting for us.'

'For me. I'm first.'

'The darkcold with that. I don't take wet mud.'

The hands released her, bodies scuffled briefly beside the cushions. SuSu spat the blood from her mouth. Instantly more welled in to take its place.

'Spit on *me* – ' He seized her and threw her on her back. Her rib shrieked in agony. Then he was on her, forcing her legs apart with his knee, dropping his weight on her body while his hands fumbled for her breasts. The first thrust made her cry out, spraying blood, and pain pierced clear to her ribs. Die . . . she was going to die . . .

Whore's rot, the dark furry voice whispered, and laughed, a laugh that turned the burning pain to cold. SuSu whimpered once and let go, drowning in the blood and the pain and the dark voice and the battering between her legs, drowning in the voices you could never hide from after all not even in the silence not ever *whore's rot you are a whore you're no better than Jamila and me* –

A scream that was not hers, and the battering stopped.

The mauling hands were torn from her breasts, and the half-eared warrior's weight disappeared, snatched upward by the barbarian giant as if the brother-warrior had been a twig. The enormous albino held him dangling above SuSu, his heels kicking inches above her eyes, his neck circled by one huge hand. The warrior kicked and flailed, his eyes bulging from their sockets. The barbarian snapped his neck and heaved the body against the wall. He stepped over SuSu and started for the other man.

The Jelite was a warrior. He had taken off his weapons belt, but even unarmed he leaped forward to meet the barbarian, knocking him sideways, and scrambled to deliver a deadly kick to his massive throat. The giant moved sideways, evaded the kick by a handspan, and caught the other around the neck. With the same practiced motion as before, he snapped his neck and hurled the body against the wall. The second before his neck snapped, the warrior screamed, a yell of sheer rage that ended in a gurgle of blood and air. SuSu tried to lift her hands to shut out that scream, heard herself cry out in pain *only it was not herself it was the dark furry voice laughing* die *die* die *die* . . .

She fainted.

The room swam back to her, buoyed on waves of hurt, but she could breathe again. She was not dead. A cloth was tied tightly around her ribs, and her own blanket covered her nakedness. There were voices, people clustered in the doorway, more tearing voices, but in the room with her there was only the barbarian giant, in merciful silence.

Silence. He tipped his head to one side and looked at her quizzically, gently, like some great quiet beast. She could feel the silence go all the way through him, as it went all the way through white rock, with no darkness or furriness, no hidden tearing voices, no sound ever. She closed her eyes and let her arms, which had been struggling to move toward her bound ribs, fall back on the cushion.

He lifted her carefully, cushion and all. Carefully, not jarring the bound ribs, he carried her toward the door.

The crowd of watchers, all citizens in this citizens' hall, scurried away. Those caught between the giant and the end of the corridor flattened themselves against the wall. Falonal, body pressing into the wrof and eyes rolling in terror, cried out to SuSu, 'I let the giant in! Don't let him hurt *me* – I went back after I – I let him in to save you, SuSu! I did – to save you! Tell him that!'

SuSu didn't open her eyes. She let herself be carried gently, tenderly, down the ladder, through the archway, away from the Jelite halls, on waves of white silence. She heard nothing: not Falonal's shouting, not the rain, not the word that flew along the sentry net from Belazir herself: *Let him pass. He is not the enemy.*

And not the later tumult behind her, as Jelite warriors discovered that while the high commander's lieutenant – who should have been checking the sentry net – had instead slipped through it and gone to the deserted Hall of Teaching, a Delysian soldier had stalked and killed a sister-warrior hunting in the dense woods. Her skull had been bashed in, and her Jelite knife lay broken beside her from having been slammed into the sleek, rain-streaked cliff of the Gray Wall.

20

Ayrys had finished making her device to keep people warm in the bitterness of Thirdnight. She sat back on her heels in her room and stared at the mass of food bowls, wires, and twisted cloth. Her cheeks were flushed with excitement, and she didn't turn when Kelovar entered the room.

'It works! It works, Kelovar!'

Kelovar stood over the device, rain dripping off his tebl. One drop landed on an exposed wire and hissed.

'Put your palms here,' Ayrys said. 'No, not there – here, on this stretch of cloth. Feel? It gets warm!'

Kelovar jerked back his hand. His light eyes narrowed. Ayrys put her own palm where his had been and laughed aloud, and slowly his head swung to study her. She laughed, the joyous, free sound that had once belonged to her glassmaking.

'I don't know how long it will stay warm. The acid eventually destroys the zinc plate, and the Ged won't tell me what to do about that. But there must be something. And *look* at it, Kelovar! It works! Hunters could take it out on the veld during Thirdnight – no, maybe not this version, it's too bulky, but they could use it at a base camp, instead of a fire. And children who are sick, or babies, could have it with them in Thirdnight. You could make a taut screen of cloth to make sure they didn't touch any of it and burn themselves. Or, no – wait! *Glass* – you could put the whole thing behind glass, the heat would still come through. What I'd give for my glass kiln! But even as it is, it *works*. Just look at it!'

Kelovar looked, his eyes narrowed to pale slits rimmed with rain. Two wrof food bowls and two Ged vessels held an acid mixture. In each, rectangles of metal were held upright by gobs of clay. More clay had fastened each bowl to a crudely shaped wooden board cut from a tree trunk and shaped to rise on two sides high enough to clear the bowls. Across the rises were stretched a triangle of multilayered Ged cloth large enough to accommodate a hunter's outstretched palms, or a newborn's small body. And there were wires everywhere, packed between the bowls and against the wood, coiled in shapes like Jelite bracelets, running directly under the cloth, where they were wrapped with some material Kelovar couldn't identify. The whole gave off more heat, more evenly, than a fire. And it could be touched. Ayrys laid her palm on the cloth and laughed again.

'There is no Thirdnight in R'Frow,' Kelovar said. His voice held a slow tightness, but Ayrys, in her pleasure, didn't hear it.

'That doesn't matter,' she said gaily. 'It *works*.'

'Where did you get all these things?'

'Bought them. Bartered for them. Took them from the Hall of Teaching. Ruined those and then went and bartered more. Grax wouldn't tell me the right proportion of acid to water – that's the kind of thing that just makes him say, "How could you discover it?" I wanted to tell him, "By magic and seduction and carrying on under both moons," but he wouldn't have understood the joke. And I found the proportion, and there the ugly ridiculous wonderful thing is, and it works!'

She took her hand off the device, made the quick salute glassmakers used in the glassyard to signal a successful firing – a half-mocking, half-triumphant flip of the thumb – and put her hand back on the device, her eyes shining.

Kelovar said nothing.

'You know, there's nothing in this thing that can't be created in Delysia, except the Ged wire, and a skillful smith might be able to figure out how to make that. It's a mixture of ores, Grax said, and even if a smith or weaponsmaker couldn't find this mixture, they might be able to create a different mixture that would get as hot without burning out. You can do that – try different mixtures of materials. I wonder why no master glassblower ever does that? We just go on using the same materials and changing only the designs. We never thought of this Ged experimenting – we just never thought of it. Maybe if I melted some . . . There's a smith in the next hall – Ondur said so. I can ask him!'

She jumped up. Kelovar, still kneeling beside the device, clamped a hand hard around her leg, and she glanced down in surprise.

'You're not going anywhere. Your childish toy can wait.'

Ayrys looked at him: his narrowed eyes, the hard set of his jaw. Slowly she said, 'It's not a toy.'

He made a noise of impatience. 'Whatever it is. You can't leave the hall. A Jelite warrior was killed an hour ago.'

She sank back down on her heels. 'Who?'

'What does it matter? There's one less now.'

'A sister-warrior?' *Jehane, reckless and overconfident . . .*

'Yes.'

'Who killed her?'

Kelovar's eyes shifted sideways. 'I don't know. But the hall below is seething with talk.'

'I haven't gone down. I was finishing . . .' She looked at her device. Warmth still flowed from it, and a faint glow.

'Not everyone was playing with toys.' He seemed to hear his own roughness, too great for the comment, and turned his head away from Ayrys. She saw the sharp line of his jaw and the strange light in his eye, gleam under gleam, light as much held back as moving outward.

'Kelovar . . . how did you hear about the killing?'

'I told you. Talk in the hall.'

'How do they know? Is the warrior boasting?'

'Of course not. Khalid forbade retaliation.'

She was silent a moment, gathering herself. 'Kelovar . . . did you kill her?'

'No,' he said. 'I only wish I had.'

She couldn't tell if he told the truth. Only the savage hatred in his voice was straightforward.

'You wish no one had killed the slime, don't you, Ayrys? You would rather we forgot Delysian pride and let the cobbler's murder pass like we were all slinking kreedogs!' He took her chin in his hand and brought her face inches from his own. '*But we're not.*'

Ayrys pulled her chin away. Kelovar laughed harshly, and then, after a moment, less harshly. It was the second laugh that chilled her. With incredible swiftness his face changed, lost it dangerous gleam, and he threw an arm around her waist and pulled her close.

'But you're not a soldier, Little Sun. You're my maker of toys. Why should you pay attention to Delysian military matters? That's a soldier's job. I'll keep you safe, so you can go on making toys.'

He kissed her neck. Violently Ayrys pushed him away. 'Listen to yourself, Kelovar. "Delysian pride, Delysian military" ' – savagely she mimicked his tone, too angry to be cautious. 'But this is not Delysia! Do you hear me? *This is not Delysia.* This is R'Frow, it's the Ged who have forbidden killing in R'Frow, and we've broken their law twice now. Don't you think they're going to do something about that?'

'Our killing was retaliatory. The only lawbreaking was done by the Jelite. "We" did not kill twice. There is no 'we' between Delysian and Jelite.'

'The Ged could exile us all from R'Frow!'

'Then let them!'

He would prefer it. For a moment Ayrys glimpsed that to Kelovar, R'Frow was different from what he had bargained for, stranger, and somehow more threatening . . . She frowned, trying to understand.

For a long moment they stared at each other. Then Kelovar smiled, a forced grimace that didn't reach his eyes. He reached for her again. 'I don't want to fight with you, Sweeting. It's raining outside, did you know? I'm all wet. Come dry me, sweet Ayrys.'

'Kelovar . . . don't.'

'Come dry me.'

She had risen and taken a step backward. He rose and lunged for her – half playfully, half not. His boot came down on the warming device, cracking the makeshift board and tipping it sideways. A wire snapped, fluid gushed onto the floor, and the reddish glow abruptly vanished.

Ayrys glanced down at the wreck of her invention, but only for a moment, and so was in time to catch the look on Kelovar's face before it vanished. Brief, bitter, unaware of itself – but she had seen it. *Pleasure*. Kelovar took pleasure in smashing the device, and pleasure of a kind Ayrys recognized. She had seen it in the glassyard, on the faces of inept glassmakers eyeing a master glassblower's batch that had inadvertently fired badly and cracked. A batch that, had it fired well, the inept could never hope to equal.

'I'm sorry,' Kelovar said, without sorrow.

'I think you should leave, Kelovar. I don't think we should bed any longer. I want to end it.'

'Because I stepped on your toy? I didn't intend to.'

'No. Not because of that.'

'Then why, Ayrys?' He was genuinely bewildered. She saw that he had not expected this, and she wondered how he could not have expected it; the frustration they gave each other outweighed the sexual pleasure. But Kelovar looked suddenly stricken, and there was something chilling in the suddenness of his change from soldier to clutching lover, something she could not name.

'Because we hurt each other. I don't want to bed together any longer.'

'You don't hurt me.'

'I don't want to bed together any longer, Kelovar.'

Bewilderment began to give way to anger. 'Do you want someone else?'

'No. No one else.'

'I love you, Ayrys.'

She looked at the broken device on the floor, and wondered what sort of love it was that knew so little about the supposed beloved. Kelovar followed her glance and his jaw tightened. 'We suit each other well enough.'

'No. We don't.'

'Because I'm not interested in Ged toys and you're not interested in Delysia?' His voice suddenly turned quiet. 'Why is that, Ayrys? Every time Delysia is mentioned, you shrink back a little. You've done it ever since we entered R'Frow. Why is that?'

She hadn't thought him that observant. They had not, it seemed, known each other at all. Before she could return an evasive answer, Kelovar said softly, 'Be careful, Little Sun. You could be suspected of more loyalty to the Ged than to your own kind. That could be a danger to you, sweet Ayrys.'

She faced him directly. 'Are you making a threat, Kelovar?'

But he was not. At the direct challenge he backed down and his face abruptly crumpled, his arms humbly loose at his sides. 'Please let me stay, Ayrys. Please.'

'No. Don't beg, Kelovar!'

But even that cruelty didn't stop him. There was something desperate in his face, a suppressed panic that she didn't understand and that slid, in a moment, back to a dangerous softness. 'You are mine, Ayrys. If I go or if I stay, it doesn't matter, you are mine. Someday you'll know that. I can wait.'

'Get out, Kelovar.' When he didn't move, she added gently, 'Please.'

He went. Ayrys stood with her hands pressed to her sides above the ruined warming device.

She was cold. Wrapping her arms around herself, she rubbed her shoulders, but it didn't help. She was cold inside, cold as she had not been even on the veld with Jehane, cold as she had not been since the south gate of Delysia had shut behind her forever. *Embry. Delysia.* *'Your own kind.'*

What would it feel like to show the warming device to one of her own kind? 'I made it like this, I tried this and this, this worked . . .' Even in the glassyard, there had been interest only in the traditional methods, the traditional shapes.

She saw again the red and blue glass helix, smashed on the stone by the river, the shards glittering in moonlight.

Kneeling, Ayrys turned over the pieces of the warming device. But this was not glass – it could be fixed. Kelovar, unlike Jehane, had done no real damage.

'Your own kind . . .'

The Ged, with their doomed prison, had set her mind free, pushed her out onto that swift river where the only currents were how things fitted together, and the only rocks her own blindness. But the Ged were not her own kind, despite Kelovar's accusation. They sat stolidly, looking and listening, listening and looking, and they were not capable of warmth.

Why was she still so cold?

Impatient with herself, Ayrys began repairing the warming device. She would have to prepare more of the acid mixture; Kelovar had spilled nearly all of it. She was wiping the floor with a cushion cover when the wall spoke, so suddenly she nearly cried out.

No wall had spoken since the choosing of thumblocks

on the first day in R'Frow, and the outer Wall had never
spoken so loud. The Ged-like voice wanted to wake up
those who slept, halt those who walked away. Yet the
voice was calm, a shout in volume but not in excitement,
an eerily quiet clamor.

'There will be no more killing in R'Frow. The humans
of Qom will make certain of this. There will be no more
killing in R'Frow, or there will be exile from the city and
no riches will be given to humans.'

Ayrys sat, wet towel suspended in midair. But there
was no more.

'There will be no more killing in R'Frow,' the wall
repeated. 'The humans of Qom will make certain of this.
There will be no more killing in R'Frow, or there will be
exile from the city and no riches will be given to humans.'

Exile from the city. Exile.

Ayrys put her hands over her face and began to laugh,
the bitter and uncontrollable laughter that had convinced
Jehane she was crazy. But this time Ayrys knew she was
not crazy. It was just so ludicrous, so absurd, so richly
impossible . . . exile from *two* cities, *two* peoples who
were not 'your own kind' . . . exile . . .

She forced herself to stop laughing.

The wall was repeating its warning a third time, and
now Ayrys heard its vagueness – deliberate vagueness?
The Ged did not say who would be exiled if another killing
took place. The killer alone? Those of the killer's city,
Jelite or Delysian? All the humans in R'Frow?

Carefully, as if care would restore sense to the situation,
she finished mopping the spilled water and opened the
door to her room. Corridor, ladder, hall below were
tumultuous with talk, with shouting, with speculation.
No one knew anything, and no two Delysians agreed on
what they didn't know.

Ayrys was halfway down the ladder before yet another
question occurred to her. The Ged always went back into
the perimeter after the Hall of Teaching was over. They

left through the only break in the entire Wall, a door in the eastern side. No one, not even the soldiers on the sentry net or the hunters in the wilderness, ever saw a Ged after dark.

So how had the Ged known there had been a killing at all?

21

'Where were you?'

'At the Hall of Teaching.' Dahar stood stiffly before the high commander; he could feel the skin on his face stretched taut and dry.

'You did not ask permission to leave the net.'

'Permission wasn't required. I checked the net at the usual time. There is no tradition of reporting how I use my time between checks.'

Belazir made a chopping motion with her left hand, unlike her usual formality. Two spots of color stood high on her cheekbones. 'Kreeshit, Dahar, I'm not talking about tradition, I'm talking about military necessity! You knew the Delysians might strike back for their bladder-muscled cobbler! What was at the Hall of Teaching more important than that?'

'There was nothing at the Hall of Teaching.'

'No Ged? No toys? No weapons?'

'No.'

'Then what the darkcold were you doing there?'

'Nothing.'

She eyed him steadily. The spots of color faded; without them she looked older. Dahar saw her waver between curiosity and punishment. It was an old scene, surprising only in that he found himself hoping for curiosity. He thought he had schooled himself long ago to indifference about which choice his commanders made.

Belazir's command room, just above the ladder from

the hall below, had the only decorated wall Dahar had seen in R'Frow. Someone had painted across it the entire spectrum of Jelite warrior ranks: crescent moon, moon with stars, one sun, two suns, three suns. What had they used that would adhere to the wrof? Dahar would have guessed whore's paints, except that he knew how impossible that was.

'I'm not going to order punishment for you, Dahar. The warriors would hold it against you, and they already hold the double helix against you. I don't want any talk of a rift in the command. Not with this group of . . . unseasoned warriors. Slipping through the sentry net is one thing – it might sharpen them to know you can do it – but going to the Ged hall alone is different. For what reason?'

'I liked to be there.'

Belazir stared levelly. Dahar waited. When she said nothing, he forced it. 'You want to know if going there is somehow connected to the Blue and Red.'

'Yes.'

'It is not. There are no strange ceremonies, no healer rituals that I slip through the net to attend. No blood drinking, High Commander. No human dissection.'

He had gone too far. Belazir did not deserve it. Her curiosity had had only the faintest sheen of distaste, and Dahar counted it as weakness in himself that he had not accepted distaste long ago. Belazir was an able high commander – that was enough. To expect understanding from her about what he did not understand himself was both indulgent and stupid.

He said, 'If I had been with a whore, would I have been any more able to stop the killing of the sister-warrior?'

'I don't expect you to be able to stop it. What I expect is for your mind to be filled with the good of Jela, and with nothing else that might either compete for that or lessen your standing among your warriors. If I thought that flogging would remind you of that, I would order it.'

It was a harsh rebuke. Despite himself, Dahar flushed.

Belazir turned away. For several minutes she stood with her back to him, apparently thinking, gazing through the open door that would always be open when a brother-warrior stood in her command room. Her back was broad-shouldered, the muscles in her neck knotted beneath the graying coil of sister-warrior's braids. He wondered suddenly what she had been like when she was young. In the dishonor of the thought and the stiffness of her back, he suddenly saw another room, another commander . . .

'But how does the double helix get into the body?' the child asked. The old man looked at him disdainfully. He wore the Blue and Red on his shoulder, and his hair – what was left of it – was cut in the fringe of a master warrior. He looked at Dahar's strong young frame with dislike.

'That is one of the mysteries. The double helix comes to each of us at birth, and departs at death. Warrior-priests wear it because when we heal we try to keep the helix in the body as long as possible. That's all you need to know, boy.'

The child peered through the crude lens in his hand. 'The blood looks the same, big or small.'

'That's because it's just blood. There is no helix in it. The helix dwells in one part of the body only, and that is the center of the life. All the rest is death, merely waiting for the battlefield.'

'Well, where is that one place?' the child demanded.

'I said you don't need to know that.'

The boy considered the master. 'You don't know where it is.'

'Don't be insolent, boy!'

'But you don't, do you? We can't find it. That's why we don't heal very many people. That's why my mother died.' He looked challengingly, without tears, at the old man, who seized his rod.

'Insolence in a warrior-priest never goes unpunished. Not by anyone.'

'You should have looked for her helix before she died,' the

*child said coldly, nothing childlike but the words themselves.
'You should have found out a way to make her another double
helix so she wouldn't have to die. It's your fault.'*

*The rod descended. Dahar took his flogging without a
sound; the master, driven to a frenzy by the boy's refusal to
cry out, left bloody welts on his buttocks and the backs of his
legs. When, out of breath, he was finally forced to stop, the
child turned and met his eyes. The look went on for a long
time. Mucus streamed from Dahar's nose and blood from his
lip, bitten nearly through to keep himself silent. When he was
able to talk again, he did.*

*'You can't find the double helix. You're not good enough.
But I will find it. When I'm a warrior-priest, I will find it.'*

*He braced himself for the second flogging, knowing this one
would go on until he fainted.*

'. . . not forbid you to go again to the Hall of Teaching,
even at night,' Belazir was saying. 'There is no horror in
retaining a lieutenant and treating him as if he were not
yet chosen for a cadre, unless I wish to call your loyalty
to Jela into question. And there is no question of that in
my mind.'

'I –'

'In *my* mind, Dahar. Look to your brother-warriors,
and look carefully. They don't like seeing that emblem
on your shoulder, and they don't like this new threat from
the Ged. You hold them by your physical skills and by
your courtesy to the monster. Be sure you continue to
hold them.'

By his courtesy to the monsters. Dahar stared at the
painted wall. The colors were too garish. Belazir understood no better than any of them. But then she surprised
him again.

'Why do you think they gave us the new weapon now?'

The question touched his own painful flickers of doubt.
'I've wondered the same thing, Commander.'

'The timing is strange,' Belazir said; she frowned
slightly. 'To demand peace, and to give a new weapon on

the same day, to forbid violence and to force Jelite and
Delysians to train together . . . if I were Ged, I wouldn't
do it like that.'

If I were Ged. Dahar said slowly, 'They don't think
like us.'

'In what way?'

'They are more . . . reasonable.'

'What do you mean? The timing of this weapon is not
reasonable.'

He concentrated on the garish wall. 'I've sometimes
thought they rely on mind, and never on body sense. On
action but not reaction. Like a warrior who is superior in
the practice yard but can't sense an advantage in actual
battle.'

Belazir nodded. 'Yes. I've felt that. But choosing this
time to give us additional weapons, when the Delysians
want revenge . . . and they've taken their revenge,' she
added grimly. 'And now that will be the end of it. No
Jelite warrior will retaliate. Not for the sister-warrior the
Delysians killed, not for those two the barbarian killed.'

'The barbarian?'

Belazir told him what had happened in the whores'
corridor. Dahar grimaced in contempt.

'I know both the brother-warriors. Yard talk is that
they were burned from their cadres in Jela.'

'I wouldn't be surprised.' Belazir rubbed her hands
over her face, pulling at the weariness. 'Choose brother-
warriors to bury them both.'

'An honourable burial?'

Dahar could follow her hesitation: She was balancing
her disgust at the night's story with her sister-warrior's
dislike of whores, a dislike Dahar knew he did not fully
understand. She was weighing, too, the effect on the
cadres of a dishonorable burial. The sister-warrior would
receive full honors, which should not be diluted by a
simultaneous ritual of disgrace. And it was not dishonorable to force a whore – merely brutish. And unnecessary.

Dahar said, 'Neither of them was respected in their cadres. I can make the burial neither an honorable nor a dishonorable one, with no ritual at all. As if they had been citizens.'

Belazir nodded. He saw what it cost her to deprive even the worst of her warriors of a warrior's burial.

'And the whore?'

Belazir's face changed. She gave him a strange look, and abruptly Dahar knew that she was wondering what she would never say aloud: whether Dahar had used SuSu, whether he had enjoyed her, about the whole murky and ambiguous relationship between the male cadres and their whores.

'Let the giant keep her,' Belazir said austerely. 'Two other citizens have applied to me for permission to become whores, since there are no whores' children here; the brother-warriors will have enough. I don't want to provoke the foreign giant. There's no way to know if he even understands the Ged law against killing. And he is not Delysian, not an enemy. Let him keep her. We stand on the blade of honor with the Ged, and no Jelite warrior is going to break that bond.'

They spent the next hour making sure of that – going over the cadres name by name, changing practice schedules and net duties, discussing what each knew about every Jelite warrior. That one warrior might have already killed against orders had shaken Belazir; that no other warriors had turned the killer over to the blade of honor shook her even more. Dahar saw that she wanted to believe that the cobbler had been killed by a fellow Delysian, but could not.

He didn't believe it either.

Belazir's lover glowered at him as he passed her in the corridor. When he stopped and met her gaze directly, she immediately dropped her eyes and flicked both wrists in respectful salute.

22

'Last night the walls of R'Frow spoke to us,' Dahar said to Grax.

The unnatural silence of the last two days had given way to a slow, angry buzzing, but as soon as Dahar spoke, the teaching room fell into quiet. Rather than go to his usual floor table, he stood at the head of his warriors; without turning, he could feel them tighten behind him. Across the room the Delysian commander shifted his weight slightly forward, turned his weapons arm slightly inward. The Delysian glass-blower looked up. Dahar saw all of them and none, saw only Grax. 'No Ged had left the perimeter. How did you know a sister-warrior had been killed?'

Grax said, 'The teaching group is not all here. We will not begin until every human in the group is here.'

Dahar held the Ged's eyes. Missing were the barbarian giant and the whore he had stolen. Those two wouldn't appear, not unless they were brought bodily by the Ged, and a stun strip would be the only way to do that to the giant. Was Grax stalling?

Dahar was wrong. The two entered, unmistakably together. SuSu's face was swollen and bruised from her battering. She walked very close to the giant, eyes cast down but her face free of a whore's paint and her black hair loose, in the manner of very young, chaste Jelite girls. The garish tebl of a whore had been replaced by a single loose garment of straight, stark white, clumsily sewn at the seams as if by someone who did not know how.

The giant's face contorted with fury. He strode straight to Dahar, who could not stop himself from flinching and silently cursed himself for it. The warriors all drew knives; Dahar signaled them to wait, fought the urge to draw his own, and met the barbarian's eyes. It was like looking up at overhanging rock.

Even Grax shrank back. *Grax.*

But the giant didn't attack. He glared fiercely into Dahar's face, anger burning on him like white heat, more terrible for being wordless. His breath scorched Dahar's cheek. After a long moment, he swung to Lajarian, the brother-warrior ranked after Dahar, and bent on him the same white burning. The warrior stood his ground, but he paled and did not sheathe his knife. The barbarian swung to Jehane, and on down the line of warriors and citizens both. Warning – it was a warning, to them all.

When he had finished, the giant sat down with SuSu at a floor table in the back of the room, not across from her but beside her. No one had spoken a word. The barbarian's weird silence, deepened by fury, circled them both so profundly it seemed they were sealed together behind it, as behind a wall of clear wrof.

Belazir had said to let him have the whore. But it was a long moment before Dahar repeated his question.

'How did the Ged know a sister-warrior had been killed, when all the Ged had gone into the perimeter for the night?'

Grax said calmly, 'The Ged knew of the second killing in R'Frow because we were informed of it. There will be no more killing in R'Frow. The humans of Qom will make certain of this. There will be no more killing in R'Frow without exile from the city and its riches.'

'Informed by whom?'

'The Ged were informed of the killing. There will be no more killing in R'Frow. The humans of Qom will

make certain of this. There will be no more killing in
R'Frow without exile from the city and its riches.'

It was no answer at all.

'Exile for the killer alone, or for other humans as well?'

The glassblower shifted abruptly in her place.

Grax said, 'There will be no more killing in R'Frow
without exile from the city and its riches.'

'You have not answered either of my questions. Who
informed the Ged of the killing? Who will be exiled if it
is repeated?'

'There will be no more killing in R'Frow without exile
from the city and its riches.'

It was like talking to the Gray Wall. Dahar's eyes narrowed; all the doubts he had discussed with Belazir surfaced yet again. Ged science might not mean Ged
truthfulness . . .

Why was the thought so unbearable?

Grax was looking directly at him. The Ged moved his
hand over the black box that controlled the floor tables,
and the top of the floor table directly before Grax dissolved
– but not the others. That was unusual. On the new top
lay a gray box of wrof and several pieces of shaped glass.

Lenses.

Grax still looked directly at Dahar. He said, 'Within
the bodies of humans lies the double helix.'

Dahar felt himself go still.

'We will teach humans what this means,' Grax continued. 'It is useful knowledge. But unlike the other
equipment, we do not have an endless supply of these.
No human may remove this equipment from the Hall of
Teaching. All who wish to learn this teaching of the
double helix must come here, to me, and share my floor
table.'

No one moved. Soldiers and warriors measured each
other across the room, and a few faces smoldered with
open hatred. *Now, after two killings, to share a floor
table . . .*

Grax repeated, 'All who wish to share this teaching of the double helix must come here, to me, at this floor table.'

Dahar felt his warriors' eyes burn into the emblem on his shoulder. *This teaching of the double helix.* He was careful not to move, to show nothing: not his anger, not his longing.

Minutes passed, while Grax waited calmly. Then the Delysian glassblower – 'Ayrys' – moved to sit before Grax. Dahar saw her clasp her hands tightly together in her lap, the one with the scarred and slightly deformed thumb stilling the trembling of the other. Her face showed defiance, and fear, and an eagerness badly hidden, like light behind clouds. She picked up one of the lenses and looked at her fingernail through it.

One of the Delysian soldiers hissed.

'This is an enlarger,' Grax said, touching the dark gray box. 'It will make the cells of your finger look much larger than lenses can. The device within must not be exposed to air.'

Dahar heard Ayrys ask something, her voice too low for him to distinguish the words.

'A cell is the building stone of flesh. It is too small to see. All life is made of cells, each a tiny wall surrounding other structures, as the Wall surrounds R'Frow. This enlarger will let you see your own cells, and also let you see other cells, the cells of sickness, that attack them.'

Ayrys held the enlarger uncertainly.

'The smallest and most important part of each cell is the double helix.'

Slowly, Dahar felt his hand move. It gave Lajarian the signal to assume temporary command. Dahar moved to the floor table, felt his knees bend and his body lower to sit beside a Delysian glassblower, in front of the Ged.

He saw, briefly, Lajarian's face.

'The teaching is open to all,' Grax said. 'All who wish

this teaching of the double helix can come to the floor table.'

Fourteen pairs of eyes flickered to the Ged's face, returned to the Jelite first lieutenant sitting beside the Delysian citizen. Only the barbarian and the whore paid no attention, walled in their own cell of silence.

Too harshly, Dahar demanded. 'How do I use the enlarger?'

The Ged showed him. He picked up a silverbell stem that had risen with the table and he sliced off a tiny piece, holding it out to show them on the tip of his finger. The greenery made a furry mote against the hard, faint shimmer of unseen wrof encasing Grax. He placed one edge of the gray box over, but not touching, the bit of plant. It disappeared.

'It is inside. There it will be separated to a single layer of plant – a layer of cells. You place your eye here.'

Dahar held the gray box to his eye. For a moment he could see nothing but Lajarian's face. Then the world exploded into its true life.

A tiny walled city, stark and miniature, perfectly formed and closed on all sides. A 'cell,' to imprison life – or to set it free . . .

Excitement that was almost fear surged through him. Pulling the knife from his belt, he didn't even see the sudden watchfulness of Grax, the stiffening of Ayrys, the immediate step forward of Lajarian, weapons drawn. Dahar sliced into the tip of his finger. Blood spurted red onto the tabletop, and he held the enlarger over it and then to his eye.

He never knew how long he stared at the round red concave miracles.

The Ged's quiet voice called him back. 'Blood cells are different from others. Living cells scraped from the inside of the cheek will show you more.'

Without hesitation, Dahar put the tip of his knife between his lips and into his mouth. Scrapings came away from the inside of his cheek. At the first sight of the cells, each a teeming city latticed and patterned and solid with life, he went rigid. It was true. It was within his grasp, as real as the veld or the sea or the mountains, filled with light.

'The dark mass is the center of the cell's life,' came Grax's quiet voice, from a great distance. 'In it lie all the orders for everything a living cell does – its birth and growth and healing and death. All the orders lie in the tiny patterns of the double helix.'

There was a great rushing in Dahar's ears. It was this, and not the quiet voice, that called him back – back to R'Frow, to the calm watchfulness of Grax. To meet Ayry's eyes, fixed with startled shock on his. To the gazes of his appalled warriors. To the bitter taste of salt in his mouth, where his hand had trembled on the knife and filled his mouth with blood.

'He could have started a *battle*,' Talot said, 'drawing his knife like that with no signal to Lajarian. No signal at all. How were we to know what he wanted us to do?'

'I wish he had started a battle,' Jehane said. She swung her threeball moodily in the direction of the target, but didn't throw it. She had practiced and raced and wrestled, but none of it had sweated the trouble off her mind the way it should have – the way it always did before – and she resented it.

Talot threw herself down by a stand of trees at the edge of the practice yard, picked a blade of grass, and chewed on it with sharp, even teeth. 'No battle. You know that, Jehane. Belazir and Dahar don't want that.'

'Then what the kreeshit do they want? Train and train, learn to use the new weapons – and a sister-warrior dies like a slug. A *sister-warrior*.'

'They want us to stay in R'Frow. If we're exiled, we'll miss the rest of the new weapons, and the Delysians won't. And Belazir doesn't want to anger the Ged. That's only intelligent. No good commander would provoke a battle we couldn't win.'

Frustrated, Jehane flung herself beside Talot. Talot was making sense – but sense was not pushing away the trouble. She stared moodily at the sisters still throwing three-balls across the field.

'What I wonder,' Talot continued in a low voice, 'is why the lieutenant did . . . what he did. Belazir orders no provoking any violence, and then he draws his knife and puts it in his *mouth*. That Delysian citizen was sitting right near him. All she would have had to do is hit him hard on the shoulder; the blade would have gone right through his face or maybe even upward to the brain – '

Unthinking, Jehane said, 'Ayrys wouldn't do it.'

Talot rolled over to gaze at Jehane. 'You know her? A Delysian?'

Jehane scowled. 'Yes. No. I don't want to talk about it, Talot.'

Talot chewed harder on her blade of grass. 'I told you what *I* didn't want to talk about.'

There was a painful pause.

'She's a glassblower. A kemburi caught me on the veld, and she threw a bottle of some glassmaking dung at it and saved my life. So I stood on the blade of honor with her until I brought her safely across the veld to R'Frow, and does *that* satisfy you?'

Talot stood and started toward the baths. Jehane grabbed at a bony ankle and held her.

'I'm sorry, Talot. I just don't like to think about it – bound on the blade of honor with a *Delysian*.'

Talot considered, standing still. 'No. I don't think so. It was an honorable bond. It would have been dishonorable if you had killed her after she saved you from the kemburi.'

'Well, that's what I thought,' Jehane grumbled, mollified. 'Sit down again.'

Talot sat. 'Why did she kill the kemburi for you?'

'Can one see the Marker set? She's Delysian, she's a crazy whore. And you know something – Dahar looked crazy, too, when he looked into that Ged box.'

Talot inhaled sharply. Jehane, hearing her own words, jerked her head upward. Both held their breaths, and glanced toward the stand of trees close beyond, but not even wind rustled the thick branches.

'No one heard,' Talot finally whispered.

'The net – '

'Too far away. Jehane – '

'I know. I know.' Jehane's scowl deepened. She felt sore with trying to understand what should not even have been, and miserably aware that her questions were not going to leave her alone. They were like redflies at dusk in Jela, circling and biting and whining in a cloud that followed wherever she moved. 'But, Talot, what could make Dahar do that?'

Talot whispered even more softly. 'There was a birth-brother to a sister-warrior I trained with. She told me. Something happened when her birth-brother was born. All his life he had moments where his mind just . . . disappeared. His face would go empty, and he would fall to the floor, and then after a while he would get up and remember nothing. No warrior-priest could heal him. A disease.'

Jehane thought about it. 'Dahar doesn't fall down. And he didn't look empty. He looked . . . I don't know he looked. But he couldn't have that disease, Talot, or he would never have risen to the rank he has. They wouldn't have let him become a warrior at all.'

'Not in Jela. But he's an outlander. How do we know what their cadres do? And he wears the double helix. They dissect dead warriors and drink their blood – and some sister-warriors say their doses can even cast spells on the mind. Maybe he gave one to Belazir.'

'Do you really think so?'

'How could I know? But the Red and Blue are strange.

Dahar looked weirdly at that Delysian woman, too, did you see? Like she was . . . I don't know. Not there. If the double helix can trance minds . . .'

Sudden distaste filled Jehane. Dahar was a brother-warrior, the high commander's lieutenant. Talot went too far sometimes. That must have been how she could once have . . . She, Jehane, didn't even believe in spells and trances; they made no sense. Fauggh! And anyway, Dahar hadn't looked to Jehane as if he weren't seeing Ayrys. Toward the end he had looked as if he saw her very well, almost as if –

'Forget it,' she rasped. 'Forget the whole thing, and don't be stupid, Talot. We shouldn't even be talking about it. He's the high commander's first lieutenant.'

Talot didn't answer. Her head was bowed; Jehane scowled at the part in her coiled hair, a clean white line through the red.

'And anyway, no one would dare challenge Dahar about the knife. If Belazir threw it open to a cadre fight, Dahar would take the challenger apart.'

'Dahar might deny it to Belazir.'

'A lieutenant wouldn't lie to a high commander!'

'Jehane – never? Not even once?'

'Not a Jelite first lieutenant!'

Talot said gently, 'You trust too much, sister-love.'

'I don't want to talk about it!' Jehane jumped up, snatched at her threeball, and hurled it. It sailed in a high, clean, uncomplicated arc and smashed into the exact center of the target.

23

SuSu sat very still. Voices approached.

She was pressed against a shallow indentation in the face of a huge boulder deep in R'Frow wilderness, where once she never would have dreamed of going. Rock stood behind her, jutted slightly above her, suggested walls on each side without being walls. Before her stood a thick tangle of brush, gaudy with unknown red flowers; she had never before seen any veld flowers. Between brush and rock was only enough room for her small body, folded even smaller. She had not moved since he had left her there while he hunted. Stillness was never irksome to her; it was a sweetness almost as great as the silence.

She had lived in the barbarian giant's hall for over two tencyles, and the dark, tormenting voice had not once broken through the clean silence. They lived chaste. He made no demands on her, not for words nor for slitting, and SuSu gave neither. She let her mind float on the quiet and the warmth and the safety, and sometimes it seemed her mind floated away from her entirely, until there was no distinction between her and the warm air, her and the wrof floor of their room, her and the heavy-scented flowers in front of her now. At such times, when he would return from hunting or bathing or wherever he went, she would blink at him with bewildered eyes, unable to remember who he was, who she was, what she had become. Then she would remember. She would smile at his anxious, upturned face brought low enough to peer upward into

hers, and stroke his white hair with a single languorous
gesture of gratitude. She would remember who he was.
He was the guardian of her silence.

But this time there were voices.

Male. Hunters. Delysian.

Without knowing she did so, SuSu let herself breathe
a little deeper. Delysian soldiers were not as sharp-eyed
as Jelite warriors. Nonetheless, for a minute the old panic
caught at her, until it slid away. He was somewhere
nearby, hunting, and he stood like a great white wall
between her and anything that might threaten the silence.

The voices stopped directly before her bush. Through
the screen of leaf and flower, she saw them as dark shapes.

'No game, Kelovar.

'There will be, farther on.'

'No. Something's already scared it off. Listen . . . too
much silence. Someone's been through here recently.'

'Jelite,' Kelovar said. SuSu heard the tone in his voice
and squeezed her eyes tightly shut.

'You think so?'

'Hope so.'

A pause, and then the other said, 'Khalid's orders.'

'So?'

'You'd defy the commander's orders?'

'Would you?'

'No,' the other said slowly, drawing it out: Nooooo.
'He's in command, Kelovar. In command, whether we
like it or not. No killing in R'Frow.'

'And if a Jelite attacks first? You wouldn't defend
yourself?'

'Of course I would. Yes. But the Ged – '

'Jelite cowardice, not Ged.'

'That doesn't make sense. The Ged rule the city.'

'It's just a city,' Kelovar said, savagely, and with denial.
SuSu felt the fear under the denial scrape across her like
nails; she could hear fear no matter what tebl it wore.

'There,' the other voice said suddenly, and a crossbow

sang. Then a high animal scream, abruptly sliced off. 'Got it.'

'Good shot.'

'Schera makes a good stew. You eat with us?'

Kelovar said abruptly, 'Let me buy it from you.'

'Why?'

'Two habrin.'

'Done. You got a woman you have to impress before she'll bed with you?'

'No,' Kelovar said. 'Yes.'

The other laughed. SuSu opened her eyes. The male shapes moved away from her bush, and then stopped dead.

'By all shit – '

'Don't touch your bow,' Kelovar said swiftly. 'Don't touch it and he'll leave us alone. He hunts here.'

SuSu leaned closer to the bush. The white giant was hurtling across the clearing toward her rock. The Delysian fumbled for his knife, but Kelovar clamped his hand hard on the other's wrist. 'Leave him alone, I said. He killed two Jelite. *Two.*'

The giant raced past the two men, toward the pale boulder. The Delysians melted off into the wood. Never even glancing at them, the barbarian tore the flowering bush up by its roots.

SuSu had once more shut her eyes against the clawing fear in the second Delysians's voice. She opened to see his face peering anxiously into hers. She smiled, and abruptly all that huge body relaxed and smiled back. Tenderly he lifted her over the wreckage of the bush.

But the barbarian had just set her on her feet when all at once his body went rigid. His face jerked into surprised stiffness, the colorless eyes wide and staring. Then he began to fall sideways into the bush.

SuSu cried out. He continued to fall, and to fall and fall – a mountain crumbling. His lips drew back from his teeth and pink froth foamed at the corners of his mouth.

For a long moment he lay spread-eagled across the bush, and then he began to flail and writhe convulsively, crushing branches that whipped back across his face and body. SuSu threw herself across his chest; he bucked and flung her off like a doll.

She crawled back onto him and clung in sheer terror, wrapping her arms and her legs around his chest. The blood frothing from his mouth smeared across her loose hair. But she couldn't hold him; he bucked her off, thrashing and jerking until, as abruptly as the fit had begun, it ended and he lay still.

Sight returned to the giant's eyes. He struggled, panting, to sit, and reached out his arms. Susu crawled into them and he held her cuddled against him as if it were she, and not he, who had had the fit. But he crooned no words of comfort, no music, and it was this silence – safe, sure – that finally brought SuSu back from the dark place of terror where his thrashing had flung her.

She drew a little back from him and ran her fingers over his face. He gazed back at her from white eyes shot with red, still a little unfocused, shadowed with pain.

Eventually she rose and tugged him to his feet. He could stand, although a little unsteadily. He looked dazed.

A great tenderness flooded through SuSu: astonishing and a little cruel. It was the same feeling as when she had pressed the Ged stun strip to his back and he had sprawled, all that fearful male power, in the dust at her feet. She wrapped her arms around him – the first time she had ever voluntarily done so. Her head came only to his waist, and so her cheek pressed against the hardness of his erection.

For a second, confusion took over: the old practiced frauds, the fear, the threat of the dark furry voice. Then the bad moment passed and she thought quite clearly, *Yes. But not here.*

It was not desire, which she had never known, but a bond of honor. *Like a sister-warrior*, SuSu thought, and the perverse cruel tenderness flooded her once more, and she led him back to their hall. He stumbled occasionally, but she held his hand firmly. Although they had the entire hall to themselves, she closed the door – the door with the lock that sealed in the silence – before she set to work.

He was awkward, obviously afraid of hurting her. SuSu led the way, and let her mind float off into the walls, the floor, the cushions, no part of what she did. Removing his tebl, she began to kiss him: neck, enormous chest, the inside of one elbow. The giant began to breathe more heavily. She took his penis into her hand. It was as huge as the rest of him. She began to massage her own loins, at the same time guiding his mouth to her breasts. But no matter what she did, he was too big to enter her without pain.

Finally she knelt between his massive legs and took him into her mouth. Her mind drifted away until she was done: part of the warm air, part of the wrof. *Ha*, mocked the dark furry voice, startling her, but only once. The voice fell silent.

But afterward, when the albino giant lay sated, sprawled loose-limbed on the floor, SuSu raised herself on one elbow and looked at him. Eyes closed, he smiled. She smiled, too. If it pleased him, she would slit for him. There was no pain if she took him in her mouth. He had not been rough. And he had given her the two great gifts, the unexpected and earth-filling miracles: silence, and the wall of safety he made by thrusting his looming bulk between her and Jela. Silence, and the wall.

SuSu wrapped her arms across his enormous chest, laid her white cheek against his whiter one, and slept.

24

The Ged had all come together in the perimeter. Once together, they all postponed what they had come to do. First came the smell of pleasure in being all together, even if undercut with the acrid odor of anxiety. The eighteen knew already what the screen would show. The Library-Mind had woken those asleep, alerted those at work, broken into the communication bands with the orbital ship. They all knew.

But first they spoke of the teaching groups, going over other strangenesses they also already knew. Which humans seemed trainable. The unmoving image from the island. The seizure suffered by the albino giant. Those things about humans that reminded them of animals on other worlds. Wraggaf, Rowir, and Kagar, who had all trained alien animals before, told anecdotes the others had not heard. The anecdotes were new, but the Ged trainers' response in each case had been what the nontrainers would also have done, and the room smelled of pleasure in the civilized mix of the new and the good.

But eventually they had to look at the screen.

Seven of the eighteen – the closest seven – moved to surround and stroke R'gref as the Library-Mind recast the event on the wall.

The monitor had been one of the glowing circles on the outside wall of the Hall of Teaching. A Delysian soldier and a Jelite brother-warrior circled each other on the wrof path, knives drawn. The light looked neither night nor day; gray as the metal path, it gleamed dully on both knives and on the fair hair of the soldier. He fought with his left arm bloody, already slashed by the Ged dagger of the other. Beneath the light hair, the soldier's face was clenched in pain. The Jelite, both younger and quicker, circled to the soldier's left side, and when the soldier turned forward to protect his damaged arm, the other warrior brought his boot up in a flashing blur and kicked the other full in the groin.

The Delysian crumpled forward. The Jelite leaped on him, tore the knife from his hand, and straddled him. The soldier struck out with his right arm, but the blow was badly directed and in a moment the Jelite had pinned the soldier's right arm with his own left. The Delysian's bloody left arm flailed weakly on the ground.

'We aren't all dishonourable cowards,' the Jelite hissed. 'The Jelite you killed was a *sister-warrior*. Do you know what that means, scum?'

'Not me . . . not me . . . I didn't – '

'No matter which of you,' the Jelite said. He moved his knife toward the soldier's right eye. The eyelid closed; the Jelite pushed the point of the knife through the lid and into the eye.

The soldier screamed, high and piercing. The warrior waited as long as he dared, then moved the knife to the soldier's chest, feeling where the rib cage ended. He thrust the point down and forward, to the heart. Once, twice. His face did not change expression. The Delysian convulsed in agony, and the Jelite pulled out his knife and disappeared off the path into the woods.

From the Hall of Teaching, another man suddenly ran toward the body.

Grax growled quietly, 'From my teaching group. Dahar' – although the others already knew it.

'He is the one with the number-rational mind?' someone said; a comment was always answered.

'Yes. I have given him the thumblock to a teaching

room. He is a primitive healer, and has been able to learn to isolate and type the simplest of their bacteria.'

'I wouldn't have thought these humans capable of that,' the other said courteously. 'Harmony sings with us.'

'May it always sing. But we have no idea of what they are really capable,' Grax said, staring at the screen. At some underscent in his pheromones the other suddenly smelled of surprise.

Dahar knelt over the Delysian soldier. He felt for a pulse, probed at the bloody eye. When he raised his head, his face was tight with fury – and with something else that had been cut off but not quite eclipsed, some light of exhilarated discovery not yet gone out. In the slowly brightening light of the coming day, the double helix on his tebl glowed red and blue.

He picked up the dead Delysian and slung the body over his shoulder. Long strides carried him beyond the monitor's eye.

Within the perimeter room, there was a long silence. Arms and legs stroked R'gref. Then Krak'gar, the poet, spoke for them all, her pheromones thick with passion. 'How can this intraspecies violence be functional? It poisons the pheromones of the mind.'

'Harmony sings in us!'

'Harmony sings in us.'

'May it always sing.'

'It will always sing. The Library-Mind does not yet abandon the Central Paradox.'

'It still finds the correlation exists.'

'Somehow this is how humans got off their world and into space.'

The smell of revulsion, edged with something else: fear. This should not happen, this should not exist in the universe, this was as wrong as if the T'Fragk Constant were to change its number-rational value.

Wraggaf said, 'The dead human was in my teaching group.'

Rowir said at once, 'It is disturbing to lose one you have worked with.'

Murmurs of agreement, although they all knew that the dead Delysian had learned nothing from Wraggaf but weapons.

The Library-Mind surprised them a little by signaling for attention. In its courteous growl it announced that the probability of significant new events within the next day-night cycle was very high. The human activity level was intense. The anticipated correlation with the Central Paradox was strong.

On the wall screen, 'day' 'dawned'.

25

Dahar carried the body of the Delysian soldier through the sentry net, toward the command hall, without once feeling the weight: not the Delysian's, not his own. He walked disconnected from his body, watching it from the outside, detaching himself from what he did in order to observe it twice. An old trick: He had begun it as a boy cut off from the other boys by his insisting on becoming a priest-warrior, and had discovered it helped him to bear the slurs and petty cruelties he had not been old enough to understand. *Dahar crossed the practice yard, ignoring the thrown jonkil head,* he would tell himself, making of it a running story, an incident happening to someone else.

Later, when he did understand the warriors' fear of him, detaching his mind from his physical body had become a habit, and then a necessity. When warriors he had tried to heal had instead died as much from what he didn't know as from their own illnesses, his mind held to one side, and watched, and tempered frustration by leaving some essential part of Dahar out of the death, out of the anger, out of the failure. Dividing body from mind. It had let him continue as a warrior-priest, and he discovered that it also made him a better fighter – able to leave his emotions out of his fighting, able to coldly observe how the emotions of his opponent could be turned to his own advantage.

He would need to do that now. There must be no false moves, no weaknesses exposed, no frustration that his opponent could use. Not this time. Not when the opponent would be his high commander.

The sentry net let him through without even the ritual challenge. No one was in the lower hall except the sentry, a very young sister-warrior set here because it was the safest duty. He sent her for Belazir. With one horrified glance at the Delysian's face, she scurried up the ladder.

Dahar dumped the soldier between two floor tables and detached himself to fight.

Belazir descended the ladder and crossed the room slowly, tying her belt around her waist, her hard-faced lover and the young sentry behind her. She motioned for both to remain by the ladder and stood looking down at the Delysian.

'By the Hall of Teaching,' Dahar said. 'Just now. I was inside, working with the Ged equipment.'

Belazir said sharply, 'Inside?'

'Grax gave me the thumblock yesterday.'

'There are no thumblocks on the doors to the Hall of Teaching.'

'There is now. Grax made one.' That gave her pause, as Dahar had intended it should; everything that kept the staggering range of Ged power in front of her mind would help.

Belazir nodded for him to go on. She had not taken her gaze from the mutilation of the soldier's eye.

'I heard a scream. By the time I ran from the hall, the killer was slipping into the brush.'

Belazir said, 'Did you stop to lock the door?' and in the dry sarcasm Dahar heard her anger, and her subtle doubt of him: Which comes first, duty to Ged potions or duty to Ged law?

He had stopped to lock the door.

For the briefest second, Dahar considered lying to her. But he pushed the thought away. *Not that way*, the detached mind warned. *Try a surprise thrust.*

'I locked the door. But I saw the warrior before he ran off.'

Belazir finally looked from the Delysian's face to Dahar's.

'You saw him?'

'Yes.'

'Who?'

'I didn't see his face – just his gait. It's enough.'

Belazir nodded; for a good first lieutenant, it was enough. 'I count three brother-warriors who move with just that gait, five at the most. It won't be hard to check on all five. Two of them were assigned to the net; they shouldn't have been able to leave it long enough to run all the way to the Hall of Teaching and back before a signal check by the sentries next to them in the net.'

Belazir said, 'Who started it?'

'I didn't see. But it had to have been the brother-warrior, Commander. Otherwise why would he slip the net?'

'You did.'

'Was there another brother-warrior who asked you for a chance to form contact with the Ged?'

She said sharply, 'Don't try to make a fool of me, Dahar. You don't study their potions to make contact with them for Jela.'

He said nothing; better to let her regret the sharpness on her own. He had her permission for study with Grax. Belazir's own sense of fairness would tell her that, and regret at her sharpness would make her more patient with whatever he said next.

He would use her fairness any way he could.

'How would the brother-warrior have known where to find the Delysian? Or even have known that this is the one who killed the sister-warrior? Yard talk is that even their commander doesn't know which soldier it was.'

'I don't think the warrior did know. I think any Delysian would have done. We know Khalid permits his soldiers to hunt in the wilderness at night – they've passed close to the sentry net before. To lie in wait near the Hall of Teaching would be reasonable. All the wrof paths end up there, and the orange circles on the outside shed enough light to see without being seen.'

Belazir stared again at the mutilated eye.

Dahar said evenly, 'The brother-warrior disobeyed not just the Ged but you. You gave a distinct high-command order.'

'And he will die for it.'

'And then so will Jela.'

Belazir jerked her gaze to his. Dahar went on in the same even tone, struggling to keep it the voice of military reason alone, fighting himself as much as her.

'Consider, High Commander. The Ged did not see the killing. But they watch who comes to the Hall of Teaching each morning and who does not, and they search for those who do not until they find them. In addition, they must have their own net of informers, or how could they have known about the first killing so fast? When we all go to the Hall of Teaching in a few hours, they will see one of two things: either a Delysian dead, or – if I kill the brother-warrior – a Delysian and a Jelite dead. The price of killing is exile.'

Dahar stopped, gathered himself together, spoke as carefully as he could. 'In each of those two situations – those two different situations – who might the Ged exile?'

'We don't know, Lieutenant. You have said yourself that they do not think like humans!'

She did not want to look at the inevitable, if it skirmished near the dishonorable. *In a high commander, that could be a real weakness*, the detached Dahar said. The other Dahar said swiftly, 'No. They aren't human. But what seems the most reasonable possibility?'

He saw her considering. 'If the Delysian alone is dead, then it would be reasonable to exile all Jelite. It's we who have broken the blade of honor – '

He caught the rage and shame under her level tone and risked interrupting her. 'Then the new weapons yet to come would go to Delysians alone. If there were no Jelite in R'Frow, Khalid could probably keep his soldiers disciplined enough not to kill each other for what's left of the year within R'Frow. Delysia would reap whatever the Ged can give, whatever power. And when the year is over and they leave R'Frow, armed with Ged power – '

Belazir scowled savagely. 'But the Ged won't see that. They will see that we have done what we can about the dishonor. They will see a dead Delysian *and* a dead Jelite.'

'Then they'll see that Jela has killed twice, and Delysia not at all.'

Belazir stared at him, and then exploded. 'You equate a killing against orders with a punishment for disobeying those same orders – '

'*I* don't. But you've just said the Ged don't think like humans. They've forbidden all killing in R'Frow. And if we kill the brother-warrior, Jela has killed twice, and Delysia not at all. Who will the Ged exile?'

Harshly, she said, 'If you have a proposal to make, Dahar, make it.'

He would not permit himself to clench his fists. 'Let the Delysians have the brother-warrior.'

'*What*?'

'If they kill him, both sides have killed equally. Any Ged decision on exile would have to – '

'You would buy R'Frow with that much dishonor? *Buy* it – like some Delysian trader who deals in life itself, and with the betrayal of a brother-warrior – '

'Who betrayed you.'

'And who deserves to die for it at Jela's hand, not at the hands of the enemies of his city – and mine! Freely given, freely returned – not bargained over like – '

'Not a bargain. An alliance. Listen to me, Commander. What is any truce but an alliance? And there is nothing dishonorable about an alliance, freely given on both sides.

Three Jelite, three Delysians, and together you and Khalid punish any who disobey the orders you've both given. The Ged see one dead from each side – and more, Commander, *much more*. They see evidence that Jela and Delysia are trying to obey the Ged law – '

Abruptly, Dahar realized he had made a mistake. *Evidence* was a Ged word; there was no human word for the methodical gathering and sifting of proof that made the Ged science everything the human dabblings were not. But the moment he had used the Ged word, growling it low in the back of his throat, Belazir's face had passed from fury to a cold contempt that he recognized as far more dangerous.

'And you could stand there in honor, *Lieutenant*, while a brother-soldier under your command is turned over to Delysia for their tortures – in order for you to study alien potions in R'Frow.'

'Not torture. Clean execution, in our presence. The warrior deserves to die, Commander. We are agreed on that. We can kill him now – and wait for the Ged to make good their own honor by exiling Jelite and arming only Delysians, who will come against Jela in much less than a year's time because we failed in our trust to protect her. Is that a position of honor? Or we can gamble that some Delysian soldier was cadre brother to this one here and retaliates before the Ged exile us. Such a gamble hopes for the death of another Jelite warrior who has broken no law – is *that* a position of honor, Commander? And can you say that while we've talked here, the possibility of it has not crossed your mind?'

She could not. Dahar saw her look at him in rage, in pain, and he pressed on, relentless.

'Or we can form an alliance. An alliance with scum, yes – but Jela already has a truce with those same scum, out beyond the walls of R'Frow, where Jelite honor has its heart. We do not stand at war with Khalid. Where we do stand is on the blade of honor with the Ged, and honor

says we do everything we can to obey Ged laws and stop
this killing – all of it, everyone's killing on both sides –
now, before the power of a Jelite high commander's orders
erodes any more than it already has.'

Belazir turned away from him. Dahar saw that she
didn't turn toward the two sister-warriors behind her but
toward the archway, to gaze out at the dim morning trees
of R'Frow. Her spine was rigid; thick muscles in her neck
worked up and down. He forced himself to stay quiet, to
let his words work on her, to not grab her by the stiff
shoulders *we stand arguing Ged weapons and you don't see
that Ged healing matters more than Ged weapons ever could,
it matters more than honor* . . .

The detached Dahar heard himself, and went cold.

'It stinks of treachery,' Belazir said, turning. 'An
alliance when there is no war may not be actual treachery,
but it stinks like it. It smells of selling flesh for profit, like
Delysians. Or of snarling over a choice carcass, like beasts.
Like kreedogs.'

'Then we'll call the alliance that. The Kreedogs,' Dahar
said harshly – and thought he had destroyed everything.
The words burst from him, past that other, watchful
Dahar, before he knew he was going to say them. They
burst from a sudden revulsion for his own desperate bargaining, a revulsion he had not known he felt – *it matters
more than honor* – a revulsion that twisted something deep
in the Dahar that was a brother-warrior of Jela. The words
burst, too, from too much longing too harshly pent up,
like the destructive gush of water blasting a dam built to
save it. Destructive – Belazir would never consent now.

He was wrong. She caught the sudden savage revulsion
in his voice, and said more calmly, 'You don't like it
either, Dahar. You smell the treachery.'

All at once he was exhausted. He had been up all night
with Grax, and he had held himself braced against strain
as against an enemy. He gave her truth. 'I see no other
plan.'

Scowling, Belazir looked again out at R'Frow. 'Neither do I,' she said finally, and Dahar saw – incredulously – that she was considering it, and that his sudden honest faltering carried a weight he had not foreseen.

'To let the Delysians get the sort of weapons the Ged have promised . . .' Belazir didn't finish. The silence stretched on. Restraining himself with all the strength he had, Dahar let the silence be.

Belazir said, 'What makes you think Khalid would agree?'

'He is being given the death of a Jelite warrior.'

Belazir flinched and turned her face from him. But her voice, when it came, held only the even note of a commander issuing orders.

'Find out who the brother-warrior was. Have him brought to me. Choose your warriors carefully, Dahar – they must be absolutely loyal. Send Ishaq to me. He will make up our third in the . . . the alliance. Khalid will have to be approached now, this morning, at the Hall of Teaching, before the Ged arrive and say . . . whatever they were going to say. And it will have to be by all three of us, and it will have to be without starting even the thought of an attack . . .'

She went on, planning in that cold, brisk voice, planning it as well as could Dahar himself, who had had days to think of it. He matched her tone, and all the while the other Dahar, detached, watched with a hard mockery he had never shown at any other death, any other failure. But this was not a failure. It was not a shame. It was a victory. He had gotten what he wanted, the chance to stay in R'Frow.

'One thing more,' Belazir said as Dahar turned to leave. 'Although you are my lieutenant, you will not speak for me with Khalid. There will be no bargaining over this, no slimy trading in life itself. Among the first words you said to me about . . . this . . . was "The price of killing is exile." A Jelite first lieutenant does not think in terms of "price". Either Khalid accepts this Kreedog alliance or he does not. I will not descend into the Delysians' mud to haggle over the cost of honor.'

But you think I will. He knew then that despite her agreement to the Kreedogs, she was not going to forgive him for it.

A strange twisted pain went through him. It was a new severing, a new and bloodier detachment: not body from mind, but the part of his mind that was a brother-warrior from the part that had been a priest and now was that other Ged word, a 'scientist'. They had after all been right, all those jeering warriors, to distrust him. To distrust all warrior-priests, who were two things and thus neither fully. *It matters more than honor . . .*

But he had not thought it would hurt so much.

Dahar straightened his shoulders. The double helix lay before him, in R'Frow. It was worth the price.

He followed Belazir through the archway into the gray morning.

26

Dreaming, Jehane felt Talot's hand on her shoulder. Even in sleep she knew the hand was Talot's: She felt the shape of the long, thin fingers, and their urgency. Sleepily she moved the hand to her breast and rolled over, but the hand returned again to her shoulder and shook it hard.

'Jehane – wake up.'

'Off . . . the net.'

'*Wake up.*'

At Talot's tone, sleep vanished. Jehane sat up. 'What is it? Talot, you look – what's happened?'

Strands of Talot's red hair straggled loose from her coiled braids. Her face was gray. and two shadowed lines cut from her nose to her mouth.

'A warrior killed a Delysian soldier.'

'Against orders? What time is it?'

'Third net. Dahar isn't sure who it was. He's asking questions.'

'Belazir ordered no more killing. Of course Dahar will have to kill the warrior, but why do you look so upset about – ' A sudden terrible suspicion pierced Jehane. 'Talot – *you* didn't kill the Delysian, not you . . .'

'No. It was a brother-warrior. But I know who it was.'

'So tell Dahar. The slug killed against orders.'

Talot covered her face with her hands. Jehane, sitting up naked on the bright cushions in the warm room, suddenly felt cold. She brought her arms across her chest and wrapped them around herself. Her stomach twisted.

'Who was it?'

Talot, hands still over her face, neither moved nor answered.

Jehane said slowly, 'It was the brother-warrior you bedded.'

Talot's thin shoulders shuddered. Jealousy crackled through Jehane like a flogging, a flogging on the inside of her skin instead of the outside. Talot had never said the brother-warrior was here in R'Frow. Talot had never said that the Gray Wall was his punishment as well as hers. Talot had never said she could shudder like this over anything that happened to *him*.

Talot had never said.

'Tell Dahar,' Jehane said harshly. 'It's your duty.'

Behind her hands, Talot shook her head.

'To the high commander. He killed against orders, Talot – *against orders!*'

Talot didn't answer. Jehane saw only the top of her bent head, the white part in the red hair, the loose tendrils above the sharp plane of cheekbone. Just last night, that red hair loose . . .

Jehane hissed. 'Then I'll tell Dahar that you know who it is!'

Talot lowered her hands. Her shuddering had abruptly stopped. She looked levelly at Jehane. 'You would do that?'

'He disobeyed orders!' Jehane shouted – but it was no relief to shout.

Talot went on gazing at her. Jehane, for something to do – it was impossible to do nothing, slugs did nothing, the burning in her chest and stomach would not let her do nothing – jumped up and began pulling on her tebl and leggings. That Talot could even hesitate, that Talot could conceal a warrior who had acted against direct orders, that Talot could . . .

Half-dressed, barefoot, Jehane stood still on the cold

floor and squeezed her eyes shut. 'Were you . . . with him?'

'No!' Not like you mean. We were on the net. He had the place next to mine, and I heard him leave it. Later I saw him return and – '

'You didn't try to stop him from leaving?'

'We don't . . . talk to each other. But when he came back, I was coming off the net and I saw that he was wounded. The Delysian's knife grazed him. I told him I was going to report his leaving the net to Dahar, and he said if I did, he would die for it, and so I came . . . here.'

Jehane asked her question fiercely. 'Do you still want him?'

'No! No, Jehane, believe me, I . . . no. But we've bedded together, we lay together in the darkness talking the same way you and I do, and I . . . I don't want to be the one to cause him to die.'

'He did that himself. He deserves to die!'

'For killing a Delysian? For how long have we tried to do that same thing, how often – '

'For acting against the orders of the high commander!'

There was no answer to that. Talot sat very still. Standing above her, her tebl in her hand, Jehane looked down on the nape of Talot's neck, white since all sunburns had faded in R'Frow, vulnerable beneath the knot of red hair. Savagely Jehane jerked her tebl over her head. But the savagery didn't help, and Jehane forced herself to speak calmly, although the words tasted like vomit in her mouth.

'Belazir might not order his death. He deserves it, but she might choose a lesser punishment because . . . because we need every warrior we've got. The Delysians outnumber us. She needs all her warriors. She might . . .' Who the dung knew what Belazir might do? She had already done things no high commander outside of this darkcold shithole would do. 'She might just order him broken in rank and flogged or . . . or something.'

Talot turned her face upward with sudden hope.

Flogged until he's half-dead, Jehane thought, and wished she could wield the whip. Picturing it gave her a savage pleasure, not as great as the jealousy.

But Talot nodded slowly, and the deep lines on her face eased. 'Yes, that's true, Belazir needs all her warriors . . .'

Jehane turned her back and groped blindly for her sandals. 'Who is he, Talot?'

She felt Talot hesitate, but she answered. 'Jallaludin.'

Jehane knew which one he was. Big, very strong with a brother-warrior's greater strength, a brother-warrior's broad shoulders and narrow hips – a deformity, it had always seemed to her, of a sister's narrower shoulders and full hips. But apparently not a deformity to Talot . . . Jehane ground her teeth, pulled on her sandals, and braided her hair in silence.'

'Jehane – '

'Tell Dahar. Now. It's a matter of honor.'

Talot had been reaching out to put her arms around Jehane. At the tone in her voice, Talot stopped the motion halfway. Instead she whispered, 'I love you, Jehane.'

'Talot – a brother-warrior!'

'You knew that before. I told you that before.'

'But not that he was here in R'Frow! And not that you could still feel like a whore for him!'

Talot stiffened. Jehane's stomach twisted inside; she wanted to hold Talot, to tell her . . . but Talot backed away, her face gone white and cold.

'I'm going to Dahar now.'

'You should,' Jehane said, with equal stiffness. Talot yanked open the door. Jehane kicked it closed again. Their arms went around each other, and they clung tightly.

Jehane made herself speak, even though the words burned her throat coming up. 'Maybe he won't die. Belazir needs all her warriors . . .' The second the words were out, she realized she didn't believe they were true. Nor should be.

Talot tried to smile at her, a curiously humble smile, and left. Jehane waited until she was sure Talot had descended the ladder, then picked up her threeball and hurled it with all her strength against the wall. *Talot and the brother-warrior, Talot and Jallaludin, Talot –*

The threeball bounced back with stunning force and rattled around the room, breaking a clay cup. Jehane struck the wall with her fist, scraping the knuckles bloody. She had not balanced herself properly for either blow, and the muscles in her arm ached in protest. But the wall showed neither mark nor damage; it was Ged.

27

Neither Belazir nor Dahar came to the practice field for morning exercises. Talot did not return. Jehane trained, bathed, ate, and strode toward the Hall of Teaching. Talot and Dahar would have to be there or the Ged would fetch them.

It began to rain, the second rain since she had come to R'Frow, floating in a soft mist from the sky – and it *was* sky, despite all the crazy talk, talk, talk that went on. Sky was what was up, and this was up there, wasn't it? It was all that stupid talk that made everything all confused: cells and forces and 'back teria.' Double-helix talk, dark talk, talk like walls. Jelite shouldn't live inside these walls like trapped animals with nothing to do but talk and think. Not even the weapons were worth it –

Another wall. The weapons *were* worth it. At her belt were the unbreakable Ged knife, a stun strip, the new tube that shot a small pellet with enough force to kill a kreedog from across a river. Jehane didn't know how it worked; she didn't care. It worked. The crazy Ged were at least good for that, as well as for making sure Talot came to the Hall of Teaching. Grax wouldn't start his drivel without the whole cadre there.

Talot was not there, and Grax had started talking.

The floor tables had risen with their crazy equipment, not toys now but Blue and Red things, dark things, that no one but Dahar, Grax, and the Delysian glassblower would even touch. Ayrys touched them alone this morning; Dahar, too, was missing.

The warriors glanced covertly at each other. Delysian citizens whispered. Soldiers glared straight ahead, faces set and cold. A sudden fear crawled through Jehane – could Talot and Dahar both have been killed, retaliation for the dead Delysian soldier?

No. If that has been so, the soldiers would not glare like that now. Their cold anger said that no retaliation had yet occurred, that Delysia still felt itself wronged. And the stupid Ged was still calmly going on with his drivel about something white in the blood.

Why? Why hadn't the monster waited for Talot and Dahar, or at least asked where they were? Unless it already knew.

Lajarian was in command. If he asked the Ged nothing, Jehane couldn't ask either. Lajarian stood tight-lipped, hand on his knife and his eyes on the Delysian commander.

The Ged went on talking, the glassblower slug asked low-voiced questions, the Delysian citizens whispered, even the Jelite laborer muttered, and Lajarian said nothing – why didn't they all *shut up*?

Only the white barbarian and the whore were quiet. For the first time in days, Jehane glanced at them, sitting alone in the back of the room, meeting no one's eyes. Two wordless rocks, one a mountain and the other a soft, rotten pebble. But this morning even they looked different.

Jehane looked more closely.

The white giant looked sick. His colorless eyes filmed over, and under his foreign tebl the huge chest rose and fell too fast, as if his breathing were shallow, or forced. His mouth had gone slack at the corners. Jehane, always healthy herself, was only dimly aware that no human had ever become sick in R'Frow – but the giant certainly didn't look good. Neither did the whore, but not as if she were sick too. Pale, her eyes raised to the barbarian, one small hand curled into a fist hard enough to turn the knuckles white.

Jehane glanced at her own knuckles, bruised from striking the wall about Talot. But to even think of SuSu and her white warrior in the same thought as Talot meant she had dishonored Talot. Now she owed Talot an apology. That was what this stupid place with all its stupid talk did to you – let you think of a whore as a person when she was no more a person than a Delysian was. It was these stupid walls –

'Euaahuh!' SuSu cried, a strange, wordless syllable. The barbarian giant was toppling sideways, falling half onto her. He grabbed at the edge of the floor table and hung there, panting heavily, pink foam suddenly frothing at his lips.

SuSu put both her small hands against him and shoved. Slowly he moved upright, and she put her arms around his body to keep it from falling in the other direction. The giant's eyes rolled backward in his head and his tongue lolled out, a wet pink slab.

'Help,' SuSu said, despairingly, in a voice rusty with disuse. She seemed not to know she had said it. Wearing the stark face of panic, she tried to tug his enormous bulk to stand upright. For a moment he seemed almost to recover; his tongue drew back into his mouth and he swung his gaze to look, bewildered, down at SuSu.

Jehane saw the look.

Somehow, the whore got him to his feet. Arms still circling him, she tugged him toward the door, every line of her tiny body straining with a desperation that Jehane suddenly recognized: a hunted lorus wounded and in pain, trying to force itself toward the safety of its lair.

The giant stumbled, righted himself, stumbled again. He stood swaying sickly, eyes closed, unable to go any farther. SuSu pushed and strained, but she could not move him.

To Jehane's surprise, the Ged did not move to help. He had that crazy listening look again, although the whole room had gone silent except for the giant's labored breathing, short huffs like cloth tearing. The Jelite watched coldly: Two brother-warriors had died at the barbarian's hands. And SuSu was a whore, a whore who had thought she was something else. Jehane saw the sister-warrior to her left – where Talot should have been – smile to herself.

On the Delysian side of the room, a fat female citizen blinked nervously.

SuSu whimpered aloud. Her arms were not quite long enough to circle the giant. Against his tebl, her hands looked like those of a doll – or a child. A child of no more than eleven.

The glassblower rose from her place by Grax's floor table. Jehane had a clear glimpse of Ayrys's eyes. They were unfocused, weird: Jehane would have sworn that the Delysian did not even see SuSu, but someone else. Putting her arms around the swaying giant on the opposite side from SuSu, Ayrys pulled him forward. When he stumbled, both women braced themselves. When he lurched to a stop, both women waited. Between them, they moved him through the door.

The whispering rose again. The Delysian citizen who had blinked now frowned after Ayrys, a disapproving frown that Jehane thought made her fat face look like a fish.

And the Ged just sat. What the kreeshit was going on? Humans not present, humans allowed to leave, that slug Ayrys helping a sick man-mountain when no one in R'Frow was ever sick, that whore with her face lifted up like . . . like . . .

Where was Talot?

28

The five of them stood in a clearing by the stream that flowed through the wilderness end of R'Frow, near the two slabs of rock where the stream rose from underground. Too low for ambush, the rocks were a landmark, and the clearing opened around them on all sides. Between the rocks the stream had swollen slightly with the rain. It fell in a light drizzle, blurring the edges of the woods.

'Keeping us waiting,' Belazir said. Along her jaw a rhythmic tightening of flesh came and went.

'They're wary,' Dahar answered.

'Talot, weapons untouched!' At the sharpness in Belazir's voice, Talot flinched and jerked her hand from the hilt of her knife. Dahar thought that the girl had not even noticed the straying of her hand. Talot looked gray, and her eyes were huge with strain. To her left stood Ishaq, first-ranked cadre leader of the brother-warriors, a stocky, silent man not troubling to hide his loathing for this meeting. Between him and Talot, bound hand and foot, stood Jallaludin. He had fought when Dahar and Ishaq had come for him; blood seeped through the cloth over his right arm. But now he stood quietly, head high, and the hatred on Ishaq's face was nothing to Jallaludin's.

Dahar felt himself detach from the scene, watching it, feeling nothing that might interfere with what he had to do. The detachment would not last. It was a wall that would, like all walls, eventually crack. But it would last long enough. The detached Dahar stood quietly to one side, and said, *Feel nothing.*

'Now,' Belazir said.

The three Delysians slipped into the clearing from three different directions, weapons drawn. They had the advantage of trees and mist. Dahar saw Ishaq stop himself from drawing a weapon, a visible spasm from years of training abruptly denied.

'We've come,' Khalid said, his voice flat with dislike. Carefully Dahar measured the three soldiers: all men, all big, one with knife drawn and the other two with Ged pellet tubes. That told him something of what their fighting styles would be. The warrior in him swiftly ran through possible attacks, countermoves, like responses from Belazir and Ishaq, the best use of their positions. Jallaludin, bound, as shield; Talot, untried, an unknown. Dahar moved a few steps closer to Belazir, bettering their defense; Khalid, without glancing at him, moved in response. He was good.

Belazir said, 'We've come as well. This is the warrior who killed your soldier.'

Khalid glanced at Jallaludin. Something moved behind the gray Delysian eyes, something more than suspicion or enmity. *He thinks,* Dahar thought, *not just reacts. He sees what he's looking at, and thinks about what he saw.*

Abruptly, another Delysian face rose in his mind.

'Sheathe your weapons,' Belazir said. 'We have not drawn ours.'

Khalid said, 'So far you've set all the terms for this meeting, Commander. We will set this. There's nothing to prevent you from having your warriors hiding in the woods.'

'Didn't you look as you came through?'

'Three soldiers do not see everything.'

'Neither do four warriors. A concealed attack would be more Delysian than Jelite.'

'Then why risk this? It was your request.'

For just an instant Belazir's face flickered in Dahar's direction. She arrested the glance almost as soon as it began, and Dahar saw how fiercely she regretted doing it at all, but Khalid caught it. His gaze rested thoughtfully on Dahar before returning to the high commander.

Belazir said, 'The Ged have forbidden killing in R'Frow. I ordered my cadres not to attack Delysians. This brother-warrior violated my orders, and for that he would have died by my hand. But Delysia' – Belazir's voice remained steady, but she lifted her jaw, and her eyes burned – 'might not have accepted that as truth. It is well known that Delysian soldiers do not always receive the punishment meted out to them, if they are well enough born.'

Dahar watched Khalid closely; he showed no reaction to the insult, which in Jela would have been deadly. But one of the men behind him suppressed a contemptuous smile. The light rain pattered on the rocks, as much smell as sound.

'Jela has broken the truce which the Ged have made,' Belazir continued, each word bitten off hard. 'To balance that wrong, the death of the brother-warrior who killed your soldier is yours.'

'Mine,' Khalid said.

'Yes.'

'You expect me to believe that?'

Belazir grew still.

Khalid said, 'I remember battles in which the Jelite killed their own wounded rather than leave them behind for Delysians. Why give me your warrior now?'

'I have told you.'

'Have you? "To balance that wrong" – no, Commander. Jela has never thought it wrong to kill a Delysian.'

Khalid was arguing Belazir's case for her. The high commander was reluctant about this alliance; Khalid was building that reluctance, pushing her to take back her warrior. Why?

Belazir said tightly, 'Jela has never before been in R'Frow.'

'Why should killing in R'Frow be any different from killing at Cold River? Jelite rigidity is Jelite rigidity.'

'And Delysian treachery is still Delysian treachery. But in R'Frow neither of us rules. The Ged do, and we stand with them on the blade of honor.'

Khalid's face hardened. 'Then offer your undisciplined warrior to them.'

Belazir didn't answer. In her silence Dahar heard more than anger; he heard the loss of R'Frow. Belazir had tried to turn Jallaludin over to Khalid; for reasons of his own, he was refusing. She would not try indefinitely. Khalid had already insulted Jelite honor, and Dahar suspected that the insults were deliberate, to provoke Belazir to do just what she was doing: take Jallaludin's death back in her own hands, where she had thought it belonged all along.

And then only Jelite would be exiled from R'Frow.

Exile . . .

Khalid pressed his advantage. 'Take your warrior to your masters, the Ged.'

Dahar watched a spasm of fury ripple Belazir's jaw. In that small movement, almost disguised by the rain on all their faces, he saw the closing of the doors of R'Frow, and all of it slipping away: all the Ged science that held the key to life itself. The other Dahar observed with detachment. *The high commander has forbidden you to speak*, at the same time that he heard himself say, 'The warrior has been taken to the Ged.'

Khalid turned his gaze toward Dahar.

'The Ged said that this meeting was a human one. They said they would not interfere with it. They also said they wished to know the outcome.

Beside him, Belazir stood like Stone. Dahar lied. Jallaludin had not been taken before the Ged.

Dahar said, probing, 'Why did *you* wish the matter taken before the Ged?'

'I did not say so.' Too swiftly – there was a weakness here somewhere, a softness in Khalid's position. What? If he were going to refuse to kill Jallaludin, why come to the meeting at all? Why not do nothing and let the Ged exile Jela?

Khalid added, 'I would have thought Jela could discipline her own. Isn't that part of her famous honor?'

It was a taunt, but serious. Dahar refused to let himself be drawn. 'It is the Ged who gave the original order against killing.'

Khalid said, 'And the Jelite who violated it.'

'For which we offer you the life of the violator.'

The taller of Khalid's lieutenants shifted his weight. Dahar looked at him more closely. He had strange, very light eyes, pale even for a Delysian, and in them the sudden flash of hatred was mindless, like an animal's.

Belazir cut in harshly. 'The death of the brother-warrior is yours. Do you want it or not?'

Khalid said swiftly, 'The question is, why do *you* want it? The Ged have said they would exile humans if there was more killing. Jela has killed and Delysia has not. Don't you offer us this death so that we, too, will be guilty of breaking Ged law? So that we, too, will be exiled from the weapons of R'Frow? Such an honorable bargain for honorable Jela!'

His tone was savage. He had played on every one of Belazir's weaknesses. Shame drove her to fury. 'By the dead – do you think I will *beg* you to take a warrior's life? Spare us all your Delysian haggling and answer now or not at all – do you kill him in retaliation for your soldier or don't you!'

Khalid's face betrayed nothing. But this time Dahar had watched not the Delysian commander but the lieutenants behind him. When Khalid had mentioned the loss of Ged weapons if Delysia killed Jallaludin, the shorter man's face had wavered: a slight dropping of the eyes, a tightening at the temples. He saw the force of Khalid's argument. But at Belazir's outburst, the wavering had vanished, and hatred again replaced it. And the other soldier, the one with the pale eyes, had never even wavered. He wanted Jallaludin's death beyond any gain or loss to Delysia, with the pure longing of bloodlust.

And Khalid could not completely control either of them.

That was the weakness in Khalid's position. That was why he had been forced to meet with Jela and hear a bargain he wanted passionately to refuse. A Delysian commander ruled partly by the agreement of his soldiers, and Khalid was afraid that if he refused outright to kill Jallaludin, his men would do it anyway. No commander could hold power after that. Khalid was trying to taunt Belazir into killing Jallaludin herself, while appearing to his own men to merely be insulting a Jelite high commander for the sport of watching her swallow both rage and honor.

All Dahar needed to do was push the Delysian lieutenants' hatred past the point where Khalid could hold it in check or could balance it with concern about what was best for Delysia. Intelligence lay on Khalid's side, bloodlust on his lieutenants'.

It was no contest.

It seemed to Dahar that he could feel Jallaludin's breath on his neck. The brother-warrior's death hung in the air, on the misty rain, on what Dahar said next. Push Khalid's men hard enough and Jallaludin died in the next few moments, here, in this wet, orangey light of R'Frow. Belazir had forbidden him to push, to speak, to tell the lies he had already told.

To keep R'Frow . . .

Feel nothing.

'Perhaps Delysians don't kill in retaliation,' Dahar said

directly to the light-eyed lieutenant, 'because a Delysian's life is worth so little. Even to his brother soldiers.'

Khalid's eyes snapped from Belazir to Dahar.

'We have made the offer,' Dahar went on scathingly, 'in all honor. A life for a life. But perhaps we should withdraw it, if even to their own a Delysian's life is worth less than a Jelite's.'

'*Khalid,*' the shorter lieutenant said.

Swiftly Khalid led his men apart. Dahar said after them, 'It is said, "Delysia for treachery." Perhaps it should be "Delysia for cowardice." '

Khalid and his men talked a little way off: low and passionate voices, the words indistinguishable. Belazir stared at Dahar, but said nothing. Ishaq watched him with open hatred. The young sister-warrior gazed from huge eyes, unguarded in their shock.

Dahar forced himself to look at Jallaludin. The brother-warrior had gone white, but he made no sound. It would have been better if he had.

To keep R'Frow . . .

The Delysian arguing was bitter and short. Khalid, his ruddy face gone redder with anger, nodded curtly to Belazir. 'The death of your warrior for our soldier.'

The lieutenants moved closer to their commander. The shorter kept his Ged pellet tube trained on Ishaq and Belazir, but Dahar saw that the light-eyed soldier kept to his knife. Khalid, too, had drawn a Delysian knife – but abruptly he jammed it into his belt and instead pulled a Ged one. He moved behind Jallaludin.

'Nooooo . . .'

It was a moan: the girl Talot, in all defiance of her training, her sister-warrior's discipline. Ishaq glared at her. For a moment Khalid hesitated, a slight drawing back from this quick and furtive killing of a bound man, while his commander looked on and did nothing . . .

It was only a moment. With a swift, practiced motion, Khalid laid his left arm across Jallaludin's throat from behind, brought his knife up to Jallaludin's belly, and drove it in hard, upward to the heart. Jallaludin went rigid and pop-eyed. Khalid held him, cutting off his air, while he died, then abruptly released him and stepped sideways. Jallaludin fell backward, his head still tilted at the angle to which Khalid's arm had jerked it, his black eyes open and staring upward into the rain.

No one spoke.

Khalid had left his knife in the body. The pale-eyed lieutenant bent to pull it out. 'Leave it,' Khalid grated. 'No – I said leave it!'

Straightening, the lieutenant smiled.

'Listen to me,' Khalid went on in the same harsh voice. 'Commander, we did this your way. Your warrior is dead, killed like a . . . but now both Jela and Delysia have broken the Ged law. Equally. It stops here. If we are not all exiled from R'Frow for this, it stops here. No more killing, on either side. We left Delysia and Jela in truce, and now the truce comes here, to R'Frow, and not only because the Ged have said so.'

The Delysian lieutenant stopped smiling.

'Stopping the killing is what this was for,' Belazir said, but all of them heard the fury in her voice, and the shame.

'Then the meeting has succeeded,' Khalid said scornfully. 'We stand even now. Life for life. You can go tell the Ged so.'

The Delysian hates this as much as Belazir does, the detached Dahar observed. Did Belazir recognize Khalid's anger as a kind of honor – a kind that he, Dahar, had just forfeited?

Feel nothing . . .

Belazir said bleakly, 'The bloodshed ends here. Jela and Delysia are at truce.'

Khalid turned to face his own lieutenants, daring them to challenge him now that he had given them what they wanted. The shorter one hesitated, shifted from one foot to the other, and nodded. The other, the light-eyed man

who had bent to reclaim Khalid's knife, met his commander's eyes levelly, and did nothing. But Khalid needed
nothing from him now; Khalid had killed Jallaludin, and
the other now had no position from which to challenge
him.

'Give us back the body of our soldier,' Khalid said to
Dahar, 'and take yours. I am done with this.'

'Wait,' Dahar said.

Khalid had half-turned. Now he turned back. Belazir
stood like stone. She could have silenced him, but she
was waiting to see just how far her first lieutenant would
depart from orders, just how much he would be willing
to lose. Dahar knew what he had already lost the first
time he spoke when she had ordered him not to, the first
time he lied, the first time she glimpsed that he would
trade – trade, bargain, sell, haggle like a Delysian trader
– his life as a brother-warrior for his chance at the Ged
science in R'Frow.

Feel nothing.

'Truces can be broken,' Dahar said to Khalid. 'Not by
treachery only, but in the same way the Ged order was
violated – by warriors or soldiers acting against their commander's orders. It could happen again. Both commanders are here now. Here, now, both Jela and Delysian
should prepare to deal with it again.'

He had said that neither commander could control the
assortment of troops, misfits and exiles that each led in
R'Frow. Humiliation: and truth. Khalid's eyes narrowed.
Dahar spoke directly to him, ignoring Belazir.

'The Ged might choose to exile us all for this double
killing. If they do not, if their patience holds this once,
it might hold twice – if we can convince them we sing in
harmony for all Jelite or Delysian.'

'Do what?' Khalid said.

Dahar felt himself flush. 'If there is another killing –
on either side – the Ged must know that neither com-

mander lies behind it, not even in secret. Not even by silent approval.'

Behind him, Dahar heard Ishaq's sharp breath. But he had not meant that Belazir would be capable of that much dishonor, or even that Khalid would be. He was thinking only of what the Ged were capable, of how they might interpret human actions, of what could be done to safeguard the staggering knowledge the Ged offered – knowledge Jela and Delysia, blind fools both, didn't see, but that could transform both of them forever.

For a brief moment he considered trying to tell Khalid directly what was at stake, trying to make him *see*. But Khalid had not understood the Ged term 'singing in harmony'. Neither had he spent those long nights in the Hall of Teaching, glimpsing the dazzling stores of Ged knowledge hidden behind the aliens' calm, discourteous silence. Khalid would not understand.

And Dahar himself realized that he could not have told him. At the thought of pleading with a Delysian commander, something in him more powerful than reason recoiled, something that had nothing to do with the detached Dahar and everything to do with the brother-warrior who waited, beyond the Wall, for Belazir's punishment. He could not plead with Khalid. He could only bargain, and at his own bargaining the brother-warrior within writhed in shame.

'It wasn't a Delysian who broke orders,' Khalid said. 'That Jela cannot control her warriors is not our concern.'

'And if next time it's a Delysian soldier who kills first?'

Khalid didn't glance at the tall, pale-eyed soldier. But something – some slight movement, some flicker in Khalid's face – told Dahar that the glance had been there, and been arrested. Khalid said, 'And if that did happen – if a soldier killed against orders – what does Jela propose?'

Belazir took a step forward. Dahar felt her fury roll toward him in waves, like heat. Swiftly he said, 'It is for the high commander to propose. I only point out that it could happen.'

Khalid spoke to Belazir. 'If a Delysian soldier kills, you propose that we turn him over to you? No. That is not possible.' He put a slight emphasis on 'that,' obvious to all – and he did not look at his lieutenants. The omission told as much as the emphasis: *Not that, I cannot do that, but something else* . . .

Khalid would favor the alliance if it did not undermine his power with his lieutenants. He had chosen poorly to include the pale-eyed soldier in this meeting. But perhaps he had had no choice.

Belazir said, 'You have killed one of ours.'

'At your wish.'

'And yours.'

Khalid said, 'What do you propose?'

Dahar saw Belazir hesitate.

He fought to hold himself steady. It rested with her now; he could do no more. He had nothing left to fight with: not reason, nor rank, nor influence. She commanded, not he, and he had staked all the rest on her being the kind of commander he thought she was – one who would choose her concern for Jela over the violence of her anger toward him. Belazir would break him, yes – but in the gray dawn at her hall, she had glimpsed the sense of this alliance with Khalid. Would she break that as well?

Khalid watched Belazir closely. The pale-eyed soldier stood behind him in the light rain, his eyes on his commander's back. Behind Dahar someone shifted weight: Talot. The moment spun itself out.

'An alliance,' Belazir said. 'Known to all. Three of yours, three of ours. If a soldier kills against orders, or . . . or a warrior does so again, we punish the killer with death. But in the presence of all six, and as swiftly as possible. An alliance to prevent killing, and so let us all stand on the blade of honor with the Ged.'

'Honor,' Ishaq spat, and the word was an oath. A small outburst, but it gave Dahar, ragged with relief, the opening he needed. He turned on Ishaq. 'Quiet! This is the high commander's decision, not yours. The high commander's.'

'And mine,' Khalid said, and there was something challenging in his voice. The shorter Delysian soldier suddenly dropped his eyes. But Dahar saw that Khalid was perfectly aware that a Jelite first lieutenant did not ordinarily reprimand a warrior in front of the enemy. Khalid knew Dahar was fighting Belazir for this – just as he was fighting his own.

Khalid said, 'The Ged have weapons that Delysia does not want to be without. Weapons that could equip Jela, if she alone obtained them, against Delysia. It is to our advantage to stay in R'Frow, and thus to keep the laws of the Ged. A truce to keep those laws is also to our advantage. For that reason – and not for any notions of Jelite honor – my soldiers and I accept your alliance, Commander. Three of us, three of you, and if any soldier or warrior kills, we will bring him here, to this spot, for all six of us to witness the death. This is all to the advantage of Delysia.'

Khalid swung his gaze to the pale-eyed soldier.

The man had set his teeth so hard, the line of his jaw stood white against the light stubble of his beard. Khalid held his lieutenant's eyes without wavering. After a long moment, the soldier nodded.

'We stand,' Khalid said – half in sincerity, half in a sudden destructive burst of mockery Dahar recognized all too well – 'on the same blade, bound – '

'Quiet!' Belazir spat. 'Don't you know any shame, Delysian? Because we are in alliance doesn't permit you to mouth words you can't understand. Now leave us with our dead.'

Khalid's eyes flared with sudden anger, and Dahar saw his strain – all of their strain. But Khalid had himself in control. He signaled to his soldiers, and the three, weapons drawn to cover themselves, moved across the clearing to the woods. The light-eyed soldier hesitated, but by leaving first, Khalid had given him no choice. He could not remain alone against four warriors. But before he followed, he spoke directly to Dahar, his voice low with hate.

'Kelovar. Remember it, Jelite.'

When they had gone, Belazir turned to Dahar. 'Pull out the knife.'

Dahar knelt by Jallaludin. The knife handle, worked with the Delysian love of excessive ornament, cradled drops of rain in its scrollwork. The grip was slippery. Jallaludin's black eyes stared up at him sightlessly. The blade pulled free, blood gushed from the heart, flowing over Dahar's hands and onto the ground. He stood, his tebl spattered with the brother-warrior's blood.

Belazir grasped the double helix on his shoulder and yanked. It ripped free. Raising her left hand, the one she did not use for a weapon, she slapped his face three times. He was a brother-warrior no longer.

On Ishaq's and Talot's faces was pure shock. They had not known what Belazir had told him beforehand, had not seen how Dahar had worked against his commander's ends, and for his own. For R'Frow. Talot's eyes were wide; Dahar saw Ishaq's, after the first shock, narrow in calculation.

Belazir stood with the double helix in her hand. Her stillness could mean wavering . . . through his own shock, he forced himself to speak. 'Commander. We have just formed the alliance. For one of the six to be barred now, when the warriors already aren't going to like – '

'Be quiet.' Belazir spoke calmly, but the color had drained from her face, and her black eyes shone with peculiar glassiness. Dahar saw that he had badly underestimated how far she would bend to gain the weapons advantage for Jela. She had been pushed right to the edge

– by him, by the Kreedogs, by R'Frow, by the crumbling away of cliffs she had built her life on and had thought to be made of indestructible work. In R'Frow she had learned otherwise. The blade of honor cuts two ways, and events had turned it against her. If the alliance – which she had agreed to – was corrupt, if her first lieutenant – whom she had trusted – was not worthy of trust . . .

Belazir said quietly, and even her voice was not the same, 'Can one see the Marker set?'

Ishaq stared at her with open amazement, Talot with bewilderment. For a moment longer Belazir stood silent on the wet grass, Dahar's double helix in her hand, her eyes unfocused, seeing what was no longer there. Then she shook her head and Dahar saw the sheer effort, the monstrous act of will, that brought her back to herself, high commander of Jelite warriors in the hostile city of R'Frow. He saw, too, that she would not be shaken again.

He said desperately, 'Commander. Take time to consider this. I'll come to you later, in your hall, to – '

Belazir threw the emblem of the double helix to the ground. Without another word, she signaled for her warriors to follow her. The signal did not include him. Dahar watched them cross the clearing toward the Jelite halls. Ishaq moved to guard Belazir's left; he was now the high commander's first lieutenant in R'Frow.

The wall within crumbled, and feeling returned.

Kreedogs.

Dahar stood beside the dead warrior, under the Ged dome, in the falling rain.

IV
DOUBLE HELIX

*I would rather understand one cause
than be a king of Persia.*
                    —Democritus of Abdera

29

Whenever the barbarian staggered, SuSu or Ayrys braced herself to support him until the other woman could again tug him down the wrof path. Standing braced into that great weight, trying to lean just enough to balance his leaning, Ayrys wondered why she was not afraid. The white hair on the giant's forearm brushed her cheek whenever she leaned into him. He smelled of male but not of sickness. From his other side SuSu's hands – the small hands of a girl, Embry's hands – clutched his waist. SuSu was afraid; even with the giant between them, Ayrys could feel her terror, and she spoke across the faltering white bulk to the girl she could not see.

'He doesn't smell sick – truly he doesn't. Has this . . . attack happened before?'

'Yes,' SuSu said. Ayrys could barely hear her.

'Do you have any doses for this? Or does he? Or one of your warrior-priests – ' Ayrys broke off. SuSu was a Jelite whore; would a warrior-priest even treat a whore, or a foreigner who had stolen her? But if not, if Jelite stupidity about sex prevented that, wouldn't Jelite whores have learned to treat themselves? But this girl was such a child. . . .

'Do you know what this disease is? Did he tell you?' Could the giant even talk? She had never heard him.

SuSu didn't answer. The giant suddenly faltered and sank to his knees, breathing harshly, great swampy gasps

of breath. Ayrys steadied him until he once more struggled
to rise, and then eased him forward.

'*SuSu*. Do you have drugs for this? Do you?'

'No.'

'Does he?'

'Nothing,' she said, and at the despair in the young
voice, compassion flooded through Ayrys. Embry –
Embry had at least been left with healers, protection,
care. . . .

They passed no one on the path under the dripping
trees. Everyone, human and Ged, was in the Hall of
Teaching. *Not everyone*, Ayrys thought, and pushed the
image away, to hold herself steady to SuSu's need. It took
a long time, with long pauses, to reach the barbarian's
hall in a part of R'Frow Ayrys had never been: close by
the north wall, just west of the Jelite halls. Gray wrof
building, open archways, floor tables – there was nothing
to see any different from her own hall.

'Lay him here,' Ayrys said, 'away from the arch. In
case the rain blows in.'

'No. Above.'

'But, SuSu, we can't get him up the ladder. Look, he
couldn't climb it, and we can bring cushions and blankets
down – '

'*Above*,' SuSu said, her soft voice cracking with desperation. Ayrys abandoned argument.

Halfway up the ladder, the barbarian nearly fell. SuSu
cried out and tried to grasp his arms from above: a single
strand of silk trying to hold an avalanche. Ayrys scrambled
to the ladder rung directly below the giant, wrapped her
arms around his thighs to grasp the gray metal, and hung
on. He shuddered, pressed backward nearly hard enough
to tear her grip free, and then at the last moment steadied
again.

They got him into his room, behind the thumblocked
door that SuSu immediately closed.

'Put him on the cushions,' Ayrys said. 'He's shaking with chills – no, ease him the other way. . . .'

There were huge blankets piled in one corner. There was everything piled in all corners, as if SuSu tried not to leave this one room any more than she had to. Ayrys looked around curiously. Food, water, blankets of bright Ged material, small furs, sandals and clay vessels – the barbarian had been a clever craftsman.

Had been. Was.

'He must have drugs,' Ayrys said gently. 'I don't know what this illness is, but he needs at least plant doses to clear his lungs and to make him sweat out the sickness. A warrior-priest – '

SuSu turned on her a look of such hatred that Ayrys, astonished, fell silent. But the hatred had not been for her. She tried again.

'At least food. It's almost time for the floor tables to rise with food. I could bring some fresh. He has to eat.'

SuSu, staring at the giant's closed eyes and heaving chest, said nothing. Ayrys opened the door.

'No! No – shut it!'

'I'm only going to – '

SuSu put her hands over her ears. Ayrys looked at the girl's face, slipped into the corridor, and shut the door.

There was a short wait in the hall below before the food rose. In the silence, in the misty emptiness, the sight was eerier than in the hall full of milling people. Everything was gray: air, light, walls. Only the bright orange circle near the ladder glowed with color. Beyond, rain pattered on the leaves of gray trees.

Taking as many bowls of hot stew as she could, Ayrys carried them back up the ladder.

'SuSu, I have food. Open the door.'

'Go away!'

Astonished, Ayrys stood in the deserted corridor, the bowls – steaming inside, cool metal against her forearms

– balanced carefully. 'But I brought the *food*. He has to eat or he'll . . . He has to eat. Open the door, SuSu.'

'Who is with you?'

For the first time, Ayrys wondered if the girl was sane. Her soft voice, muffled by the door, was hard to hear.

'No one is with me. Only I, Ayrys, the Delysian woman who helped you from the Hall of Teaching.'

Woman. Delysian. Would that make SuSu more afraid, or less?

Ayrys waited. The gray corridor was dim and silent. Finally SuSu, her small face white with terror, opened the door a crack. Ayrys slid in, and SuSu slammed the door.

The sick man would not eat. Patiently Ayrys tried, then SuSu, then Ayrys again. He would take water if they placed it, drop by drop, in his mouth, but he seemed to lack the strength to chew. His breathing had quieted once he lay down, but his skin was clammy, and out of all that vast sprawled bulk only his eyes moved. Colorless, preternaturally intense, they followed SuSu whenever she moved, but Ayrys couldn't tell what they really saw. She thought that he was drifting in and out of his mind, and he never spoke.

SuSu never spoke to him.

As the hours of tending the barbarian went by, Ayrys became unnerved by the silence. The closed room, the wordless suffering, the *silence* – like a grave, although she could not tell if the barbarian was dying or not. Why didn't SuSu talk to him, or croon, or whisper the reassurances that comfort as much by tone of voice as by pathetic lies?

Finally, the giant stirred.

His eyes flickered from SuSu to Ayrys. One huge hand rose from his side, faltered, dropped back. His face mirroring an effort terrible to watch, the giant again brought the hand into the air above his chest. He held all five fingers pointed sharply upward and pantomined their rising from his chest up into the air in a fast, clean arc.

'What?' Ayrys said. 'I don't . . .'

The giant repeated his pantomime. Ayrys shook her head. His colorless eyes closed in despair.

A few moments later he opened them again; again came the terrible battle to raise his hands to his chest. Once there, he tapped with all ten fingers on his chest, one finger at a time hitting an imaginary surface at great speed, tapping out . . . what?

'I don't understand,' Ayrys said. 'Is it a dance?'

The enormous white hands fell back to his sides. The giant gazed at her with deep, lucid sorrow. Ayrys had the sudden strange thought that he gazed at her across some great gulf he could see and she could not. Once more he tried the high arc, some object rising fast into the air . . .

The giant suddenly gasped. He struggled to sit up, clawing at nothing. His eyes bulged and pain contorted his face to white agony. Then he fell back among the cushions, closed his eyes, and began to breathe in fast, shallow pants, not at all like his breathing before the attempt to tell her . . . what?

'I'm going to find drugs for him,' Ayrys said firmly. 'SuSu, do you hear me? He must have medicine.'

'No!'

'Yes. He has to have a healer, or he'll die. Not a warrior-priest, I won't bring a warrior-priest.' As if she could. What had the Jelite done to this child to make her hate them like this? 'I'll find Grax, or one of the other Ged. The Ged are teaching things about illness, about blood and bacteria. You've heard them in the Hall of Teaching. . . .'

SuSu had stopped listening. How much would she have understood anyway of what the Ged taught of bacteria those small, deadly miracles? The only one who really understood was Dahar. Ayrys saw him bent over the enlarger, his dark, coarse face burning with discovery, and saw too his empty place in the hall this morning. How

long ago? What time was it now? If the hours for the
Hall of Teaching had ended, all the Ged would have
disappeared back into the Gray Wall.

'I'll bring Grax. Or a Delysian healer, one like – '

'No!' SuSu shrieked, and suddenly put her hands over
her ears, pressing the palms desperately against her head
as if she were trying to crush some sound out of existence.
'No, no!'

'Then no. Hush, SuSu, you're scaring your lover.' But
the barbarian had gone blank-faced, as if he no longer
heard nor saw. He still breathed, but quietly now, and
irregularly. 'Hush, no one will come that you don't want
here – '

A beating sounded on the door.

SuSu froze. Ayrys turned to face the door.

'Open this, please. Open this, please.'

Relief washed through Ayrys. 'It's a Ged, SuSu. They
can help him!' She rose to her feet.

Instantly SuSu was between her and the door, leaning
against it with her thin arms spread across the metal, her
eyes wild, the orange circle on the wall streaking one
cheek with sickly color.

'It's a Ged,' Ayrys said. 'He can help.'

'No!'

'Without medicine – '

'No!'

'Open this, please.'

Ayrys stood, uncertain what to do, helpless and troubled. SuSu pressed her small palms flat against the metal.
On the floor the barbarian giant began to breathe more
heavily. The door opened by itself.

SuSu tried to push it closed. She didn't have nearly
enough strength, and was thrust back into the room as
the door opened. Grax entered, an orange strip of fabric
wrapped around his thumb. Behind him stood Dahar.

Something turned over in Ayrys's chest. Dahar's face
sagged with exhaustion. His mouth was drawn in a grim

line, and in his eyes was an expression she had never seen there: Taut and feverish as panic, it was nonetheless not panic but something else, something she could not name. His tebl was streaked with dirt, rain, and splatters of dark brownish red. When he saw Ayrys, he stood still.

'He must be carried inside the Wall,' Grax said.

He meant the barbarian, and he spoke to SuSu. Ayrys thought the girl might throw herself across the giant, but she did not. When Grax crossed into the room, all the fight seemed to go out of her. Her face went blank with despair, and her small body seemed to fold inward, toward some other place. Moved to pity by that terrible giving up, Ayrys put her arms around Susu and held her. It was like holding a child.

'SuSu, the Ged will help him inside the Wall. Grax is right, that's the place he should go – they must have equipment and medicines. You can help him, can't you?' she asked Grax.

His face did not change. 'He must be carried inside the Wall.'

The Ged lifted the giant's shoulders, Dahar his legs. Of course, Ayrys thought, that was why Grax had brought Dahar – the Jelite lieutenant was strong enough to help carry the huge barbarian. But why not another Ged? And Dahar didn't look strong at this moment; he looked like a man pushed to the limit of what he could bear. What had happened while she had sat for hours trying to get the sick man to drink, trying to lend to SuSu comfort she didn't want?

The giant sagged in Dahar's and the Ged's arms. He was almost too big for even both of them to carry. SuSu watched, her face gone cold and empty. Ayrys couldn't stand it.

'Grax, tell her the Ged can help! Your knowledge of sickness, what you've been teaching us . . .'

Grax glanced up briefly, but said nothing. He wore his listening look. Dahar stared at Ayrys, her arms around

SuSu, and suddenly Ayrys remembered that SuSu was a whore and Dahar a brother-warrior, and what that meant. Remembering filled her with fury, the same reckless fury she had felt on the veld with Jehane; and like that fury, this one thrust on her a heedless courage she already knew would not last.

'I said, will you give him medicines? Drugs? *Will you?*'

Grax, despite his burden, looked at her evenly for a long moment, his face intent with listening.

'We will give him drugs.'

'SuSu, listen to him, they'll help him . . . don't cry. . . .'

She was not. Dry-eyed, soundless, she followed the giant from the room, and she did not glance back at Ayrys. Neither did she close the door. Ayrys saw that the locked room, sanctuary against her terrors, was sanctuary no more. *But who knew the Ged could open any door in R'Frow?*

Grax and Dahar carried the giant through the archway and toward the north wall. The rain had stopped. The grass lay slippery under their feet. From the light, Ayrys thought it must be late afternoon, but she could not be sure.

At the Wall, the Ged pulled from somewhere inside his force shield a small, dark box. At first Ayrys thought it was an enlarger, and involuntarily she glanced at Dahar. But this wrof was darker than that of enlargers, and shallow depressions indented two sides. Grax put his fingers into three of the indentations, and a section of Wall vanished.

'Your air fills this part of the perimeter,' Grax said to Dahar. 'Bring him in.'

A large room, plain and empty except for the smells. Ayrys's nostrils flared: kreedogs, the scent heavy and rank, and from somewhere she heard their faint frantic yelping. Overlaying the kreedog smell was a different one: the stew that was not stew. Were the bowls filled here, for the floor tables of the halls? She saw no bowls. But then, a moment ago she had seen no break in the Gray Wall.

Fear of the Ged, lulled by tencycles of familiarity, stirred again. The power they held . . .

Grax and Dahar lowered the albino giant to the floor. At another touch on the dark box, a large table rose under him. His breathing had worsened, and Ayrys could hear the yelping kreedogs only between those tortured gasps.

'You must leave,' Grax said.

SuSu did not move.

'Can't she stay with him?' Ayrys asked.

'No.'

Ayrys said angrily, 'Why not?'

'No,' Grax repeated, but he was not looking at her. He looked at Dahar.

'But she won't – '

'No.'

SuSu clutched the giant's hand. With his own hand the Ged separated them, not ungently. SuSu whirled on him in sudden desperate fury but still without sound, battering her fists against the clear wrof that covered Grax completely. There was something horrible, unnatural, in the silent attack. Ayrys moved forward, but even before she could reach SuSu, Grax pressed his gray box and the three humans no longer stood within the Wall.

It had slid upward from the floor between them and Grax, between them and the stricken giant, on three sides, until it met the ceiling. Dahar and Ayrys and SuSu stood in a cave of wrof, a cubic dimple in the Wall, open on the fourth side to the fading gray light of R'Frow.

So fast . . .

SuSu gave one despairing sob and ran from the cave toward her hall. Ayrys grabbed for the girl but wasn't quick enough. Dahar clamped his hand over Ayrys's arm. 'Let her go.'

Ayrys turned on him. 'Like that? Alone and half-crazy? Or doesn't it matter, because she's only a Jelite whore?'

'Not for that.'

'She hurts!'

'Is that your concern, Delysian?'

'My name is Ayrys!'

'I know your name,' Dahar said. Their eyes met and held.

His hand lay hot on her arm. When she said nothing, Dahar repeated, with a peculiar intensity, 'Is her pain your concern?'

'Yes!'

'Why? She is Jelite.'

This time Ayrys heard the intensity. She saw that he was asking more than this question, more than she understood – but she didn't know what. In Dahar's exhausted face the dark eyes were hollowed with strain. Something had happened, then, while Dahar and the red-haired warrior, Jehane's friend, had been absent from the Hall of Teaching. Something had happened. . . . His closeness dizzied and confused her, and she didn't answer. Dahar's hand tightened on her arm.

'Why does a Delysian glassblower concern herself with a Jelite whore, Ayrys? Do you have a reason? *Why?*'

She had never seen him like this. In all the long hours of bending together over the Ged equipment that only she and Dahar seemed to see as more than toys, they had never spoken to each other. They passed ideas and questions, when ideas and questions had to be passed, through Grax. Yet Ayrys knew how his mind moved: what question he might ask next, what test he would propose in order to discover what he wished to know. With a jolt, she realized that Dahar's was the mind she knew best in all of R'Frow. A strange way of knowing – like being able to make glass in the darkness, sure of each step in the process but never seeing the glass sparkle in ordinary sunlight.

But she didn't know him like this. Not with this panic, this unknown despair.

'Dahar,' she said slowly, 'what happened this morning? What have you done?'

To her astonishment, the hand on her arm shuddered. For one sharp moment the strained face above hers seemed to break up, go all to pieces. Then he had turned and was striding off, his back to her, stiff as a blade.

Ayrys started to run after him. Then fear – the fear she should have reasonably felt all along, and had not – struck her in a rush. *A Jelite brother-warrior . . .*

It was Dahar who turned back, his face under control. In a quick, harsh voice, he said, 'There's a drink that will soothe her, or at least dull her mind past the worst. She wouldn't take the dose from me, but you can make it for her. Fourteen balloonweed leaves, they grow close to tree trunks in the shade – do you know the plant? It grows in Delysia. Boil the leaves hard for at least half an hour. Add more water whenever it boils away, until you get a thick paste. Mix it with enough crushed linberry to cover your thumbnail in a thin paste – '

'But linberry is poison!'

'Not mixed with the balloonweed, although it may give her mild visions. But dissolve the potion in a full bowl of water and make her drink it right away. Don't let it precipitate.' He growled the Ged word; the sudden shift from plant healing to Ged science caught at them both. Dahar grimaced with a sudden bitterness Ayrys did not understand.

'Handle the linberry paste carefully. Don't use too much, and don't get it into any open cuts on your hands.'

He glanced down at her hands. Ayrys raised one, tentatively, a gesture going nowhere. Something flickered behind Dahar's eyes. Then he strode toward the trees, in the direction of the Jelite halls.

Ayrys wrapped her arms around herself and shivered.

In a little while it would be dark. Something struck her gently from behind.

It was the Wall. The back of the cubic cave was swelling, pushing her out. Ayrys hurried ahead of the moving wrof, to stand blinking on the wet grass. In a moment the Wall was again straight and impenetrable, shimmering faintly with a glow of its own.

30

Behind the Wall, Grax hurried away from the albino giant, releasing the molecules of his wrof outer suit as soon as he had passed through the airlock back into true atmosphere. His pheromones smelled of bewilderment and dismay.

Humans had destroyed another section of the Fleet. They had erupted into space where no Ged had expected them to appear, wielding weapons neither the Ged nor any of their ancient allies had ever seen. Ged ships had been lost. Lives had been lost.

And on Qom, the mating ceremony for the dead could not even be held until the eighteen and the Library-Mind were done with this bewildering matter of the 'Kreedogs.'

The humans in R'Frow, who had been consistent only in behaving as if they were two species, had suddenly had seven members cooperating as if they were one species. *Why?*

The Library-Mind had contacted all eighteen Ged at the start of the morning's teaching. One by one the Ged had fallen silent. Grax had felt his pheromones slide out of control, had arrested the shock, and had immediately contacted young R'gref – as had every other Ged. But the cub had stayed in control.

As much as any of them could. This 'alliance' was as shocking as if the non-number-rational jonkil had begun signaling prime numbers. It contradicted months of data. It could not be.

It was.

The Ged had each stood and walked to the Wall, ignoring the disruptions among the animals left behind. All day they had been discussing it, pressing the Library-Mind, searching for answers that did not come. How could the humans switch so fast to behavior that contradicted everything they had done before?

When the Library-Mind again interrupted the discussion to show the albino giant motionless on the floor of his room, pheromones actually radiated relief. This, at least, was understandable. From the beginning, Decontamination had shown the tumor pressing against the giant's brain. The tumor was only the expected result of the radiation on the island, radiation the giant must have lived with all his life. This was only predictable death, number-rational when considered in view of the biological skills the human 'healers' did not possess. And for the human Ayrys to help the white one might add a new fact to the Library-Mind, but it did not contradict what was already there. The white one belonged to neither of the subspecies that were not.

'He should be brought into the perimeter.'

'Yes. He should. Harmony sings with us.'

'Harmony sings with us.'

'May it always sing.'

'It will always sing. We could learn much about the human brain.'

'Should he be brought now?'

'The Library-Mind says now.'

'I think now. Harmony sings with us.'

'It will always sing.'

Grax had been the one to go. It was a wrench to leave the perimeter, when all eighteen were together and the ceremony for the lost matings of the dead trembled on the edge of the pheromones like cool mist. But the giant had been in Grax's teaching group. And the Library-Mind had said that the human Dahar waited at the Hall of

Teaching, in the deserted room. It was for Grax, the Ged all thought, that Dahar must be waiting. He could help carry the giant.

Dahar stood rigid in the corridor outside the teaching room, which he could lock, but only Grax could open. He spoke even before Grax had fully rounded the corner, and he spoke without a vestige of civilized calm, without speaking in harmony for even one other of his kind, his hairy and two-eyed human face gone an ugly white.

'Will the Ged exile humans from R'Frow for today's deaths?'

Grax stepped closer. 'What has happened?' The Ged already knew, of course; the two flat white rocks in the wilderness clearing held the environmental-control system and thus were part of the Library-Mind itself. Grax listened as Dahar told him what he already knew – alliance, 'Kreedogs,' death and violence – and smelled his own pheromones, and smelled surprise. A human, telling him what he already knew . . .

Dahar finished. 'Will the Ged exile humans from R'Frow for today's deaths?'

Grax said nothing.

'Will you? Grax . . . we have done what we could to prove our . . . our good faith.'

'No. No exile.'

The muscles of the human's face shifted in a way Grax had not seen before, did not understand.

'You wish to stay,' Grax said, and again smelled himself. 'For the science. To learn.'

'Yes,' Dahar had said, and this time his facial muscles had not moved at all.

But no other human had shown such a strong desire to learn, and yet others had agreed to this new alliance. Not even the Library-Mind understood how the new human cooperation could relate to the Central Paradox.

Grax hurried into the midst of the strongest smells he could remember on Qom: bafflement, sorrow, anger. The

Library-Mind continued to growl the news about the Fleet disaster. Pheromones washed over him, drawing him in, triggering his own smells, as strong as if the perimeter were a nest and he a recovered cub.

'Grax, you are here – '

'We sing in harmony – '

'Grax has come – '

'Grax – '

'Harmony . . .'

It was hours before the number-rational discussion could even begin, hours more before the Ged reached their one decision: While they were needed for study, no human violence must end the lives of the six who had made the alliance. The Library-Mind would act to protect them, if necessary, even within R'Frow. And the Ged who led the teaching groups of the six would try to learn directly from the erratic animals all that the humans would say.

The room reeked of exhaustion. Finally, with relief, with sorrow, with the civilized sense of leaving painful light for a close and dim mat, the Ged blanked the wall screens and slid into the trance of Oneness to mate for their dead.

31

No sentry challenged Dahar at the outer net, nor in the dark woods beyond. At the edge of the clearing around the command hall, he paused. The hall loomed across the grass, a black bulk with sharp, precise corners.

Ishaq spotted him even before he left the trees. The older warrior waited, pellet tube and knife both drawn, within the deserted arch.

Dahar stopped six lengths away. He drew no weapons. 'I want to see the high commander, Ishaq.'

'No.'

'Is that her order or yours?'

'Hers. She is not seeing Jelite citizens.' He gave Dahar a moment to react to that; Dahar did not. 'But she's given me a message for you.'

'What is it?'

'This is the last time you will be allowed through the net. You are not permitted to take anything from the brother-warriors' hall except the weapons you wear. Either move to the citizens' hall or stay outside the net completely and don't try to return. If you try the net again, the warriors have orders to kill.'

Dahar said evenly, 'As if I were a citizen under warning.'

'You are a citizen under warning.'

'Even a . . . citizen may request to see the high commander for a good reason.'

'The high commander has already turned down your request.'

From reflex, Dahar's eyes measured the distance to the ladder. Ishaq said quietly, 'Don't try, Dahar.'

Dahar asked nothing, but Ishaq seemed compelled to answer.'Yes. I would.'

'You could not have stopped me without that pellet tube from the Ged.'

'But I have this pellet tube from the Ged. I have it.'

'Yes,' Dahar said. 'You do.'

He could not fight. He could not think. He had been awake for nearly thirty-six hours, all of a – for a moment his exhausted mind could not even find the word – *three-day*. With effort, he stopped himself from swaying on his feet before Ishaq, who would stop him from fighting for his life as a Jelite warrior by using a Ged weapon Dahar had fought to keep for Jela.

'One thing more, citizen,' Ishaq said, 'Belazir told me, as her first lieutenant, why she burned you. For that direct disobedience, I would have first had you flogged until you couldn't stand. And for this "alliance" – but she takes full responsibility for that herself. She shouldn't. You betrayed us, and now we who have any honour left have to live with the results of that betrayal. But think of this, Dahar – think of it whenever you see a Delysian. Their soldier Kelovar watched with pleasure while Jallaludin died. With pleasure and triumph. Not the clean triumph of death, but the filthy triumph of dishonor over honor. And now every time one of them lays eyes on a Jelite warrior, he's going to be reliving that triumph that *you* gave them.'

Dahar stared straight ahead.

'Belazir sends one message more. You were a healer; you may heal still. But not warriors. Citizens, whores. Delysians. Ged if you choose – but not warriors. You are not fit to touch them.'

'Is that last part Belazir's or yours?'

'Move, citizen.'

'Ishaq – hers or *yours?*'

Ishaq took a step forward and raised his pellet tube. Everything that was warrior in Dahar tensed and readied.

But he was not a warrior.

Slowly, Dahar made himself turn from Ishaq.

He went back the way he had come, not stumbling until he was beyond the sentry net. In the darkness the wrof path shone faintly. He fumbled along it, forcing his mind awake, forcing himself to think. The Hall of Teaching. That would be safest.

But no place in R'Frow would be safe for him once Khalid's soldiers learned that he had been burned from Jela. They could hunt him in packs.

The barbarian giant would have sealed all the thumb-blocks in the only empty hall, to lessen the chance of ambush from inside. There were no doors left unlocked in R'Frow.

Dahar dragged himself to the end of a corridor in the Hall of Teaching. Not an open teaching room – from inside a teaching room, he wouldn't see or hear who entered the archway. Instead he hunkered down in a corner of the corridor, where walls formed a shallow alcove that gave him both darkness and a clear view of two entrances. In the most shadowed place at the other ends of the corridors, between two sets of the glowing orange circles, he spread a few light twigs, brittle enough to snap easily. He put his weapons where he could find them in the dark. Despite his exhaustion, sleep didn't come immediately; for a long while he lay awake, in isolation.

Isolation. It seemed to him that this isolation – gray, dim, as metallic as the wrof beneath him – was his natural condition, his for all his life, risen finally around him like cold fog rising from ground where one misstep could sink a warrior in muck. He had misstepped. He had been fool enough to try to serve two masters – the Ged science and the brother-warriors' blade of honor. But the science was without honor, without brothers, without anything but this cold metallic pain.

When he finally slept, it was to plunge into dreams.

He was a boy again, hunting on the veld with the others not yet cadre-chosen. They knew they would receive beatings from the master when they returned, for slipping away from the practice field. It was Lastlight, and the sky was hot and blue. He shot an arrow straight up into the blueness and somehow it hit a kreedog, a deformed three-eyed monster with hidden fangs. He couldn't see the fangs, but he knew they were there. The others wanted to kill it, but he blocked it with his own body, shouting, 'No! No! I've got to take it to my mother! She'll die without it!' But the others pushed him aside and killed the thing, and the moment the shoving boys touched him, he felt Kelovar's knife eager at his throat.

Someone stepped on a twig.

Dahar woke instantly. Without noise, he shifted farther into the shadows, knife in one hand and pellet tube in the other. He fought to clear his mind of its crippling exhaustion.

A figure stood at the other end of the corridor, backlit by the dim archway. Not tall enough for a Jelite warrior, nor for any male Delysian soldier Dahar had seen. A woman? Not a sister-warrior. And even though the shape was mostly obscured in the gloom, it seemed too wide in proportion to its height to be a fighter.

Back against the wall, Dahar eased himself to standing and silently maneuvered for the best possible position. His body tensed for battle.

Suddenly a light shone directly in his face, blinding him – an orangey light, with no warmth.

'You can't stay here without a lock,' Grax said. In his hand was a strip of orange fabric. 'All humans in R'Frow have thumblocks, Dahar. You can't stay here without one.

'It would not be safe.'

32

When Dahar left her by the Gray Wall, Ayrys had gone to find the plants for the mind-numbing dose to give SuSu.

She remembered seeing balloonweed along the path to the Hall of Teaching, on the day of the first rain within R'Frow. It had bloomed behind the showier silverbell, in the deep shade close to the trunk of a tree. The silverbell might have bloomed again in this new rain, but even if it hadn't, Ayrys thought she could find the right tree. It had been close to the Hall of Teaching, at one of the curving bends in the wrof path. Ged paths, like their cushion designs, curved and swirled; only their walls were straight.

She could still feel Dahar's hand hot on her arm. What had happened during the hours she had spent with the sick giant?

A shadow moved beyond a group of trees, and Ayrys froze. The shadow moved closer, and became a stone-mason Ayrys knew slightly, a big, red-faced man whose mouth was set in an unusually grim line. He nodded to Ayrys and kept walking.

She found the balloonweed without trouble, behind the silverbell. The silverbell were all dead.

Kneeling on the metal path, holding the tall grasses apart with both hands and peering into the gloom at the base of the tree, Ayrys studied the plants. Silverbell grew in Delysia. The leaves should have been pale green, lightly veined with red and hairy to the touch. These were gray. Holding one up to the dome, she could just glimpse the green color still within, like a shadow of itself. The veins were pale and thin, and the short stems – which should have been tough and woody – hung limp.

Ayrys felt the soil around the tree. It was moist enough. Standing, she waded a little way into the brush until she came to a bush the same height she was. The bush was one she remembered seeing all over the veld; wouldn't that mean it was tough enough to withstand cold, heat, drought, flood? She examined the bush. The wood was still firm, but the leaves were sparse; Ayrys could feel the tiny projections where leaves had fallen off. The remaining leaves were pale, and there was no new growth.

A sentence Grax had uttered just days ago, as he showed her and Dahar the dividing nucleus of a cell through the enlarger, came to Ayrys's mind. What does not grow, the Ged had said, dies.

Was R'Frow dying?

Ayrys looked at other plants, but she could not be sure which were not healthy and which were supposed to look like that. There were few plants in a glassyard; the only plants she knew about were either ornamental or those burned for the ash used in glassmaking. But it seemed to her that many of these plants held a subtle droop, a languishing that was not death but not growth either – like veld plants brought within Delysia's walls for their bloom, and then mistakenly planted in too much shade.

A *year* – the Ged had meant R'Frow to last a year, and Grax had never said different. But she had never realized that the reason was the light, that warm and unnatural light that made everything so much easier than it had been in Qom's harsh days and endless nights.

The light – there was something else in her mind about the light . . . it teased memory a moment, and then was gone.

The balloonweed seemed healthy enough. She gathered it and the other plant Dahar had named, linberry, and carried them to the constant tumultuous bazaar overflow-

ing the Delysian halls. There were always hot fires burning
just beyond the arches, where for a price women cooked
game caught in the wilderness, adding herbs and attention
the hunters themselves did not want to give. For a few
coins, someone would boil Ayrys's leaves according to
Dahar's directions. Would a cookwoman recognize the
combination as a drug to dull the mind? Probably not –
not even Delysian healers came anywhere near the skills
of Jelite priest-warriors.

SuSu had been alone now for an hour with her pain
and grief. That poor child . . . Ayrys quickened her step.
But at the edge of the market, she stopped in amazement.

Chaos. Shouting. Delysians arguing and yelling and
smacking their fists one into the other in anger. She could
hear a dangerous edge in the anger; it reminded her of
that first night in R'Frow, when Khalid had gathered the
rage and fear in both hands and made for himself the
leadership of Delysian soldiers.

Ondur, Ayrys's friend from the sleeping room beside
hers, stood at the edge of the crowd with her soldier lover,
Karim. When she saw Ayrys she broke away and came
toward her with both hands outstretched.

'You're safe! When I didn't see you, I was afraid. . . .
Where have you been, Ayrys?'

'Ondur, what's happened? Why all the shouting?'

'Don't you *know*?'

'No, I–'

'Khalid has betrayed us,' Karim said grimly.

'No,' Ondur said, equally grimly, 'he hasn't.' The two
exchanged a look that had nothing to do with Ayrys, a
look of hostility and longing.

Ayrys seized Ondur's arm. 'What are you talking about?
Have the Ged . . . exiled us?'

'The Ged? No, no, this is Khalid – and the Jelite commander. They've made an alliance to stop the killing. And
they're *right*,' Ondur said, with a fierce look at Karim.
'It's not a great price for peace.'

Karim said contemptuously, 'Craftsmen have no more
military sense than birds.'

Ondur gave her lover a long, troubled look, the gaze of
a woman afraid of what she is seeing in her man. Pointedly
she turned to Ayrys. 'Six of them made an alliance.
Khalid, Sancur, Kelovar–'

'Kelovar!'

'Not Kelovar,' Karim said grimly. 'This cowardice was
none of his.'

'–and three Jelite: their commander, her second, and
one other. A Jelite warrior murdered a soldier early this
morning or late last night, and the Jelite let Khalid kill
the warrior who did it. They *gave* him to us. If anyone
else on either side kills again, the six will find the killer
and . . . execute him all together. Until it stops.'

Ayrys stared at her. Ondur gave a mirthless smile. 'It's
hard to believe, isn't it? A council, that's what it is, a city
council. With Jelite and Delysian both.'

'To weaken us,' Karim said.

'No. To make the Ged see that we're all at least trying
to live by their laws. To do what they say so we can stay
in R'Frow.'

Karim sneered. 'And you like it here that much.
Enough to let Jela rule you.'

'Yes,' Ondur said fiercely. 'I like it here. I like having
enough to eat and not being cold and being where my –
where no one can find me. And Khalid leads us, not Jela.
Khalid and Sancur and Kelovar.'

'Not Kelovar.'

'He agreed,' Ondur said. She had been standing turned
toward Ayrys, sideways to Karim, as if looking straight
at him hurt her. But now she whirled to face him, and
her fists clenched at her sides. 'Or are you saying, Karim,
that Kelovar would disobey Khalid? His commander? Is
that how your "military sense" works? And *you* – if Khalid
gives you an order about this Kreedogs, will you defy
your commander?'

Karim scowled.

'Answer me! Will you?'

Karim's face betrayed his struggle, fierce but brief. 'If Khalid turns a soldier over to those scum and orders me to be part of it . . .'

'You'll what?'

He spat out, 'I'll obey my commander.'

The tension left Ondur. She touched Karim's arm gently, almost humbly, as if in apology. 'I knew you would.'

'But Kelovar might not. He might not, Ondur.'

At Kelovar's name, Ondur turned back to Ayrys. 'You haven't said anything, Ayrys. I know you and Kelovar aren't . . . don't . . .'

Ayrys's throat had gone dry. She got out only one word. 'No.'

'You could say,' Ondur went on thoughtfully, and Ayrys could see that she said it for Karim to hear, testing the victory she had just won over him, 'that it's worse for the Jelite than for us. They never understand bargaining; trying to get the best price for something just enrages them because they don't have any freedom to do it themselves. My mother traded with Jela. They can't bargain, they don't understand the smart way to get around treaties–'

'Because they're stupid,' Karim cut in. 'Dumb as stone. Not letting male and female warriors bed together because she might get pregnant; not letting warriors bed citizens because citizens are supposed to be beneath them; making the women fighters bed each other – although that's not something I'd mind watching . . .'

He had gotten even with Ondur. She clenched her fists and said to Ayrys. 'Come eat with us.'

'No, I . . . I have to do something, I . . .'

'You look pale. Are you sick?'

'No one is sick in R'Frow,' Karim said. He looked

more sharply at Ayrys. 'Tell us, Ayrys, what you think about the Kreedogs. You haven't said.'

Ayrys found her voice – low and strained, but again hers. 'I think they're brave. All of them, all six. To try to stop the killing, no matter what it takes . . . Killing is not what R'Frow is *for*, and Dahar is right to see that!'

'Khalid,' Karim said. His eyes narrowed. 'Khalid speaks for Delysia.'

'She meant Khalid,' Ondur said. 'Can't you see she looks exhausted? Go lie down, Ayrys.'

'I will. Soon.' But all the while she stood by the cookwoman boiling the silverbell and linberry near the back of the market, she tried to picture it, and then to feel it.

'Why does a Delysian concern herself with a Jelite whore? Is there a reason?' And again, more intently, '*Why?*' Reassurance – Dahar had been asking for reassurance that some sort of connection was possible between her and SuSu, between Delysian and Jelite – between himself and Khalid? 'It's worse for Jelite than for us,' Ondur had said. 'They never understand bargaining.' Yes, Ayrys thought, because they intend to *keep* their bargains. She thought of Jehane, bringing a Delysian safely across the veld because she thought she was honor-bound to do it. But when Jehane had killed Ayrys's attackers and Ayrys had asked her 'But what if they had been Jelite,' even Jehane, uncomplicated and young, had glimpsed the terrible possibility of two loyalties crushing her like opposite boulders, and had stalked angrily away.

Dahar was neither young nor uncomplicated. Ayrys thought of that quick mind, fierce for what the Ged could teach, and felt again his hand on her arm. He had been in some complex pain when he laid the barbarian inside the Wall. His efforts to hold himself steady had nearly broken when she questioned him: What happened this morning? What have you done? It had only been half the question. The other half would be, What has it cost you?

A bargain – or couldn't a Jelite let himself think of it that way?

That would make it even worse for him.

'There you are,' the cookwoman said. 'Two habrin.'

'We agreed on one,' Ayrys said.

'No, we didn't. Two,' the woman said. 'That was the bargain.' Her eyes glittered slyly at Ayrys.

Ayrys dropped one coin at the woman's feet and walked away from her curses, cold with anger all out of proportion to the little incident. The anger sustained her along the path away from the Delysian halls, until she was stopped at the sentry net.

It was nearly dark. They would not let her through. She was turned back inside the net.

Angry, frustrated, picturing all too clearly, the grief SuSu must be feeling alone in her locked room – that child, smaller even than Embry – Ayrys returned to her own room. Because of Dahar's warning not to let the dose precipitate, she had not mixed the plant parts, but carried them in separate bowls. She could take them tomorrow, when the sentry net let people through to go to the Hall of Teaching. SuSu, alone all night . . .

Carefully Ayrys set the two cups in a far corner of her room, behind the jumble of wires, electromagnets, simple motors she had learned to build from the Ged. Resting her back against the wall, Ayrys sat on a cushion and closed her eyes. Pictures crowded her mind. The white giant, the terrified and desperate child, Dahar by the Wall, SuSu begging to stay with her lover, and Grax, so good at explaining the world, refusing without explanation, barely hearing SuSu because he was so busy listening to whatever it was no one else could hear, so busy listening–

He *had* been listening.

Ayrys's eyes flew open and she sat up straighter. Of course, that's what Grax had been doing – listening. There was equipment inside his clear wrof helmet that let him listen to . . . something. She herself had learned to build electromagnets that emitted clicks and buzzes; the Ged must have equipment that could make other sounds. But where were the wires and electric cells?

She almost laughed at herself. The Ged dissolved walls and built sky. They would not need wires.

Well, then, what was Grax listening *to?* Clicks? Voices? Was that possible?

There was no way to know what was possible for the Ged, no measuring rod. But it they were listening to voices, whose?

There were no answers. Ayrys puzzled over it until she could no longer think straight, and still there were no answers.

She could ask Grax.

But the Ged had not told her about hearing voices inside their helmets. On the other hand, they usually answered only what had been asked. Why tell humans about this? Why *not* tell humans about this?

No answers.

She tried to sleep, and could not. She was lying awake on her cushions when her door opened.

'Hello, Ayrys.'

Kelovar stood in her room. Involuntarily – stupidly – she glanced behind him at the door. But of course she had closed it. Once thumblocks were exchanged, there was no way to ever undo the exchange.

'Kelovar. I told you not to come here anymore.'

'I know. But I had to come.'

She stood up, glad she had not undressed, and looked at him more closely. His pale eyes shone strangely, but the skin on his face sagged with exhaustion. Like Dahar's. But unlike Dahar, Kelovar radiated something frightening, something that made her move no closer. She had the sudden fanciful impression that like the bush beside the balloonweed, the months in R'Frow had make Kelovar less whole than he had been, as if he had lost soft and green layers of himself that had withered in the dim Ged

light. She pushed the fancy away. The richness of Ged
science might leave most humans untouched, but how
could it make a man worse?

If he knows he can't share in it, a part of her said, out
of nowhere.

'I had to come,' Kelovar said, 'to warn you.'

A thrill of fear shot through Ayrys. Had anyone seen
her talk with Dahar, his hand on her arm . . . ?

'Don't try again to pass through the sentry net at night,
Ayrys. Not to fetch things for your Ged toys, not for any
reason. The toys can wait till the net is open. Don't try
it again.'

'How did you know I had?' Stupid, stupid – if Kelovar
had become Khalid's lieutenant, of course he would know.

Kelovar looked at her intently. She recognized the look,
but before she could speak, the walls around them began
to growl.

'Humans of R'Frow. There have been two killings in
R'Frow, against Ged wishes. The Ged have promised exile
for this. Humans are trying to stop the killings. The Ged
will wait and watch this trying. None will be exiled while
the Ged wait and watch.'

Kelovar's jaw tightened with sudden fury. Ayrys
backed a step away from him. But he said nothing, made
no comment on the walls' message, which, like all other
Ged messages, repeated itself in the same calm tones three
times. Because they had three eyes? Ayrys wondered, and
felt a bubble of insane laughter – or relief – rise in her
throat.

Kelovar spent the time while the walls spoke in looking
slowly around the room, packed with Ged science – Ged
'toys'. When the growling had finished, he put both hands
on Ayrys's shoulders. 'Be careful, Ayrys. I still want no
harm to come to you.'

She stepped backward, and his hands fell empty at his
side.

'Ayrys–'

'No, Kelovar. I'm sorry, but no. Not tonight, not ever.'

'I don't believe that.'

'Believe it. Please. Not ever.'

He left. Ayrys lay down on her cushions and tried to sleep.

33

'Talot,' Jehane said. '*Don't.*'

She knelt beside their cushions and put out one hand to stroke Talot's hair, then withdrew the hand helplessly. Talot was not crying. She lay face down, motionless on the cushions, asking for no comfort. She had asked for nothing. She had come back from the Kreedogs in mastery of herself, dry-eyed and white-faced, strong in her control. Yes, she told Jehane, the story flashing through the Jelite halls was true. She had identified Jallaludin to Dahar, and Belazir had let Khalid kill him. Dahar had been burned from the brother-warriors. It was all true.

'Talot–'

'Leave me alone, Jehane. I am a sister-warrior. Don't insult me with the softness of a whore.'

Jehane turned mute. Talot was right. Talot was a sister-warrior, and softness was for citizens and whores. That was the way it had always been. Only . . .

Only why was it all so much more treacherous in R'Frow than it had been in Jela! Fauggh! R'Frow was as treacherous as Delysia itself. Sister-warriors should know what to do and what to feel, and then go do and feel it. Jehane should. Talot should.

But that was the treachery – Talot *was*. A sister-warrior should be left alone with her own failures, and that was what Talot asked. So why did it make her, Jehane, feel so slimy to do it? Why was she eaten up by this stupid

desire to do something for Talot, when Talot wanted
nothing done for her, and there was nothing to do anyway?

This was not how it was supposed to be. Nothing in
R'Frow was how it was supposed to be.

Throughout the walls' growled message of no exile,
Talot neither raised her head nor moved. She seemed not
to have heard. Jehane listened in stony silence. There was
nothing else to do. Or if there was, she couldn't think of
it.

34

SuSu opened the door a tiny crack and peered into the corridor. It was empty. She waited, heart pounding, fighting against her own hands. Again and again they twitched to slam shut the door, and again and again she forced them to be still. Fear made her vision blur so that the walls of the dark corridor seemed to waver in and out, a horrible metallic breathing. But even that could not stop her. And despite the horrible wavering, the corridor was silent. She still had the silence.

The silence he had given her.

He was not coming back. Huddled in the corner of her room all night, too paralyzed by fear to cross the floor and wrap herself in a blanket, she had waited for the dark furry voices to once again begin to torment her. He was gone. He had kept the voices away. Now the voices would come back; tearing at her, urging her to do things that would hurt her, as once they had made her lock her room against the brother-warriors, as once they had made her cross the veld to R'Frow, as once they had told her she did not have to be a whore.

But the voices had not come. And in the blessed silence, toward morning, there had come periods when the fear went away a little, just a very little, and SuSu had been able to think.

He was not coming back. The reason he was not coming back was that the monsters had him behind the Wall. He was a prisoner behind the Wall.

But she had been a prisoner, too, and he had saved her.
He had taken her away, and given her safety and the
beautiful silence. He had saved her.

Whenever her mind reached this point – slowly, painfully, shivering in her corner – SuSu suddenly saw what
thought came next. Then the black fear howled over her,
scattering all thought. As long as it raged through her
mind in wave after wave, she did not have to see what
she had seen.

But eventually the fear receded, and the thought came
stronger, and then again stronger yet – until it was as
strong as the dark, furry voice had once been, and like
the dark furry voice, this other thought was telling her
what she had to do.

And as with the dark furry voice, there was no escape.
She had to do it. He had saved her.

Her small bare feet made no sound. She listened a long
time at the top of the ladder, finally descended, stood
shivering in the hall below, thin arms wrapped around
herself and black eyes wide with terror.

It was not quite dawn. The hall was dim and cool, all
edges shadowed in gray except for the glowing orange
circle high on the wall beside the ladder. Unlike the circle
in her room, it protruded a little from the wall, an orange
blister.

Suddenly the circle frightened her. It was too bright
against the gloomy dimness of the rest of the hall. It was
too orange. Brightness, orange – they were both suddenly
loud to her, both suddenly as bad as noise in the silence
he had given her. She put her hands over her ears, but
she could still see the orange noise.

White – it should be white. If the circle were white, it
would be like him. It would not be loud. It would not
hurt.

SuSu pulled her white tebl over her head. She wore
nothing underneath. Her fingers, scarcely thicker than her
collarbones, twisted the tebl convulsively. With a desper-

ate flurry of motion, she scampered back up the ladder nearly to the top and draped the tebl over the orange circle.

Now it was white. SuSu clung to the ladder, breathing hard.

Below, a single note sounded. The tops of the floor tables dissolved and other wrof arose, each carrying four bowls of steaming food.

Slowly, SuSu descended the ladder. She picked all four bowls off the closest table and laid them on the floor. At the smell of the food, her stomach lurched violently. The fear swept back over her.

But there was no escape. The other thought was there, too, the one that had come again and again in the night. There was no escape.

Susu climbed onto the floor table. She lay on her side, her knees drawn up to her chin, folding her tiny body as small and flat as she could, careful not to protrude beyond the table's edge. She squeezed all the air from her lungs. Naked, tiny as a child, she waited.

After a measureless time, the note sounded again. The tops of the floor tables dissolved themselves, and the unclaimed food bowls slowly sank. The sides of the floor tables began to slice inward from the edges above her. For a terrified moment she thought she was not flat enough, and the closing metal would not close. Then the last of the gloomy light disappeared, and she lay locked in darkness, small and naked in the wrof womb.

No alarm sounded. No children had been dragged across the veld to R'Frow. The Ged, number-rational knew the food chutes were too small for even the dismaying range of body sizes produced by wildly variant genes. The Library-Mind had computed the deviations on a probability curve. SuSu's tebl covered the monitor. No alarm sounded.

SuSu whimpered, and fought the black fear. She could almost hear the dark furry voice now, hidden in the fear like warriors in mist, waiting for her. But she saw the other thing, too, the other thought, and her mind reached out and clutched it with both hands. There was no escape from it, but now there didn't have to be. She was doing the thought. She was not a whore any longer. He had made her not a whore, so there was no escape from the thought. It was the one thing standing solid in the howling black mists that filled her mind, the one thing that kept mind and bone and muscle from dissolving completely. It had always been there, always.

What is freely given must be freely returned.

He had saved her. And now he was locked inside with the monsters. What is given must be returned.

SuSu rode noiselessly inside the Wall.

35

Jehane stalked past three sister-warriors resting at the edge of the practice yard. Although it was barely full light, first-net warriors had already finished morning practice. Threeballs, crossbows, pellet tubes, knives littered the grass beside them.

'You're going the wrong way,' one of them called to Jehane, who scowled and kept walking.

'She's going hunting in the wilderness.'

'No game left in the wilderness. Hardly, anyway.'

'You'll miss the Hall of Teaching,' one of them said. Another called, 'Where's Talot?'

Jehane stopped and faced them. 'What do you care?'

An older sister-warrior, not a cadre leader but in charge of this morning's practice, said warningly, 'Sharimor . . .'

'Let her answer like a sister-warrior. Where's Talot? She missed practice.'

'In our room.'

'And where are you going?'

'Anywhere but sitting here!'

The older warrior said placatingly, 'You've hardly been sitting, Jehane. You've practiced hard enough for a whole cadre.'

'We all know Jehane is indestructible,' Sharimor said with angry malice. They were all angry, all tense, edgy with the undigested events of the day before; Jallaludin, the Kreedogs, the burning of the first lieutenant. 'Nothing wears down our Jehane.'

'Enough,' the older one said. 'Jehane, don't leave for the Hall of Teaching alone. We should be cautious–'

Jehane lashed out. She had been looking for someplace to lash out; the practice-yard targets had not provided it. 'Cautious! So now being a sister-warrior means being cautious! When did that happen? Or is it just another word for cowardice?'

The warriors rumbled angrily, but the leader got to her feet and kept her voice even. 'The next attack, Jehane, will probably be Delysian against Jelite, a retaliation for . . . for yesterday.'

'Or a gloating over it,' someone muttered.

'We can't afford to lose any more warriors. You know how those slime are about keeping treaties. If you walk to the Hall of Teaching alone–'

'Let them just try,' Jehane said fiercely. Stupidly. She knew it was stupid, and knowing it made her feel even angrier, so that she stamped away. The sister-warrior had been *right*, she should not be fighting with her, and she should not be going alone to the Hall of Teaching. That was the trouble with this darkcold piss-hearted place – you couldn't do anything. Couldn't hunt, couldn't fight, couldn't leave. Walls. Everywhere you went, there were walls. You couldn't do anything.

She couldn't do anything for Talot.

Talot had refused food, refused sex, refused – unthinkably – to go to the practice field and smash threeballs into targets. When Jehane had asked Talot if she was going to the Hall of Teaching, Talot had not answered, just went on lying face-hidden on the cushions, her red hair straggling out of the warrior coil she had never brushed out the night before. Looking at those bedraggled tendrils had filled Jehane with a furious helplessness she couldn't stand one minute longer. Talot was in pain, and Talot's pain had somehow become Jehane's as well. How? Talot had become one of the walls, fencing off Jehane from where she had been before, diverting her this way and that until she walked smack into a place where someone else's pain hurt her as if it were her own.

The worst was – she couldn't *do* anything for the pain. Nothing helped Talot. But if she, Jehane, didn't do something and do it soon, she would go as crazy as everybody else in R'Frow. Crazier than she had already become in this slimy city where walls sprang up and stopped you from being what you had already been before.

Viciously Jehane swiped with her knife at the heads of a patch of tall rillweeds. Instead of snapping free at the blow and scattering seeds on the ground, the heads bent and swayed limply.

She swerved away from the Hall of Teaching and turned instead toward the wilderness. No teaching cadres for her this morning – no monster drivel, no first lieutenant who had somehow become not the first lieutenant, no smug Delysian glances with Jallaludin in their eyes. She wouldn't go – she would *not*.

She traveled rapidly, moving for greatest safety close to the north wall. The air brushed her cheeks, but without cooling them. She shook her head, but instead of clearing it, the simple action only increased her misery. Her hand tightened on her bow. If she could only see some game, if she could only hunt, if she could only do *something* . . .

Ahead of her and to her left loomed the gray bulk of the unused hall. No, not unused – the barbarian giant lived here, with his stolen whore. Jehane could not see around the corner of the hall; cautiously she slowed her pace.

She heard male voices around the corner.

She fitted a quarrel into her crossbow, took it out again, and instead drew the pellet tube at her waist. Her unfocused fury left her, replaced instantly with cold concentration. Using a stand of scrub brush for partial cover, she stepped quickly around the corner. Delysian *soldiers* – and something at last to do.

But the men were Jelite.

Two of them – citizens, not brother-warriors – standing with their backs to her. Citizens? Jehane lowered her pellet tube and prepared to demand why they were here and not on their way to the Hall of Teaching. Then one of them moved, and beyond them Jehane saw a woman. The Delysian glassblower, a food bowl held in either hand, her face gone white.

The citizen took a step toward Ayrys. Jehane saw her glance at the bowls in her hands, at the man's face, back at one of the bowls. The man reached out a burly arm. Ayrys threw a bowl at his face, whirled, and ran.

She missed, of course, as she had missed with the blue glass bottle on the veld. Both men broke into a run, and in a moment they were on her.

Jehane was back on the veld, by the river, on the other side of the Gray Wall. Ayrys leaned dizzy and sick against a tree and said, 'What if they had been Jelite? Would your protection have held then?' But she owed Ayrys no protection now. It was Talot she had wanted to protect from pain – and had failed. And a high commander gave a warrior to the enemy to murder, and a first lieutenant was burned from the ranks, and all the old right rules had become walls that did not hold.

Ayrys cried out. The two threw her to the ground; one pinned her arms over her head and the other picked up a rock.

Killing a Delysian in retaliation had been forbidden. But Belazir had said nothing about maiming short of death.

Ayrys suddenly worked one leg loose and thrust her knee upward, hard. She caught the man in the groin, and he howled in pain. The other man, surprised, shifted his grip on her arms. Ayrys wiggled from his hands and tried to roll free.

Fighting – the glassblower was fighting. Blindly, stupidly – she had no hope of rolling free with enough time to get up and run, not from that position – but she was still *fighting*. Afterward, going over it again and again in her mind, Jehane knew that had Ayrys lay there passively, had she wept or begged, Jehane would have gone away and left the Jelite men to their Delysian sport. But Ayrys fought. She was doing *something*.

And because the woman was doing something to help herself, and because there was nothing Jehane could do to help Talot, and because all the walls in this bladder-slimed place were somehow different anyway, and because helplessness was driving her crazy – Jehane raised her pellet tube.

The man Ayrys had kicked seized her right leg, while the other regained his grasp on her shoulders. The first Jelite then grabbed her knee in his right hand and her ankle in his left and with one violent motion flipped her over. He held both ankles in one hand, raised the rock, and smashed it down on the left leg, halfway between ankle and knee. The bone broke with a loud *crack!* and Ayrys began screaming.

Jehane ran forward. 'Stop! Now!'

The man at Ayrys's head, facing Jehane, gaped in astonishment. The other turned slowly. When he saw a sister-warrior, his face puckered with confusion.

'Get away from her. Back away, and move slowly.'

Neither man would be armed – they were citizens, not warriors. Wordlessly, like citizens, they obeyed a sister-warrior.

Jehane said, 'The high commander said no killing.'

'We weren't going to kill her,' the first man said. His confusion was turning to a sullen rage, which Jehane could see he dared not show. *The next attack will probably be Delysian against Jelite*, the practice leader had said. This was not the way it was supposed to be.

The man repeated, more strongly. 'We won't kill her.' Jehane saw that Ayrys had fainted. White bone stuck up from her leg, higher than the pooling blood.

'The high commander meant no violence at all,' Jehane

said icily. 'It's not for you to twist her words! Go to the archway in her hall and wait for me there.'

One man, clearly frightened, turned to go. But the one who had broken Ayrys's leg laid a restraining hand on the other's arm, licked his own lips, and did not move. His eyes met Jehane's.

Jelite citizens. It was unthinkable that a Jelite citizen would disobey a warrior – but then, in this darkcold place the unthinkable just kept *happening*. If they disobeyed her order to stop doing what had always been right to do – killing Delysians – would she kill them? Could she?

Coldly, Jehane knew the answer. She would not kill them. Flog them unconscious for disobedience, gladly – but not kill. Not Jelite citizens she was sworn to defend. Not what was left of the way it was supposed to be. Not over a Delysian glassblower.

For a second her hand quivered on her weapon. A small quiver, but the man saw it. From inside his tebl he pulled a Ged knife he should not have had, and he stood up.

But he, too, was Jelite, and Jela was bred into him as much as into Jehane. He in turn hesitated, and in the small bit of time Jehane fired not her pellet tube, nor her crossbow, but her threeball. It wrapped itself around the citizen's knees and dropped him on the grass. Jehane had already swung her pellet tube to cover the other man, who looked terrified and did not move.

'Take his knife and throw it down, and yours, too!'

He did. Jehane said furiously to the fallen man. 'I could have broken your leg with it – remember that. You, over there, as you value your life, crawl away from her and toward the warriors' halls. Tell the first warrior you see to come here and bring a Blue and Red. And if you don't, I swear I'll hunt you down myself.'

He went. Jehane watched him out of sight, bound the other citizen wrist to ankle – he gave her a look of so much confused fury that she scowled in warning – and bent over Ayrys.

The glassblower was coming out of her faint. She paled, and clammy sweat sprang out on her forehead. She barely had time to turn her head before she vomited. Her hand convulsively clutched Jehane's, who recoiled in distaste. She didn't mind the vomit, but Ayrys's weak grip, tightening and untightening with all the strength of a child's, disgusted her. Didn't glassblowers do any work at all? And after Talot's hand, so strong and firm . . .

'Don't move,' Jehane rasped. 'Your leg is broken. A healer is coming.'

Ayrys tried to speak. It came out a whisper, and Jehane had to bend closer to hear. 'Why?'

'Why did I help you?' Jehane frowned; there was no answer. She tried to yank her hand away, but Ayrys's grip had tightened surprisingly; she kept her hold on Jehane's hand. Jehane said, 'Because of the high commander's orders, Delysian. Not because of you!'

'Dahar . . .' A wave of pain crossed Ayrys's face. 'He will have to . . . the same to them. . . .'

Jehane stared at her. Gloating – the slug was *gloating*. The Delysians wouldn't have heard yet about last night's burning of Dahar from the ranks, but Ayrys saw what Jehane had not – that now, for the second time, the alliance would force Jelite to betray Jelite. By all – what had she *done*? She hadn't even seen it. In stopping the two citizens, she had only made sure that Belazir would know who they were, and would turn them over to the Kreedogs for the same maiming they had inflicted: Khalid would break their legs. And she, Jehane, hadn't even seen it. But the Delysian slime had, and she was *gloating*.

Jehane's knife itched. In the fiercest battle of her young life, she stopped herself from plunging it into Ayrys. It wouldn't help. She didn't understand how she had come to this Wall where the fighting she had been trained to do wouldn't help, but somehow she had. It wouldn't help.

'I did it for Talot,' Jehane said aloud. Ayrys had fainted again and didn't hear her. The Jelite citizen looked at

her without comprehension. Somehow, the words eased
Jehane a little, and that made no sense either. Talot was
not helped by Jehane's helping Ayrys, and now Khalid
and his slime could . . . But nonetheless, in some stupid
crazy darkcold way, the words were true. Looking down
at this other woman who was alive because of her, Jehane
thought of Talot, and the hard knot of panic in her breast
loosened just a little. She had done it for Talot.

Figures broke from around the corner of the hall. A
brother-warrior and a very young warrior-priest, the
double helix sewn to the left shoulder of her tebl above a
crescent moon, ran toward her across the grass.

36

Within the Wall, the Library-Mind began to signal. Ged, waking or sleeping or eating, stopped, looked at each other, and moved closer. Every screen in the perimeter except that of the island probe, no matter what had been on it a moment before, began to show the same images. The Library-Mind signaled urgently: 'Significant data, Level Prime. Significant data, Level Prime.'

'Level Prime' meant the Library-Mind had learned something that would modify the Central Paradox.

Ged began to run.

37

SuSu rode sideways into the Wall. All at once there were bowls of stew pressing into her before and after, smearing her with still-warm liquid. Light appeared at the end of the horizontal shaft and she was dumped naked down onto a pile of bowls and food, the pile itself already sinking even farther beneath the floor. Other piles from other halls stretched to her right and left. SuSu felt the precise edges of the wrof bowls beneath her begin to dissolve. Scrambling off the pile, she stood blinking in the sudden light, her hands clapped to her ears.

There was a horrible din. Kreedogs barked and yowled in clear pens all along one wall. They hurled themselves against the clear wrof, fangs bared and mouths slavering, trying to get at either her or the food. SuSu shuddered violently, and it was a long time before she could make herself either open her eyes or move.

The room was larger than when they had brought the barbarian giant into it; walls had been moved. SuSu looked around in bewilderment. She saw nothing that looked like the same room. What if it were not the same room and she couldn't get to where he was? The black fear almost swamped her.

She groped through it until she found that other thought, and hung on to it: *What has been freely given must be freely returned.*

She had smelled kreedogs when the Ged had brought

him here. And now she heard them. This was where he was.

At the opposite end of the room from the kreedogs stood a series of low partitions. SuSu set out toward them, her bare feet noiseless on the floor.

The partitions formed a series of irregularly spaced cubicles. The first held a floor table covered with a jumble of equipment, all meaningless to SuSu. In the next cubicle was another clear pen, this one with a top bored with small holes. Two jonkils inside had built a nest; the female ruffled her feathers protectively as SuSu passed. Behind the third partition plants were growing under a light so bright SuSu blinked. She had seen no light that bright since threeday on the veld.

At the next partition, she put her hands over her mouth. A kreedog lying on a floor table, its belly and head cut open and the dead eyes staring at her shiny and wild-eyed. SuSu felt her gorge rise, but there was nothing in her to vomit. She had not eaten in two days.

Cubicle after cubicle, Ged equipment, Qom plants and animals, boxes and ovals of dark wrof, strangenesses she could not even guess at.

Where?

It did not even occur to her to call out for him. Sound was the kreedogs barking, was hard hands and the dark furry voice, was herself screaming when they took him behind the Wall. She searched in silence. Where?

She rounded another partition, and found him.

The giant lay where the first lieutenant had placed him, on his back on the immense floor table, his huge white hands at his sides and his white hair falling forward over his shoulders. The top of his skull had been removed, just above the eyebrows, and convoluted tissue bulged outward. There was no blood. But in among the brain tissue tiny orange lights twinkled, glowing to illuminate folds and depressions, like minuscule embers in gray and white ash.

SuSu reached out one hand to touch him. She could not; he was encased in a clear wall, cool to her touch. She picked up a gray metal rectangle lying amid a jumble of equipment and struck the clearness with all her strength; the heavy metal had no more effect than her hand. Patiently she searched for something to stand on. From the next cubicle she dragged a wrof cube, not heavy, and climbed upon it. But the top of the giant was sealed with the same clear wall.

Leaning over, she circled her arms as far around that clear shield as they would reach. She felt nothing, thought nothing, gone as motionless inside as the stasis unit, frozen in mind and bone at the moment she rounded the partition. She laid her cheek against the wall around his.

After a long while, SuSu stepped back off the box. She dragged it one-handed back to exactly where it had been; in the other hand she still clutched the dark gray rectangle that had not dented the wrof shield. Her fingers had frozen around it. She didn't know she still held it. She left the cubicle.

The kreedogs still hurled themselves at the invisible barrier. SuSu stood before them. She could not remember what she had been going to do. The animals slavered and howled and she watched, almost dreamily, not remembering what she had been going to do, not remembering, not thinking.

Eventually she turned and padded in the other direction, frowning a little in distraction, as if trying to remember something, although she was not. There was no memory, no something. She circled the room aimlessly, a naked, stew-smeared figure delicate as glass.

When she reached the food shaft, the tiny frown of concentration returned. Without thought, she lay down on the floor in the same place from which she had risen. The bowls and stew had disappeared; this piece of floor was smooth as the rest.

Eventually, the floor moved. Beneath SuSu, stew bowls

rose, four by four. The bowls themselves were cool, but where the hot stew touched her, her skin burned enough to blister. She did not feel it.

The shaft carried her sideways beneath the floor of R'Frow, then abruptly upward. Light broke over her head. When she opened her eyes, the first thing she saw was her white tebl, draped where she had left it, the protruding orange circle glowing sickly through the fabric like light within white tissue.

The frozenness shattered.

38

'Now they not only cooperate between the subspecies, they switch subspecies,' Krak'gar said. Her smell of bewilderment mingled with all the others'. The Library-Mind had been requested to pause a moment. None of the Ged liked it when the Library-Mind outstripped their thoughts and reactions too far.

They had all seen the images: the 'Jelite' female Jehane stopping violence against the 'Delysian' female Ayrys *by attacking two Jelite*. Then the Delysian had been assisted by a Jelite healer, and the Jelite Jehane – instead of staying with this new membership in the Delysians – had gone back to the Jelite, and been accepted. Unlike Dahar, who, for bringing about the cooperation of the 'alliance,' had been rejected by the Jelite. Even though the violence done by the alliance had not been intrasubspecies, but in the accepted pattern of Delysian against Jelite. Meanwhile, the Delysian Ayrys had tried to help the Jelite SuSu, who had changed to the third subspecies of the sick giant from the island.

It made no sense. The Ged had come to accept the humans' behaving as if they were two species at territorial war, like the Ged and humans in space – and now some humans were behaving as if those two species were one.

'No species in the known galaxy shows greater loyalty to another species than to its own,' growled Rowir, in the configurations of absolute fact.

'None. Harmony sings with us,' said R'gref.

'Harmony sings with us,' said Wraggaf.

'None.'

'None. May it always sing.

'It will always sing. But they are biologically *one* species, not two.'

'But they think they are two.'

'The female Jehane talks to her mate as if they were still both "Jelite." '

'But she acted as if she had become "Delysian." '

'Harmony sings . . .'

'Harmony . . .' with pheromones of fear.

It was beyond the number-rational, almost beyond the expressive capacity of the pheromone glands. Evolving in a slow, stately dance where solidarity meant survival and change came slowly, over millennia, the number-rational mind and the communication of smells were supposed to perform in harmony, the rational with the moral. Wraggaf and Krowgif felt themselves slipping toward biological shock. The rest pressed close, surrounding and stroking, smothering the two with reassuring smells until the threat passed. Then they all returned to the discussion, starting it around yet again, with the slow and ponderous assimilation of race that had once taken a millennium to move from the idea of one wheel to the idea of two.

The wall screens revealed humans entering the Hall of Teaching, waiting in puzzlement for Ged who did not come, drifting away again.

Eventually, when they were ready, the eighteen requested the Library-Mind to offer its modification to the Central Paradox.

And that, too, took hours to discuss.

The Library-Mind had not found an answer to the Paradox – nor a negation of it. Intraspecies violence was too great a biological liability for a number-rational species to survive long enough to reach star drive; yet humans had. No answer.

Instead, in the grammatical configurations of facts

arranged into a tentative hypothesis, the Library-Mind had upset all pheromones by recommending skipping over the lack of an answer.

'Humans can change loyalties from one species to another, or from what they think is one species to another,' it growled softly. 'Ged represent a different species. Thus, humans may be able to change loyalties from human species to Ged. Such humans aboard ship may be better able than the Ged to predict what the human fleet will do. This project may then succeed even without a resolution of the Central Paradox.'

The eighteen sat stunned – and yet not stunned. They had not thought of this desperate course of action themselves, yet as they watched the wall screens, essentially the same reactions had occurred in each of them, essentially the same perceptions, essentially the same patterns, sensed if not yet given grammatical configuration. The odors had been there – elusive still, overwhelmed by general revulsion, but there: a whiff of desperation, an odor of resolve upon action, the smell of being cornered.

But – humans aboard a Ged ship? Living, eating, working with those violent and erratic gene-diversifieds, who were so pathetic they did not know what species they belonged to, and so immoral they could be brought to not care?

A babble of voices broke out. 'They might switch their loyalties' – the words sounded makeshift; there was no grammatical structure to permit their linking – 'yet again, and without a Wall between . . .'

'. . . have to treat them as Ged . . .'

'. . . atmosphere requirements . . .'

'The ship's weapons . . .'

It went on and on. They crowded closer to each other, and when the room began to smell of panic, they knew without words that they were moving toward acceptance of the Library-Mind's recommendation. The underscent of desperation grew stronger. It was a desperate idea.

A long time later, they began to discuss safeguards. They called on the Library-Mind, and they tried to think how humans might react aboard ship. But how could even the Library-Mind know how humans would react, if they really could both forget something as basic as what species they were and create something as complex as a star drive?

A star drive that was taking Ged territory and Ged lives.

At last, exhausted and strained, all pheromones smelled of resignation, of resolve, of the subordination of disgust to their species' desperate need. They would try to make a small number of intelligent humans switch loyalty to the Ged. They would do it the same way 'Jelite' and 'Delysian' and the mute albino giant apparently had – by extending aid. By keeping the chosen humans from violence. By offering to them, and not to the others, whatever seemed to be desired.

Presently they began compiling names.

39

The pain in her leg and spine had gone, swirling away down a liquid river. In its place was the river itself, a dark rush of water moving in two directions at once, rising between its banks, rising up to the light.

'Give her another dose,' someone said, 'she's moving Fauggh – don't let her move until I'm done setting the bone!'

A cup was held to her lips. Ayrys drank, gagged, tried to turn her head. The cup followed, roughly; someone poured bitter liquid down her throat. Jehane? But Jehane was not a healer. Who was? Someone was. She couldn't remember. . . .

The river rose and flooded over her.

'Ayrys,' Ondur said. 'Ayrys?'

Ayrys opened her eyes. She lay on her own cushions, in her room. A small group of Delysians crowded in the doorway, quiet and watchful. Ondur and Karim knelt near the pallet, Ondur's pretty face creased with concern.

'I'm not here,' Ayrys said stupidly, and thought: *How foolish*. The thought moved sluggishly, flotsam on turgid water.

'Yes, yes, you're here,' Ondur soothed. 'It's the dose she gave you. The . . . warrior-priest. But she said once you woke, it would leave you fast. No, don't try to sit.'

'What . . . happened?'

From the doorway, people began to push into the room, eager to see and to tell.

'Two Jelite men–'

'One of their own warriors, a girl from–'

'Khalid–'

'Their high commander–'

'Be quiet!' Ondur shouted. She scowled fiercely at the babblers, and Ayrys thought stupidly that when Ondur did that, she looked like Jehane. *Jehane . . .*

Karim pushed the crowd back into the corridor and closed the door. Ondur said gently, 'Can't you remember? You were attacked by two warriors–'

'Not warriors,' Karim said. 'Citizens. Scum.'

'And then a sister-warrior from your teaching group – Jehane? – stopped them. But don't you remember, Ayrys?'

'It's that dose,' Karim said grimly. 'Don't give her any more. How the darkcold can we know what it does to her mind? Their priest-warriors do things–'

'Be quiet, Karim,' Ondur said.

'I . . . remember,' Ayrys said. The balloonweed leaves, SuSu, the corpse with Jehane's arrow in his neck – no, that was on the veld . . .

'She remembers,' Ondur said to Karim, and a little of the worry left her face. 'It was only a dose to dull pain.'

'SuSu, Ayrys said.

'What, dear heart?'

'Nothing. How did I get–' The pain suddenly surfaced from the river onto her leg, and she gasped.

'Do you want another dose, Ayrys? The warrior-priest left more.'

'I wouldn't give it to her,' Karim said. 'Kelovar said–'

'Kelovar has no concern in what she chooses. Do you want the dose, Ayrys?'

'No. Tell me . . . what else happened.'

Ondur said, 'The slime broke your leg. That Jehane sent for a priest-warrior, who set it, and carried you to their high commander. She and Khalid met at the Hall of Teaching with the Kreedogs–'

'Don't call them that,' Karim said sharply.

'–and Belazir turned you over to Khalid, and turned over the two men as well. Kelovar said she looked sick as death.'

Karim said, 'Of course she looked sick as death. She can't hide now behind any claim that Delysia attacks first. Two attacks since the Ged law, and both by Jelite!'

The effect of the dose was fading, and Ayrys's leg hurt agonizingly. But she had to know. 'Who . . . what did the Kreedogs do?'

'Broke the Jelites' legs, same as yours,' Karim said immediately, but his eyes did not meet Ayrys's.

She whispered, 'Who?'

There was a little silence. Then Karim said, 'Kelovar.'

'Not . . .'

'Khalid? No,' Ondur said, with heat. 'Even a commander might not have the stomach to maim bound men.'

But Kelovar would. Ayrys saw his face, not the weary face of the soldier who had helped her at the Breel's so long ago, but the one Kelovar had come to have in R'Frow: close, narrowed, like a river channeled into murderous straits by rocks it could not move. That Kelovar would not hesitate to maim.

Dahar had not done it. Had not had to do it. But somehow he bore the responsibility, or had borne it yesterday by the gray Wall: *What happened this morning? What have you done?* The Kreedogs were Dahar's plan, and not his high commander's, she who had looked sick at its execution. Yet he had turned back to tell her how to make the dose for SuSu.

'Ayrys – are you all right? You look . . .'

'Will I be crippled? Forever?'

Ondur and Karim exchanged glances.

'Will I walk again?'

'Of course you will,' Ondur soothed, but for once Karim overrode her and leaned closer to Ayrys.

'The healer couldn't say. It depends on how the bone grows together. And although I hate the truth of it, their healers are better than ours – they've saved warriors that . . . But she was young, Ayrys, just a girl, she could be wrong. You're supposed to lie still and not move the bone.'

Ondur said quickly, 'I'll bring you your food. And help you shit or piss. Just share your thumblock with me.'

Karim said, 'How can she, if she can't move to the door to stick her thumb in with yours?'

Ondur said, 'Ayrys, you haven't said anything. You're not thinking of . . . I had a lover once who was wounded in battle, and rather than live crippled, he . . . you wouldn't . . .'

'No,' Ayrys said, surprising herself. 'I wouldn't. I would not seek more pain.' But that had not been true on the veld; when had it become true?

'A better healer than that young girl,' Ondur said. 'They caused this, they should have sent for a warrior-priest older, more experienced–'

Karim's face tightened. 'No.'

Ondur cut in, obviously trying to divert Ayrys's mind from her leg. 'Their first lieutenant, that warrior-priest, has been stripped from their warriors. You didn't hear that, did you, Ayrys? Do you know it's evening, and you've been out all day from that dose? Wasn't their first lieutenant in your teaching group? You must know which one he is then. He's been stripped from their warriors. Completely out.'

Ayrys turned to Karim. 'Why?'

He shrugged. 'No one knows. How can you understand minds like the Jelite? Murderous, all of them.'

'Ayrys, you look . . . are you in much pain?'

'Yes. I think I could sleep now, though – I'd like to sleep.'

Ondur stood. 'I'll come in the morning. Take the Jelite dose if you need it.'

Karim said, 'Try not to need it.'

They had reached the door when Ayrys said, 'Ondur, Karim . . . thank you both. For your kindness. There isn't . . . I sometimes think there isn't much kindness in R'Frow. Thank you.'

For an instant Ondur's pretty face grew strained and taut, and Ayrys saw the woman beneath the bright cheerfulness, who covered whatever grief she had left in Delysia with determination not to look back. Then Ondur forced herself to smile, and the instant passed. She turned off the light.

Alone, Ayrys squeezed her eyes shut. The pain in her leg was growing worse. Was the Jelite dose still in her blood? How much worse would the pain get if the dose wore off completely?

'Crippled . . .

When she opened her eyes, the orange circle stared at her in the darkness. Her thoughts skittered wildly: Was that, too, the dose wearing off? The jumble of equipment piled on the floor – wires, prisms, cells, magnetic rods – looked weird in the faint orangey light.

Light. R'Frow was dying from lack of light. The Wall and the dome, which kept out the light and cold of Qom, had made R'Frow. And now were killing it.

There was some echo about the word *light* . . . in her pain she could not find it.

The Ged had made R'Frow. The Ged, who listened inside their helmets, without wires, to . . . something. To what? How could any sound get into the helmets without wires? The idea was staggering. Wasn't there anything the Ged couldn't make, anything they didn't know? *Listening* . . . a babble of voices, wondering how the Ged knew of the first killing in R'Frow when they had all been shut up inside the Wall for the night, how Grax knew the barbarian giant had become too sick to walk to the Wall without being carried. When the giant had left the Hall of Teaching, he had been walking. No one could have told Grax how rapidly the giant worsened; there had been only she and SuSu who knew, and they had not even talked about it, because of SuSu's weird silence. . . . Not even listening could have told the Ged *that*. . . . Was there nothing they could not make? . . .

The orange circle glowed on the wall.

Ayrys looked from the circle to the tangle of prisms and electromagnets on the floor, back to the orange circle, back to the prisms. Back and forth.

If she put both palms flat on the floor on either side of her cushions and then pushed, she could raise herself to a sitting position. Pain knifed through her leg, but now she was hardly aware of it. She inched the cushions across the floor to the wall.

The orange circle was seamless with the wall, although not made of the same wrof. There was no raised surface to pry out, no way to examine what lay behind. Ayrys put her palm flat over the circle; a faint orange glow shone through the back of her hand.

Nothing the Ged could not make. Orange circles all over R'Frow, in every hall and corridor and room, on the outsides of the Hall of Teaching. The ones beside the ladders in the hall larger, protruding from the wall, to watch down and across and miss nothing. And in the rooms, watching SuSu and the barbarian, Ondur and Karim, herself and Kelovar naked in the warm air . . .

Teeth gritted with both fury and pain, Ayrys dragged herself toward a pile of her equipment. The orange circles in the rooms did not protrude. All she could do was fold a piece of cloth sixfold, until no orange showed through, and stick it over the circle with chonde, a sticky sap she had squeezed from a plant because she wanted to see what it looked like in the Ged enlarger.

And the Ged had never said. *Never said*. What do we

look like to them, eating and bathing and bedding, under this greater, secret enlarger? And why secret?

Or was it? The Ged answered no questions until the questions were asked. Would Grax tell the truth if she asked about the orange circles? Or – what was the truth?

She had only speculation, not tested answers. And it was the Ged themselves, with their science, who had taught her the difference.

Confused, afraid, in pain, Ayrys lay back down on her cushions. Her mind circled feverishly, and sleep was a long time coming. As it finally did, the last image in her mind was Kelovar, smiling at the sharp crack of rock on Jelite bone.

Later, much later, the door opened.

Ayrys, sleeping fitfully, awoke at once. A sliver of dim orangey light appeared on the wall. *No*, Ayrys thought, *I don't want him here*. . . . The door closed almost instantly, but not before she had seen the silhouetted figure slip through. *No*.

'Kelovar,' she said wearily.

There was a long silence, taut and black.

'No. Dahar.'

She gasped and tried to sit up. Pain leaped along her leg. He had not moved, a dark bulk by the closed door, sensed rather than seen in the complete blackness.

'Kelovar,' he finally said. 'And you. Kelovar.'

'No. No – not anymore.'

He said nothing.

'How . . . how did you get in?'

'Grax. He gave me a thumblock device. The same one he used to open the barbarian's room.'

'Why?'

Dahar said harshly, 'Why did he give it to me, or why did I use it to come here?'

Ayrys drew a deep breath. 'Both.'

Abruptly, light exploded the darkness; Dahr had pressed the orange circle through the sixfolded cloth. Ayrys blinked against the sudden brightness. When her eyes had refocused, Dahar stood over her, staring at her leg.

'The warrior-priest who set the bone isn't very skilled. Let me see it.'

He didn't look at her face, but she could see his. Bitterness, exhaustion – and something else, a desperation she recognized from her first days on the veld, her first days of exile: *Keep moving, don't stop, keep moving.* If she hadn't been there herself, she would not have recognized the place where Dahar stood now. But she had been there, on that empty veld with the gates of her city locked behind her and night falling. She had been there.

She whispered, 'You shouldn't be here. It's too dangerous.'

'I can reset the bone. More skillfully.'

'Dahar, did you hear me? If they find you–'

He repeated, with a kind of exhausted doggedness, 'I can reset the bone. More skillfully.'

'Will I walk again?'

'Let me see. I can reset the bone.'

She nodded. He knelt by the cushions, untied the splint the sister-warrior had put on Ayrys's leg, and probed at the break in the bone.

Ayrys screamed.

Instantly he stopped, head bent over her leg, still not looking at her. When the pain subsided, she found both her hands clutching his arm hard enough to turn the knuckles white.

If anyone heard her, if anyone brought Kelovar to open the door . . .'

Moments passed. No one came.

'Dahar. You can't. If I scream and anyone comes . . .'

'Who else has your thumblock? Besides Kelovar?'

'No one. But Kelovar–'

'I know Kelovar,' he said, with a curious lack of feeling, completely unlike his first response at the door. His voice was dull: exhaustion pushed to the brink. 'I can reset the bone. More skillfully. If I don't you'll never walk straight again.'

She shuddered, and tried to think. 'Wait. Wait – there's a dose your warrior-priest left me–'

'Not mine,' he said, and now the harshness was back in full and he looked at her levelly, his dark Jelite eyes blank. 'What dose? Where?'

'There. In that bowl.'

He held it to his face, sniffed the dose, took a drop on his tongue. 'Yes. Good. It will help with the pain.'

'Last time it put me out for the whole day.'

'It won't do that this time. It's been standing too long. But your mind may wander.'

'If it does, and if I scream anyway and someone brings Kelovar to open the door . . .'

For a moment, with the measuring glance of a soldier, his eyes moved to the door. But then the glance dissolved and he turned his face away from her, as if he did not want her to see whatever was mirrored there. Then he turned back and held the dose for Ayrys to drink.

She gulped it all.

The room began to fade. Then there was confusion: blackness that was not blackness, and cries that might have been inside her head or outside, and waves of pain without images.

When she fought herself free of the worst of it, she sat leaning against Dahar, her hands gripping his arm so hard that her nails had cut through the tebl sleeve to the hard muscle below. She had bitten through her bottom lip; blood streamed down her chin and her eyes watered.

'Did I? Did I . . .' The moment she spoke, she knew that the dose still held her; she could not remember the word for what she was asking, or why she was asking it.

'No. No, you didn't scream. Wait, I need to tie this.' He tied it, and she watched the leg as if it belonged to someone else.

It was a strange sensation. She was both herself and not herself, and although she knew that the dose had done that, she didn't care. She said, almost easily, as if it didn't matter at all, 'Will I walk straight now?'

'After it heals.'

'Dahar–'

'Do you want to vomit?'

'No.' Suddenly she laughed, a light, high laugh like a girl's, so shocking against the blood and pain that she frowned, and then laughed again. 'Not vomit. Talk.'

'That comes from the dose.'

'No. Yes. Will it really heal?'

'Yes.'

'Why did you come to set it?'

He didn't answer. Exhausted bitterness had settled over his face like a mask.

'You came because you think you caused it. That because you planned the Kreedogs, the two Jelite attacked me.'

Dahar's eyes narrowed. Ayrys heard herself as from a great distance, knew that this was in part the dose talking, and that without it she would not have been able to say that truth to him. Realizing so much made her – perversely – determined to say more, and she realized that this, too, was the dose – but only partly.

He said, 'Kelovar told you that?'

'No. I already told you, Kelovar and I are done with each other. I saw it for myself. By the Wall. They've exiled you, haven't they? From Jela?'

He rose and started for the door. She said after him – quietly, still from that great distance – 'But that's not the only reason you came to help me. No, Dahar. You're doing violence to yourself, aren't you, by coming here? Risking death, and to help a Delysian. You came *because* I am Delysian. Like deliberately grinding glass into your thumb.'

He had turned; he was staring at her from across the room.

'Yes,' she went on, smiling faintly, from somewhere out at that safe talkative distance the dose had taken her. 'Maiming a hand. Helping a Delysian. There's a saying in the glassyard, Dahar – a proverb. "When the kiln is too hot, it seeks the impure fault." Did you ever hear that? No, of course not. You've never worked glass. Embry asked me what it meant. She was making the blue bottle. . . .' What was she saying? *Embry–*

At the sound of her daughter's name, the two places collapsed, the one at a great safe distance and the one in the room at R'Frow, with her leg on fire and an exiled brother-warrior staring at her from such a great height that she was suddenly dizzy, dizzy and sick. Ayrys looked back at him, her eyes gone wide and undefended with the shock of Embry's name.

'I never said it aloud in R'Frow. Never,' she whispered, and had just time enough to turn her head before she vomited, a thin stream, dark with the last of the Jelite dose and followed by dry heaves that should have sent lacerating pain through her leg.

He was a healer; neither vomit nor dry leaves repelled him. He knelt again beside her and she fastened one hand on his wrist until, weak and dizzy, she had finished. He helped her lie back on the cushions, but she kept her hand on his wrist.

Softly he said, 'Who is Embry?'

Ayrys closed her eyes. 'My daughter. My daughter in . . . in Delysia.'

He was silent a moment. 'Why did you leave her behind?'

'I was forced to. I was exiled from the city.'

'Why?'

'For making a glass ornament. A double helix in blue and red. A Jelite warrior-priest double helix.'

His wrist stiffened under her hand. Dizzy and weary,

Ayrys kept her eyes closed. 'I made it because it was beautiful. Not because it was Jelite, but because in glass it was beautiful. Beautiful. Don't you find that funny, Dahar? The beauty of a warrior-priest healing emblem exiled me from Delysia to R'Frow, where an exiled warrior-priest risks death to heal me because I am Delysian.'

She heard herself and thought clearly, *Not all the dose was vomitted up*. But she didn't know if that were, or were not, the truth. She opened her eyes.

They looked at each other.

Dahar, said, 'I didn't come because you are Delysian.'

'Yes,' Ayrys said. 'You did.'

Dahar looked down, at her right hand circling his wrist. Over the tencycles the scars on her thumb had faded from red to white, long stringy ridges of thickened skin.

'Yes,' Dahar said, at last. 'I did.'

Ayrys felt cold and lost. But at the unguarded grief in his voice, her anger was stopped. She didn't know what grief would mean to a brother-warrior, to Dahar. The strangeness of the situation – previously lost in the strangeness of the dose – rose up strongly. Her leg ached and throbbed. Dahar's face was in profile, the cheekbone stark and the skin pasty with exhaustion.

But then he looked directly at her. 'But I was wrong. You are not Delysian.'

She frowned, not understanding.

'Not any longer. Delysia exiled you. They couldn't see what your glassmaking was, they can't see what the Ged science is – no more than Jela can. *No more than Jela can*.'

His gaze swept around the room, as if he saw for the first time the jumble of Ged equipment – wires, cells, prisms. He picked up the heating device with both hands. 'What is it?'

'For heat. Hunters on the veld, or babies born in Thirdnight.'

Ayrys watched how his eyes moved over the device.

'Grax told you how to build it?'

'No. Except for what he showed us in the Hall of Teaching.'

He put the device down, and spoke savagely. 'You see what the Ged could mean for Qom. Not toys, not weapons, not gems – *science*. Things we never thought we could know, things we didn't even dream could be known . . . Why can't they see it? Belazir, Khalid, Ishaq – they aren't stupid, so why can't they *see*? Nothing we knew before in Jela – or in Delysia – can measure up to the Ged. Nothing that happened on Qom is as important as the Ged's coming – *nothing*. This is R'Frow. This is . . . R'Frow.' His voice quavered, very slightly.

Ayrys heard that small wobble in his certainty, and it moved her as nothing else had: more than his risk in coming to set her leg, more than his exile from the warrior's place that had been his. Dahar, too, was uncertain about the Ged. He recognized with an awe that was almost despair the vastness and richness of the Ged science, the power that could seize and shake a human mind as devastatingly as an earthquake could shake up a stagnant pool. For that earthquake he would pay any price – he, who had been taught to think not in prices but in honor. But even so, even as the earthquake cut the familiar ground from under him and he gathered all his courage to meet the devastation – even then, he knew it was for an unseen landscape, a new plain of incredible fertility but as yet no sustenance, no shelter. The power of the Ged raged underfoot, and there was no place to hide.

Ayrys saw his courage. But it was the quaver that moved her, because it meant Dahar, too, was afraid. He looked at what the Ged could do, saw clearly the abyss between that and his own arts as a warrior-priest – and did not look away. Sight of the abyss had not turned him murderous, like Kelovar; not made him cringe, like SuSu; not led him to dismiss the Ged as unimportant, like Karim, Dahar saw, and recognized, and in his fearful recognition

Ayrys saw the intelligence and courage she had seen nowhere else in R'Frow.

Carefully, she removed her hand from his.

Dahar said, still without looking at her, 'But you see what the Ged science is, Ayrys. Don't you? I watched you, in the Hall of Teaching–' He stopped.

She saw why he stopped, better than he could ever see it. The room seemed filled with fragility, as if the air itself were made of glass. A brother-warrior did not watch a Delysian woman, not with what Dahar's tone had carried: respect. Did a brother-warrior watch any woman with respect? The sister-warriors, probably, whom he never touched. He had probably bedded only whores, like . . .

It was the same connection that had angered her in the morning, by the Gray Wall. How many whores were there in the Jelite halls? SuSu, her small body bruised from beating–

'I watched you,' Dahar said, almost roughly, 'and I did not see Delysia. I saw R'Frow. The Ged science, and R'Frow.'

She stayed very still. Dahar sat beside her, the heating device in his hand, his weary face averted. The tension grew, tangible and fragile as glass. If she reached out to touch him – what? He was not a soldier. He was, until yesterday, a Jelite warrior, an enemy, and he touched only whores.

She said, more harshly than she intended, 'I am not R'Frow. I am not anything. Not Delysian, not Jelite, not Ged. And neither are you. Exiles.'

He was silent. Then, to her astonishment, he said softly, 'How old is your daughter?'

'Eleven. She is eleven.'

'Who takes care of her now?'

'My mother's sister. She will be looked after well. Only . . .' She couldn't finish.

'Only without you.'

'Only without me.'

'Who is her father?'

'A soldier. He's dead. He died long ago.'

He said, in a different voice, 'In battle?'

'No. No – of a sickness. The healer didn't know what it was. Delysian healers aren't as skillful as you are . . . were. . . .'

'Were,' he said, with so much bitterness in his voice that she looked directly at his face. But it was controlled, carefully blank. 'He was your . . . mate?'

'It's not like Jelite citizens,' she said clearly, and gripped her two hands together. 'He was my lover then. We were not mated for . . . for life.'

Dahar was silent. Ayrys heard herself speak again, wanting to make clear what was so natural to her but not to him.

'Children live with their mother's family. Lovers come and go, but children and sisters and brothers . . . Embry is with my mother's sister, and my brother is there, too, when he is not . . . away.'

Dahar said, tonelessly, 'He is a soldier.'

A small anger, born half of strain, took her; she felt that he was judging her, and she didn't like it. 'Yes, of course he's a soldier. What else would he be, with things as they are between Delysia and Jela?'

'Citizens do not become warriors.'

'They can become soldiers. In Jela, mothers must be warriors for children to become warriors?'

'Mother and father both. Children in Jela know what caste their fathers are.'

'Especially if they are the children of whores.'

'Yes.'

'Whores like SuSu, who live as outcasts, who get used as you choose, even if the "whore" was a Delysian captive taken in battle–'

He said coldly, 'Does that seem worse to you than having male fighters who breed from physically weaker citizens, and female fighters who must leave their cadres to bear children?'

'Yes!' Ayrys said. 'Much worse!' Fury was rising in her, born of frustration and disappointment. *A brother-warrior after all.*

But Dahar had spread his hands in front of him, palms down, studying the fingers in pointless weariness. 'I said this isn't Jela, but R'Frow. The Ged have . . . the Ged are . . . I don't know, Ayrys. Many things I was sure of once . . . I don't know.'

He had said too much. She saw him think that, and then rise stiffly, anger kindling behind the exhausted strain in his face. Before he could get to his feet, Ayrys reached up her hand and caught the tips of his fingers in hers. Lying immobile, her leg throbbing even under the drug, she could not reach up any farther. She closed her eyes tightly, childishly, and immediately regretted it.

Dahar stood still a long time, his fingers in hers. Then suddenly, with a violence born of weariness and despair, he knelt beside Ayrys's cushions and put his free hand over his eyes. His lips trembled.

She drew his head to her breast, until he lay beside her, and held him. Once he shuddered – a long, powerful spasm – but only once. She held him a long time, neither of them speaking, clinging together, exiles.

A long time later, after he had slept, she felt Dahar raise his head and look at her. He had slept as if dead, the motionless, heavy sleep of the exhausted. Ayrys could not sleep; she had slept all day. She had been afraid to move because she might waken him, afraid to let him sleep because she couldn't tell how close it was to morning. But Dahar, with a warrior's honed instincts, could tell. He awoke by himself and lifted his head off her breast to see her face. Great dark hollows ringed his eyes.

Ayrys whispered, 'I am not a whore.'

'No. *No.*'

'I choose for myself, Dahar.'

'Your leg . . .'

'I don't even feel it now. And I choose for myself. As you did in coming here. How did you know which room was mine?'

He smiled faintly. 'Last one on the right in the third corridor. I overheard you say so once to a woman in the Hall of Teaching.'

'And you remembered.'

He looked around the room slowly, at the piles of Ged equipment, at the devices she had made to harness the power neither of them understood. 'And I remembered.'

But still he held back: uncertain, confused. Ayrys raised her mouth to his.

40

Grax watched the blank wall screen. 'And I remembered,' said Dahar's voice with complete clarity, but the screen showed only the swirling Ged patterns of the cloth Ayrys had stuck over it. The other screen isolated by the Library-Mind for anomaly was silent, and the cloth that covered it hung in white, crumpled folds.

Grax frowned: a quick slight downturn of the muscles at the corners of the mouth, a slight contraction of those below the central, slightly larger eye. Grax did not realize he had done it, and so his pheromones did not change odor. Rowir and Krak'gar had their backs turned, absorbed for the moment in their own work; neither noticed. Neither had spent the long hours alone with humans that Grax had spent with Dahar. They might not have even recognized Grax's version of the human gesture. Had Grax seen it on one of their faces, he might not have recognized the grimace either.

He went on staring at the empty screen, frowning.

41

Ayrys lay alone in the dark, staring at the door, which had just closed. A bar of dim orangey light slanting into the blackness, the bar shrinking, and Dahar was gone.

I never told him, Ayrys thought, eventually. I never told him about the listening helmets, or the Ged circle eyes. . . . *'I watched you, and I saw R'Frow.' 'Nothing that has happened on Qom is as important as the Ged's coming, the Ged science.'* I never told him.

She touched her fingers to her mouth. The door opened again; Ayrys jerked herself upward and grabbed for a blanket to draw over her nakedness.

'Ayrys,' Ondur said, 'I came to help you wash. Are you hungry? How does your leg feel?' Behind her in the corridor stood Kelovar, a silent dark shape; he had opened the door for Ondur, who otherwise could not have come in.

'What's wrong with your lamp? There's a cloth over it. Go on, Kelovar, Ayrys needs to wash. Why did you cover the light?'

'It . . . hurt my eyes.'

Ondur pressed the circle through the cloth. She balanced a bowl of warm water on one hip, and cloths and food bowls on the other arm. She said cheerfully, 'It might have been that dose. Kelovar, are you going?'

He had not moved. Ayrys did not dare look at him. After a moment Ondur, with a little clucking noise, stuck her foot out behind and shoved the door. It swung gently closed. Ondur grinned. 'Sometimes that's the only way to deal with men! Now, how is your leg? I'm not going to undo the splint, but I'm going to set this water here and then–' Abruptly she stopped.

Ayrys had been staring at the covered orange circle. Now she swung her gaze to Ondur, who had set down the water and knelt by the cushions, wide-eyed with surprise. Ondur's nose wrinkled. Ayrys understood: Ondur smelled sex.

The two women looked at each other.

'Kelovar?' Ondur said doubtfully.

'*No.*'

'Then who?'

'Ondur, don't ask me who.'

Ondur had begun to smile slyly; but at the intensity in Ayrys's voice, the smile vanished, and Ayrys cursed herself. Stupid, stupid – making mysteries where there didn't have to be any. She felt shaky and tired, and her leg began to ache. Ondur fumbled with her towels.

'Of course. I didn't mean to pry.'

Ayrys covered Ondur's hand with her own, and forced herself to smile. After a moment Ondur chuckled.

'And with your leg like that. You must be pretty lusty, Ayrys – and him, too!'

A bubble of hysteria rose in Ayrys; she beat it down. Careful, she had to be careful – *Dahar, be careful* – this shakiness, sprung from too much feeling and too little sleep, could betray her. She felt her own vulnerability. And Ondur's kindness, a simple clean kindness sturdy as grass, further unsettled her. She had almost forgotten it could exist, among the dangerous and tendriled plants that seemed to flourish in R'Frow.

'Ondur, why are you helping me like this?'

Ondur began washing Ayrys's good leg. 'Why not? You would help me if I'd been the one attacked by those – oh, I'm sorry, I didn't mean to bump into that . . . object. Ayrys, do the Ged know you have all these wires and things here?'

Ayrys couldn't stop herself; she glanced at the covered orange circle. 'They know.'

'As long as they don't care that you're hoarding all these wires and things. Brace yourself, I'm going to turn you a little left. Does that hurt?'

'Yes,' Ayrys gasped. 'Ondur – do you trust the Ged?'

'Trust them? How?'

'To do what they say they're doing: helping us because we know so little and they know so much.'

'We know enough,' Ondur said. Ayrys heard in her tone the now-familiar refusal to let the Ged matter: *We are not less because they are more*. 'We got along in Delysia before the Ged came, and we . . . Delysia will get along after the year has ended and they go.'

'Will you go back to Delysia?' Talking, she had to keep talking about Ondur or she would say something dangerous. *Dahar, be careful*. . . .

But Ondur's face closed like a box. After a moment she said, 'A question for you instead, Ayrys. I didn't ask you yesterday. What were you doing alone by the deserted hall? It's much closer to the Jelite net than to ours.'

'It isn't deserted. There's a girl there, alone now. She's . . . in pain. I was bringing her a dose for the pain.'

'A girl? What girl?'

Ayrys said carefully, as if she were connecting a wire to an unknown arrangement of cells, 'A Jelite whore.'

'A Jelite! Why were you . . . oh. I heard about that. It's that one you helped with her lover when he was sick, isn't it? She ran away from the Jelite warriors to him. That huge white barbarian, and that tiny girl . . . she looks about eleven years old. Why is she there alone? What happened to the giant?'

'Dead.'

Ondur wrung out her towel. 'A child like that . . . I could almost feel sorry for her. Their warriors only enjoy it if it's by force, you know. Animals. She could be captured from a barbarian tribe herself – she's tinier than any

Jelite I've seen in R'Frow. And I never heard anyone say
she could speak real words. Can she?'

'Yes.'

'With a Jelite accent?'

'Yes.'

'Then why were *you* helping her?'

Be careful. 'Because she's so small. Ondur, have you
ever had children?'

Again Ondur's face closed, a shuttered room. She stood.
'I've finished. There's food there, Ayrys. You should eat
it while it's still hot. I'll come back later, after the Hall
of Teaching.'

'I'm sorry, Ondur. Now I was pry–'

'Forget it!' Ondur shrilled. She turned her back on
Ayrys and stayed that way for long moments. When she
turned back, she was smiling: brightly, determinedly. 'I
should go now to the Hall of Teaching. Although did you
know that yesterday all the Ged walked out after not even
one hour? All of them, and they never returned. So of
course we all left, too. I should . . . I need to . . .' Trai-
ling off, Ondur's voice made a strange, uncertain rise,
like a traveler reaching a bump in the road, before she
walked abruptly from the room.

'Ondur!' Ayrys called after her. But Ondur did not
turn.

Ayrys lay for a long time without moving. She thought
of SuSu, alone in the deserted hall, in silence; of Ondur,
fled perhaps to her own room with Karim and not to the
Hall of Teaching; of Dahar – above all, of Dahar, because
she did not know where he had gone for safety, she had
not asked; there had been no time. To his soldiers' –
warriors' – hall still? Would they let him in if he was no
longer a brother-warrior? With the Jelite citizens? To the
Hall of Teaching, with the Ged?

The Ged, watching them all, wherever they had gone,
in whatever room in R'Frow. Unless she was wrong, and
the orange circle eyes were not eyes but something else

entirely, something made from parts of the Ged science that she had not yet even begun to glimpse.

Ayrys gripped her hands together. She was not sure she saw anything right.

When she slept, her sleep was troubled. She woke from dim dreams with a jerk that sent pain shooting through her leg – real pain, sharper than at any time since Dahar set it. The Jelite dose had finally worn off. How long had Ondur been gone? She had no way to tell; she lacked a warrior's bone-and-muscle sense of time.

Someone kicked the door, hard.

Ayrys found that she could drag herself across the room to open it, although the movement nearly made her faint. Karim, a stained bundle filling his arms, pushed past her. The smell made Ayrys gag.

'Put her there, Karim – no, there in the corner, away from Ayrys's wires,' Ondur said. 'Bring me water from the baths, lots of water, and a clean cushion cover from our room. And a bowl of fruit gruel – Farima was selling some fresh this morning. Ayrys, do you have another towel?'

The bundle was SuSu, smeared with Ged stew and her own shit. Naked, small body stiff, eyes open but unseeing, she looked dead. One side of her face was irritated and red, as if she had lain on it for a long time without moving.

'We found her on the floor of the barbarian's hall, beside a floor table,' Ondur said. Karim scowled he obviously had wanted no part of this. 'Just lying there. She didn't move even when Karim picked her up. None of the other soldiers would do it. I could pick her up myself. Look at that hand – a twig has more flesh on it.'

But Ayrys was looking at SuSu's other hand. Ondur saw it at the same time, and pried open the rigid fingers. 'What's this? . . . The smell! Now why would she have one of those Ged enlargers?'

Ayrys went very still.

In the brief space of time when she glimpsed the dark

gray metal brick in SuSu's right hand, there was time for endless thoughts: that Karim had been carrying SuSu with her right side crushed against his chest; that the rectangle would thus have been hidden from the orange circles in the corridor and the hall below; that Ondur had said 'enlarger' because that was the only Ged box she had seen. But this was not an enlarger. Ayrys saw again Dahar and Grax struggling with the huge body of the sick barbarian, saw the Wall opening, saw Grax press indentations in the dark gray rectangle that dissolved and reshaped wrof.

Stretching to full, painful length, Ayrys reached out and pried the box from SuSu's fingers. Her head swam. . . . *How?* Grax had pulled the dark box from inside his clothing, within the force shield that carried Ged air. How could SuSu have taken it from one of the impenetrable Ged?

Beyond her, the door opened yet again. Kelovar – it could only be Kelovar. Ondur's body, bending over SuSu, blocked Kelovar's line of sight. Ondur turned to see him come in, and in the moment when her gaze left SuSu, Ayrys thrust the dark box underneath the cushion on which she lay.

'I told you, Kelovar–' Ondur began, and found herself fussing not at Kelovar but at Grax.

Ondur, who had never seen the orange strip wrapped around Grax's thumb, caught her breath and took a step backward. Ayrys felt her heart begin to thump in her chest, even as a part of her mind noted coolly that once she would not have been completely sure that she could distinguish Grax from the other Ged. When had she learned to tell them apart?

'How did you get in?' Ondur demanded, then remembered to whom she spoke, and bit her lip.

Grax said at once, 'This orange wrof opens any room in R'Frow.'

Karim made a slight, dangerous noise. Grax seemed not to have heard. In his other hand he carried something made of cloth and metal tubes, the metal gray and the cloth – unlike the cushion covers that provided most of the cloth in R'Frow – a deep black.

'This is for you, Ayrys,' Grax said calmly. 'It is meant for damaged Ged limbs, but I have altered it to fit you.'

He set the thing on the floor and touched one tube at a place where the wrof swelled into a sudden oval. The tubes spread into an open lattice slung with two pieces of cloth. Ondur jammed her fist against her mouth – the thing floated an arm's length above the floor.

In one swift motion Grax bent and picked up Ayrys. Pain stabbed through her leg and she cried out through sudden panic as strong as the pain: All she could see was the barbarian being carried by Ged arms through the Wall. Grax's arms around her were not arms but wrof – the hard, clear shield that encased both him and his air. Ondur sprang forward, but by the time she reached Ayrys and then halted, uncertain what to do next, the Ged had lowered Ayrys into the chair and the miracle had already happened.

Ayrys sat on one stretch of cloth, her back supported by the other. The rest of the tubes cradled the leg out-stretched before her – her broken leg, from which all pain had vanished.

'*How* . . .'

'Your leg rests in a charged field,' Grax said. 'It is not in the same . . . place-time as the pain is.'

Ayrys stared blankly, first at the Ged and then at her leg. A faint layer surrounded it, not the shimmer that covered wrof walls but a slight thickening of the air itself, like clear fog.

Grax said, 'This is a force you don't have the ideas to understand yet, just as once you couldn't have understood electricity. The same force that holds your leg carries the Ged ship between worlds. You sit in the only such . . . machine in R'Frow, the only such machine on this world. I will show you how to move it.'

He showed her how to press the black oval with her left hand. The chair moved forward, moved to the side, turned in a slow, perfect ellipse. Ondur shrank against Karim.

Ayrys thought, out of all the things she might have thought – *But I am right-handed*.

The stupidity, the sheer ingratitude and shortsightedness of the thought hit her almost immediately. It was followed by a moment of terror, the same as she had felt her first time in the Wall, when the magnetic rods had leaped toward each other and she had thought them alien beasts, alive and devouring. But then both terror and pettiness fled. This was a Ged invention, a Ged use of forces as natural in the world as sunlight, hidden from humans only because they had not yet rounded from darkness into Firstmorning. It was not magic. *It was not magic*.

Ayrys put her hands more firmly along the arms of the chair, and for once failed to notice the intent listening on the face of the Ged as Grax looked at SuSu, rigid in the corner. Karim drew his pellet tube.

'This is only a chair for the wounded,' Grax said to him calmly. 'It is nothing to fear. Watch. She can move in it.'

'It's all right,' Ayrys said to Karim, and wondered if it was.

Grax said, 'The chair cannot go down the ladder to the hall below. You will need to be carried down. If you are carried while you are still in the chair, you can avoid both pain to the leg and changing the position of the bone that the Jelite healer set.'

Ayrys stopped moving the chair. *Which* Jelite healer? Did Grax somehow know that Dahar had reset her leg, or did he mean the young sister-warrior Jehane had sent for? The orange circle in her room had been covered, but there were circles in the corridor through which Dahar would have walked, by the ladder he would have climbed. . . . She had to know.

'Grax, thank you for the chair. The Ged science has

great healing arts. Will you look to see if my bone is set well?'

A short silence: He was listening inside his helmet.

'It is set well. Ged medicine could not tie the bone any more carefully than the healer has done.'

Ayrys said carefully, trying not to emphasize the second word, 'Then she did it right? I will not be crippled?'

'You will not be crippled.'

'How do you know?'

'The Ged who studies human healing has seen the bone set.'

'When did a Ged see it?'

'There was a Ged brought to the place where you were attacked.'

That was true – now Ayrys remembered seeing, through the haze of pain and drugs, a shimmering face with three eyes looming closer to her own. But that setting of her leg had *not* been done well; Dahar had said so when he reset it. Did that mean that the Ged could not tell a good bone set from a bad one? Or that they knew the Jelite woman had set it badly and Grax was lying to her now? Or – a third possibility – that the orange circle had been able to see through the sixfolded cloth anyway, and the Ged had watched Dahar reset the leg, but did not want her to know that they had? 'You will not be crippled,' Grax had just said – but how did he know?

Ayrys studied the Ged's face through the clear helmet: the sharp skull, stiff mouth, two calm eyes, and third high, monstrous, filmy one. She could not tell if the alien features lied.

She said, 'Why didn't you give me this . . . machine for pain yesterday, if Ged came to where I was attacked?'

'It was not made yesterday. The parts can become other machines, the same as these wires and electromagnets you have here, depending on how they are put together.'

'Other humans in R'Frow have been in pain. The white

giant – you didn't give this machine to the white giant. Why not?'

Another silence, this time longer. 'His pain was not in a leg but in his brain. You can't put a brain in another place-time from a body, no more than the Delysian commander could be in another place from those from whom he sings in harmony.'

There was no way to tell if it – any of it, all of it, none of it – was lies. Frustration welled up in Ayrys. From the corner of her eye, she could see SuSu, still curled rigidly in the corner. The room reeked of her.

Ayrys looked directly at Grax. 'Are the orange circles all over R'Frow eyes that can see everything humans do?'

Ondur gasped. Karim, weapon still drawn, went white, and then red. Grax's face did not change, but he took on that listening intensity for so long that Ayrys thought he was not going to answer at all.

'Yes. The orange circles are eyes.'

After a moment of shock, Ondur began to yell. Privacy, lies, sex, perversion – indignation tumbled from her in a torrent, sweeping away any uneasiness she might have felt with the Ged. But Ayrys sat in a glow of relief so strong she wanted to close her eyes against its brightness: The Ged had not lied to her. All they said was truth, made true by this one truth, in the same way that one drop of dye could color a whole batch of glass. Grax had no reason to tell her that the orange circles were eyes, except that she had asked. If others of their actions looked questionable, it was only because humans had not asked the right questions, didn't know what the right questions would be to these strange, strange minds. But about the orange circles Grax had not lied. The Ged could be trusted.

'. . . and not tell us?' Ondur shouted.

Grax said, looking not at her but at Ayrys 'You did not ask.'

'I ask something now,' Ayrys cut in, before Ondur could start yelling again. 'This Jelite girl – SuSu – since you took her lover inside the Wall, she doesn't move or speak. I know there are drugs to break shock, but Delysian healers are not as good as . . . as Ged science. You blocked all the pain in my leg; can you tell me how to make a dose that will bring SuSu back to her own mind?'

Grax swung his gaze to SuSu. 'There are drugs to change how a mind is thinking?'

Even Ondur and Karim heard the un-Ged-like intensity in his words. No one answered.

Grax repeated, 'Humans have drugs to change the way a mind is thinking?' He spoke directly to Karim.

The soldier said coldly, 'Battlefield shock can be broken with the right drug.'

Grax knelt by SuSu. He did not touch her, but it seemed to Ayrys that his three eyes traveled over the delicate lines of the girl's skull as if it were a foreign country. Ayrys said, not as a question, 'The white barbarian died.'

'Yes. I will take this girl inside the Wall. We could not help the giant, but perhaps we can help her.'

Something moved in Ayrys, some dark chill beneath her giddy relief.

'Why not help her here?'

'It needs study.' Grax straightened.

'You don't know the drug to break shock, do you?'

'No. It needs study. Let me take her.'

The chill grew stronger. Before, the Ged had not asked – they had simply taken the barbarian. Why ask now? And why ask her, who was not of SuSu's people nor in command?

Experimentally, Ayrys said, 'No. Let her remain here. She needs . . . human talk to help break the shock. I've seen this before, not on the battlefield like Karim, but after an accident in the glassyard. In Delysia. Let her stay with me.'

'If you want,' Grax said. And he frowned.

He frowned. But Ayrys had never seen a Ged frown

before – and for a moment she wasn't sure she had seen Grax do it, either. A quick contraction of the face, not quite right, like the witless imitation of the simpleminded: but still a frown. And letting her choose whether or not SuSu remained outside the Wall – why?

'You will come to the Hall of Teaching tomorrow,' Grax said to Ayrys. 'The teachings to all humans in R'Frow have finished, except for the teachings of weapons. That will continue. The other teachings have finished, and only those humans who choose to will come for new teachings in the Ged science. The new teachings will go on faster, and clearer, for those who have the mind differences to understand.' Again the small frown, and this time Ayrys sensed that Grax did not know he had done it.

But Grax had not adopted human courtesy. When this speech was done, he abruptly left.

Ondur sputtered, 'Watching us! In every room!'

Karim said quietly, 'Aryrs. How did you know?' He looked at her with the eyes of a soldier, measuring and a little hard.

'I didn't know. I guessed, from what the Ged can build.'

Karim glanced around, at the piles of things Ayrys could build. His expression did not soften.

'*Watching* us,' Ondur said. 'Even sex! I'm going to do what you did, Ayrys, and hang cloth over the circle! Karim, where are you going?'

'To inform Khalid.'

'It makes my skin crawl,' Ondur said. 'Ayrys, why was that Ged trying so hard to please you?'

Karim, halfway to the door, stopped and turned. 'What?'

'The Ged was trying to please Ayrys. The chair for pain, and letting her decide about this girl, and inviting her to these other teachings – he was trying to please her. Why, Ayrys?'

Ayrys said slowly, 'I don't know.'

'Will you go to these special teachings?'

'*For those who have the mind differences to understand.*'
Dahar.

'Yes. I'll go.' She turned her head to look at Karim, to
see his expression, but he had already reached for the
door and opened it. There was a crowd in the corridor
where Grax had passed. Karim closed the door.

Ayrys pressed the oval on the arm of her chair, made
it rise, moved it to the left. *Too far.*

'Don't go to any teachings alone, it's dangerous,' Ondur
said. Ayrys moved the chair to the right. *Too far.* 'Did
you notice that Ged didn't even smell the whore? I guess
they can't smell through their helmets.' Ayrys brought
the chair directly over the cushions on her pallet. 'They're
not human, I don't trust them,' Ondur said sharply, all
brightness gone. 'I'd trust a Jelite before I'd trust monsters who would spy on us, so help me I would!'

'Is that why you made Karim bring this Jelite girl here
after all?' Ayrys's fingers fumbled at the oval on the arm
of her chair. Knocking began on the door.

'No. I have . . . what you asked me before,' Ondur
said, her voice splintering with sudden pain. 'I have borne
children.' Quickly she whirled and yanked at the door.

Ayrys lowered the chair squarely onto her cushions,
trapping SuSu's dark rectangular box tightly underneath
her own weight, just as Khalid T'Alira pushed past Karim
toward Ayrys, his face hard with questions about the Ged.

42

The wall screens were blank – all but one.

Grax, R'gref, and Fregk had been in the room when the Library-Mind suddenly illuminated one wall screen. In one day the humans had covered every orange circle in R'Frow with cloth, wood, chonde, clay – anything that would blank the monitors. The three Ged had been listening to a sightless conversation that, out of the hundreds it simultaneously monitored, the Library-Mind had identified as significant enough to bring to the attention of all Ged either within the perimeter or wearing their communications helmets outside.

'She charged me eleven habrin,' said the voice of the Delysian female Ondur. 'Greedy kreebitch. But the other healer wanted even more. For one food bowl's worth! Here's your change, Ayrys, I'm sorry I couldn't get it for less.'

'It doesn't matter,' said the voice of Ayrys. 'How do we get her to swallow it?'

'Oh, she'll swallow,' said the voice of Ondur, grimly. 'You just have to massage her neck in the right place. Watch.'

The Ged pheromones smelled of frustration. What was 'the right place?' And they could not watch.

Yet the Library-Mind had been right to advise Grax to tell Ayrys the truth about the orange circles. All agreed that it would aid her in changing species loyalties – even though there was no way to put 'change' and 'species loyalty' grammatically in the same thought unit. Krak'gar, the poet, released faint pheromones of aesthetic dissatisfaction.

And one circle remained uncovered.

Grax looked steadily at the images on the single wall screen the Library-Mind had illuminated. Dahar bent over a floor table in the Hall of Teaching, not in the empty locked room where he had finally slept all day, nor in the room of the Red teaching group, but in another locked room, where he and Grax kept the work they had done together during all the long nights in the empty hall. The room was filled with equipment, brought from Biology. Some pieces had been given invented human names for concepts human language had not possessed: enlargers, growing bowls, blood tubes, helix-hearts. Some bore alien names: bacteria, antitoxin, culture broth. Their Ged growl in Dahar's throat disturbed Grax's pheromones.

Dahar peered into an enlarger modified for human eyes. The fingers of Dahar's right hand – to Grax, deformed in shape and gross with fat – unknowingly spread and curved, as if to physically take hold of what he saw in the enlarger. His left hand, holding a tissue sample, remained steady as stone. Grax watched the two human hands.

From the other, blank screen came Ayrys's voice. 'She won't drink it, Ondur. It's all coming out the side of her mouth.'

'She'll drink it. She *will*. Hold her head higher. That's better – it's going down now. Hold her tight, Ayrys – when that dose hits her brain, she's going to thrash and kick and maybe bite. Can you hold her, with your leg like that?'

'It's as if the leg doesn't even exist. I can hold her . . . she's so small.'

'Yes,' Ondur's voice said grimly. 'She is.'

Dahar rose from the enlarger and crossed to a second floor table. On it lay the body of a kreedog, with a large open sore on one flank. The animal was freshly killed; a little pus still oozed from the sore. Carefully, as Grax had taught him, Dahar scraped pus from the sore and smeared it on a circle of clear wrof. He laid another circle on top of the first; they leaped together to trap precisely a single layer of cells.

Ayrys's voice said, 'It's starting.'

'Hold that side. Oh–'

Another voice moaned, low at first but rising quickly, higher and higher, a keening shrill wail of grief and darkness cresting into higher registers than the Ged had ever heard humans go. R'gref shielded his ears, smelling of pain; the Library-Mind dampened the volume.

'Hold her, Ondur!'

'I've got her. . . .'

Ayrys's voice gasped, 'How long does this part last?'

'A few minutes more – don't let her bite you! The dose . . .'

'SuSu . . . *SuSu* . . .'

On the screen Dahar inserted the pus cells in the enlarger, adjusted it until the image was clear, and studied the cells intently. His fingers curved and spread.

SuSu's wailing rose to a shriek, splintered, and sank into a long moan, a whisper of desolation. 'Pity,' whispered Ondur's voice. 'By all pity . . .'

'Give her to me, Ondur.'

'She knows us. Look at her eyes – her mind has come back. She knows us.'

'Oh, yes,' Ayrys said grimly. 'She knows.'

Dahar removed the pus sample from the enlarger, and the circular cover from the pus sample. With a tiny dropper he added to the diseased tissue a single drop of a simple antitoxin from a growth bowl Grax had helped him prepare. He replaced the circular wrof, inserted the sample into the enlarger, and bent again over the eye opening.

'She bit me!' Ondur cried.

'She can't help it – give her to me . . .'

Silence. Then a woman's crying, heartbroken but no longer demented, on and on.

'By all pity . . .'

'Did she break the skin when she bit you?'

'Yes. But it's only a scratch. Why does she let *you* hold her, Ayrys?'

'I don't know. I helped her once. Ondur, we could have left her as she was. . . .'

Ondur's voice was shocked. 'She would have starved. We had to bring her mind back. She was in . . . in darkness!'

'And what is she in now?'

The blank screen did not answer.

Dahar stared for a long time into the enlarger. Grax knew what he must see: the antitoxin destroying the bacteria cells in the tissue sample. It was the simple biology that cubs would be shown as soon as they asked any questions even remotely related to the phenomenon, simple biology the Ged had taken thousands of years of evolution to discover, so many thousands of years ago that the Library-Mind bore no records of it. Simple biology that, routinely, Grax had seen save an infected animal population on a new Ged world from the ravages of disease, to give them to the ravages of overpopulation. Simple biology.

Dahar raised his head. The strange, distastefully dark eyes shone in a way Grax had come to know meant human emotion. The gross fingers trembled a little; Grax saw the tremble clearly. Dahar turned toward the orange circle on the wall – the only orange circle left uncovered in R'Frow, deliberately uncovered, although Grax had told Dahar just what he had told Ayrys – and looked at it directly. He looked for a long time, longer than humans ever took to glance at something casually, as long as a Ged might look. His eyes met Grax's, whom he could not have known was watching. The human eyes, black as space, were filled with a light like stars.

Ayrys's voice said unsteadily, 'What will the dose do now? She's quieter.'

Ondur's voice answered. 'She'll be quieter until all the dose has worn off. She's . . . you can tell her to do anything now, Ayrys, and she'll probably do it. She's in a sort of daze. The healer told me that in Delysia battle shock isn't the only use for that drug. In the worst of the traders' halls–'

'I don't want to know,' Ayrys said violently. 'Don't tell me.'

SuSu cried softly.

Dahar stared from the wall screen at Grax. The other two Ged had stopped moving to also look at Grax. Smelling their pheromones – startled, wondering – Grax suddenly smelled his own. Immediately the others' pheromones changed: Courteously they exuded acceptance, covering their startlement. Grax knew their thoughts: On Ged he had been a teacher of cubs; a teacher of cubs became used to the movements of immature minds; a teacher would take pride in the mastery of even the simple. It was number-rational that Grax would stare at his pupil. It was understandable – and forgivable – that for a moment the number-rational movement of a human mind should occupy a teacher to a greater extent than the uncivilized and immoral human nature. It was understandable – and forgivable – that for a moment Grax should forget himself and smell of pride.

For a moment.

'Significant data,' the Library-Mind said suddenly. 'Significant data – Level Prime.'

43

The image from the monitor probe on the island began to move.

The bearded old man rose slowly and hobbled forward. His face swelled on the wall screen until the dirt in the seamed cheeks formed a grid of black lines. Five-fingered hands groped upward, closed on the screen, dropped away.

'From where?' the human whispered. The Library-Mind adjusted for a different accent, for the raspiness of old vocal cords. 'Why *now?*'

The probe shifted to the left, taking in as much of the room as possible without losing the human face.

The man suddenly squared shoulders stooped and rounded with age. 'Fahoud al-Ameer, United Space Navy, 614289FA. Off of the *Star of Mecca*, United Space Navy hired medical ship escorting dissident colonists from New Arabia to . . . to . . .' He hunched forward, coughing.

The probe shifted a little more left. The room, built against one side of the immense ruined contaminated ship, glowed with the light of a makeshift and primitive screen. Screen, nondrive electrical generator, flat rudimentary manual pass-key controls.

The man wiped his mouth and tried again to pull his shoulders straight. He whispered, 'She went down.'

The probe turned in a slow circle to record everything.

'She went . . . down. The enemy hit us. Ged. And the stasis generator . . . What year is this?'

The probe completed its circle, returned to the human face.

'*Who* are you?'

The old man put out one hand; the fingers, thin as wires, trembled. 'Please . . .'

The probe moved closer to the primitive keyboard, switched to close scope.

'Please . . . who won the war?'

The image froze.

V
DISEASE AND ANTITOXIN

Nothing exists but atoms and the void.
—Democritus of Abdera

44

Ayrys sat in her Ged chair in the Delysian hall, eating breakfast with Ondur and Karim. Three or four people ate at other floor tables; more wandered down the ladder to carry steaming bowls of food to the rooms above. They glanced sideways at Ayrys, who went on chewing. Karim met each pair of eyes, his hand casually on the heat gun that was the newest weapon from the Ged. The gun would sear flesh, but only at close range. Ayrys had noticed that the Ged weapons which humans could duplicate at year's end – pellet tube, threeball – were deadlier than those they could not.

Sometimes Karim, grown more silent and somber over the two tencycles since the forming of the Kreedogs, spent an entire evening cleaning his weapons while Ondur chattered to Ayrys with desperate brightness.

A soldier entered the hall through the southern arch. When she saw Ayrys, her upper lip drew back over her teeth. Karim stared until she dropped her eyes.

'I'll walk with you to your teaching.'

'That's not necessary,' Ayrys said.

'Let him go with you,' Ondur said. 'Another Delysian has come down with the itching disease.'

'Who?'

'Arquam, a soldier in the next hall. He got it last night.'

'How do you know, Ondur?' Ayrys asked. Ondur always knew such things; it was rumored that even Khalid came to her for information on what was happening in the Delysian halls. Ayrys had never asked Ondur about this, and in turn Ondur never asked what the six humans and Grax did within the Hall of Teaching. Ayrys understood. Too much knowledge could destroy the fragile kindness.

'What are his symptoms?' Ayrys asked.

'You talk like a healer,' Karim said, unsmiling, and Ayrys flushed. Of Karim, too, she asked no questions.

Ondur said, 'The same as the other two. Red splotches on his skin that spread fast and itch painfully all the time. He keeps clawing at his skin. His lover is afraid he'll scratch out his eyes. Let Karim go with you as far as the Hall of Teaching.'

'But, Ondur, how could Karim defend me against a disease? Not that I'm not grateful, Karim, but I don't–'

'Oh, don't argue, Ayrys! How do we know where this disease came from? It started at the same time those Jelite scum attacked you, and then their first lieutenant, who knows all their perverted doses and has the Ged to help him with more, moves into the Hall of Teaching. A disease is just a poison – isn't that what the Ged say? This itching disease could be a Jelite poison!'

'A –'

'What did that Ged call it, Karim? A back something? No reports say any Jelite have come down with it!'

Karim stared hard at Ondur, who suddenly flushed and dropped her eyes, but not before Ayrys had caught the look. *Ondur had said too much. She was not supposed to tell me that.* A little wave of nausea washed through Ayrys. But . . . it made sense that Karim would be suspicious of her. She went each day to the Hall of Teaching, even against mutterings from those who shared her hall, to study arts few understood, in the company of one of the Ged who had spied on Delysians and two of the Jelite who were Delysian enemies. She moved around R'Frow in a Ged chair that many – even in the face of all they had seen of Ged inventions – regarded as a fearful magic. And there was SuSu.

Not all Delysians looked with the same compassion as Ondur on the Jelite whore. SuSu, ever since the mind dose forced down her throat had worn off, had not spoken. She ate, washed, slept, and followed Ayrys wherever Ayrys went, but in her dark eyes was a horrifying blankness, like a blackened city burned empty of all life. She would not be touched, not even by Ayrys. Twice someone had tried: Karim, steadying her down the ladder, and Ondur, with a sudden compassionate caress. Both times SuSu had begun to rage, kicking and biting and scratching with long, pointed nails, all in a silence more frightening than any ferocity in her tiny body. That silence, unnatural and eerie, made Delysians already on edge mutter and look at her sideways. *Jelite*, some said. *Spy*.

What, Ayrys wondered, did they say about her? Or the three other Delysians who still went daily to the Hall of Teaching: Ilabor, Tey, Creejin?

'Ondur,' Ayrys said gently, 'bacteria cause disease, yes. But it's not like a poison dose – the Jelite couldn't just make bacteria and put them on whoever they want.'

Karim shifted his gaze from Ayrys to the blank wall.

Whatever she said would only make his suspicions, whatever they were, worse. And Karim didn't even know about that one night with Dahar. . . .

Ayrys gripped her two hands together hard. The thought of Dahar hurt. Pressing on the arm of her chair, she made it rise slightly and back away from the floor table. 'I'm going now to the Hall of Teaching.'

'Go with her, Karim,' Ondur said. She did not look at Ayrys.

Karim went. He and Ayrys moved unspeaking along the paths of R'Frow, past the trees that dropped more leaves each day, the withering scrub. SuSu followed silently behind. When the Hall of Teaching was in sight,

Karim said abruptly, 'Kelovar doesn't like you having that Jelite whore in your room at night.'

'It is not Kelovar's concern!'

'He doesn't like it.'

Ayrys twisted in her chair to look up into his face. 'And where would Kelovar have her sleep? Where would *you*? What do you think would happen to her if she weren't behind a thumbblock?'

Karim flicked his hand, an impatient flash of rough skin. His glance fell on SuSu, and he looked away again. In his face Ayrys saw confusion: He both pitied SuSu and agreed with Kelovar, with no way of reconciling the two. She could see that he resented the confusion, and Ayrys for being the cause. Only Ondur held him.

'It's not Kelovar's decision, is it, Karim? Does Khalid forbid me to keep SuSu in my room?'

He scanned the brush beside the path, hand on his pellet tube.

'Does Khalid forbid it?'

'Not yet.'

'What does that mean? That Kelovar will try to persuade him to forbid it?'

Again Karim didn't answer. In the stubborn set of his jaw, Ayrys read only his own resentment, not any clue to what Khalid might decide. She hadn't told Khalid about the enlarger that was not an enlarger; she hadn't told him about the listening helmets; she hadn't told him about the resetting of her leg . . .

Abruptly she was sick of all of it, the suspicions and uncertainties and mysteries. It never ended. She said roughly to Karim, 'I'll go on from here alone.'

Karim kept beside her floating Ged chair.

'By all pity, the Hall of Teaching is right in front of us! Not even Ondur would think I could be attacked by a horde of bacteria in fifty lengths of wrof path!'

She expected him to turn patronizingly superior, as Kelovar would have, or furious, as Jehane would have.

But Karim did neither. He squatted beside her chair, bringing his face level with her own, although he never stopped scanning the woods and brush. Over his features lay the sudden openness of a man determined to speak honestly.

'Listen, Ayrys. Be careful. There are many Delysians who . . . I think Ondur is right when she says you just come to the Hall of Teaching because you're a glassblower and the Ged inventions remind you of making glass. Ondur is good at knowing things like that. But I'm a soldier and I've seen . . . Be careful.' He stood and strode back down the path.

Be careful.

Both chilled and touched, Ayrys twisted her body in the Ged chair to watch him out of sight. Then she moved into the Hall of Teaching and down the corridor – and stopped short in the arched doorway.

The floor tables stood sharp and clear; there was no known way to damage wrof. Tables, floor, even walls were smeared with the wreckage of equipment the six humans had used over the last tencycle: smeared tissue samples, twisted copper wires, spilled liquids and vials, smashed lenses that Lahab, the former Jelite laborer, was learning to grind from glass Ayrys had made. The eyeless mangled head of a kreedog grinned horribly from the floor, spilling blood and viscera. In the middle of the destruction, Lahab, the left side of his face bruised purple and blood streaming from his left arm, stood motionless while Dahar, his back to Ayrys, carefully lifted and examined the eyelid. Grax, the only other one in the room, started immediately toward Ayrys.

'Nothing is dangerous. All the pathological bacteria for study had been encased in wrof last night.' He pointed: On the smeared floor just before Ayrys's chair lay a cube of clear wrof holding four vials; all four had spilled within the cube and trickled down its inner walls, like ink within a square bottle.

Ayrys said tightly, 'Who?'

At the sound of her voice, Dahar turned from Lahab and Ayrys saw his face. He was holding back a storm of emotion she could not name, fighting it with all his strength; she had the eerie impression that even though he turned toward her voice, the dark Jelite eyes didn't see her at all.

Grax answered, 'It was two human males and a female.'

'How did they get in?' Ayrys asked. Only the six of them shared the thumblock.

Grax said, 'They ran in while only Lahab was here and began their violence. Lahab came early to work on his lenses. He left the door open. I arrived and sent the humans away.'

Ayrys caught her breath, staggered not only at what Grax had said but at what he had left out. She made herself ask. 'Humans – Delysian or Jelite?'

Grax said calmly, 'Jelite. They do not like Lahab coming to the Hall of Teaching. I told the human Belazir has sung in harmony for them.'

At the name of the high commander, Ayrys saw the hard mass of shoulder under Dahar's tebl clench, release. Ayrys said, 'And you just sent them away. . . .'

'Yes.'

It was stupid to ask how. If the Ged wanted someone gone, he would be gone. Ayrys remembered wrof forming to cut her and SuSu off from the dying barbarian, the Wall bumping her gently out of the perimeter.

There were gasps behind her; the rest of the six, all Delysians, had arrived together. Ilabor, the former soldier, drew his weapons and moved to have the wall at his back. Tey, the little trader with the musical voice and eyes like shiny beads, took in the room with a glance and looked suddenly thoughtful. The very young gemcutter, Creejin, who had recently become Tey's lover, did not try to hide her fright.

Grax repeated, word for word, his maddeningly

unruffled recital of what had happened. Tey walked over to Lahab and Dahar. 'Is your citizen badly hurt, Healer?'

Ayrys felt, rather than saw, Dahar stiffen. Tey was the only Delysian who would address Dahar directly, and whenever he did there was that slight mocking undertone, that faint pleasure in using Delysian titles to an exiled Jelite warrior. Tey often smiled when he looked at Dahar, and did not seem to care if Dahar stared levelly back. Ilabor ignored Dahar completely, and Creejin, who, after Dahar, showed the greatest passion for the biological science, often assisted Dahar for hours without once looking at him. But worst of all, Ayrys suspected, was Lahab, the other Jelite. Silent and slow-moving, his laborer's face too heavy for mockery, the citizen still treated Dahar with the deference due the high commander's first lieutenant, and Ayrys suspected that under that misplaced courtesy Dahar writhed.

But only suspected. She and Dahar spoke only in the words of the Ged science, and in all the long hours in the Hall of Teaching, he did not once let his eyes meet hers.

Lahab, in his slow and heavy speech, said to Tey, 'I am not hurt. Grax came just after the warriors.'

Tey gave one of his sly smiles. 'That was fortunate.'

'Yes,' Grax agreed calmly. 'We sing in harmony. I will arrange for new equipment to come from within the Wall. This will take a little time.'

'But the *experiments* . . .' Creejin said.

'We will begin new experiments. There is a new experiment we will begin.'

Ilabor said sharply, 'What is it?'

'We will find the bacteria that has begun to cause this itching disease.'

Slowly, Dahar turned from cleaning Lahab's wounds.

Grax said, 'There have been outbreaks of the disease in five of the nine human halls. You know now how disease is caused by bacteria. We will find the bacteria and develop an antitoxin.'

The growled alien words hung a moment in the air.
Then Ilabor said, 'There has been no disease in R'Frow
until now.'

'No,' Grax agreed. 'When each human first fell asleep
within the Wall, he or she was given a powerful antitoxin
to kill bacteria in the body. You know now, as you did
not then, what that means. But this bacteria is new; the
Ged have no antitoxin for it. We will try all those we have
and then look for new ones. You will learn how this
testing of knowledge is done.'

Ilabor said, almost angrily, 'Can humans learn to do
that?'

'Yes,' Grax said.

Ayrys was watching Dahar; he stood very still, and his
eyes glittered as if with fever.

Tey said, 'Are all these antitoxins something humans
could make without the Ged, after the year in R'Frow is
over?'

'For a profit?' Ilabor asked roughly, and then laughed,
his anger suddenly vanishing.

Grax said, 'Humans can learn to make antitoxins to use
after the Ged have left. But our teaching must not be
interrupted by more violence. Lahab's attackers waited
until he had unlocked the room to do him violence. They
did not expect anyone else to be here early. I will give
you each individual thumblocks to another room, and you
may sleep and eat there if you choose. Floor tables can
be created to bring food to each room. You will be able
to work at whatever times you choose, and you will be
safe.'

'Hidden away like the healer here,' Tey said with a tiny
smile, at the same time that Ilabor burst out, 'Why do
the Ged want us here in this hall instead of with our own
city?'

'We do not,' Grax said. 'We offer the choice. The choice
is yours.'

Sudden tension filled the room. Grax looked first at

Lahab. The laborer's stocky frame and heavy face, both masking a passion for lenses and light so tenacious that Lahab had often worked sixteen hours straight in the Hall of Teaching, betrayed no emotion. The battered left side of his face had begun to swell: purple-blue, half-closing one eye. Lahab said, 'I will stay in the citizens' hall.'

Dahar turned on him harshly. 'Why?'

Lahab struggled for words. Dahar, caught in his own struggle, did not let him find them. 'I asked you why, citizen!'

Tey answered in his musical voice, 'Presumably because he is a Jelite.' After a moment he added, 'Citizen.'

Dahar did not move. Tey turned toward Creejin, smiling faintly. 'We, too, will stay in our own hall, Little Sun?'

Creejin, eyes downcast, nodded wordlessly.

Grax said, 'Ilabor?'

'I stay with my own!'

'Ayrys?'

All eyes were on her, even Dahar's. Ayrys did not dare look at him.

Grax said, 'Your chair cannot go up and down the ladder of your hall without being carried. Here there is no ladder. That is a greater reason for you to stay here in the Hall of Teaching.'

Grax was making it easier for her. Or was he? He must know about the night Dahar had spent in her room, must know from the orange circles then uncovered in the Delysian corridor. Did Grax know how dangerous that had been for both of them? Did he know . . . there was no way to know what he knew. He treated Delysian and Jelite exactly the same, as if political differences did not matter to the Ged. Perhaps they did not. But she had once thought they did not matter to glassblowing either, and the red and blue glass helix had lain smashed in the moonlight beside the dark river.

Ilabor said tightly, 'Ayrys?'

'Grax,' Ayrys said slowly, 'you said that Lahab came very early to the Hall of Teaching and opened this room, to grind his lenses. His attackers didn't expect to find anyone here yet. But you came and saved Lahab. How did you know to be here?'

Grax pointed at the wall. He used the last of four fingers, not the second of five. 'You know the answer. Dahar left the orange circle uncovered when he and I worked last night late. The Ged saw the violence done to Lahab.'

'But you must have seen all the other violence in R'Frow – the killings. There were orange circles all over R'Frow, until we covered them. You must have seen the first killing that started all the . . . you must have seen it. Why interfere now, and not before?'

The others stared at her. Grax was silent for a long time. *Listening.*

'We did not stop the other killings because we did not have time. They all happened very fast. This attack on Lahab was slow. The only other violence that happened slowly was the attack on you, Ayrys, and the Jelite female Jehane stopped that before a Ged arrived.'

It sounded reasonable. It *was* reasonable. Ayrys glanced at the others, and only two faces stood out: the Delysian Ilabor, looking at her with sudden hardness at the reminder that she had been aided by Jehane; and Dahar, his dark eyes gone equally hard at the tone in which she questioned Grax.

'It is fortunate you did come early,' Tey said to Grax, 'or otherwise we might have had another killing – and another task for the Kreedogs.'

But for once his baiting of Dahar misfired; the soldier Ilabor, hating the bargain Khalid had struck as much as Kelovar or Karim did, rounded on him ferociously. 'Watch your tongue, trader, or you won't have it much longer!'

Tey moved quickly toward Grax. The Ged made no

move toward either man. Ayrys could not stop herself from glancing at the uncovered orange circle; were there Ged watching this even now, through some unimaginable tubes and lenses of light?

'I will go now to arrange for the new equipment we need,' Grax said calmly, 'and we will bring it here. Dahar and Lahab will come and help me carry what is too large to come through the floor table. Ilabor and Tey and Ayrys and Creejin will remain here until I return. Lock the door behind me' – Ilabor bristled slightly – 'if you choose. I will return here very soon. We have much teaching to give humans. The Ged are eager to help you find the antitoxin for this itching disease.'

Why? Ayrys thought, and held her hands tightly together, and watched Dahar turn as much away from her as if she had spoken aloud. Or perhaps he only turned toward the new equipment, and the antitoxin, and Grax.

45

They were all so tired of the alien mind.

The galaxy held many number-rational species that altered their own genes, and some that used chemicals to alter the perceptions of their minds. The Ged met both with tolerance and faint distaste, the distaste of those who know that civilization resides in perception of the vast ordered patterns in the universe, for those who believe it resides in perception of the variations from the patterns. But even among the Ged's gene-altering or mind-shaping allies, the variations created or perceived were small. Solidarity came first, the solidarity of slow evolution, of creeping forward through the endless millennia by minute steps. Number-rational, even those gene-altering species had introduced to their biology nothing disruptive to their solidarity. Nothing wrenching, nothing more than the species – or the individual – could bear.

Nothing like what they had seen a primitive plant-derived drug do to SuSu.

The human 'Jelite' had been brought to a different *behavior* by some primitive chemical. Not just to a different appearance, or to a different behavior that sprang from a gene adaptation, but to a different behavior while the rest of her biology remained the same. This was not just a matter of stimulating the pleasure centers of the brain, as some species did, nor just a matter of counteracting biological shock. SuSu had been brought to a state where

she would behave as the two other humans suggested –
at least while the chemical remained in her body.

It was a difficult concept. The Ged had struggled with
it, trying to fit it into what they knew of humans. Violent,
gene-variant, number-rational, likely to act against loyalty
and solidarity even when those would have been useful to
them – and then all that altered to suggestibility by a
primitive chemical distilled from plants. And the moral
implications, indistinguishable to the Ged from the factual
ones, were staggering. How could a human ever know
who he was? Identity came from behavior – that was
fundamental to physics, to weaving, to all the most
important activities of mind. It was fundamental to
number itself. If human mind behavior could be altered,
if human species loyalty was not fixed, if human solidarity
could turn in a moment to violence against the individual
– then what could the individual depend on? Not his
species, not his place in the world, not even his own mind.
Nothing but flux, without pattern, without solidity. The
humans must be perpetually lost. To do that deliberately
to the members of one's own was a depravity that the Ged
hadn't known even humans were capable of.

But animals controlled by chemical tranquilizers would
be less a danger aboard ship than animals controlled by
only their own bewildering wills.

Wraggaf said, 'We will need a great number of human
subjects for the experimentation.'

'Yes. Harmony sings with us.'

'A great number of subjects.'

'A great number. It will always sing.'

'Harmony . . .'

The six humans to be brought abroad ship must be
given help, protection, teaching, stimulation that would
bind them to the Ged enough to permit them aboard ship.
The last was a difficult concept – that stimulation and not
solidarity would 'create' loyalty – but the Library-Mind

agreed. The six were thumblocks to the humans warring in space.

And if necessary, mind-suggestible organics, once tested on enough subjects, were the thumblock to the six.

The room smelled of hope.

46

Jehane and Talot sat at a floor table in the sister-warriors' hall, eating. Jehane, who noticed what she ate only when there wasn't enough of it, shoved two large chunks of 'stew' into her mouth, chewed, and licked her fingers. Talot picked up one chunk, held it a while, put it back with long, too bony fingers. Jehane scowled. Talot was still losing weight.

'Eat something!'

'I am eating.' Talot bent her head over the bowl. Her red hair sprang aside from the white center part as unruly as ever, a bright vitality around a face from which vitality had gone. Love twisted in Jehane's chest, followed by exasperation. Talot was too thin, too thoughtful, too . . . something. If she would just stop all this darkcold thinking and *eat* . . .

'Let's go,' Jehane said. 'They're waiting for us in the practice yard.'

After a moment Talot looked up and said, 'Do you think they're waiting for us on the practice field?'

'I just said that! Shit, Talot, you have to stop this stupid trance! What are you, a bladder-brained citizen? Stop it!'

Talot should have been angry – Jehane would have welcomed anger. Anger was good, anger was *alive*. But Talot merely rose from the floor table. Her food bowl was untouched.

The hall had nearly emptied. Jehane stalked toward the archway, Talot following. The walls began to speak.

Jehane's hand shot to her weapons – the walls had not spoken since the forbidding of violence in R'Frow. But what was she going to do with her pellet tube, shoot the wall?

'Humans of R'Frow,' the walls said in their expression-less growl, 'seven humans have developed a disease on their skins. The disease shows red splotches that cause itching and pain. The splotches start on the backs of the knees and elbows, the folds of skin on the neck, between the thighs, in the armpits. Then they spread. Any human who has this disease should come to the Ged in the empty hall by the north wall. The diseased human will be taken within the Wall, healed as soon as possible, and returned to R'Frow. The disease does not kill. It can be spread from one human to another by touching. A human with the disease should come to the empty hall. A human with the disease should not touch another human.'

After a short pause, the walls began their message again. Jehane did not wait for them to go through the whole thing three times. She turned to Talot. 'Do you have any itchy splotches?'

Talot said, with sudden violence, 'No. And if I did, I wouldn't go inside the Wall!'

'Neither would I. Not that I'm afraid of the Ged.'

'I am,' Talot said tonelessly, and started toward the practice yard, unwrapping her threeball from her waist as she went.

47

Dahar awoke as soon as the knocking began on the door, and even before he opened it, he knew.

They had worked late into the night in the Hall of Teaching, all but Ilabor, who had left at the end of the afternoon. Ayrys had gone next, still tiring easily from her injured leg, and Grax had gone to create for her a thumblock on another room in the Hall of Teaching. The whore SuSu had followed Ayrys. The other four humans had worked on, astonished at the corridors of knowledge Grax opened into a biology not even his own.

Again and again Dahar's chest had tightened and clutched, as if from a hard blow. So much knowledge – *and if only they had known*. If only the warrior-priests had known what Grax showed them so effortlessly now – the lives that could have been saved. The pain that did not have to be. The mistakes that the Red and Blues, in blundering ignorance, had made over and over.

By evening the humans' minds reeled; they could not remember any more. But it had been Grax who stopped.

'I will return inside the Wall until tomorrow. I am very tired.'

Dahar had looked at the Ged, and realized he did not know how a Ged looked when he looked tired. There were no changes in the skin under Grax's eyes; in the set of his thick, short body; at the corners of his inflexible mouth.

Dahar had thought he could not sleep. But the moment

he reached his own room, sleep overwhelmed him, until
the quiet knock on his door.

She sat motionless in her chair, looking up at him.
The corridor behind was dim and still, gray 'night' from
beyond the four arches the only light. From long training,
Dahar moved to a better striking position while scanning
the dimness; when he shifted, Ayrys moved her chair past
him into the room.

He closed the door.

In this, his sleeping room, Dahar had covered the
orange circle. They could not see each other. It was, and
was not, like that other time, when he had come to her:
exhausted, despairing, not sure what he did, or why.
Some of the confusion of that night rushed in on him,
but he didn't need it; he had confusion enough already,
all the confusion he had not looked at for tencycles.

'Dahar,' she said quietly, and stopped. He felt himself
tense in the darkness, but said nothing. The old habit
came over him, and the detached Dahar waited to see
what she would say next.

'You have not looked at me once in the Hall of Teaching,' Ayrys said. Her tone surprised him: as quiet as a
Ged's, without either fear or submission. 'If you looked
at me, would you see R'Frow?'

His own words. Dahar flushed in the darkness. He said
nothing.

'I think not,' Ayrys said, and now he heard the note of
strain, held in check by a kind of violence different from
Jelite forthright emotion. *Different.*

'I think,' Ayrys went on carefully, 'that if you looked
at me, you would see a Delysian whore.'

He had not realized how much courage she had. Intelligent, brave, desirable. And when he looked at her, he
saw Kelovar, he saw the others that must have preceded
Kelovar. A lifetime of thought rose in his brain, solid as
a wall. *Whore.*

'No,' he said.

'Don't lie to me, Dahar.' Unexpectedly, she laughed. 'You lie badly, did you know that?'

'Yes. Ayrys,' he said suddenly, surprising himself, 'I know sister-warriors, mother-warriors, citizens, and whores. . . .'

'And no one can learn to know something he didn't know before. No one in R'Frow can learn a new way to think, a new way to form a hypothesis.' At the growled Ged word, for which there was no Qom equivalent, she faltered a moment. But only a moment. 'Or perhaps you should not change your hypothesis about women because it has worked so well. I have SuSu as proof of that. Weren't you one of the honorable brother-warriors who made her into what she is now?'

Again he said nothing, and he heard her small gasp in the darkness.

'Did you force her, Dahar? *Did you?* Because if you forced that child – '

'I have never forced any woman!'

She was silent. She could feel her thinking, like palpable heat rising in the darkness. He felt confused, hot, obscurely ashamed. That she had made this a battlefield – or he had, or they both had – was evident, but he did not know how she fought, or for what. It seemed to him that she was at home on this battlefield, sure of her ground, had perhaps fought over it many times . . . *whore*. He could not guess, as he had been able to do with Belazir, what she would say next. The detached part of his mind realized that she was at that moment more alien to him than the Ged.

'Have you even wanted any woman you were not supposed to want? Ever felt the stirrings of desire for a sister-warrior, or a citizen?'

The snickerings of boys in training, the masculine talk on the veld. But a woman wouldn't know about that, unless she *was* a whore. . . .

'Answer me, Dahar. Have you ever looked at a sister-warrior and wanted her?'

Sudden anger filled him. 'You babble of things you don't understand!'

To his utter surprise, Ayrys laughed: a loud laugh of genuine amusement. 'Jehane said that same thing to me on the veld. It must be something your warrior teachers say. Is it?'

It was. But her laughter, which sounded all at once like Tey's mockery, turned his fury colder, harder. And from her . . .

Ayrys stopped laughing and whispered, 'Oh, Dahar. No playfulness, no love, no real sex . . . Oh, you stupid fools.'

Through his anger and confusion, he heard the authentic note of sorrow in her voice, and he caught the doorknob before she could reach it.

'Let me out,' Ayrys said, her voice now as furious as his, ready to strike out however she could.

'No.'

'Why not? Or are you ready to force your first woman? You can't use a Jelite whore anymore, can you, Dahar? How long has it been? Are you hard?'

'Only whores talk like that!'

'Why?'

The question startled him. But the moment she asked it – furious, accusing – he caught a glimpse of what her mind must see: that talking of bodies in sex was no different from talking of bodies in science, and if he had torn apart everything he thought he knew of healing, he should be able to tear apart everything he thought he knew of sex. Discuss it, change it – she expected him to understand the same freedom of body that the Ged had brought him of mind. Brought them both.

A sudden strange humiliation came over him, unwelcome and a little sore. She had seen him as more – more flexible, more capable, more far-seeing – that he was.

'Let me go back to my own room,' Ayrys said.

'No. Please Ayrys . . .'

She heard the change in his voice. For a long while they stayed motionless, unable to see each other in the darkness.

Finally she said, in a voice shorn of all anger, reasonable to the point of gentleness, 'I wanted you. We say so frankly in Delysia, yes. But I am no longer . . . Delysian. And you are no longer Jelite. And after you came to me that first night . . . I want to go. Let me through the door.'

Dahar said, before he knew he was going to, 'Why aren't you afraid of me?'

'I am.'

And that made no sense at all. Baffled, Dahar pressed the orange circle. Ayrys sat with one hand cradling the lacerated thumb of the other. At the burst of light, she raised her head. Tears filmed her eyes.

He knelt beside her chair, and she twisted hard to put her arms around his neck. Her breasts pressed against his chest, and then he felt her hand on his penis, already stiff.

It was a whore's trick. The image of her with Delysian soldiers rose again in his mind, but this time he pushed it away. *Not Delysia. R'Frow.* In the exhaustion and pain of that other night, he had spoken better than he knew.

But somewhere within, the image remained.

Ayrys gave a small sound, between a laugh and a whimper, and tried to push him away. 'Think, Dahar – if we become lovers, you'll think of me as a whore; and if we don't you'll think of me as a bladeteaser.'

The word was Delysian slang; he wasn't sure what she meant. But a sudden longing rushed over him, longing and tenderness and a bursting hardness of more than physical need. He didn't understand that either. But in the sudden rush of longing, he saw Ayrys in the Hall of Teaching, wrapping coils of wire to electric cells, reaching out with both hands to the Ged science with the same courage she reached out toward him.

He said roughly, 'I don't know how to bed a woman who isn't a whore. I'll hurt you. I hurt you last time.'

Ayrys shook her head. 'It's all right. I wanted you to.'

He didn't understand that either. But he pushed away the image of Kelovar, lifted her from the Ged chair, and carried her to the cushions spread brightly on the wrof floor.

48

People began disappearing into the Wall.

The trees in R'Frow stood motionless and dusty; it no longer rained from the wrof dome. No wildflowers bloomed. The scrub brush, tougher than the flowers, did not die but began to look limp and a little blurred. The grasses, tougher yet, neither grew nor withered but became spiky and dry, each blade a separate tiny knife.

Panic spread along with the skin disease. Just enough humans had paid just enough attention at the Hall of Teaching to understand that these *bacteria* were invisible, and therefore might possibly come from spirits on the Island of the Dead. But spirits played so small a part on Qom that most Delysians and Jelite alike regarded the itching not with superstition but with skepticism, with anger, with fear. Mudpacks, healing ointments, the priest-warriors' doses secretly sold by a few Jelite citizens to a few Delysian traders – nothing eased the itching.

A knot of Delysians on a wrof path. A musician, still holding her flute in her hand, is pushed forward by hands that touch her only briefly, She stumbles a few paces, then turns to look piteously back, her face white around scabbed and reopened red splotches.

'Go to the Ged,' *someone says firmly, not unkindly.* 'Some are always in that empty hall.'

'But it's near the Jelite!'

'Go to the Ged.'

'Don't make me! Don't make – Ahmed! We shared thumb-
blocks, don't let them send me there!'

Ahmed stares at the ground and says nothing. At the back
of his neck, the flesh works up and down over the collar of
his tebl.

'Go now!' a slightly built man barks suddenly. 'You
could . . . I sat eating next to you yesterday at the hall! If
I . . .' He does not finish.

The musician plants her feet firmly. 'I won't. I won't.'

Muttering rumbles through the group. The slightly built
citizen stoops and picks up a rock. He takes a menacing step
forward, but his voice has a whining, almost apologetic edge.
'We could all get it from you.'

The musician does not move. The man takes another step
forward. The musician screams something no one hears clearly,
turns, and runs toward the empty hall.

Behind her there is silence. Then a soldier on the edge of
the group says abruptly, 'I'll follow her. Near that hall is
where the slime attacked the glassblower.'

The soldier draws his pellet tube and follows the musician,
walking with the light step of the trained fighter. The knot of
Delysians moves worldlessly back to their hall. Ahmed stays
where he is, fists clenched at his sides, head bent to hide his
face.

'The only broth that cleared is the one in Ayrys's
glassmaking acid,' Dahar said wearily. 'None of the ones
in healing doses, none of the ones in Ged antitoxins.
None.' He looked up from the enlarger, his frustration
clear on his face. The enlarger rested on the floor and
reached to his waist, a dark gray cube with the Ged lack
of adornment, so heavy not even Dahar could lift it. It
did not open. There was only one.

'Let me see,' Creejin said in her timid voice. She didn't
approach the enlarger until Dahar had moved away from
it, but her voice lost its timidity when she spoke about

the antitoxins. 'The acid would eat away the skin as well as the sore. No use.'

Ayrys, preparing more broth to turn dark with the maddening bacteria they couldn't find, said, 'If we cut the acid with water . . .'

'It would still be too strong,' Creejin said. 'No use.'

'None of it is any use,' Ilabor said harshly.

'That's not true,' Tey said. 'We know now what won't work. That's more than we knew before.' He smiled faintly, lounging against a far wall.

The little trader spent more time in the teaching room than anyone but Dahar – and never prepared a broth, never added pus from the sores of diseased humans who came to the Ged, never tested an antitoxin. Lounging, watching, Tey was merely *there*, Ayrys thought. She didn't think he was really interested in the strange new Ged way of thought that was systematic experimentation, and she had wondered why he was so often present – until she realized that the disease born in R'Frow would not stay in R'Frow when the year ended. Unless all diseased humans were thoroughly cured, they would carry the bacteria to Delysia, to Jela. A cure would become a profitable ware.

'What if,' Creejin said, 'we cut the acid enough so it doesn't damage living skin permanently. How much . . .' She fumbled after her idea. 'How much acid is too much?'

Dahar said thoughtfully, 'But how could we test it? We can test how much damage the acid does to the bacteria, but we can't test how much damage it does to skin unless we put it on skin.'

Tey said in his musical voice, 'I thought that was the sort of thing that gave warrior-priests their reputation.'

Dahar flushed. Ayrys saw the hand that shifted, as if by itself, toward his weapons, and the effort to stop it. Dahar clenched his jaw and glanced at Grax. Grax looked back with his calm, unmoving gaze, and the rigid line of Dahar's jaw relaxed a little.

Ayrys said, 'We've tried all the doses and all the antitoxins. But we haven't tried mixing them. This is a bacteria new to Qom and new to the Ged; maybe it needs a
new combination of . . . of things to attack it.'

Creejin said, 'But we've tried tens and tens of doses,
and twelve antitoxins! To make every possible mixture,
in every possible proportion . . .'

'But one might work,' Dahar said thoughtfully. His
dark eyes lost their weariness.

Lahab, grinding lenses across the room, looked up and
said in his quiet, heavy voice, 'We have no pus left. All
of it is used.'

Ilabor snorted. 'No shortage of diseased skin.'

Creejin said, 'Grax, can you bring us more from the . . .
the sufferers inside the Wall?'

'Yes.'

Yes. Ayrys swung her chair toward Grax, to a better
position to see his face. 'But you told me yesterday, Grax,
that the humans inside the Wall don't suffer. You said
they are in stasis – like when we were put to sleep, or like
my leg – so they wouldn't feel the itching. If they're in
stasis, how can their sores ooze more pus?'

The room became very silent.

Grax's expression grew intent. Finally he said, 'You
have not understood the explanation I made to you about
stasis. I told you that you did not yet have the ideas to
understand the ideas that make up the idea of stasis. There
are many kinds of stasis. The stasis of cold sleep, what
took you in the perimeter, is not the same as the stasis
around your leg. That is not as complete. Think, Ayrys.
Your bone continues to grow together, although more
slowly; if it did not, the stasis would be useless in healing
you.

'In the same way, the humans within the Wall continue
to ooze pus. But they do not itch. You do not feel the
pain in your leg; they do not itch.'

Again the room fell silent. Loud in the silence, Ayrys

heard the question Grax had not asked: *Why do you think I would lie to you?*

She glanced at Creejin, at Ilabor, at Tey. The same question was on their faces.

And she had no answer.

Finally, she looked at Dahar. He stared at her in surprise. As she watched, his black eyes hardened and narrowed.

A Jelite citizens' hall. Within a sleeping room, a too thin man, no longer young, sits with his head buried in his hands, listening to the kicking on his door. Beside him sit seven wrof bowls full of water and a large basin of Ged stew, now cold. In the corner is a bowl used as a shitpot, the smell dampened by lime from the stream bed.

The pounding on the door continues. The man looks up; his face and forearms are covered with red splotches. He itches frantically, forces himself to stop, cannot. His nails claw at his face and neck until he draws blood.

Abruptly, the kicking stops. The citizen draws in his breath, staring at the door. But the thumblock does not open. No one comes for him. As long as he does not try to come out, the door will stay closed.

He gazes at the seven bowls of water and one basin of food, until the itching starts again.

'I don't understand,' Dahar said, 'why none of the antitoxins work. I don't understand.'

Ayrys didn't answer. She felt sleepy, and sated, and indisposed for conversation. They lay in Dahar's room in the dark, Dahar full length on his back and Ayrys curled against him, her thumb tracing lazy circles on his smooth chest. At the corner of her mind, more remembered sensation than thought, hovered the memory of Kelovar's chest, the hair growing in fine, thick whorls. Ayrys's jaw tightened. She would not have remembered Kelovar except for the suspicion, undiscussed, that Dahar did.

'It must be because the bacteria are so small,' Dahar said. 'Too small to see. If the antitoxins kill all other kinds of bacteria but these – '

'We don't know that,' Ayrys said.

He considered. 'No. We don't. But Grax said this is the only bacterium he's ever seen untouched by at least one of the antitoxins. And the only one too small to see. Are those two things connected? How?'

'Maybe they're not bacteria,' Ayrys said, to say something. But once the words were out, the idea caught her. She stopped tracing circles on Dahar's chest. 'How do we know they're bacteria?'

'What else could they be?'

'I don't know. But six tencycles ago we'd never heard of bacteria. Why couldn't it be something else we never heard of?'

'Grax would have heard of it. He would say so.'

Ayrys lay silent a moment. Then said said, very carefully, looking for words that would not open another gap between them, 'Grax said the Ged had never seen any bacteria that couldn't be killed by Ged antitoxins. Maybe it's something human. Ged don't have this disease, whatever it is. Only humans do.'

She could feel him thinking beside her in the darkness, and groped for his hand. It tightened on her own, without hesitation or reserve, and something painful flickered in Ayrys's chest. It was always like this. When their bodies joined, there was a holding back on Dahar's part, an awkwardness that had nothing to do with the hard pleasure the sex brought both of them. He desired her, he caressed her, he pleasured her – but she never asked him what he thought while he did so. She didn't want to know.

But there was no holding back, no doubt, no confusion when they talked of the Ged science. The strange, growled words did not sound strange in each other's throat. They took pleasure in following the swift flights of each other's minds, pleasure that often mounted again to passion – and then Dahar would again turn guarded, his mouth closing on her breast with a violence that Ayrys suspected was not all passion, and that she was afraid to tell him she liked because that, too, might have been what Jelite brother-warriors expected of whores.

They did not talk about it. Ayrys remembered Jehane saying, 'You babble of things you don't understand,' and clenched her fists, lying beside Dahar in the darkness.

Now Dahar said, 'But even if it's not bacteria, if it's something else, why can't we see it in the enlarger?'

'Maybe it's too small.'

'We can see parts of cells, even the smallest cells. It would have to be smaller than even parts of the smallest cells. And then how could it live?'

'I don't know,' Ayrys admitted. 'But Grax said that was another reason for the Ged breathing suits – to protect Ged from human microorganisms.'

'But it would have to be smaller than any microorganism the Ged know about,' Dahar argued, as much with himself as her. 'Smaller than even *parts* of cells.'

'Why couldn't it be?'

'I don't know.'

'A tiny microorganism, different from bacteria, unknown to the Ged, too little to see in the enlarger?'

She could feel him frowning into the darkness. 'But if it were that small – if a cell that small could exist . . . But it couldn't. Not unless you left parts of it out.'

'What if you left everything out that the cell didn't need? What would you have?'

'But if the cell didn't need it, it wouldn't be there. Grax is clear on that.'

'Could it not be a cell?'

'All living things are cells. The Ged have never found anything alive that was not.'

'If . . . if . . .' She groped for the picture she wanted, couldn't find it. 'If it's not a cell, if it has no parts the same as a cell . . . I don't know, Dahar. We just don't *know* enough!'

'But isn't there any living thing too small to see with the enlarger? That Grax already knows of?'

When he answered, his voice was a little forced. 'Only the double helix.'

'But the double helix couldn't live . . . naked. Without the rest of the cell.'

'No. Grax says not.'

Ayrys didn't answer. There was no reason to doubt Grax. If there were other, small microorganisms, he would have told them. Everything the Ged had told her had been proved, time and again, to be truth. There was no reason to doubt Grax.

But Dahar felt her doubt, and she felt him stiffen slightly beside her. Carefully, as if handling glass too fast fired, too fast cooled, Ayrys removed her hand from his, not touching him while she spoke.

'Dahar. What will happen when the year in R'Frow has ended? R'Frow is dying. I can't return to Delysia, to Embry. . . .' She faltered a little, and then pushed away the pain that lessened but never stopped. 'And you can't return to Jela as a warrior. Will you go back as a citizen?'

Without me. She could not say it.

'Maybe the year won't end.'

'What?'

He seemed to be gathering himself in the darkness. Even without touching him, Ayrys felt the tension in his muscles and the moment of its release, like a spark leaping the space between them. He knew something more; he had decided to tell her.

'Grax and the Ged are from another star. They will go back to it, across space, in their . . . starboat. Today I asked Grax if the Ged plan to ever return to Qom, and he said yes, in a year or two. We – you and I, Ayrys – could spare a year or two.'

'Spare . . .' She could not even repeat it. Staggered,

she sat up in the windowless, closed room and felt as if she were falling endlessly through blackness without walls. *Starboat* . . . She made a sound, a small strangled, meaningless gurgle.

Instantly Dahar laid his fingers across her mouth. 'Don't say anything, Ayrys. Not now, not yet. It may not be a choice we can make – the Ged may say no when I ask them – and for now, for the time that's left in R'Frow, what matters is to learn all the Ged science we can, so if that is all we ever . . . Don't say anything now. Your child in Delysia . . . don't say anything now.' After a moment he added, his voice gone grim, 'There is no reason to refuse a choice we might never have.'

He put his arms around her, and in the suddenness of the movement Ayrys saw his clutching after more than her, after more than he thought he could gain or hold.

'I love you,' he said roughly, tentatively, with the awkwardness of a boy.

Joy rose in her, like water from rock, immediately, muddied by what he said next.

'Does anyone else . . . am I the only one who has the thumblock to your room here, in this hall, besides SuSu?'

She was astonished, then angered. 'The only one . . . of course you're the only one with the thumblock. Do you think there's a constant parade of soldiers through the Hall of Teaching to my room? Do you think that because I am – was – Delysian, that . . . kreeshit!'

He was silent for a moment, his arms still around her – she was miserably conscious that the oath was one she had picked up from Kelovar. Dahar said, 'Why are you angry? You told me Delysians talk frankly between men and women about sex.'

He did not understand. Ayrys saw the ravine between them and tried to control her anger. 'Yes. But, Dahar, when sister-warriors finally bed with men and bear children, do they do it with great numbers of men? Dozens?'

'No.'

'Neither do Delysian women, soldiers or citizens. And especially not when there is . . . love.'

'Mother-warriors usually love only their sisters. Despite bedding brother-warriors.'

Ayrys had not realized that. 'And go on having sex with their sisters, too?'

'Of course.'

'With both men and women?'

'Why not? Once they retire from a fighting cadre, there is no reason not to.'

She tried to picture a lifetime of bedding women for the sake of warriors' vows, followed by having sex with men for children and women for love. She couldn't picture it. But another thought came to her. Quietly she said, 'You would prefer I'd bedded women instead of men, before you.'

'Of course.'

Of course.

She saw him realize, as she had, the size of the abyss between them, and the dark currents at the bottom. Then, in a voice that suddenly reminded her sharply of Jehane – the same refusal to be sidetracked, the same determination to push past all obstacles – he said, 'All that is over. Delysian, Jelite – we're exiles from both, and nothing of either has to hold us. This is R'Frow. The rest is over, the brother-warriors and . . . Kelovar, the Kreedogs, all of it – *over*. You and I have done with it.'

He had turned his back on the abyss, the currents. In the Hall of Teaching, he missed nothing, grasped complexities no one else could see; here, the same mind refused all complexity, all dark and shadowed places. Ayrys tried not to see them either. His hand caressed her breast; she pulled him toward her in the darkness, and his mouth came down hungrily on hers.

'Kill her,' Belazir said.

The bound Delysian soldier stared at the Jelite high com-

mander. She showed no fear, only the flaming defiance with which the least imaginative of warriors met death, the ones too young to have grasped that dead fighters win no battles. The soldier's chin rose; her eyes flashed hatred. Such youthful stupidity deserved both disdain and pity, but Belazir had neither left. Like all else, they had drowned in weary shame.

The Kreedogs stood above the bound soldier in two lines, three and three, Khalid's mouth drawn into a tight line. Sancur's face gone gray, Ishaq and Syed stiff with silence. Only Kelovar's eyes burned.

Ishaq stepped forward, grasped the soldier's hair, and jerked her head backward to expose the neck. He put his pellet tube against the skin from which all suntan had faded long ago. At such short range — no range at all — the pellet slammed the body backward, tearing the hair from Ishaq's grasp. The soldier gurgled once, then lay on her back on the grass, her eyes open to the dim clouds.

Belazir had committed the dishonor of turning away from the execution, which she should have watched unflinchingly. There was no end to it. This hated alliance was supposed to end hostilities between Jelite and Delysian; instead it mired them all further in blood. Belazir was a fighter; blood did not bother her. But not like this, in dragging, weary passivity.

Not like this.

'What has been given has been returned,' Ishaq said woodenly.

No one answered.

49

Jehane stormed into her room and hurled her threeball into one corner; it struck the wall, clattered, rolled across the wrof floor. 'Idiots – bladder-brained kree-lice *idiots*. They forget why we come here, all our precious sisters; they lie around the edge of the practice yard and chatter like whores and get fat like citizens – no, fatter. Fauggh, most of them couldn't take a Delysian child armed with a twig. They all need Belazir to order them a good flogging. I tell you, Talot, ever since that drivel in the Hall of Teaching stopped a tencycle ago . . . Talot?'

Talot sat in a corner of the room, legs drawn up to her chest and forehead resting on her knees. Even before she raised her head, Jehane knew. Coldness, real as ice, slid down her spine.

'Talot. You have the splotches.'

Talot nodded. The movement started a bout of violent itching; she clawed at her neck, knees, neck again, arms. Tears of shame in her eyes, she scratched between her thighs, shuddering violently. On her chin and in front of her ears spread irregular red splotches, bloody from her nails.

'How long?' Jehane whispered.

'Since last night. I didn't want you to know – '

'Of course I had to know. How bad?'

Talot made a gasping noise. 'Worse than any flogging. And it doesn't stop – don't come any closer.'

'Don't be stupid.' Jehane crossed the room, but Talot stood up, Ged knife in her hand.

'I mean it, Jehane – don't come near me. I don't want you to get it.'

'I won't. And even if I did, it wouldn't be as bad as you. They're saying in the halls, "The lighter the skin, the worse it is." ' She stopped. Stupid, stupid thing to say. Fear and love roiled in her, turning her furious.

'Don't be stupid, Talot – I'm not going to get it. Badr caught the disease early and her lover, Safiya, never did. And that brother-warrior, what's his name, hid his cadre brother in his room for nearly a tencycle until the others – until he didn't hide him anymore. They were together all that time and he never got the disease.'

Talot seized on Jehane's words like a kreedog on a bone; it hurt Jehane to see it.

'Then I could . . . I don't want to go to the Ged, Jehane. None of the humans who have gone inside the Wall have come out yet, not one. I went inside the Wall once, to pass into R'Frow, but that was before there was you, and I was different then, I was' – her voice dropped suddenly – 'I was stronger.'

Jehane felt a stinging in her throat, and scowled all the more fiercely. It was true. Talot was weaker now, as if something in her had worn away with her part in Jallaludin's death, with the whole shameful birth of the Kreedogs into Belazir's command, where neither birth nor shame should ever have come. But Talot's weakness did not make Jehane despise her, as it should have – it made Talot dearer, and that, too, was a shame and a puzzle in this place of puzzles, Fauggh! When would she be done with this endless thinking!

'You don't have to go to the Ged, Talot. You don't. I'll bring a warrior-priest – ah, don't, love!'

Talot had begun another violent bout of scratching. She clawed at herself with both hands, and bloody welts followed her clawing. When the worst had passed, she said roughly, 'Don't leave me, Jehane.'

'Never.'

Jehane brought a warrior-priest, the same one who had attended Ayrys. The young healer shook her head and did not meet their gaze. 'There's no dose I can give her.'

'You gave something to help that Delysian! But for one of our own you stand there shaking your head like a – '

The warrior-priest said tartly, 'If I had something to cure the sickness, I would give it to her. I don't. If she won't go to the Ged, there's nothing. Unless . . .'

'Unless what?' Jehane said.

The warrior-priest hesitated. 'Yard talk is that they're making a new dose in the Hall of Teaching, that Ged and those six.' Her mouth tightened. The burned first lieutenant, the double helix torn from his shoulder, was among the six. 'You can ask there about the dose, if you want. I think it would be a waste of muscle.'

'Why?'

'What do star monsters and Delysians know about healing? Foreign bodies and treachery. And not all the treachery from Delysians, either.'

She left. Jehane slammed the door after her – slimy Blue and Red, the stories about them drinking blood were probably true – and turned to kneel beside Talot as gently as her churning muscles would permit.

'Don't come any closer, Jehane.'

'By all . . . I won't. Listen, Talot. I'm on the net tonight, but I'll be back after watch. I won't leave you, I won't let anyone take you inside the Wall. Stay here and keep the door locked.'

'I can't. I can't, Jehane – the *walls* all the time, closing in without even a window, day after day until the disease goes away . . .'

They were both warriors, used to hard exercise and the emptiness of veld or wilderness; Jehane understood.

'Then run only at night, move quickly, don't touch anyone, and keep close to the Wall.'

'I will.'

'I love you, Talot.'

Talot made a choking noise. 'Like *this?*'

'Like any way. We stay together, no matter what.'

'*Yes*, Talot said, but the hideous itching had started again, and Jehane had sentry net. She slipped down the ladder, her face so ugly that no sister-warrior dared speak to her.

Never had the watch seemed so long.

As it wore on, Jehane found herself to be a burden. Pictures chased themselves in her mind relentlessly: Talot raising her splotched head from her knees; Ayrys's white face as she ineptly tried to fight her attackers; the strange flat faces of the Ged, monsters with three eyes; the red hair springing from the white part along Talot's head . . .

Something lurched through the brush to her right.

Jehane raised her pellet tube in one hand, knife in the other, and tensed. The lurching form came closer, breaking branches indiscriminately, low to the ground, until it broke cover and staggered onto the wrof path not far from where Jehane stood hidden. It was a kreedog, just past cub, scrawny and patch-furred. Jehane watched with amazement; after all the hunting, she hadn't known there were any left in R'Frow, and what the darkcold was this one doing? It whirled madly on the path, snapping at its own back with salivating fangs; it rolled against a rock again and again; it wiped at its face with both front paws – all silently, in obvious torment but without the relief of howling. Swiftly Jehane considered the air drift between them, the branches that might deflect her pellet, the chances of the kreedog's smelling her. . . .

But it showed no awareness of her smell, and, finally, she understood.

She took as clear aim as she could, and fired the Ged pellet tube. The pellet struck the animal in the head.

Then it did howl – a single, drawnout, shuddering note that echoed from the dark dome above and seemed to go on, note and echo, forever.

Jehane waited a long time before breaking her cover; it was just possible that the kreedog had been enemy bait, more possible that the howling would bring humans. But finally tedium outlasted caution, and she slipped onto the path and squatted with drawn knife to examine the body. She had to know.

Even in the gray half-light, she could see that the kreedog was female. Its gray belly skin, where there was little hair, was splotched with open sores. How long? Humans had had the disease over a hundred days – nearly three tencycles; she was losing the habit of thinking in cycles here in R'Frow where there weren't any. Had the game had it that long? But there was hardly any game left in R'Frow. In fact, Jehane would have sworn there were no kreedogs left. This one was so thin its flanks stuck out in bony knobs. Couldn't it find anything to eat, or had it been so crazed by itching that it hadn't hunted for even a sluggish Delysian citizen, or did the disease kill appetite?

Jehane shuddered. *Talot* . . .

But she could not stand here a clear target – stupid, stupid. Again Jehane hid and willed herself to become part of the net, motionless and lightly tranced, a willed alteration of time that let her remain preternaturally alert even as her mind became too detached for boredom.

But tonight she could not hold the warrior's trance. Her mind skittered, making picture after picture: Talot raising her splotched head from her knees; Ayrys's white face as she tried to fight her attackers; the strange flat faces of the Ged, monsters with three eyes . . . Beyond, the body of the kreedog lay lumpish and diseased on the wrof path.

For the first time in her life, her warrior's timing deserted her. She could not tell how much of the endless watch was left, how much had gone. Over and again she thought she heard the whistled signal of her replacement. But when the actual signal came, she didn't hear it, and her knife was drawn when the outraged brother-warrior slipped in beside her.

It was near morning. The gray half-light brightened slowly, filtering from the dome through the sickly trees. Jehane ran over the paths within the outer net, barely stopping to give the signals to the warriors on the inner net. She hurled into the hall and up the ladder – *faster, faster* – jammed her thumb into the lock, and flung open the door. The heel of her hand slammed into the covered orange circle to send light exploding into the room.

The light showed her nothing. Talot was gone.

50

Dahar leaned against the wall and closed his eyes. He dared not rub them; he hadn't scrubbed yet. The time when he had not known about disinfectant seemed both remote and painful, a part of that other life as a priest-warrior. Dahar thought that he should scrub immediately, before he fell asleep standing up, but at the moment he was too tired to move.

For twenty hours, long after the others had gone to sleep, he had been bent over enlarger and samples – for nothing. No mixture of antitoxins, or of doses and antitoxins, had stopped the growth of the bacteria that could not be seen but must be there because they turned pus solutions cloudy and kreedogs crazy.

The room, crowded now with equipment, smelled of pus, of disinfectant, of a dissected kreedog, of the four humans who had toiled there. Ilabor, a soldier first, no longer came to the Hall of Teaching, and Tey did not toil.

Dahar dragged himself to a floor table that had, when Grax was alone in the room, become a wrof spring. Water flowed ceaselessly up from one side, down the other. Ayrys had been fascinated, and had immediately begun to construct a cruder version of the artificial spring using tools and materials that did not depend on Ged science. She moved between that and the search for an antitoxin, even as Lahab moved between the search and his lenses.

The search that had failed. There was no way to stop the bacteria from growing.

The bacteria could not be bacteria.

There was nothing else they could be.

Dahar was too exhausted to trudge around the weary circle yet again. Ayrys would have long since gone to his room, waiting until the corridor was empty, safe behind both the door and the knowledge that in R'Frow, no one could know behind which door she lay. By now she would be asleep. Dahar thought of her, lying curled on his cushions, with that slow tenderness that could still bewilder him. With tenderness – but not, tonight, with desire. He was too tired.

If the bacteria were bacteria, antitoxins should have had some effect on their growth.

They were not bacteria.

There was nothing else they could be.

Walls, Dahar thought. Of our own ignorance. We understand nothing, we will never understand anything. Next to the Ged we are barbarians. And should be.

But the Ged did not understand the not-bacteria either.

He wanted to stretch out and sleep without having to stumble along the corridor to his room, but he also wanted to lie beside Ayrys. Wearily he crossed to the door. The warrior in him held; before opening it, he drew his knife and shifted, without thinking about it, into the best position for sudden defense.

In the corridor, huddled against the doorway, SuSu slept.

She had the thumbblock to Ayrys's room and usually slept in it, but she would never go there unless Ayrys was locked behind Dahar's door. If SuSu somehow became locked out of the teaching room while Ayrys was in it, she simply crouched in the corridor until the door was open. Tonight she must have thought Ayrys was still inside, and fallen asleep there.

Dahar stood over the tiny girl, her delicate face wiped

smooth by sleep. He had spent tencycles trying not to see her. *I have never forced a woman*, he had said to Ayrys. But the truth was that now, after the nights with Ayrys – nights of sex, of talk, of that strange and bewildering tenderness – the memory of using whores felt like force, although he did not remember that SuSu had ever cried out. Dahar smiled sardonically – as if he had ever believed that force could not act in silence.

He didn't want to leave her lying unprotected in the corridor. She looked so small. But if he touched her, she would become a raging animal, and he was too exhausted for that. And, he discovered, he did not want to touch her.

Because she was Jelite? Because he had never noticed, until Ayrys pointed it out, how much of a child SuSu still was? Because when he remembered using her, he remembered Ayrys with the Delysian soldier who had given her a child not much younger than this?

It didn't matter. Such distinctions were stupid; this was neither Jela nor Delysia. This was R'Frow. In R'Frow, this girl spent her days with Ayrys and the Ged. This was R'Frow.

He clung to that.

Dahar bent and lifted SuSu, trying not to wake her. She weighed nothing. He didn't want her in his room; he carried her along the corridor to Ayrys's.

SuSu had wakened and lay in his arms, looking at him.

The look pierced his exhaustion and crawled along his mind. He might have expected madness – but this was not madness. Not fury, not fear. It came to him that this was the look he might have expected to see in the eyes of the three-eyed monsters from another star, and never had: the blind enmity of one type of being for another that it considered totally alien, where no truce and no talk was possible. He had seen eyes like that glitter in the darkness beyond a campfire, in the cold and hunger of the veld.

Chilled, Dahar set SuSu on her feet. She ran around

the corner of the corridor, her unbound black hair a swift lash behind her.

The first touch of Ayrys, sprawled across his cushions but waking as soon as he lowered himself beside her, made a lie of his lack of desire. This, too, was desire – strange, troubling – this sudden violent longing to hold her against him and poor out his exhaustion and discouragement against a woman's ear. Nonetheless, Dahar had a sudden vivid memory, as he had not had when he carried SuSu, of her small naked body straining beneath him. Remembering SuSu, touching Ayrys, he found himself suddenly aroused, completely bewildered.

'Dahar,' Ayrys said, gladness in her voice. She turned her face sideways and kissed him in the darkness.

Her mouth was warm. Ayrys's mouth, SuSu's eyes . . . the thing he had seen in SuSu's eyes, primitive and violent . . . He rolled on top of Ayrys and brought his mouth down hard on hers. Too hard, harder than necessary, and that, too, came from the thing in SuSu's eyes and the weary hours of failure and inadequacy in the Hall of Teaching. Beneath him, the soft body did not flinch. Dahar tightened his arms around her. She was not strong as a sister-warrior would be; she had light ribs, delicate under his, delicate enough that if he were not holding his strength in check, he could easily crack them with his bare hands.

Ayrys gasped and pulled her mouth from his. 'Dahar . . .'

With a kind of horror, Dahar realized that he had forgotten which woman lay beneath him, forgotten what he was doing. Abruptly he let her go. 'Ayrys . . . I'm sorry!'

His hand fumbled for the orange circle, found it. Ayrys sat up, blinking in the sudden light. She looked flushed but not frightened.

'What happened?'

'I wanted to hurt you. I wanted . . . I wouldn't hurt you, Ayrys!'

'No,' Ayrys said gently. And then, 'Yes . . .'

They looked at each other, suddenly wary. After a while Ayrys said slowly, 'I watched you in the Hall of Teaching, the first time Grax brought the small enlarger. Cycles and cycles ago. You took a cell sample from your inner cheek by scraping it with your knife. The knife was very sharp, and you slid it into your mouth. . . .'

Weariness, failure, the thing he had seen in SuSu's eyes – all crashed together in Dahar's mind. He grabbed Ayrys's left wrist and wrenched her hand palm upward to the light. At the base of the thumb and across the heel of the hand ran a maze of scars, white ridges like tiny worms.

'The glass you ground into your hand was the glass that exiled you from Delysia, the double helix – wasn't it, Ayrys? Wasn't it?'

'Yes – '

'The double helix. *Why?*'

'Because I had lost Embry. Because I had lost . . . everything. Delysia, Embry, glassmaking.'

'So you did deliberate violence to yourself.'

'Yes. Hurting myself made it more bearable. . . . Don't look at me like that. I hurt myself then. I don't now,' Ayrys said, with too much force. Under the force, the fright scraped clearly. They both saw what lay on the path ahead; it had been there since the first night they had bedded.

Dahar said, 'You severed the muscles and nerves in your hand. You turned your violence on yourself.'

'I did. But not any longer. Not in R'Frow.'

'No. Not in R'Frow. In R'Frow, you bed men who do violence. Kelovar. Me.'

Ayrys tried to remove his fingers from her wrist. He tightened them, hard enough to bruise, his face cold. She tried again to pry his hand loose, and could not. She was breathing a little harder, her head bent.

He said, in a voice that didn't sound like his own, 'Were all your lovers in Delysia soldiers, Ayrys? All of them?'

She didn't answer.

'No glassmakers, or potters, or anything but fighters? Ever? And during sex you like . . . answer me, sweet Ayrys.'

'Don't call me that!'

'Only soldiers,' Dahar repeated. 'And a Jelite warrior might provide more thrill yet – '

Ayrys flung up her head. 'Is that what you think, Dahar? You are – were – a warrior, but you were a healer, too, and when I watched you with the Ged science in the Hall of Teaching . . . I don't know! What exactly are you asking me? Why I turned the pain of being exiled into violence against myself? Would it be better to turn it into blind hatred, like Kelovar? or against my own mind, like SuSu?'

He had again the image of SuSu struggling naked under him, of forcing his way into her, and he dropped Ayrys's wrist. Red bruises circled it.

'Loss and violence,' Ayrys said furiously. 'They grow together in strange ways. Especially in R'Frow. But you won't see it, you won't look at what R'Frow is doing to humans – '

'No,' Dahar said harshly. He turned away from Ayrys. 'I have to return to the teaching room. I left the door unlocked. I was carrying SuSu.'

'SuSu – ' Ayrys said sharply. Again the women merged in Dahar's exhausted mind. Neither was what she had seemed; both pierced him with weapons that he could not counter, Ayrys with her words and SuSu with the deadly violence in her eyes. . . .

'She fell asleep in the corridor. She looked at me – '

'I know. I know how SuSu looks. The loss and violence all inside, knives and daggers slicing her inside with every breath she takes. How did she get that way, Dahar? What happened in your honorable brother-warrior halls to do that to her? A Jelite whore – she couldn't put her violence anywhere else but in the way she looks at you, could she? And you turn your back on me. Would you rather I had done *that* to myself when I lost Embry? Or hated you, like Kelovar? Or turned myself into a two-eyed pretend Ged, like you?'

She hit him in the chest, a flailing, ineffective blow. Dahar caught both her wrists and tried to hold her still. She continued to fight, more seriously now, lunging her upper body toward him even though she couldn't really move her legs. Her teeth closed on his shoulder, biting viciously through tebl and skin. Roughly, much more roughly than necessary – he was strained to the breaking point, and she was untrained – Dahar threw her to the floor. Ayrys cried out in anguish. He had forgotten her leg – or had chosen not to remember. *Loss and violence.*

He knelt and gathered her to him. She didn't fight. They stayed that way a long time, unmoving. The unsuspected ravines yawned around them.

Finally Ayrys said, with difficulty, 'I would have wanted you even if you were not . . . a warrior. In the Hall of Teaching, when you looked at the Ged equipment . . . Does it matter why I wanted you? If a warrior uses any whore available – '

'Stop it,' he said coldly. 'All that is done.'

She didn't answer.

'Loss and violence – kreeshit!'

'It's R'Frow. They . . . grow here. R'Frow gave us the science, but that wasn't all.' He had stiffened against her, but Ayrys struggled on. 'You don't want to hear it. But there's something in R'Frow. . . . When I first came here an exile, it was like sunlight on glass. I was dazzled. The science, the food, the warmth: that wonderful warmth. I had been so cold on the veld, so cold without Embry –

no, just listen to me, Dahar. But the longer humans were in R'Frow, the more the violence grew.

'Was there this much killing between Delysia and Jela outside, when we weren't actually at war? Delysian traders and Jelite citizens traded; Tey told me he has been inside the gates of Jela itself. Glassyard talk said that in the mountains Jelite and Delysian miners dug ore together even when we *were* at war. When either city broke the treaty and there were border attacks, it still wasn't like this is in R'Frow. This is more violent, more savage – even with the Ged forbidding violence. The violence grows anyway, like some disease, like the itching bacteria that didn't exist until humans were in R'Frow. It keeps on growing.'

He said tightly, 'R'Frow has given us science that we could not have discovered for ourselves in a hundred years.'

'I know. I know that. But the violence grows. The trees and grass die, and the violence grows.'

Dahar lay still. He saw in his mind the wrof vials clouded by pus and bacteria, the bacteria growing and growing. 'You're wrong, Ayrys. Delysia and Jela have always fought. What the Ged have made, what has grown in R'Frow, is just the opposite: cooperation between Delysian and Jelite. Creejin and Lahab and us in the Hall of Teaching with Grax. The Kreedogs' – he stumbled a little over the name, went on coldly – 'that both Belazir and Khalid agreed to, for whatever reasons. And you and I, naked here together. For . . . whatever reasons.'

If his last words hurt her, she kept it out of her voice. 'But the violence has grown, too. Cooperation and violence – they've grown *together* in R'Frow, in a way they didn't outside, as if . . . I don't know! As if R'Frow added something to the way people are.'

He heard the stumbling frustration in her thoughts, and heard, too, that the thoughts were not new. She must have turned them over in her mind for a long time, gone

around in circles with them in the same way he had
trudged in circles with the bacteria that were not bacteria.
Dahar felt a cold, exhausted fury. She was attacking
R'Frow. She was attacking him.

'And what is it you think R'Frow has added to people?'
'I don't know.'
'I do know. Science. Healing. Knowledge. Some of
which you have claimed to find important.'

Ayrys said, very low, 'Yes.'

'So you attack what you love. "Delysia for treachery."
Perhaps they should not have exiled you after all.'

She neither answered nor shrank from him. Even
through his anger, and through his bewildered weariness
at the violence they were doing to each other – was it
always this way with women? Dahar felt a reluctant admiration. She had said what she would say, regardless. From
admiration to anger to exasperation to desire to violence
– she confused him in ways he didn't understand. And
he was so tired.

'Ayrys,' he began, a little sullenly, but she interrupted
him.

'Not added, Subtracted.'

'What?'

'R'Frow didn't add something to humans to make this
savagery between Delysian and Jelite. They took something away. Room. There isn't enough *room* in R'Frow for
warriors and soldiers to avoid each other. We're thrown
together. Jehane and I. You and I. Belazir and Khalid.
R'Frow subtracted something humans had on the outside,
and got death.'

Her voice had grown quiet, with the kind of detachment
that comes from furious thought. Dahar felt a slow prickling at the base of his skull.

Ayrys said, 'Something subtracted that was there
before, and the violence grew.'

The prickling increased, something trying to get in. It
was the sensation brought by a new leap of mind in the

Hall of Teaching, a new revelation in the Ged science. But he couldn't quite see it. . . .

'Something taken away,' Ayrys said again. 'Not added – *taken away*.'

Dahar saw it. His hand closed tight on her arm. 'A growth. You called the violence a growth, Ayrys – you called it that. Something subtracted and you get a different kind of *growth*.'

They stared at each other, she – not yet seeing that he had shifted roads, or where he was going – bewildered by his sudden excitement; he with an intensity that made his coarse, exhausted face look wild.

'Ayrys – something taken away in R'Frow and you get a different kind of growth. . . .'

She saw it. 'The bacteria . . .'

'Or whatever they are. Not something added to make the disease grow in R'Frow, but something *subtracted*.'

'But what?'

'I don't know. Something that was on the skin outside R'Frow, and isn't on the skin now. River water – outside R'Frow we bathed in the river. Maybe the water in the baths is different – '

'No. I asked Grax. The river was just diverted under R'Frow into pipes for the baths and the stream.'

'But the bacteria must have been filtered out of it. No one got sick in R'Frow before. . . .' He shook his head violently to clear it. Red fogged his vision, and the combination of exhaustion and excitement sent a sudden tremble through his upper body. Ayrys watched him with concern.

'Not water. No – it could be water. Moisture. The itching first appeared in R'Frow, where the air is moist all the time. What would happen to a skin sore on a dry day at the height of Lightsleep, on the veld? The air would be baked dry. We could test that with a potter's kiln, bake the air dry!'

Ayrys said slowly, 'At the height of Lightsleep . . .'

But Dahar wasn't listening. His mind raced. A kiln

would bake the pus sample dry, but it would also make it very hot. How would they know if the dryness or the heat caused the change in bacteria growth, if there was a change? And the high heat generated in a kiln wouldn't have been on human skin outside R'Frow. The vial would need to be close enough to the kiln to be in moisture-free air, but far enough away for human skin to be able to stand the heat. Or if not heat, there were other substances that touched skin outside R'Frow but not inside. Perhaps the skin itself could grow bacteria, as rotten meat could grow worms, in their absence. Pollen from the flowers, something in the rain, something from the plants excluded from R'Frow, maybe the kemburi . . . there were no kemburi within the walls of R'Frow. . . .

Unknowing, he had stood up. Slowly he became aware of Ayrys sitting below him, preternaturally still, and touched her shoulder. She raised her face to his. Her expression was stunned, as if from a blow she had not yet fully absorbed. She looked from him to the covered circle on the wall, back to him, back to the circle. *Something taken away.*

'Light,' she said.

51

Grax stood alone within the perimeter. There were no
corridors here; one area flowed into another, as one Ged
mind flowed into another, without unnecessary obstruc-
tion. But for the moment Grax, on his way from one place
to another when the Library-Mind contacted him, was by
himself. He stopped walking, limbs loose by his sides,
third eye ceaselessly scanning the empty ceiling.

The Library-Mind gave him the two human voices,
not much muffled by the cloth over the sensor: Ayrys's
thoughtful, in the slightly higher pitches that, for the first
time, Grax consciously registered as distasteful; Dahar's
deeper, closer to a satisfying growl, but ragged with contradictory emotion. No verbal capability for harmony, no
precision of grammar, no concern for the moral response
to order, the basis of what was moral.

Yet . . .

Intelligence. Number-rational intelligence, in the two
humans' whole unimaginable chain of reasoning. Dahar
and Ayrys could not, either of them, discover the concept
of 'virus' – they lacked the equipment, they lacked the
theory, they lacked the knowledge to build either theory
of equipment. But as Grax listened, Ayrys and Dahar
pushed around the barrier of their ignorance – bypassing
all order, all sequence – to consider what might be the
ecology of a virus before they knew that viruses were
possible. The needs of existence before existence itself –
how could minds think in such a way? Grax could follow

their bizarre reasoning, but he knew that no Ged could have initiated such thought. It would be as if the Ged tried to design a weapon to subdue the animals on a new planet before the planet itself was discovered. Inefficient, inharmonious, wasteful, frustrating – such thought processes could lead only to futility.

Such thought processes could lead Dahar and Ayrys to stopping the itching disease.

It was possible. Inefficient, inharmonious, wasteful, frustrating, slow, a disorderly and distasteful perversion of number-rational thought – but possible.

'What would happen to a skin sore on a dry day at the height of Lightsleep, on the veld?' Dahar said inside Grax's head. *'The air would be baked dry. We could test that with a potter's kiln, bake the air dry.'*

'At the height of Lightsleep . . .' Ayrys said.

The concept of testing a concept had been unknown to either of them until Grax had shown it to them.

The others, alerted by the Library-Mind as he had been, would be gathered in the meeting place. They must discuss what to do next, what they should have done before. Had they foreseen that treacherous number-rational-that-was-not-number-rational reasoning, they could have chosen a different virus, one more impervious to ecological influences. But even the Library-Mind, patterned by Ged reasoning, had not foreseen it.

The Library-Mind began a mathematical analysis. Grax requested it to fall silent. He could smell his own pheromones: chagrin, concern, bewilderment, fear. But he had been the one to teach the humans, and he wanted a moment to bring his odors under control before he hurried to the other Ged. His chagrin must smell stronger than theirs. He had been the one to teach Dahar.

Chagrin, concern, bewilderment, fear – and the shameful smell of pride.

52

The fire that Dahar built in the central courtyard of the
Hall of Teaching gave off an intense, dry heat, and light
brighter than any of them had seen since coming to
R'Frow.

'Blinding,' Tey said in his musical voice. He lounged
against the wall near Ayrys, his arms folded across his
chest. 'Do you think it will work?'

'Why don't you help Creejin with that wood?' Ayrys
said irritably. She liked the little trader no better now
than she had tencycles ago.

'Creejin is doing well without my help,' Tey said. He
smiled to himself; everything he said seemed to have a
double meaning, whether it did or not. 'And I don't think
the brother-warrior would welcome my help. A woman's
help, of course, is something else.'

Ayrys eyed him warily. There was no way to tell what
Tey meant, or guessed: possibly nothing at all.

Creejin had been skeptical at first about subjecting the
'bacteria' to light and heat. The deftest of them all with
the vials and reeds of wrof that a year ago she had not
dreamed existed, Creejin had a mind that Ayrys thought
of as a small burrowing animal. She worked diligently,
tirelessly, but did not like to move to new ground. She
had wanted to continue combining Ged antitoxins with
warrior-priest doses to stop the disease. Ayrys had watched as she was swept along by Dahar's forceful argu-
ments, and Grax had watched her watching.

Lahab continued to work on his lenses. Grax answered
Lahab's questions, answered Dahar's questions, answered
promptly and fully whatever he was asked.

And watched.

'Add dryness and light and the growth of the bacteria
slows down,' Dahar said after the fire had been tended
constantly, in shifts, for two days, 'but it does not stop.'
He held two vials at arm's length and studied them. One
was cloudy with pus in solution; the other less cloudy,
but not clear. Creejin entered the teaching room from the
courtyard, carrying two more vials.

'These are the ones farthest from the fire. Look – they
seem to be equally cloudy.'

'Not enough heat.'

'Or enough light,' Tey said. 'How will you know
which?'

Dahar didn't answer. He went on studying the vials,
his coarse features intent.

Creejin said, her soft voice gone flat, 'But none of the
flasks is completely clear. We haven't found anything. As
long as the bacteria grow at all, they will infect people.'

Dahar grimaced. 'We could try leaving the vials out a
few days longer. Maybe the time counts. Staying longer
in the light . . .'

'No,' Ayrys said. 'It's been in firelight for two days and
nights. That's as long as a threeday. It's not the time
that's different from outside R'Frow – it's the kind of
light. Firelight isn't the same as sunlight. I said so before,
but Grax wanted to try the test this way.'

The room fell silent.

Ayrys floated her Ged chair closer to the vials Dahar
held, studying them but not meeting his eyes. 'We need
to take the vials outside R'Frow, onto the veld. That way,
we can see if real light kills the bacteria. And if it does,
then we'll know the altered light of R'Frow made it grow.'
A faint echo of something struck in her mind – *altered*

light – but she pushed it aside. It wasn't important; what was important was what Grax said next.

Dahar said, a little coldly, 'Grax answered that. If the gates to R'Frow are opened, bacteria for the itching disease may go out on the air. We could contaminate Qom. And if the disease *isn't* cured by light . . . Grax says there are still people in the camps just beyond the gates. What if one of them took the vial during the threeday it remained out there?'

'I thought about that,' Ayrys said. She drew a deep breath. She had thought about it during the hours last night when Dahar had not come to her, when he worked instead in the teaching room with Grax. She had had a long time to think it through.

Ayrys turned her chair to face Grax directly. 'We want to put the vial with the bacteria in the light outside R'Frow. You say if we open the gates, we'll let out air, which might contain bacteria. But there is a way to let in light without letting out air. Ged can make the walls dissolve and then form again – we've all seen you do it. And if you know there are people beyond the gates, there must be a part of the Wall that's clear wrof, to look through. Make the Wall bulge into a bubble of clear wrof, right at ground level, on the south wall, where the sun strikes unshaded. Put the vial inside the bubble. Light will pass through the clear wrof and hit the vial, but no air will go out from or come into R'Frow.'

They were all staring at her. Ayrys ignored them all, even Dahar, and kept her eyes on Grax.

The Ged said, 'We don't see outside through clear wrof. We use orange circles, like those within R'Frow.'

'But is it possible to replace part of the gray wrof of the Wall with clear wrof? Could you do it? If you chose to?'

Grax did not answer immediately. His face took on the old listening intensity – and something more. Ayrys, watching as closely as she had ever watched anyone in her life, saw on the alien face slight shifts that once she would have missed entirely, and it seemed to her that for the first time she knew what Grax was thinking. He was weighing the bargain.

For bargain it was: a true Delysian bargain, the price as much as she thought she could exhort, free from any distractions of Jelite honor. *This for that – no, too much – done? Done!* Alter the Wall to let sunlight stream onto the vial, and Ayrys would stop questioning Ged trustworthiness to herself – and to Dahar. Do the bacteria test Ayrys's way, no matter the consequences, and she would strangle all doubt. For temporary Ged obedience, she would trade the scientific skepticism that had been the Ged gift.

Obedience for freedom of mind. It was the trade she had refused to make in Delysia, when she had insisted on her right to create a Jelite double helix in blue and red glass.

It seemed to Ayrys that she could see on Grax's unhuman face the moment he made his decision.

'Yes. It is possible to make a bubble of clear wrof on the outer Wall of R'Frow.'

Done? Done.

Creejin said excitedly, 'That would work.'

Dahar said, 'We could separate light from moisture, too. If there were two vials, one with pus in water and one with just a smear of pus so that the moisture bakes out in the first hours – '

Lahab interrupted him: Lahab, the laborer who never said anything, and who still kept the downcast eyes of a good Jelite citizen whenever Dahar was in the room.

'The clear wrof would act as a lens. It would make the heat more intense. It would not be the same as having the pus exposed directly to sunlight.'

They considered this. Creejin began to speak; Dahar interrupted her. Tey stopped lounging against the wall and moved toward the circle, some of the secret slyness gone from his face. The four of them argued, speculated, suggested possibilities. Creejin's hands sculpted some idea in the air with quick flickers of her arms. They talked more loudly, even Lahab, his slow voice rumbling under the three quicker ones. He shook his head at something Creejin suggested, and said it would not work. Tey asked why not, and Dahar explained.

Grax watched them, his gaze moving from Delysian trader to Jelite laborer, from brother-warrior to gem-cutter. It was the first time no walls had risen between them, no bazaars nor battlefields nor blades of honor. Delysia and Jela, momentarily, were forgotten.

Except by Ayrys. Grax had met her price, he was as straightforward as Dahar had said. Ayrys waited for the wave of relief to break over her. It did not come.

Delysia for treachery. Even though Grax had answered her question honestly, even though what she felt was senseless, even though it puzzled her – Ayrys knew she could not keep to her silent bargain with Grax. She distrusted him still.

'*Light*,' Dahar said exultantly, and she forced herself to smile.

53

The withered human on the island began to move.

For the second time he hobbled close to the floating monitor probe. His dark eyes in their shrunken, shadow-rimmed sockets examined it closely.

'We had nothing like this. Nothing. Is there another ship on the continent where they all went . . . however long ago it was?'

The probe floated away from him, toward the primitive keyboard on the opposite wall. The human turned to follow the probe with his eyes. 'Makeshift. Like all of it. But the best we could do. And I taught the ones who could learn – I taught my own son. . . .'

A child peered around the doorway, a little boy with black curls and bright black eyes. At his shoulders were stumps of flesh ending in two flaps of weathered skin. The probe moved toward him; he cocked his head to one side and gazed up at it.

The man said, all in a desperate rush, 'Are they still there on the continent? Are they? There were so many, military, medical, and all those damn colonists, heretics every one, dissident no-pasts . . . are they there? Still?'

The child grinned. Abruptly he flipped onto his back, raised his right leg, and beckoned to the probe by wiggling five dirty toes. Somewhere a woman's voice, high with either exasperation or fright, called, 'Ali! Ali – where are you?' The child's grin widened.

The old man said, 'You must be from the continent.

Or an orbital lander. My son and the other young ones took the lander, three days ago – they repaired it somehow and stole it. They *stole* it. My son. A son of Allah.'

The probe floated to a position just above the child. He touched it experimentally with his big toe.

'Did my son send you back here? There were five of them; my son is the giant – "Giants shall walk among you." ' His voice changed. 'Mute. They all . . . did the others tell about the stasis field? Did they tell how it is with us?'

The child put both feet on the probe. Dirt smeared across the gray wrof; a pebble scraped loose from the bottom of one foot clattered to the floor. The woman called, 'Ali,' farther away now. The old man began to chew the inside of his cheek.

'A son of Allah. Not like the ones who couldn't get away fast enough from the ship. Even the officers, abandoning their posts – put that in your data banks!'

He closed his eyes and began to chant softly in another language, his voice rising and falling in wails that matched nothing in the Library-Mind's memory scans. He wrapped his arms around himself and swayed.

The armless child, lying on his back with two dirty feet cradling the probe, looked over and giggled.

The image froze.

VI
AN ALIEN LIGHT

The universe is stamped with the adornment of harmonic proportions, but harmonies must accommodate experience.

— Johannes Kepler

54

Four days after Talot disappeared, Jehane slipped toward the Hall of Teaching just after daybreak. In one hand she carried a Ged pellet tube, in the other her threeball. Knives and heat gun were thrust through her belt. The dim light turned her face as gray as the weapons.

Four of them in there now. All night she had crouched in the woods, counting and calculating. The Delysian soldier Ilabor had neither entered nor left the hall – where the shit was he? If he was inside, she had to know it; it could make all the difference. Ayrys, Dahar, and the Jelite whore had not emerged from the hall all night; maybe the Delysian soldier had a room inside, too. Maybe Ilabor slept with Ayrys, or with the whore.

Grax, the Jelite citizen Lahab, and the two Delysian citizens hadn't yet come to the hall. Ayrys, crippled, was no threat; neither was the little whore. That left Ilabor and Dahar. Once Jehane would have thought it impossible that a Jelite first lieutenant – even one disgraced, even one who would create the Kreedogs – could be a threat to a sister-warrior. She didn't believe that anymore. There were a lot of things she didn't believe anymore.

So guess two fighters: Ilabor and Dahar. Keep Ayrys as a shield between herself and the Delysian soldier. Dahar, better trained, would be the worse threat; she would lose her edge if she thought too hard about facing down Dahar. So she didn't think about it.

She did think about waiting for Grax to come to the

Hall of Teaching. If, instead of Ayrys, she kept the Ged and his invisible armor between herself and Dahar, Dahar would have to move around Grax to try body combat, and that would give her an added few seconds. But in the end she rejected the idea. No one could ever be sure what a Ged would do, and there were enough unsurenesses in this plan already.

Like Ilabor. Was he inside or not? She could not afford to have him come in after she did, at her back. She could handle that from the puny trader and the Delysian woman, but not from a soldier. It had taken hours to assure herself that no Delysian soldiers held the Hall of Teaching from the outside. But then, why would they want to? They already held it from the inside, four to two. No, four to one. She would not count Dahar as Jelite. All along his actions had aided Khalid, corrupted the cadres, gone after dishonorable alliance with Delysian slime –

Like she was going to do now.

Jehane scowled savagely. *Talot, Talot, only for you . . .* Where the kreeshit was Ilabor?

She had waited too long to find out. Another figure strode up the path to the Hall of Teaching, and Jehane faded back into the woods. But it was only a Delysian woman, who hurried along with the stupid carelessness of a citizen who thought that glancing nervously around was a substitute for concealment and weapons. Another bladder-brain.

The woman vanished into the Hall of Teaching, and Jehane followed. No one in the corridor, but voices in one room. Jehane slithered closer to listen: Ayrys and another woman. *Good. Now.*

She moved swiftly into the doorway. 'Stand still!'

The Delysian woman; Ayrys sitting in a pile of metal sticks; Dahar; the tiny whore huddled in a shadowed corner. No Ilabor. Jehane kept her pellet tube on Dahar.

'Weapons down, Lieutenant! Without drawing them!'

The title had slipped out. Dahar's face hardened. He didn't move.

Jehane wondered coldly if she would kill him if he tried to draw his Ged gun instead of untying his weapons belt, and decided that she would.

He saw it on her face. But still he didn't move, until Ayrys cried out, 'Do it, Dahar! Don't make her kill you!'

The other woman's eyes suddenly widened.

Dahar dropped his weapons belt to the floor and stepped away from it. Jehane kept her pellet tube on him but moved farther into the room, where she could cover the doorway. Then she turned to Ayrys.

But Ayrys, for whatever reason, had started toward her. The metal sticks rose into the air and flew forward – were they *alive?* Despite herself, Jehane jumped and her aim wavered toward the attacking metal. She recovered – *just another Ged toy*, unnatural but not alive; but in the second it took her to realize that, Dahar sprang forward and closed on her.

The floor became time.

Afterward, Jehane could not really remember what happened or what it felt like, only that it *did* feel, that there was something real rising from the floor more swiftly than Dahar springing toward her, more swiftly than her hand closing on the trigger of the Ged gun. The realness was invisible. No shimmer, as with Grax's armor, no anything except time slowed, and she and Dahar had a long moment – the longest moment, a moment out of time – to look at the impossible: a Jelite first lieutenant closing in body-to-body combat with a sister-warrior who would kill him. And her mind did not slow; there was time in the unshimmering realness to think: *The Ged did this, protecting him*, and then there was time to realize that the Ged wasted their power.

For she had eased off the trigger even before the time-slowing took her, and Dahar had checked the deadliness of his attack. A Jelite first lieutenant closing in body-to-

body combat with a sister-warrior who would kill him –
it would not have happened. Jehane's body, trained to
discipline and loyalty in muscle and bone, had faltered,
and so had Dahar's, and they were left staring at each
other an arm's length apart.

Through her confused shock, Jehane had a sudden
piercing glimpse of what it must have been like for Dahar
to cause Jallaludin's death. Or for Talot –

The stasis field sank again into the floor. Jehane swayed
on her feet, momentarily dizzy. Chaos swirled around her;
the Delysian woman screamed, and Ayrys cried out to
Dahar. Then order returned – Dahar must have silenced
both women – and Jehane felt the blessed relief of anger.

'I'm going to talk to Ayrys, and I'm going to do it
alone,' she grated. 'In the corridor. The rest of you will
stay here!'

Before Dahar could say anything – had he, too, felt the
time-that-was-not-time? He must have – Ayrys had moved
her Ged-tube thing toward the corridor. Jehane followed
her, keeping her back to the wall and her weapons covering both the room and Ayrys.

She stopped Ayrys halfway down the corridor, with the
glassblower's body as shield between her and the two left
in the teaching room. But it wasn't Dahar or the Delysian
citizen who slunk around the corner and down the corridor; it was the whore SuSu, following Ayrys.

'She won't leave,' Ayrys said quickly. 'Don't hurt her,
Jehane, she won't interfere. She's . . . deaf. What do you
want?'

'I saved your life from . . . the two citizens. We stand
together on the . . .' She couldn't say it. Not again, not
to this crippled slug who lived with monsters, not when
the words of honor came from this bile at the heart. Not
when she – a sister-warrior! – was begging. And knew it.
Talot . . .

Instead she said, 'One of them has killed himself. One
of the two Jelite you made cripples. Did you know that?'

Ayrys went white. But she said steadily, 'I did not cripple them.'

'No. The Kreedogs did it for you.'

'What do you want, Jehane?'

No escape. She would have to say what she had come to say. Hating it, Jehane choked out, 'Yard talk says you're making a new dose in this place. A dose for the itching disease . . .'

Ayrys leaned forward. 'Do *you* have the itching disease? Where?'

'No. Not me. But if you six work with the Ged on a dose and carry it inside the Wall to the sick . . . Do you go inside the Wall? Is there a way in?'

Ayrys stiffened. She didn't answer. Jehane said, 'Is there a *way in?* I saved your life, Ayrys. . . .' She heard herself begging, and writhed.

Ayrys said quietly, 'Why do you want to go inside the Wall?'

'That's nothing you need to know!'

'There's someone inside, isn't there? Someone you . . . love, who left you outside the Wall and went inside for help from the Ged.'

'She didn't leave me! She didn't go inside by her own choice!'

Ayrys's eyes sharpened. 'How do you know that? It's the tall red-haired girl from our teaching group, isn't it? How do you know she didn't go by her own choice?'

'I *know*.'

'Please, Jehane, it's important. How do you know she didn't go freely into the Wall?'

'She was going to fight out the sickness – we promised each other. . . . You wouldn't understand, Delysian. A sister-warrior doesn't curl up like a kemburi at Firstnight. Talot has *courage* – ' Jehane heard herself shouting, and then abruptly heard herself whisper in anguish, 'I know she was taken inside.'

'Taken? By whom?'

'Ged. Who else? She was going to exercise along the Wall, at night, and if Kelovar's soldiers had killed her, I would know by now.'

Ayrys gripped the Ged tubes and said, '*Kelovar's* soldiers?' but Jehane scarcely heard her.

'Or else I would have found her body. For two days I've searched. . . . She's in the Wall, and the Ged took her there, and if you six can enter the Wall, you're going to get me in there, Ayrys. You are.' Jehane still held heat gun and pellet tube; she met Ayrys's eyes straight on.

Ayrys said, 'No one but the Ged go into the Wall.'

'Then Ged dragged Talot into it. And you work with the Ged. The six of you are Ged pets – you can trail at their heels and go into the Wall after them. And I'm going in after you.'

Ayrys was silent. She sat gripping her wrof tubes so hard that her knuckles turned white, and Jehane had a sudden confused memory of the glassblower's hand bloody with shards of glass in lost moonlight.

'I can't help you, Jehane. I would if I could, but no one goes into the Wall but the Ged. And even if we six humans did, the Ged would not let you just follow along. They could keep you out – they can keep anyone from doing anything. But listen to me. We are very near a cure for the itching disease. They almost have it, Dahar and Creejin and Grax, and then the Ged will cure everyone within the Wall. They'll cure Talot. You'll have her back soon. And meantime she doesn't suffer, she's asleep inside the Wall.'

Jehane heard the change in Ayrys's voice. 'You're lying. You don't believe that.'

Ayrys looked at her, and even through her fury Jehane saw the sudden sharp anguish in the Delysian's eyes. Ayrys didn't believe her own words, but she wasn't lying either. It was something else – everything in R'Frow was something else, and the enemy kept changing. Delysia, Dahar, the Ged – there was no way to tell who to attack

and who to trust, and so how the darkcold could you fight
for anything?

'You won't get me inside the Wall?'

'I can't!' Ayrys cried, and now Jehane could not tell
whether Ayrys lied or not, Jehane dropped her threeball
and drew her knife.

But before she knew what she was going to do with it,
or who the enemy was this time, once more time began
to rise from the floor to hold her immobile. Ayrys had
already turned her Ged tubes and started back along the
corridor; her shoulders shuddered, and it came to Jehane
that she didn't know about the time-that-was-not-time, or
that the Ged were protecting her as well as Dahar. If
Jehane's knife had caught her in the back, she would not
have died surprised. *Stupidity. Courage.*

When Ayrys had rounded the corner back into the
teaching room, the stasis released Jehane. Grax stood
beside her, carrying some sort of bottle.

The Ged did not speak. He did not have to.

Jehane rushed from the Hall of Teaching and tore along
the wrof path. Morning surrounded her, choked her, pur-
sued her: The morning air of R'Frow, all of R'Frow, was
the enemy. The wrof path curved cleanly to the south
Wall. Jehane hurled herself against that gray cliff, right
shoulder slamming into the wrof, the rest of her body
shuddering under the impact.

'Talot!'

No answer.

She hurled her threeball at the Wall. The clanging was
loud enough to make her ears ring; she hurled it again,
and again. Neither wrof surface nor weapons so much as
scuffed, but eventually the cloth strap on the threeball
gave way and one sphere crashed into the wood of a dying
tree.

'Taaaaaallloottttt!'

People came running, Jehane turned to fight but then
saw that they were armed Jelite and sheathed her weapons

when the first sister-warrior warily approached. Too late, she saw through the raging red in her brain that the emblem had been ripped from the woman's shoulder – from all their shoulders – and then that they were not warriors at all but citizens. *Citizens armed*. The woman, though carrying a knife, was an untrained slug. Jehane dropped her with one blow.

The red fury left her instantly. She maneuvered for battle.

The men closed in on her. She kicked one in the groin and he fell, howling, but the other three carried Ged knives and they overpowered her. Even then she felt the hesitation, the citizens; awkwardness at handling a sister-warrior, and she turned it to advantage and nearly broke free.

'Hold her!' the second woman shrieked. 'Shit – *hold* her! She'll see – '

'She won't see anything,' one of the men gasped. 'Not till it happens.'

Jehane had his knife. But she had no room to turn, the other two still held her, and even for a sister-warrior the odds were too great. There was only time to hear the woman spit passionately, '. . . not trample on citizens anymore – this is *R'Frow*' before the man she had disarmed yanked back his fist and struck her, clumsily but hard, on the jaw. She went down with the word *R'Frow* closing around her like a kemburi.

55

SuSu walked across the open stretch of withered grass toward the hall where she had lived with him. She did not hurry; she did not leave the exact center of the wrof path, cool under her bare feet; she did not think that in the cloudy light her white tebl made a clear target. She did not think.

And yet, as Ayrys had said, she was not mad. She remembered everything that had happened, as it had happened, without distortion. But something in her mind had burned to extinction, as fully as wood burned in a too-hot kiln. Feeling was gone. SuSu remembered it all – the veld, the brother-warriors. Him, the place within the Wall – without reaction, as a series of pictures flickering in firelight, and as untouchable. She looked in dark silence at the pictures, but did not touch them, and missed the touching no more than the kiln misses the wood.

She stopped to remove a pebble from between her toes. Somehow it had come onto the smooth path. Her black straight hair swung sideways, cutting the air.

The pebble was smooth and round. The picture flickered again, the same one that had brought SuSu to this path: the sister-warrior with the weapon like three round pebbles: *Talot is in the Wall and the Ged took her there.* A sister-warrior. But sister-warriors did not push against the silence with words that anguished, and this strangeness had held SuSu for a little while before it, too, danced back into the wordless fire.

She tossed the pebble into the woods.

There was no one in the hall when SuSu strolled through the archway. Ged used this hall now, for humans to come to when they had the itching disease, but just now the hall was empty. SuSu did not wonder why. But someone had left something behind, so SuSu stooped to pick it up from the floor. She didn't know, or care, what it was: some small bit of strangely shaped wrof. But nonetheless SuSu held it for a moment against her cheek, not because it brought flickers of the Ged but because it brought flickers of Ayrys, who sat all day in wrof tubes of the same coolness as this piece of nothing much.

Ayrys was the one picture that did not flicker, did not change. Ayrys was the center of the fire, the white rock that did not burn. Once a huge man had been, but now it was Ayrys, because it must be somebody. She, SuSu, had once dragged Ayrys through the streets of Jela and Ayrys had been dead; now she was not dead. That seemed strange, sometimes.

But no stranger than the other pictures flickering in the silent fire.

Ayrys was the white rock. She was there even when she was not there, when the brother-warrior used her behind the closed door, as he had used SuSu in the Whores' Alley in Jela. But Ayrys would always come out from behind the door, back to SuSu. She had come back from being dead; she would come back from the closed door. She would always come back. She was not a sister-warrior, and she was not a man.

SuSu tossed away the bit of Ayrys-wrof.

The floor tables growled softly, and bowls of food arose. SuSu regarded them unblinkingly while pictures flickered in her mind: cool firelight that did not burn, words that did not hurt the silent because they were Ayry's.

'I can't help you, Jehane! I would if I could, but no one goes into the wall but the Ged!'

SuSu frowned.

Something made her glance at the wall beside the ladder. There was nothing there; the Ged, not wanting to upset the human who came for help with the itching disease, had covered the orange circle in the same way the humans had covered all the others.

SuSu removed four of the food bowls. Lying on the floor table, she curled herself as small as possible and waited. After a moment, she put her thumb in her mouth.

When the wrof closed over her, it struck her right shoulder and immediately stopped forming. SuSu hunched her shoulder smaller yet. The floor table seemed to shudder, as if undecided, and then closed her into darkness. She sank into the floor.

After being dumped onto a pile of food bowls, SuSu leisurely stood up, wiped herself off, and looked around.

Kreedogs: The image flickered coolly in her mind, faded. There were no kreedogs here. The room had changed dimension yet again, larger but lower, and now the partitions reached from floor to ceiling, clear wrof with one horizontal slit in the front of each. Voices called out to her: frenzied, angry, desperate, pleading. Hands reached through a few of the slits.

Carefully SuSu picked a chunk of stew out of her hair, turned back to put it on the pile of discarded food bowls.

She strolled closer to the pens. Behind the first, a naked Jelite woman sat slumped vacantly. Behind the next, a naked Delysian man was jumping up and down. He faced away from SuSu, toward the back wall, where a picture of a man moved. The picture jumped on one foot; the Delysian jumped on one foot. The picture put its hands on its head; the Delysian put his hands on his head. The picture sat down; the Delysian sat down.

SuSu watched him awhile. It seemed strange that the wall picture should move, that the man should put his hands on his head. He didn't notice her. After a while the strangeness faded, and SuSu walked along the other pens.

Humans crying. Humans in stupor. Humans dead. It
was all strange – for a moment.

'You! Whore!'

It was a naked red-haired woman in one of the pens,
her face incredulous. She thrust an arm through the slit
in the wrof. Long and bony, the arm nearly reached SuSu,
and she melted backward.

'Come closer! You, come here!'

SuSu didn't move. Her black eyes watched without
expression.

Talot's eyes glittered dangerously. Then she knelt to
bring her mouth closer to the slit and said clearly. 'You
are . . . SuSu. From the Hall of Teaching. Come closer,
I'm, not going to hurt you. You weren't brought by the
Ged – how did you get behind the Wall?'

SuSu said nothing.

'Can you leave again?'

Still SuSu said nothing. She remembered the red-haired
woman, in the same way she remembered everything else.
She was Talot, a sister-warrior. In a moment she would
fade.

Talot bit her lip. 'SuSu – if you can get out again, will
you take a message? To a sister-warrior from our teaching
group, Jehane? Do you know who she is? Answer me!
Shit on you, can't you hear me at all, you whore?'

A flicker of movement caught SuSu's eye. A man in
another cage had begun to have convulsions. For a
moment something terrible shrieked at the edge of SuSu's
memory, something that was not a flickering picture but
a howling solid – but then it was mercifully gone. SuSu,
too, turned to go.

'A message to Jehane!' Talot said desperately. 'You
know who she is, whore – she helped the Delysian woman,
Ayrys. The same Delysian who helped you!'

SuSu had begun to stroll away. At the sound of Ayrys's
name, she turned back, frowning a little.

'Yes, *Ayrys*,' Talot said. 'A message to Ayrys. Tell her

people are prisoners of the Ged. Tell her the Ged cured the itching disease but keep us here and force us to swallow doses – ' She shuddered, the tight and abruptly cutoff shudder of a person refusing to give in to fear. 'Tell her there are Delysians here, too, and tell her . . . Can't you hear me? By all – can't you *hear* me at all, you whore?'

SuSu stared flatly, waiting to hear Ayrys's name again. When it didn't come, she turned to go. Talot clenched her fists.

'Wait! You can't hear . . . take this to Ayrys. See, you know her name, you can hear her name. How the shit can you . . . Carry this to *Ayrys* SuSu. To *Ayrys*.'

Talot fumbled at her hair, freeing it from its warrior's knot. Lacing her fingers in a long red skein, she yanked viciously. A hank as thick as a finger tore loose. Talot winced in pain, knotted the tress deftly, and threw it out the slit in the wrof. It landed at SuSu's feet.

'To *Ayrys*,' Talot said.

A box: She had carried a box from this place. The memory flickered coolly. This was not a box, it was hair. That was strange. But the sister-warrior had said *Ayrys*, and SuSu picked up the hair and sauntered back the way she had come.

She lay on the same place on the floor, dreamily unbothered by either the waiting or the humans calling desperately from the pens. Eventually new food bowls rose from below. SuSu winced; they burned. But she didn't move.

When she had risen in the still-deserted hall, she rinsed herself and her white tebl in the baths, pulled on the tebl, and walked back to the Hall of Teaching. Along the way she frowned slightly. She could not find a picture in the cool flickering fire of memory. There had been a dark gray box, that other time. Now there was no dark gray box. What had happened to it? She searched, but could not remember.

But other memories flickered clearly: brother-warriors, sister-warriors, Whores' Alley and the hoping against hope for silence while warriors' hands reached for her mother . . .

Warriors.

She had nearly reached the Hall of Teaching when she tossed the knot of red hair behind a clump of dying brush.

56

After Jehane rushed from the Hall of Teaching, Ayrys faced Ondur.

She led Ondur down the corridor to her own room; there was no other way. Dahar was in the teaching room, and soon Lahab, Tey, Creejin, and Grax would come in.

Ondur's eyes burned. 'A Jelite brother-warrior. That's who it was that night you broke your leg, after *they* tried to kill you, and in our hall – *in our own hall* –'

'Ondur, listen to me –'

'Or did it start even before that? How could it start? A Jelite first lieutenant – how could you do this, Ayrys? It's like letting an animal touch you – you're diseased, you're not sane . . .'

Ayrys gripped the arms of her chair. It was Ondur's loathing that seemed animal: It twisted not only her face but her whole body, so that she stood with her spine drawn back and her face thrust forward, the upper lip wrinkled over bared teeth.

'I wish the Jelite had killed you instead.'

The words hung a moment in the closed room. Then Ayrys said coldly, 'What are you going to do about it?'

'Go to Kelovar. I came to tell you that he . . . You don't deserve to know!'

'Ondur, you can't.'

'You're a traitor to Delysia!'

'Am I? How? Do I know any of Khalid's plans? And what would Dahar do with them if I did? He's not a warrior any longer, and I'm not in the Delysian halls. Think, Ondur – it makes no difference to Delysia.'

But Ondur was beyond thought. 'You're a Delysian. And you let a Jelite put it between your legs – '

'If you tell Kelovar, you murder us both.'

'That would be cleaner than this.'

Her voice turned cold. Ayrys recognized the coldness; she had heard it in the council hall in Deylsia, with First-morning falling blood-red through the coloured glass windows. Exile.

'Then while you're thinking about Kelovar, think about this, Ondur. If he hunts down Dahar, it might be Dahar who kills Kelovar. And you would be responsible, you would have caused it . . . You were kind to me – you couldn't throw away three lives . . .'

Ondur's face did not soften. 'Who taught you to beg, Ayrys? Him? You sound like the whining Jelite citizens – is that the way it is between you two? He plays at still being a warrior and you play at being the cringing citizen, a brother-warrior's whore?'

'Ondur – '

But abruptly. Ondur broke. She put her hands over her face, and Ayrys floated her chair forward to grasp the hem of Ondur's tebl. Ayrys's voice came out in a whisper, but even so a part of her mind planned wildly. The dark box SuSu had once clenched in her hand never left the pouch in Ayrys's tebl; it was hard and sharp-edged. If she hurled it at Ondur's head . . .

'Please . . . don't tell Kelovar or Khalid, or anyone. There's no need, Ondur, there's no *reason* . . .'

Ondur took her hands away from her face. Ayrys saw there the same closed desolation she had seen when they had both nursed SuSu, and suddenly, irrelevantly, she knew that even if she and Ondur had come to know each other for years. Ondur would never have told what lay behind the desolation, or what had driven her from Delysia to R'Frow. Ondur had walled it away, and behind the wall lay only darkness.

'Please . . . there is no way I can threaten the Delysian halls, and no way Dahar can either.'

'You don't exist,' Ondur said. 'You are dead. You are an exile forever, and I never knew you.'

Ayrys sat motionless after Ondur had gone. Then she made her chair carry her to the teaching room.

They were all there. Dahar's eyes sought hers: *Danger?* She shook her head imperceptibly. There was no way here to explain, to question, and Dahar's face was already full of a different emotion, a different situation. She felt Grax's eyes on her. The Ged spoke directly to Ayrys in his calm, monotonous growl. He held the flask that the six had left in a bubble of clear wrof on the outside of R'Frow, the flask they had made cloudy with the bacteria-that-could-not-be-bacteria.

The flask was clear.

'You reasoned well, Ayrys. The light of Qom killed the unknown microlife. Whatever this life is, it cannot survive in the light of the Qom sun.'

'Light,' Dahar said fiercely. '*Light.*'

'Now if we can just turn it into a cure,' Tey said.

'No need,' Dahar said. 'Sunlight is free.'

Tey, lounging against the wall, said nothing.

Ayrys moved closer to Grax. Seen close up, the solution in the flask still looked clear, with only faint tracings of something that was no longer there.

They had done it. A victory, a triumph. They had killed the bacteria – or the not-bacteria – and so found the cure for the itching disease. They had, in this one tiny thing, gone beyond the Ged. They had triumphed.

'*It cannot survive in the light of the Qom sun,*' Then where had the microlife come from? From the Ged, from somewhere, from anywhere.

An exile.

'I think,' Tey said, 'that I have had enough biological science for today.'

The others looked at him. Ayrys saw what she had not seen before: that under his smooth indifference, Tey was furious. The pupils of his eyes had shrunk to pellets. Tey had expected a dose to cure the disease, as easy to carry to Delysia as the disease itself would have been.

Grax was watching Tey thoughtfully.

'I am tired too,' Ayrys said. She dared not, under Tey's fury, glance at Dahar. Carefully she turned her chair and made her way along the corridor. Her own room – with the other humans close behind her, she could not risk going to Dahar's. She would have to wait until he thought it safe to come to her to tell him what Jehane had said, what Ondur had threatened. But SuSu would be in her room.

SuSu was not there.

Ayrys closed the door. Lowering her chair to rest firmly on the floor, she swung her good leg from its supports. Then she eased the broken one from the stasis field. It did not ache – but she already knew, from leaving her chair to sleep or bathe, that healing had progressed that far. Now she wanted to know something else.

Sitting perpendicular to the arrangement of Ged tubes, Ayrys steadied herself on them and tried to stand. Her injured leg buckled and she fell, crying out with sudden pain.

Sprawled across the floor, she waited for the pain to subside and then crawled back into the Ged chair. The stasis field, unknowable mystery, surrounded her leg and the pain disappeared.

Now she knew. She could not do without the Ged numbness. She needed it.

The same as Dahar did.

He was a long time coming. And when he did, he looked stunned. For a long moment he stared at her with such naked intensity that Ayrys would have put out her arms except for the certainty, complete, that he did not see her at all.

'Belazir is dead.'

'How . . . how do you know?'

'Grax told me.'

He went on staring over her head at the wall, and for the first time Ayrys noticed that he carried the vial of clear broth, his knuckles white around the neck of the unbreakable bottle. She expected that when he finally looked at her – fortifying herself against it, fighting the sickness swamping her – she would see in his eyes the old resentment, the endless wall: *Delysian*. But it was not there. She saw his numb pain, and slithering behind it some other horror, and a new suspicion occurred to her.

'Not Delysian soldiers. It wasn't, was it, Dahar? The Ged killed Belazir.'

'The Ged?' he repeated, not taking it in. Then he did and fury swept his dark face, the swift and violent anger that must go somewhere and is viciously glad of a target. 'Why would you say that? Why would the Ged kill her?'

'I don't know. The disease – '

'We just found cause and cure for the disease. Weren't you there, sweet Ayrys? I thought I saw you there. Why would you even think that the Ged would kill the Jelite high commander? Why?'

Ayrys said nothing.

'Because you hoped it. Didn't you? You hoped Grax would finally justify all your suspicions and give you a reason to distrust him. But you didn't need a reason, did you? You've distrusted him from the first, even after he gave us what humans couldn't hope to discover on our own for lifetimes, gave us the entire *world* – and I thought you understood. I thought that out of all the minds in R'Frow, *you* understood . . . "Delsyia for treachery." '

She saw that he wanted to hurt her, and her patience, strained by Jehane and Ondur, snapped. 'What "treachery," Dahar? Whose? The Ged taught us to question and reason, and when I do, you call it treachery. You didn't hear what Jehane told me. She said her lover, Talot, had been taken behind the Wall by the Ged. Talot didn't go by choice, she was *taken*. Why? How do we know the humans behind the Wall are in stasis? How would we even know if the Ged had lied to us from the beginning?

'You believe the Ged because you want the science, but taking the science isn't enough; your twisted Jelite training demands you "honour" them as well. "Honour" doesn't come from the Ged science, Dahar. It doesn't come from any reason the Ged taught us, any forming of theories and making of tests. It comes from Jela. But you're bargaining with it as ruthlessly as Tey would – "Give me this science and I'll honor you Ged like a true brother-warrior, no matter what else you do in R'Frow."

'But you're not a true brother-warrior. Not anymore. And even if your high commander hadn't exiled you, you wouldn't be an honorable brother-warrior while you bargain like a Delysian, and decide that no price is too great to pay!'

She saw the violence her words did, and took pleasure in it.

He said through lips gone white, 'There is no price. You see one because you are Delysian, you see everything with a price on it. Like Tey with a cure – as if healing were a bit of worthless glass to be haggled over in a marketplace. You dare to talk of reason and tests – what reason do you have to believe Jehane? An untried sister-warrior, in love for the first time, too excitable and arrogant to make even a practice-yard leader . . . Belazir could see that with one glance. But you – *you*, who said you deserted your own halls for Ged science and reason – believe her with no proof, no testing, no reason. Except that you want to believe the Ged mean us harm. Why? Why do you want to believe that, sweet Ayrys?'

'Don't call me that!'

'Why do you want so badly to believe dishonor of the
Ged?'

'I don't *want* to believe dishonor of the Ged. I just . . .'
She faltered, seeing where the trap lay.

'You "just do." Without reason or evidence or theory
or proof. Very Delysian, sweet Ayrys.'

'Is it? Is it, Dahar? " Delysia for treachery" . . . Then
tell me this. Who did kill Belazir?'

He said nothing; not even the sudden anguish on his
face could stop her now.

'Not Khalid's soldiers. Not Ged. That leaves Jelite. Her
own warriors, over the Kreedogs *you* created? No. It was
Jelite citizens, wasn't it? Like SuSu and Lahab. Battered
on by your brother-warriors and sister-warriors and warrior-priests until they finally came to a place like R'Frow,
where warriors are not rulers anymore because the Ged
are, and suddenly you don't look so invulnerable anymore.
Your battered citizens see that the Ged are the real masters
in R'Frow, and they see their high commander turn over
two citizens to Kelovar, and Jehane – '

'Rescued you from them. You.'

'Yes! *Delysia* for treachery? And when Jehane comes to
ask for help because the Ged have taken one of your
warriors, the first thing you do is call her a liar!'

'Not one of *my* warriors,' he said coldly. 'You've made
that very clear.'

'Wasn't it clear before? But just because you're no
longer Jelite doesn't mean you can become Ged!'

'No more than just because you are no longer Delysian
means you are capable of any loyalty at all.'

His contempt scorched her. The nails of one hand dug
into the wrist of the other until blood flowed.

'Answer me this, Dahar. The new microlife that caused
the itching disease – Grax said it could not survive under
the light of Qom's sun. Those were his words. So if it did
not live on Qom, where did it come from?'

His eyes went still.

'It must have come to Qom with the Ged, on their starboats. Where else could it come from? Yet Grax said the Ged had never seen it before. How could that be, with all their vast science that can take apart the littlest pieces the world is made of? How could that be?'

She saw his mind, despite its fury, snag on the question, and refuse to either discard it or lie. Watching that, Ayrys knew she had never loved him as much as in that moment, when she hated him.

'I don't know. I will ask Grax.'

'Would you ask Tey how much he was cheating you, and expect to hear truth?'

'Don't try to trap me with my own hatreds, Ayrys!'

'Only with your own sense.'

'Don't try to trap me at all. I'll ask Grax about the microlife.'

'Ask him as well why he never told us about the orange circles.'

'He never lied about the orange circles.'

'To withhold knowledge is a kind of lie! Watching us . . .'

Dahar, raised in the communal watching of a brother-warriors' hall, grimaced in contempt.

'Then ask Grax where Talot is.'

'I don't need to ask him that. If she went to the Ged, she's being turned out right now from R'Frow, into the sunshine of Lightsleep. The veld will cure her. The Ged are opening R'Frow.'

Ayrys stared at him. 'How do you know?'

'Grax just told me.'

'The year is not over!'

'Their gift to humans is. But not for all of us, Ayrys. Not for the few human minds that can both understand and appreciate a gift like the Ged's . . . a gift, Ayrys. Not a bargain. Grax will take us on the starboat when the Ged leave Qom.'

The breath went out of her. Dahar, hard-eyed, watched

her without pity. 'Now. Today. Tey and Creejin have refused. He would rather return to Delysia and his filthy . . . He's not worth talking about. Lahab will come. And I. And you.'

The last was a question – rock-edged, without softness. Dahar folded his arms across his chest and waited, the wrof bottle still held by the neck in his right hand. Ayrys saw again that other bottle, blue and ill made, glinting in the moonlight as she hurled it at the kemburi plant on the veld. *Embry.*

'Let's at least have no treachery now, Ayrys. A straightforward question. Are you going on the Ged starboat?'

She looked at him. He hid nothing, with the passion a Jelite warrior counted first as courtsey, and then as virtue. Belzair's death, the pain they were causing each other, the dazzle of the Ged starboat – all hardened even as she watched into a determination no reasoning could touch. He would go with Grax. He would go on the starboat. He would look at nothing that dimmed that vision.

He was, in a differing way, as blind as Kelovar.

'Are you going on the starboat, Ayrys?'

She clamped her lips shut and looked down. Dahar gripped her chin with one hand and wrenched her face upward to meet his gaze.

'Are you going to the starboat?'

Ayrys shuddered; he was hurting her. 'If I say no . . . you will go without me.' It was not a question.

Dahar released her chin. He stood looking at her bleakly, from a great height.

She said, suddenly drained of fury. 'The Ged science. At any price.'

Emotions warred on his face. But when he finally answered her, it was with the same quietness, and there was no victory for her in how much his words conceeded.

'Yes. At any price.'

They could not look at each other.

'Dahar. Be careful, until . . . you leave. Kelovar may be have been told about . . . me.'

'Will he – '

'No. He would kill you, not me.' Kelovar would never be able to admit she had chosen a Jelite warrior over a Delysian soldier. He would remake the truth to suit what he believed.

As Dahar was doing.

'Be . . . careful.'

She heard his struggle to answer. 'Grax will take us behind the wall. Now. Lahab and me. We were only waiting for . . . you.'

Ayrys squeezed her eyes tightly shut. When she felt his hand on her shoulder, she knocked it off so violently that she wrenched the muscles in her shoulder. Dahar drew in a quick breath.

She heard the door open, and close.

57

Someone had turned up the temperature ten units, almost
to celebration levels. Pheromones hung redolent and lush
on the warm air. There was a persistent undersmell of
anxiety and uncertainty, but none of the seventeen Ged
asked the Library-Mind to lower the temperature. Celebration was more important than correctness.

They were going home.

Going home with humans aboard ship, going home with
the last news from the Fleet a massacre by those same
humans, going home without an answer to the Central
Paradox – but *going home*. Voices growled in the configurations of fact, breaking occasionally even into those of
deliberate unfactual whimsy, which none of them had
used since coming to this wretched and immoral planet.
Hands stroked backs, limb, heads. The powerful, subtle
fragrance of the premating smells teased the skin.

Only Grax was absent, talking still to male humans who
would have to come aboard ship.

The celebration was especially sweet because none of
them had expected to be able to leave Qom before the
entire 'year' had passed. But after hours of circular discussion – so satisfying in itself – that had taken all 'night,'
it had been decided they must take the five humans that
remained of the six who had felt loyalty to the Ged.

That grammar still grated on the ear.

There was no reason to delay. The experiments in
suggestibility, to chemically control the humans aboard

ship, had failed. All the chemicals that produced compliance had destroyed intelligence; all those that had left intelligence intact had not made the captive humans any more suggestible.

'If we had time to refine the test . . .' said Wraggaf.

'Harmony sings with us.'

'Harmony sings. If we had time – '

'Time is what we don't have.'

'Time. May it always sing with us.'

'It will always sing. The experiments with minds were useless.'

'Useless.'

'Harmony sings with us.'

'It is the human intelligence,' said Fregk, deliberately using grammars that did not quite fit together, smelling of distaste.

Krak'gar said, 'Human intelligence. It's like a black hole, sucking up ideas that took the Ged the lives of suns to form. Powerful. Destructive.'

The others saw the rest of the metaphor immediately, and completed it: the poetry of civilization, in which all created together.

'Ged intelligence.'

'A steady sun.'

'Burning slowly, giving light.'

'Nourishing life.'

'Permitting moral solidarity.'

'Harmony sings with us!'

They were going home.

The three humans to be aboard ship were a problem. Ged had transported animals before, of course – but not like this. The three humans would need to move freely, believing themselves allies of the Ged; they must also be confined, since they were not Ged. It would strain the pheromones of all, particularly the Ged who had stayed aboard ship all along, to whom the humans were so far only images transmitted over the Library-Mind. It was a problem. And there was, as always on this malodorous planet, no time.

And then they learned that there was even less.

The Library-Mind said, 'Significant data.' It had been asked not to break in on the celebration unless something urgent happened; the next moment Grax spoke directly, through the Library-Mind, into the room.

'Two of the humans refuse to come aboard ship. Tey and Creejin.' At the same moment the Library-Mind said, 'The human who sang in harmony for the "Jelite" has been killed by them.'

There was a whimper from Grax.

They all heard his strain, out beyond the walls with the beasts, and immediately smells reached out for him, laced with the frustration of not being able to reach him. The anxiety undersmell increased. The Ged began to growl softly in reassurance, but the Library-Mind was not transmitting to Grax, only from him, and the priority of significant data overrode all else.

'. . . kill her,' a voice replayed: deep, unexcited, with such deadly pleasure that the Ged heard it even in that alien grammar, that alien mind.

A sound, unidentifiable. Then the thud of something striking the floor.

Grax began to talk, too fast, to the human Dahar. Three Ged at once said to Grax, through the Library-Mind but not wanting for its corroboration, 'Bring the other three humans safely inside the Wall now.'

Grax said, '. . . to tell Ayrys alone, Dahar? I will tell her.'

'No. It *is* necessary. She . . . I will tell her?' The human voice was shaky with the excitement the seventeen had learned to recognize by sound, and with emotions they had not.

'*Now*,' the Library-Mind said in configuration of greatest urgency.

Grax said, 'Because you are mating partners? Coming with the Ged is a sexual communication?'

The seventeen heard Dahar laugh, and this time none of them knew what the human sound meant.

'I'll bring her here.'

The Library-Mind said to Grax, 'When you bring them inside the perimeter, don't enter by the Ged door. Humans are committing violence by the east wall. Dahar should not see it. Bring them through the Wall behind the empty hall, north of the room holding the experimental animals. An airlock chamber will be ready with human atmosphere.'

Dahar said – at a greater distance from the sensor, as though he had begun to leave and paused in the doorway – 'Grax. I have never told you . . . you are what the Jelite warrior-priest masters should have been. You, and the Ged . . .' A long pause, and then, painfully, 'We stand on the same blade, bound in the honor of life itself. What you have given freely I can never return. But for whatever measure it has, I would serve you any way I could, Grax. And I will.'

For a while, there was no sound. Then the Library-Mind began to transmit the conversation between Dahar and Ayrys. It would not have done so if it had not found the content significant.

Ayrys's voice: '. . . didn't know what Jehane told me. She said her lover Talot had been taken behind the Wall by the Ged. She didn't go by choice, she was *taken*. Why? How do we know the humans behind the Wall are in stasis? How would we even know if the Ged had lied to us from the beginning? . . .'

Someone told the Library-Mind to lower the temperature of the room.

58

Afterward, Ayrys never knew how long she sat there in the dark.

When she came back to herself – back from the empty place where there was no R'Frow, no Dahar, no Embry – it was to a slow thumping on the door, steady yet tentative, as if the knocker were both afraid to have the door open and afraid to have the door not open. Numbly, Ayrys moved her chair across the room. SuSu crouched in the orangey light of the corridor, her black eyes huge in a dead white face.

'You saw him leave,' Ayrys said, realizing. SuSu had seen Dahar, a brother-warrior armed, leave in anger, and what memories had it touched in her child-whore mind? Yet she had not run to hide, had not left Ayrys, just as once she had not left the dying barbarian who could no longer protect her from her own kind.

Gently she said to SuSu, 'I'm not hurt. He didn't hurt me,' and heard the mockery in her own gentleness.

'Where did he go, SuSu? Dahar – did you see where he went?'

The black eyes stared at her, no longer terrified but opaque and shiny, unreadable as a wall.

The sudden smell of burning filled the room. Next to the two women, the cloth covering the orange circle began to smoke. Singeing first in the center, where it was stretched tautest over the wrof, the cloth charred until it burst into flames. Shreds fell to the floor and burned harmlessly on the metal. When the orange circle was free, the fire went out.

'They wanted to see us again,' Ayrys whispered. She held her hand toward the wall; the orange circle was still warm, although cooling rapidly.

SuSu had barely glanced at the burning circle. She seized Ayrys's hand and tugged her forward.

Too harshly, Ayrys said, 'There's no place to go, SuSu. Don't you understand? There's no place to go!'

But Ayrys suddenly didn't want to stay in the sight of that orange circle, between these walls of Ged wrof – yet there *was* nowhere else to go. Not even exile was possible when the place of exile died. This, then, must have been what Kelovar had felt, all these cycles: trapped in a rotting city, no escape possible, shut away from the Kelovar he had once been. Watching himself grow into something else, as surely as the diseased microlife had grown in the hectic heat and dimness away from open light.

Light. There was no light anywhere, not in R'Frow nor Jela nor Delysia . . .

SuSu had led her out the archway. A weird yellow brightness crawled across the dome overhead.

'SuSu – what is *that*?'

SuSu didn't answer. Overhead the brightness leaped, and in the distance smoke rose toward the colorless wrof that was not sky. Shouts and cries rose with the smoke.

They were burning R'Frow.

'Who?' Ayrys said aloud. The fire burned south of the Hall of Teaching, away from both Jelite and Delysian halls. '*Who?*'

'Jela,' SuSu said clearly.

Startled to hear SuSu's voice, Ayrys turned sharply. SuSu was smiling, and in another burst of brightness overhead her white teeth gleamed, sharp and small.

'Jelite citizens,' Ayrys said slowly. 'The ones who killed Belazir. Because of the way the warriors . . . ruled . . .'

SuSu's smile widened.

Ayrys reached down and fingered the grass. The fire was not close, and the bursts of light reflected off the dome seemed bright only to eyes that had spent a year in dimness. The grass was very dry, but even as her fingers closed on it, water began to fall: the gentle drizzle that passed in R'Frow for rain. Did it start in response to the fire? Was the fire why the Ged finally burned the cloth off the orange circles?

If they did it now, they could have done it anytime they chose.

More shouts, this time very close.

SuSu disappeared into the brush; one moment she was there, the next not. Two Delysian soldiers, male and female, tore around the corner of the Hall of teaching. They caught sight of Ayrys, and the woman stopped.

'Come on!' the other shouted, grabbing her arm.

'Wait. This is one of *them*.' Her eyes, gray under braided fair hair, raked Ayrys.

'One of who? Come on, she's Delysian!'

'She's not Delysian. She's Ged. She's one of the traitors that slits Ged, like that slug Tey.'

The man hesitated, glanced toward the fire. 'Leave her. Khalid's going to need every knife.'

'No! They're traitors, living with the Ged to get closer to Jela!' The woman twined her hand in Ayrys's hair and brought her knife closer. 'A Ged knife. A Ged death for a Ged traitor, yes, Ayrys?'

'Ayrys?' the man said. He stopped staring at the fire and looked at Ayrys. 'That's her?'

'Let me go, Urwa! Damn it – '

'Don't be stupid! You know what Kelovar said – '

'Shit on Kelovar!' the woman hissed. 'How will he know?'

'Don't touch her, I tell you,' Urwa said, and now his voice, heretofore hurried and indifferent, held such deadly warning that the woman hesitated. 'Kelovar means it.'

The woman let go of Ayrys's hair. Urwa began again

to run toward the fire, but the woman, frustrated of her prey, grabbed the wrof tubes of Ayrys's chair, dumped Ayrys to the ground, and raised the chair over her head. With all her strength she slammed it on the ground.

Wrof was not bone. Nothing broke.

She tried twice more. Urwa cursed, seized her arm, and dragged her forward. The woman glared down at Ayrys, gasping on the ground – and took the chair with her, toward the fire.

Ayrys lay still until the ache in her leg subsided. It was not bad, not as bad as she expected, if she put no weight on it. She looked after the soldier, running bizarrely toward battle with a Ged stasis field in her arms, and closed her eyes. *R'Frow*.

When she opened them, SuSu had reappeared, squatting beside her on the path. She put her small hands in Ayrys's armpits and began to pull.

'No, don't . . . don't, it only makes it worse. I have to crawl.' But she leaned a moment against SuSu's small body.

The shouting was continuous now. From the distance a scream came, too far off to prickle the spine. Ayrys began to crawl back toward the Hall of Teaching. There would be, at least, a door to lock. Panic rose in her like bile, and more figures came around the Hall of Teaching.

They ran past her. But Ayrys had already begun to hide, dragging herself off the wrof path into the scrub brush. A pounding foot nearly stepped on her bad leg. Then that group was gone, but shouts rose again, closer.

Ayrys pulled herself deeper into the scrub. Rain slithered into her eyes, and twigs snapped her face. Fear took her. She was back on the veld, hunted; she was back by the deserted wrof hall, her leg seized and raised above the rock. Panic blinded her as much as rain. With both hands she grasped the thorny base of a bush and squirmed under it as far as she could.

Her forehead struck something hard.

She nearly cried out, stopped herself. At the same time that blood began to trickle down her forehead, her hand closed on something slippery and soft.

The something hard was a projection of wrof, rising from the forest floor close to the trunk of the bush, and hidden by it. Ayrys explored the projection with her fingers. It was cylindrical, with nothing to break its even surface. No orange circle for seeing; there would be nothing to see this low to the ground and hidden by thick foliage. Nothing to see, even though the projection was only meters from one of the most traveled paths in R'Frow. Nothing to see.

The something soft and slippery was a knotted hank of red hair.

All traces of panic and fear suddenly left her. She ran her hand over the rippling red hair. '*You believe Jehane with no proof, no testing, no reason.*'

No proof.

The bushes parted quietly. SuSu, so small she barely disturbed the scrub, slipped through and squatted by Ayrys, looking at the rainsoaked hair.

To anyone else, the girl-child's unchildlike expression would not appear to have changed. But Ayrys, shadowed by SuSu for tencycle after tencycle, caught the tensing of the soft curve of jaw, and the glint that came and went over the empty blackness of SuSu's eyes.

'Talot,' Ayrys said. SuSu raised her face. The two women stared at each other: Ayrys stretched on her stomach on the wet ground, streaked with dirt and blood; SuSu with her black hair plastered flat to her skull by the rain, impassive as white stone.

'How did it come here, SuSu? How did Talot's hair get here?'

No answer.

'Did you see it? Did you see the Ged take away Talot?'

Silence.

'Did you see the Ged take Talot into the Wall?'

No answer.

Ayrys drew a deep breath. Her fingers grasped SuSu's wrist and she was shocked all over again by how much thumb and forefinger overlapped. This was a child. How far could she push a child? And without clear explanations, without revealing words. Sound – unlike light – would go through a cover of cloth, or a projection of wrof. And it would be at least as clear as listening inside a helmet.

'SuSu. You are Jelite. Not a sister-warrior' – again that furtive glint, all that SuSu had been permitted of hatred – 'but still Jelite. I have saved your life when you lay helpless, and helped you with the . . . with your lover while he lived – do you remember?'

There was no response.

'I helped you. We stand on the same blade, bound in the honor of life itself. What is freely given must be freely returned.'

SuSu did not move. Ayrys, not sure what SuSu understood, or what the effect of this desperate obscenity would be on a mind Ayrys could not have understood even when it was whole, tightened her grip and blundered on. She could not – *You babble of things you don't understand. Delysian* – remember the correct words. The rain fell harder, but the weird brightness still crawled across the dome.

'You have to help me, SuSu. In all honor. What is freely given must be freely returned!'

With a violent wrench, SuSu yanked her wrist free and backed away, branches whipping closed behind her.

Ayrys squeezed her eyes shut and made herself count while she waited. *One, two, three, four* . . . Lights danced behind her eyelids.

Brush crackled. SuSu had returned, blood and rain on her white face, her black eyes glittering with resentment and pain and something hard and Jelite that Ayrys knew she had never understood and never would. Alive. The flat black eyes had come alive. Ayrys forced herself to not look away from that life. *I am sorry, SuSu.*

'Help me to the path,' Ayrys said. She did not need the help, but she needed to keep SuSu close. Slowly she crept through the brush at an angle to the path, ending beside it but as far as from the listening projection as she dared take the time to go. The dragging sent dull pain along her leg.

She put her mouth close to SuSu's ear and whispered. The tiny girl was not trembling; what seethed in her showed only in her eyes.

'SuSu. Is Talot inside the Wall?'

SuSu nodded.

'Did the Ged take her there?'

Another nod.

'Did you see her taken away?'

SuSu shook her head.

'Then how do you know she's inside?'

A sudden tightening of every muscle in the small body. SuSu ducked her head, and her breath came faster. All at once Ayrys saw that it was *words* SuSu was afraid of: sound, speech. She could see whatever she had seen, go wherever she had gone to see it, but breaking her silence with words to describe it filled her with terror.

'SuSu. Dear heart . . . how do you know Talot is inside the wall?'

SuSu gasped. 'Saw her.'

'You . . . *saw* her? You went inside the Wall?'

SuSu nodded.

'*How?*'

'In a food table. I . . . wanted to find . . . Don't let the voices, don't . . . let the *voices* – '

'I won't. I won't let anything hurt you. You went inside to find your lover, didn't you? That first time. That's where you got the wrof box.'

SuSu tried to nod. Ayrys put her arms around her and held her tight, and instead of fighting, SuSu clutched at her and clung. Overhead the dome brightened; the rain was losing to the fire. Somewhere in the distance a woman screamed.

'Don't let . . . voices . . .'

'No. No, it's safe here, dear heart, it's threeday again, I'm here, I'm here . . .' She might have been comforting Embry. But the crooning did not seem to help, and after a moment SuSu pulled away and looked at Ayrys with her old look, flat and black, and whispered, 'What is given . . . must be returned . . .'

She was not Embry, and she had seized her own bizarre comfort.

Ayrys, her voice husky with pity and admiration, whispered, 'Where is Talot now?' Is she inside the same part of the Wall where they took your lover?'

SuSu nodded.

'Is she alive?'

Another nod.

'Is Talot the only one there? Or are all the humans who took sick with the itching disease in there?'

'All.'

'Are they all alive? SuSu?'

'No. Some are dead. Some are . . . alive but not whole.'

'Alive but not whole? What do you mean?'

SuSu took a long time to answer. 'Like me.'

Ayrys couldn't answer. SuSu looked at her with flat black eyes.

'Did Talot give you the hair? What did she want you to do with it? Take it to Jehane?'

'Sister-warrior,' SuSu said, and her eyes were no longer flat.

SuSu hated the sister-warriors more than the men, Ayrys realized, and realized also that she did not understand why. She was not Jelite, and there were mazes and walls, shadows and variations of light, her Delysian eyes did not see.

'SuSu. You must take this message for me. Not for Talot, for *me*.'

'Not to a sister-warrior. Not.'

'No. To Dahar.'

SuSu sat wordless while Ayrys held her breath. Then SuSu picked up the hank of Talot's hair and melted into the brush.

What is freely given must be freely returned.

Ayrys laid her cheek against the wet ground. They had none of them, from the moment they entered R'Frow, been free.

The Ged had used them all – Dahar, her, Belazir and Khalid, the humans inside the Wall. But *why*? 'Like me,' SuSu had said. The Ged had done something to the minds of the humans with the itching disease – but not to those who remained within R'Frow. What had they done to the others? Doses . . . the dose Dahar had first given her for her broken leg had done things to her mind, made her talk, and it was long rumored that warrior-priests knew doses that would poison or drive mad, some subtly and some not. And what humans knew, Ged must know even better . . . but perhaps not for human minds. Human minds must be different to them, just as human lungs breathed different air, different in blood and muscle and bone . . . Ayrys saw again the white giant being carried into the Wall, to die there, and gripped her hands together hard.

Dahar . . .

But the Ged had also given them riches beyond measure, all the riches of their science, patiently leading whatever humans who wished out of ignorance they had not even known they had. Why? What did the Ged gain from it?

She saw that she was thinking like a Delysian trader, like Tey. *Jela for honesty. Delysia for treachery* . . . but not treachery like this. This was new on Qom. But why? What did the Ged hope to gain?

Abruptly, she smelled smoke.

The dome still crawled with weird light, red and gold, flickering as the fire flickered. But already the light was darkening with smoke. A sudden gust of wind bent the bushes around Ayrys – real wind, where there had never been wind before. Some device of the Ged to blow away the smoke? How big was the fire? And how big the combat around it?

More smoke blew toward Ayrys. If SuSu became frightened of the fire, or if she was caught by Delysian soldiers or Jelite warriors, or if she went to lock herself in Ayrys's room, behind the safety of a door . . . SuSu's mind was such fragile glass to lean against.

But was it? To go into the Wall inside a food table . . . the Ged had not thought of *that*. They put the orange circles everywhere to watch humans, but they had not thought of a girl tiny enough, or a mind different enough, to do that. And once inside, SuSu had seen . . .

Why?

Ayrys tried to think calmly. The Ged had said, from the first day, that they wanted to learn how humans thought. But they had learned only in part, as she had learned only in part what strangeness moved in Jelite minds. Even Dahar's. Even Kelovar's, who was not Jelite but whose thoughts had grown more opaque to her as she lived with him. Firstnight falling over his mind . . .

'Humans of R'Frow,' a voice growled from the wrof projection hidden in the brush. 'You will stop this violence. A cure has been found for the itching disease. All the humans within the Wall will be cured of the itching disease. The cure is sunlight. The sunlight of Qom cures the disease; its biology is not adjusted to the light of Qom. In a few hours the gates of R'Frow will be opened and all humans will pass out into the sunlight. You will stop this violence. This burning and killing.'

The distant shouting did not stop.

'Humans of R'Frow . . .'

Ayrys stared at the brush, in the direction of the wrof she could not see.

Darkness. Sunlight.

Light . . .

Light was the thumblock, had always been the thumblock. *Its biology is not adjusted to the light of Qom.* No, because the microlife came from somewhere else, some other light, along with the Ged. So much had she said to Dahar.

But now she stood again looking on R'Frow for the first time after waking from stasis, Kelovar beside her with a day's stubble on his chin, the same as he had had in the camp beyond the Wall. She saw again for the first time the gray clouds of R'Frow, the orangy dimness, when it should have been Darkday. She felt again her own ignorant, animal terror: *They had altered the sun.* And she heard the calm Ged voice growl words she was not then equipped to understand: *The light has been adjusted to match your biological pattern, sixteen hours of light followed by eight hours of darkness.*

Not then equipped to understand. Not then.

The microlife had not taken to Qom light because it came from elsewhere, from some half-believed other world out there in the stars. But the humans of R'Frow had taken easily to sixteen hours of light and eight hours of darkness – so easily, like kemburi to Firstmorning. Kemburi did not open to Darkday, did not try to stir to wakefulness in the cold and dark . . . *The light has been adjusted to match your biological patterns, sixteen hours of light followed by eight hours of darkness.*

The microlife biological pattern came from elsewhere. The human biological patterns . . .

Ayrys's mind reeled.

Carefully, as if thoughts were molten glass and could maim by their own heat and brightness. Ayrys backed away from her reasoning. It could not be. Yet, at the same time, she thought that this same reasoning, this careful

chaining of one idea to the next, was Ged science, and
she would not even have been able to do it had the Ged
not taught her how. She breathed deeply; the air smelled
of smoke and decay, and the rain that was not rain brought
down ash in gritty, sodden flecks.

She reached again toward the molten glass.

The Ged wanted Dahar aboard their starboat. Dahar,
herself, Tey, Creejin, Ilabor, Lahab – the best human
minds in R'Frow. But even the best human minds could
not think of any science the Ged did not know. Had the
Ged already known that the new microlife would be killed
by Qom sunshine? They must have. They knew about
human biology and light . . .

They knew about human biology and light. *Before* they
studied humans in R'Frow.

Suddenly dizzy, Ayrys closed her eyes for a moment.
The Ged wanted Dahar and the others aboard the starboat, sailing through the sky to other worlds, thinking
like humans out away from Qom, where humans were.
Out where humans must be, where sixteen hours of light
were followed by eight hours of darkness. Where other
humans must be, not on Qom but somewhere else, under
other and kinder suns . . . under alien light. But, no, it
was the light of Qom that was alien to humans; some
other sun was the one adjusted to human biology, and
Jelite and Delysian were the aliens on Qom, under an
alien light . . .

She could not grasp it, could not hold it. The idea was
too large. Ayrys felt the reasoning slide away from her,
melt into doubt and questions, even as the brush parted
and SuSu crouched there alone, black hair plastered wetly
against her skull and Talot's hair in her hand.

'Gone,' SuSu said. 'Brother-warrior and citizen. Gone
inside the Wall with Ged.'

59

On the screens within the perimeter, the fire burned.

The artificial drizzle had finally dampened it from leaping flames to a fitful and sullen burning. Humans moved, blackened and bloody, in and out of visual tracking. Burned flesh came away in patches on withered grass.

A Jelite citizen crept from behind a building and stood over two fallen, facedown figures. Cautiously, poised to run despite his drawn knife, he turned one figure over with his foot. The Delysian soldier stared from one dead eye; the other hung over his cheek by a bloody shred of flesh.

The Jelite stared downward for a long moment, and did not touch the body. With the same caution, he turned over the other figure.

The sister-warrior still lived, though barely. The soldier's knife hilt stuck from her belly. She looked up at the face of the citizen and then past him, to the smoke and light of the dome. Her lips moved, without words. From the harsh shape of her mouth, the wordless utterance was a command.

Swiftly the citizen knelt. He pulled the knife from her belly, spat on it, waited to see that she saw, and cut her throat.

One of the watching Ged moaned, the kind of noise made only by cubs. The other four in the room, though equally sickened, tried to move closer and soothe him, but the body did not obey the mind and went into genetic

shock: *an intelligent species slaughtering its own kind*. There
was not in this morally and biologically depraved killing
even the artificial idea of two human subspecies: This was
'Jelite' killing 'Jelite.' That artificial idea, imposed on the
body by the mind, had been more protection to the Ged
than they had realized. Now it had failed, and the genetic
recoil – as much an evolutionary survival mechanism as
an opposable thumb – reasserted itself: *an intelligent species
slaughtering its own kind*.

The Ged lost control of his pheromomes. Smells
vomited out of him.

'Significant data,' the Library-Mind said. 'Significant
data, Level Matrix.'

60

Ayrys grasped SuSu's hand, as if afraid the girl would melt back into the brush. But SuSu sat stolidly, her white tebl blackened in smoky streaks, the cloth torn over one small naked shoulder. She still held the knot of Talot's hair.

It had stopped raining.

'SuSu, how do you know Dahar and Lahab have gone into the Wall? Did you see Grax take them inside?'

'Yes.'

'By . . . by force?'

SuSu shook her head.

'Where? Through the Ged door in the east wall?'

Again SuSu shook her head. 'Fighting there.'

'Then where?'

'The place.'

Ayrys tried to think what SuSu might mean. 'The place where Grax and Dahar took the giant through the Wall? The same place?'

SuSu nodded.

Ayrys touched the hank of wet hair in the girl's hands. 'You must take another message for me, SuSu. You must. To Jehane.'

'No.'

'What is given – '

'No!' The black eyes leaped again into life, and glittered.

Ayrys clenched her fist around the hem of SuSu's tebl,

but the girl did not try to leave. What words would move her, would grab and hold something solid in the slippery darkness of that mind, as for a moment SuSu had been held by the bizarre perversion of the warriors' oath of honor? Ayrys tried to think, tried to speak without fear, and knew she failed. 'You would have gone to Dahar for me, a brother-warrior who used you as a whore. How could it be worse to go to a sister-warrior who never bedded you, never forced you to . . . SuSu, Dahar is in danger, like your lover was in danger. And like that, he is my lover. Just the same.'

For a giddy moment Ayrys thought she had convinced her. Something moved behind SuSu's eyes, and she looked down at the hair in her hand, as if she didn't see it but something else. If SuSu would bring Jehane . . .

But when SuSu looked up, her black eyes were unreadable. She opened Ayrys's fingers, one by one, and freed her tebl.

'Then I will bring your other man.'

'My *other* . . . SuSu, you can't – '

But SuSu had already gone, passing soundlessly into the brush.

Kelovar. She could only mean Kelovar. She had listened to Ayrys and Ondur, listened to the Delysians who had tried to smash the Ged chair, listened for tencycles to rumours no one had thought she could understand. But there was no way she would be able to get to Kelovar. He would be where the battle was, fighting by Khalid's side, and SuSu would not go into the fighting . . .

SuSu had gone into the Wall. Twice.

Ayrys gripped her hands together hard. She could not sit here and hope for SuSu's return. SuSu was too small, and whatever lights flickered in her mind were too unsteady, strange washes over a bleak and unknown landscape. No one could rely on SuSu.

Keeping to the very edge of the path, Ayrys began to drag herself toward the Wall.

61

'This is an "airtebl." '

Within the small, newly created room in the perimeter, Grax handed Dahar and Lahab rectangular plates of clear wrof, roughly the size of a man's palm. They took them awkwardly.

'You will place it here,' Grax continued. The plate was flexible and very thin; when the two humans pressed it to their chests as Grax had indicated, it molded itself to the body and clung.

'Press first on the thin bottom edge, at both corners, like this . . . no. Lahab, use this finger and the thumb. You will need to keep your excess finger away from any contact.'

The fifth finger could be amputated aboard ship, if the humans wished; Grax did not think they would. Activating the wrof was a deliberately complex maneuver, so it would not happen accidentally. The humans would be wearing the lifesuits aboard most of the ship, since only their own rooms would carry human-breathable air; they would become accustomed to the sequence of fingerings. Already Dahar's fumblings were better than most cubs.

Grax smelled himself, and looked away.

He had broken the link with the Library-Mind and instructed it not to override except in life-threatening emergency. Now he thought of a story that would have been part of Dahar's instruction, had he actually been a cub. It was a teaching, terrifying and strong, of a Ged lost

alone in the blackness of space, his Oneness mates all
dead, and even his pheromones of loneliness vanished –
because there was no one else left to smell them. Solidarity
did not exist without perception of it. Without solidarity,
reality itself did not exist.

Dahar would never smell pheromones. He would never
go into Oneness trance, never sing in the harmony of
solidarity. His was the most number-rational mind Grax
had ever taught, and it was the mind not of a cub but of
an animal.

Paradox was inherent in the physics of the universe,
even in the configurations of certainty; it was rational. But
paradox never existed in the configuration of Oneness and
solidarity. Watching Dahar's ugly face twitch and distort
– too many facial muscles, too much subcutaneous fat –
as the human probed at the wrof, Grax smelled his own
shame at longing for what was both impossible and
obscene: to share the trance of Oneness with this number-
rational mind to which he had taught so much, of so much
lesser importance.

He watched Dahar turn over the wrof plate with wonder
and passionate intelligence, and met the animal's eyes
across an impossible void, more lightless than space.

'Like this,' Dahar said, and fingered the entire
sequence. From the wrof plate, the lifesuit formed around
him.

62

Ayrys had crawled halfway to the Wall when darkness fell: not the gradual false twilight of R'Frow nor the murky gray that passed for night, but a sudden total blackness, deep as in the windowless rooms of the halls. There was no glow on the dome; the fire must have been put out by the rain. To her left the orange circles on the outside of the Hall of Teaching bit through the blackness, fangs of light in midair. Somewhere, not close, screams rose to meet them.

Why the blackness? To stop the slaughter? But battle had been raging for – how long now? Long enough; the killing must be mostly over. If the Ged hoped to stop the fighting, why hadn't they cut off the light when the fighting first started? Or was the blackness due to something else, some failure of the unimaginable devices in the dome?

In the blackness, her leg pulsed with pain. Ayrys laid her cheek against the tough, withered grass.

If the false light had failed because the Ged machinery was not built to deal with large fires – if SuSu could enter the Wall because the Ged machinery was not built to deal with madness . . . if that were true, the Ged were not invincible.

Suddenly, as abruptly as the plunge into darkness, there was light: a weird orange glow, much dimmer than had illuminated R'Frow before and with a strange thickness, as if light could be heavy. Under that errie and lurid half-light, the smooth path became a twisting orange mirror. Trees and bushes looked as if they were underwater, drowning in a poisoned sea.

Pointless gusts of wind began to blow.

Ayrys heard footsteps behind her, and then Kelovar stood over her with another soldier behind him, dragging SuSu by one powerful hand clamped over her wrist. Blood saturated Kelovar's tebl and leggings. Ayrys struggled to turn her leg over and sit up.

'Ayrys,' Kelovar said tonelessly, not releasing SuSu. His eyes, preternaturally pale in his smoke-blackened face, were shards of light. In his watchful tonelessness Ayrys saw how dangerous he was. To do whatever he had been doing, he had cut off all thought, and on his face was the unthinking blankness of pure action. Ayrys thought that he would be as likely to kill her as help her, and without thinking much about either. What had Ondur said about the doses soldiers took before battle?

She shuddered inwardly and fought to keep her voice strong. Any sign of weakness would be lethal. She must sound as strong as the Ayrys he thought he remembered, the Ayrys he had forbidden Urwa to harm.

'Let SuSu go, Kelovar.'

He did, flipping her to the ground like a tossed pebble. Ayrys saw that SuSu still held the hank of Talot's hair; what had Kelovar made of that? The other soldier looked toward SuSu, shifted slightly toward her, glanced at Kelovar, and remained where he was. SuSu slid sideways into the bushes, but not before Ayrys caught the look of pure terror on the girl's face.

'You were right about the Ged,' Ayrys said, as firmly as she could manage. Where in the brush was the nearest wrof projection? Were the Ged listening? 'I've come to see that you were right – and for reasons you don't even know yet.'

'What reasons?' Kelovar said, still tonelessly.

Ayrys made herself keep her eyes from his bloody knife:

How many? Jehane? More blood matted his hair, and in the random gusts of wind, sticky locks blew stiffly across his shoulders.

'You heard the Wall. It said the Ged had found a cure for the itching disease. But I've been with the Ged in the Hall of Teaching for tencycles now. I know they already knew how to cure the disease – and kept it from humans.'

Something flickered behind his eyes. 'Why?'

'To have a reason to imprison humans behind the Wall.'

'We are already imprisoned behind walls.'

She had a sharp and poignant memory of him the first day in R'Frow: *'What is that Wall, ten times a man's height? And the trees grow right to the base. We can leave if we want to.'*

'But not imprisoned like this, Kelovar. The humans inside the Wall are penned and . . . tortured. Delysians, soldiers – how many of Khalid's soldiers have disappeared inside the Wall?'

'Khalid's soldiers are my soldiers now,' Kelovar said, more violently than he had spoken before, and behind him the other man suddenly grinned. Ayrys looked at Kelovar's knife – she could not help herself – and fought off a wave of nausea. But perhaps Khalid had only died in the fighting by the fire. Perhaps.

'Then how many of *your* soldiers have disappeared inside the Wall? And how much could you use them now?'

She saw him considering.

'Kelovar. Who won the battle?'

'Standstill.'

'And who started – '

'It was theirs to begin with. Citizen against warrior.' His lips moved, relishing it. 'But not for long.'

'Soldiers of . . . yours are inside the Wall. I can help you get them out.'

'How?'

She couldn't tell him too much. He sickened her, frightened her, dizzied her, and she would bargain with him as hard as she dared. 'The Ged will let me inside the Wall.'

'Why?'

'I worked with them. There is a special signal for those of us who remained in the Hall of Teaching. Lahab, Dahar, me. I can enter the Wall.'

He said swiftly, 'And the two Jelite?'

'Yes. They are already inside. With . . . Lahab must be with the Jelite soldiers. Going to free them.'

'You did this "work" as much with them as with the Ged, didn't you, Ayrys? With the two Jelite. With their first lieutenant. He wasn't really stripped from their ranks at all, was he? They just wanted us to think so. And you helped him.'

Alarm coursed through her. *Ondur*. If Ondur had told Kelovar about Dahar, or even told Karim . . . Had Ondur had time to do that? Would she do that?

Ayrys made herself meet Kelovar's eyes. 'No. I never helped Jela. I worked with the Ged. And I can enter the Wall because of it. Do you want to free your soldiers, Kelovar? Do you want to enter the Wall?'

'Tell me first why you do.'

She remembered his boot smashing through her first crude invention, his jealous contempt, and was astonished to find that this deadly haggling could include the truth. This was truth Kelovar would welcome. 'The Ged betrayed me. They gave us the teaching, but never said it was to bind us, to make us trust them, until the moment they decided to imprison and torture some humans while others . . . They want to take humans aboard their ship-boats, Kelovar, the starboats they came to Qom in, and I think I've guessed why . . .' Despite herself, Ayrys faltered. *Dahar, forced again into one more betrayal of his own kind.* She caught her breath; she had not meant to falter before Kelovar, had meant to show not even the smallest weakness.

Kelovar's expression changed. He spoke a short word

to the other soldier, who immediately strode away. Squatting on his heels beside Ayrys, Kelovar reached out one hand and touched her cheek. His fingers felt sticky, but their movement was a caress.

Wrong – she had read him wrong. He preferred her weak, had always from the very beginning preferred her weak, and there was still tenderness for her weakness somewhere in what he had become. What R'Frow had made him. It was a horrible tenderness, feeding desperately on her weakness in order to feel strong. Ayrys's flesh crawled.

'No Ged slime will take you anywhere, Ayrys.'

He smelled of ash and blood. She forced herself to look at him straight. 'Will you carry me to the Wall, Kelovar? I can't walk. And I can't fight.'

'Why do you want to enter the Wall?'

'To get even for the lies. And you will get to free your soldiers. A . . . bargain.'

'No. An alliance.'

She would not let her gaze flinch. 'Yes. An alliance.' Like the Kreedogs.

'I told them you were still Delysian. I told Karim and Urwa and – all of them.' He did not put his arms around her. Instead he brought his face to within a handspun of hers, not to kiss her but to let his eyes bore into hers. Ayrys could not look away. Flecks of orange light from above slid over the top half of his light eyes, followed by shadows of branches writhing in the perverse winds. From inches away he smiled at her, a suddenly humble smile, horrible in his bloody face. 'I told Karim – '

'Stand still,' a voice said.

Ayrys felt Kelovar stiffen, fumble for his weapons, arrest the movement. His face tightened in fury. Ayrys jerked her head to peer around him, and saw why he did not move: both a red stun strip and the point of a knife touched the back of his neck.

'Rape? Or love?' Jehane said.

Ayrys stared at her.

'Which is it this time, Ayrys? *This* one' – although her voice flickered at SuSu, her hands never wavered – 'says rape. But that's not how it looks to me. So you *can* get into the Wall, Delysian whore. And I believed . . . If this is rape, I kill him and you take me to Talot. If he's your lover, I don't quite kill him and you do the same thing – or he dies. Which?'

Ayrys saw SuSu cowering at the edge of the path, away from Jehane. SuSu's terror then had been for *her*, for Ayrys. She would not go to Jehane to save Dahar, but when she thought that Ayrys had been threatened, she had hunted in desperation for the sister-warrior she hated.

And so had destroyed everything.

Jehane said again, 'Love or rape?'

Ayrys met Kelovar's eyes. She did not need him now to get to the Wall. Jehane could carry her, Jehane could fight, Jehane would be no harder, nor easier, to bargain with. Only the trade would be different. She did not need Kelovar now.

Ayrys closed her eyes to shut out Kelovar's face.

'Love,' she said, and Jehane pressed the Ged stun strip to Kelovar's neck.

63

The armless child on the island moved again. He closed his dirty feet on opposite sides of the probe and tugged. The probe let itself be dragged down. The child laughed and his black eyes shone. The old man stopped chanting and swaying to yell 'Go away!' The child ignored him.

'No respect!' the old man shouted. He picked up a small pebble and threw it at the boy. The pebble missed. The voice outside the ruined ship went on calling, 'Ali!' The child laughed again, released the probe, and flipped to his feet. As he disappeared out the door, tears of rage stood in the old man's eyes.

'They taunt me and break things. They break what's left of the machinery, what I could save . . . Their fathers never did that, my son never did that – he was brilliant, brilliant – ' He began to cough, bending his ragged body nearly double, arms clutched across his stomach. The probe moved to the machinery and began scanning it from centimeters away.

'My son,' the old man said when he could. 'They took the lander and repaired it and went to the continent because they thought the jolt of takeoff might finally crack the stasis field. It's not made for gravity. Did you see my son on the continent? A giant among men, brilliant; he showed me the stasis equations. Not like the young ones now, not like them.'

He sucked in his cheeks. The probe finished its close scan, moved back to an arm's length from the human's face. The hollows in his cheeks quivered even after his tongue released them.

He said quietly, 'The equations were wrong. Not enough jolt. Sta – '

The quivering cheeks froze.

64

Within the chamber, newly fitted as an air lock, Grax watched as Dahar and Lahab felt the lifesuits spread around them in a clear, nearly invisible layer. The wrof formed a completely flexible shield from the neck down, but did not seal to the neck; without the helmet, it was armor but not life support. Into the neckband of the clear wrof helmet were built the mechanisms, half number-rational and half semiorganic, that could indefinitely hold the atmosphere to its composition at the moment of sealing, compensating for emitted and consumed gases. The neckband also controlled temperature and pressure, and held the communications link with the Library-Mind.

In the helmets made for the humans, the link transmitted only one way.

Dahar fumbled for his knife, and could not draw it. 'I've seen you take things from inside your airtebl, Grax. But if anything goes through . . .'

'Nothing in a state of matter goes through the airtebl. But there can be accessible pockets of wrof on the outside.'

'Can be? Aren't they always there?'

'No. You will need to start again to make your weapons accessible. To remove the airtebl, the sequence is different. Like this . . . No, Lahab, that is wrong. Sing in harmony with Dahar.'

Lahab gave Grax his slow, heavy, deliberate gaze. Dahar mastered the sequence; the wrof flowed back into the flat plate. He whispered, stunned, 'In all honor . . .'

'It can be understood,' Grax said. 'It is number-rational, Dahar. You can understand it.' There was no emotion in the Ged growl. And Dahar could not smell his pheromones.

'Teach me how to create the pockets.'

Lahab still stood with the plate of wrof in his hands, holding it a little away from his body, doing nothing. Dahar drew his weapons from his belt, laid them on the ground, and again activated the wrof. Grax saw the long, deformed fingers tremble.

'Teach me.'

'You will not need pockets for your weapons aboard ship. You will not need your weapons.'

Dahar did not answer. He was fiercely absorbed in the wrof, in the teaching Grax had given him, in the teaching that was all an animal could know of Oneness.

Grax showed him how to create accessible pockets in the wrof, and Dahar turned to show Lahab.

65

Kelovar's eyes opened when the stun strip wore off. Jehane had bound him wrist to ankle. SuSu crouched beside Ayrys, and Kelovar's gaze traveled slowly over the three women, one after another. The thick orange light washed down over them, bathing them all in lurid color and casting their shadows on the wrof path that had never reflected shadows before.

'Listen to me, Delysian,' Jehane said. 'We're going into the Wall. You're going to carry *her*' – she jerked her head towards Ayrys – 'so I can fight. I have your weapons. If you decide to drop her and turn on me anyway, you die. As fast as that.'

Kelovar said nothing. His gaze continued to crawl over the three women, one after another, one after another.

'Kelovar,' Ayrys said, 'I did not plan this.'

'Shut up,' Jehane said. 'Untie him. Pull on that cord – no, *that* one!'

Ayrys did as she was told. Free, Kelovar did not attack. He stood looking from her to Jehane.

'Carry her to the Wall,' Jehane said. She held both pellet tube and heat gun trained on Kelovar. He bent down and picked up Ayrys.

The smell of blood on his tebl and body was overwhelming. Ayrys fought off nausea. In a moment he would drop her, and Jehane would kill him. Or his soldiers would come looking for their commander. But neither happened. Kelovar began walking toward the Wall, Jehane behind him. He had not said a word. Ayrys expected to see his face contorted with rage, but Kelovar walked with a set, rigid expression, his pale eyes impassive.

He did not understand what was happening.

How could he? She, Jehane, SuSu – there was no way for him to know what any of them were doing. If Jehane had killed him, he would have understood. But this he did not understand – no more than he had understood the equipment littering Ayrys's room in the Delysian hall. Nor wanted to.

Yet he carried her carefully, her hurt leg braced along his left side to jostle it less, and this concern baffled her. Was it concern? She did not know what it was.

She did not know anything. Her hand tightened on the Ged box within her tebl.

The four of them approached the Wall.

66

'Significant data, Level Matrix,' the Library-Mind repeated. 'This is a resolution of the Central Paradox. This is a resolution of the Central paradox. This is a resolution of the Central Paradox.'

Twelve Ged fighting off biological shock tried to listen over the sensory clamor of their own pheromones.

'The Central Paradox. Darkside: Species that practice intraspecies violence do not survive to reach star-drive technology. The wide genetic variations that cause their rapid evolution also cause their intraspecies violence to persist past the point of simple evolutionary selection. They blow up their planets.

'Sunside: Humans have reached star-drive technology. They are a wide genetic-variant race. They practice intraspecies violence. They did not blow up their original planet before they migrated to others.'

The Library-Mind had been growling in the configurations of observed fact. Now it switched to those of a tentative hypothesis – but the grammatical connectors said it was a wild hypothesis, flying against all reason.

'Under the right conditions, biological evolution can convert a liability into an asset. There must be some aspect of human violence that is unique to humans. There must be some aspect of human violence that *aids* their advancement even past simple selection of the most fit.'

The Library-Mind, patterned by Ged, paused. Then it

repeated the statement of what must exist – this time in
the configurations of a hypothesis proved.

67

Both Lahab and Dahar stood encased in wrof to the neck. Dahar tried the point of his Ged knife against his chest, first gently and then not; wrof turned away wrof effortlessly.

He cannot forget his violence even in his number-rational intelligence. Grax smelled his own bitterness, and handed the two humans their helmets.

Lahab held his up to eye level, squinting through the clear wrof as through a lens. Dahar fingered the neckband, where the hidden life-support 'equipment/organisms' 'lived/functioned' – not even the Library-Mind had devised an appropriate translation into human of what the life support was, or did.

Perhaps Dahar would.

'Put them on,' Grax said, and at the human harshness in his growl, even Lahab looked up.

Dahar said quietly, 'What does not sing in harmony, Grax?'

'Put on the helmets.'

They did, awkwardly. The neckband sealed itself to the lifesuit, and a spasm of panic crossed Lahab's usually stolid face. But Dahar traced the nearly invisible lines of the helmet with his fingers, and Grax recalled suddenly how Dahar's face had spasmed in the Hall of Teaching the first time he had seen human cells in the enlarger. The same.

'You can hear me,' Grax said. Both humans looked

startled at the voice inside their helmets. 'These helmets allow limited talking, within the walls of this room.'

' "These"? You mean there are helmets that allow talking through walls?'

There was no Library-Mind to ask how much he should tell the humans; Grax would not reopen his link with it. Not until he had done the shameful thing he was not going to stop himself from doing.

'Yes. There are helmets that allow talking through walls.'

'Yours?'

'Not now,' Grax said, and knew that a Ged would have been able to smell the undertones to the answer, and know what it meant. Dahar did not. Dahar was not a Ged.

'Keep your helmets on your heads. I will change the air to what fills most of the starboat.'

'Now?' Lahab said nervously. Dahar moved closer to him. Grax caught the protective movement – it was almost Ged, he told himself, and was flooded with the reek of self-disgust. He ran his fingers over an indented section of the wall. A shelf unfolded from the wrof. Grax fingered it in a complex sequence, and there was a slight whooshing sound as the air of Qom was sucked from the room and replaced with true air, thick and fresh.

68

'. . . and the lililiv,' the Library-Mind said, finishing the list of precedents of biological liabilities converted into assets. Three Ged writhed in reeking shock. But the wall screens had been turned off; two others had begun to recover.

'Within R'Frow, only twenty-six of the six hundred humans showed any response at all to number-rational science. Humans at star-drive level are assumed to be the same. Intraspecies violence destroys many of these genetically erratic minds. But humans have reached star drive. This could not happen unless intraspecies violence had become a human asset. It must not be merely at equilibrium temperature, it must be sunside, to make up for the destroyed genetic-variant intelligence.

'Equations follow. . . .'

69

'There is no door here,' Kelovar snarled. 'The door the Ged use is on the east Wall.'

Ayrys could not hear Jehane behind her, so silently did the sister-warrior move. But when she glanced around Kelovar's bulk, Jehane was there. Kelovar stood so close to the Wall that Ayrys could have reached out and touched it, but she suddenly knew that for nothing in the world would she be able to lay her fingers on that faint electro-magnetic tingle ever again.

She drew the enlarger-that-was-not from inside her tebl.

Kelovar stiffened until he saw that it was not a weapon. He did not recognize it – but SuSu did. From the corner of her eye, Ayrys saw the tiny girl, cowering behind a tree, fasten her gaze on the dark box – and then her white face dissolved, broke up. Somewhere in her terrified silence, SuSu remebered things Ayrys could not guess, brought back by the sight of the Ged box. She remembered.

'SuSu,' Ayrys said softly, 'go hide. Go to my room in the Hall of Teaching, no one will be there. . . . There will be killing here.'

Kelovar made a low noise. SuSu, her eyes on the dark box, did not move from behind her tree, and there was nothing more that Ayrys could do for her now. There was no time – there was never time! – and at any moment Kelovar might . . . Ayrys turned her face from SuSu's stricken one, toward the Wall. She spread the fingers of both hands to cover as much of the surface of the enlarger as she could, and pressed down.

The Wall went crazy. Up its entire height and for twenty lengths to each side the wrof shuddered, convulsed in waves, and began to open in crazy holes: tens of them, all perfectly round, opening and closing like the surface of boiling water. A shrieking noise tore the air, backed by a sudden cacophony of human cries from beyond the boiling holes. SuSu screamed, a high, childish wail nearly lost in the din, but Kelovar said nothing. Ayrys felt his powerful body shudder and then go rigid.

She removed one hand from the box. Half the holes sealed themselves; the others grew larger, opening and closing even more rapidly than before. Desperately Ayrys moved her fingers, trying different combinations. The holes rushed together into one jagged opening starting a meter and a half off the ground, its edges wavering and thinning like a drooling mouth. Ayrys shifted her fingers again, Jehane shouted something, and the drooling hole rose even higher, moving over the wrof out of their reach.

With shaking fingers Ayrys reversed the motion, and the traveling mouth dropped to ground level, quivering with sharp edged wrof.

Jehane shouted again. But Kelovar would not move. His rigidity had grown until his arms holding Ayrys felt like stone. She twisted to see his face; it had gone white as the barbarian's, and his pale eyes were blank as not even SuSu's had ever become.

'Kelovar! Go in!'

He did not move. He did not seem to see her. Jehane jammed her heat gun against the side of his head, and still he did not move.

Ayrys saw that he could not believe it. It was too different. It was not there.

Jehane held the gun against him while she shoved past, through the hole. Ayrys saw in her face the fraction of a second when she nearly fired. There was no reason, now, not to. But then a human scream, more piercing than the rest, rose above the shriek of alarms, and Jehane rushed through the slavering hole into the Wall.

'No,' Kelovar whispered.

'Put me down!' Ayrys said. She struggled in Kelovar's arms, but she could not break his paralyzed grip.

The hole began to close itself.

Ayrys tried again to hurl herself to the ground. But Kelovar must have seen the same thing she did: humans in invisible cages within the wall, glimpsed through the shrinking hole, and it broke his rigidity. Ayrys thought wildly, *He can understand torture*. Kelovar raced through the mouth in the Wall just before it snapped shut behind them both.

70

'. . . End equations.'

The Library-Mind left the configurations of certainty and returned to those of facts arranged into a probable pattern. 'First hypothesis: We thought when we built R'Frow that intraspecies violence meant there was no species loyalty at all. But humans within R'Frow sometimes worked in cooperation, and sometimes sang in harmony.

'Second hypothesis: We thought that humans mistakenly believed the subgroups are subspecies, "Jelite" and "Delysian," and showed species loyalty to their subgroup. But humans killed members of their own subgroups.

'Third hypothesis: Humans act with loyalty to subgroups, but the subgroups are not constant.'

There was a long pause. The Ged listening – those still capable of listening, those not in shock nor aiding those in shock nor fighting their own gene-deep nausea – had never heard the Library-Mind pause so long. It was making radical rearrangements of facts, barely within its capabilities.

'Humans act with loyalty to subgroups, but the subgroups are not constant. The 'Jelite' SuSu aided the giant of no subgroup. The "Delysian" Ayrys aided the "Jelite" SuSu and the giant. The "Jelite" Belazir helped the "Delysian" Khalid to kill a "Jelite" for whom she had sung in harmony. The "Jelite" Jehane interrupted viol-

ence toward the "Delysian" Ayrys by the "Jelite" Salah
and Mahjoub. The "Jelite" Belazir ordered violence to
the same "Jelite" by the "Delysian" Kelovar. The "Jelite"
Dahar offered medical help to the "Delysian" Ayrys, *and*
to the "Jelite" SuSu. The "Jelite" Dahar and Lahab sing
in harmony in the Hall of Teaching with the "Delysians"
Tey, Creejin, Ilabor, and Ayrys. The "Delysian"
Khalid . . .'

71

Grax watched Dahar and Lahab. Lahab made some sound, low and frightened, and Dahar spoke sharply. Lahab nodded, and did not speak again. But it was not words of comfort Dahar had offered.

They were animals.

And he himself was, too, Grax thought through the rising tide of his own pheromones. Bitterness, disgust, shame, longing – there was no way to support such contradictory smells for long before going into biological shock. He reeked to himself, and thought through his bewilderment that he *should* reek: a thought so alien he could not hold it. But no more alien than the other thought, the loathsome one he was acting on now: that number-rational intelligence could outweigh solidarity.

Until this desperate project on Qom, it had not been possible to believe that the two could ever not be the same.

That was the greatest immorality of all. There was no grammatical configuration to express it, there were no pheromones except the stinking mixture of fear and yearning and repulsion Grax smelled on himself now. To do what he was going to do, with an *animal* . . .

The exchange of oxygen-based human atmosphere for true Ged air was complete. Grax moved closer to Dahar, released his own helmet, and removed it. He breathed deeply.

But it was too late. The only pheromones in the air were his own. No trace of Dahar's remained.

72

'. . . The "Jelite" Jehane attempted to cooperate with the "Delysian" Ayrys, and was refused. The "Delysian" Kelovar killed the "Delysian" Khalid. The "Delysian" Ayrys protected the "Jelite" SuSu. The "Jelite" SuSu refused contact with the "Jelite" Jehane but did seek out the "Delysian" Kelovar. The "Jelite" Jehane . . .'

'Kelovar, I did not plan this,' said Ayrys's voice from another part of the Library Mind. 'Shut up,' said Jehane. 'Untie him . . . Carry her to the Wall.'

'They cannot get in,' said the Library-Mind, over its own recitations of the bewildering shift of human alliances within R'Frow. 'There is no way they can enter the Wall. Origin of the red hair carried by the "Jelite" SuSu is not anywhere in the memory images. Scanning again . . .'

'. . . The "Delysian" Ayrys in alliance with the "Delysian" Kelovar and the "Jelite" Jehane . . .'

73

Ayrys saw where she and Kelovar had entered the Wall, and gasped.

She had misjudged. This was not where Grax had taken Dahar, but somewhere farther west, where the itching victims were, and she had lost.

Naked men and women pushed their faces to slits in the clear wrof and shouted incomprehensibly, flailing like insects against glass. Kelovar started toward them at a run, and Ayrys pointed the dark box at the pens and pressed it. She had no more control than she had had outside the Wall, but the clear wrof reacted differently: No matter where or how she fingered the dark box, the wrof disappeared entirely. For a choking moment Ayrys wondered what would happen when the force from the dark box struck the people behind the dissolving wrof – but nothing happened. Humans swarmed into the chamber.

Jehane appeared beside Ayrys. 'This way!' she shouted over the blasting noise. 'Talot is here!'

Ayrys twisted in Kelovar's arms to look at Jehane. A Delysian woman, released from her cage and heavily pregnant, stumbled dazedly between Kelovar and Jehane. Taking advantage of the momentary screen, Kelovar dropped Ayrys, bent swiftly, and drew a hidden knife from his boot.

Ayrys landed heavily, and pain whipped through her leg. For a moment she could see nothing, and then she saw Kelovar above her with the knife. She would die then, after all, in R'Frow, with the echo of Dahar's voice mocking in her head: *You. And Kelovar*.

But Kelovar had no time for her. He straightened just as Jehane knocked the pregnant Delysian into him. He spun free, off-balance, and Jehane's shot missed. The next moment he was on her.

In avoiding a second shot from the pellet tube, he had had no time to fully recover his balance. Jehane countered to throw him even more off-balance, and they both crashed to the floor.

Time slowed down, grew as malleable and thick as molten glass, flowed in directions Ayrys had never seen. What was happening? Kelovar had dropped her two lengths away; how had she dragged herself this far, away from Jehane's battle and toward the wrof pens? The dark box still rested in her hands. Ayrys looked up – slowly, with the invisible slowness rising from the floor – and saw Talot, her red hair writhing around her naked body. Talot was shouting in her pen, but Ayrys could not hear her – nor anything else. From all that screaming and shrieking chamber within the huge perimeter, she had found her way into SuSu's silence, and it was suddenly so horrible that she pressed – slowly, slowly – the dark box.

The silent slowness shattered. Talot leaped forward, hurtling over Ayrys, toward Kelovar and Jehane. Ayrys saw the flash of Talot's long naked legs above her. And she saw the small hole that she had, at this closer range, blasted in the back of Talot's pen, in the wall to the west.

To the *west*.

Both palms flat on the floor to drag herself forward, Ayrys crawled through the hole. On the other side Dahar cried out something she could not hear – she only saw his mouth open wordlessly behind the wrof helmet of a Ged. He had become a Ged after all. He smelled Ged, the room smelled Ged, with a thick strange smell that was choking her . . . she could not breathe – the air was not breathable; this time they had altered not only the light but the air.

She tried to back out through the hole. It was gone.

Grax stood at a shelf in the wall, without a helmet. Ayrys groped for the dark box, but it was gone, she had dropped it to drag herself forward; it was sealed on the other side of the wall.

On the other side of the wall . . .

Dahar was coming toward her. But there was no time, no air, they had both shattered into red and blue shards on the stone, and all light failed.

74

'. . . the "Jelite" Jahane and the "Delysian" Ayrys and the "Delysian" Kelovar in an alliance to breach the perimeter . . .'

75

Dahar sprang toward the crumpled human Ayrys and seized her wrist. Grax saw him shouting within the helmet, but, his own helmet off, could not hear the words. He did not need to. The female was choking on real air, and Dahar's erratic solidarity with her had returned with her biological shock.

How had Ayrys breached the Wall? The pressure of Ged atmosphere was greater than that of human; already air would be leaking through the hole. The Library-Mind sealed the break; Grax watched the hole behind Ayrys swiftly close. But the Wall had somehow been breached by humans. *How?*

Grax reached to the floor for the helmet he had just laid there. It was gone.

Panic swept from him, reeking even stronger than the shame of a moment ago. He had heard the Wall's monitors shriek while Ayrys had crawled through the hole. What was happening in the perimeter? *The seventeen . . .* Grax turned toward the door at the far side of the room. But before he could move toward it, it flew open and Fregk and Krak'-gar burst through, suited and armed. Reassured, Grax's panic smell subsided and he turned back to Dahar, bent over Ayrys.

Their eyes met and held.

Black human eyes and cloudy Ged ones, and they needed neither of their languages:

Change back the air! 'She will die!

She has broken through the Wall. She is a danger to the Ged.

Grax watched Dahar's face change, watched realization twist that squirming mass of unnecessary facial muscles, and Grax's pheromones suddenly smelled of pure astonishment. Dahar thought it was *possible* for Grax to choose to help Ayrys. He actually thought it was genetically possible to choose saving a human over protecting Ged. He thought Grax might do that, could do that. He thought the Ged biologically capable of human shame.

The concept itself was almost inconceivable. It flickered at the edge of Grax's grasp and winked out, and in the second of its going, Grax knew he was the only Ged to have ever even glimpsed the full strangeness of human thought. It was more alien than any of them had thought, and more perverse than even speculative configurations could have put into speech. The Library-Mind could speculate on animal thought patterns, but for animals to expect Ged to . . .

For that, there was no grammar.

He did not even try to ward off Dahar when the human sprang.

76

'Answer to the Central Paradox: How does human violence transform into an asset to human intelligence?

'The humans shift loyalties no matter what their previous subspecies loyalties were. The mechanism they use to do this is violence. Through violence the superior minds, carrying the best technological ideas, can leave one subspecies and sing in harmony with another. The destruction of superior minds is overbalanced by erratic loyalties, in exactly the same way that the lack of solidarity is overbalanced by wide genetic variation. Without wide genetic variance in their early periods, the humans would not have evolved so fast. Without changing loyalties in their later periods, they would not have avoided planetary destruction.

'Instead, superior minds have switched loyalties to channel technology into paths that led to a star drive. The chances of this happening are small. The margin by which humans must have avoided planetary destruction by this shaky path is even smaller. In number-rational configurations . . .'

77

'She can't breathe the air!' Dahar had shouted. 'The air – change it back!' But the moment he spoke he realized that Grax could not hear him; the Ged had removed his helmet with its talking equipment.

But Grax would *know* no human could breathe this air, would know it was killing Ayrys –

A door on the far side of the room burst open and two Ged ran in. Dahar saw that although the room contained Ged air, although the two humans they had expected to find within had been named allies, although Grax had removed his helmet and could not have summoned them – despite all that, the Ged were suited and helmeted, and they held in their hands weapons different from any they had given humans in the Teaching of Defense. Grax did not look at his brothers – his gaze still held Dahar's – but he moved his hand and beside him the shelf disappeared into the wrof.

It was enough to see.

R'Frow heaved and shuddered around Dahar. Then it righted itself, blacker than before. Ayrys had been right about the Ged.

The most profound sorrow of his life pierced him, hot and sharp as a heated blade. For a moment he hated Ayrys, for making him see the loss, even more than the Ged for being that loss. She lay choking on the wrof floor beside him, that clean and precise wrof that had just slipped away from him, and Dahar's hand tightened on her sooty wrist in resentment, and rage, and loss.

Then he leaped to the wall and began pressing it with outstretched palms. Nothing he did made the shelf reappear.

Strange growling filled his helmet: the two Ged talking to each other, in the alien language he had never heard. Dahar turned on Grax.

The Ged grabbed for his helmet, but it was no longer there. Lahab had snatched it and backed into a far corner, the helmet held behind his back, his heavy face pasty with fear. Dahar thrust Grax's hand toward the wall where the shelf had been, and then wrapped both hands around Grax's neck.

He felt thin bones, in strange places, sheathed by almost no fat. The hard edge of the wrof airtebl rose high around the neck – but not high enough. Neck enough, vulnerable enough, squeezed between his hands.

'Change the air!'

Grax still could not hear him. But the other two could, and the growling in his helmet rose sharply. Grax did not move. Blackness filled Dahar's mind, a warrior's rage, and he heard himself cry out as he tightened his hands to break Grax's neck.

And could not.

Slowness overtook him, a thick slowing of time itself, so that he could not move his fingers, nor see why not. It seemed to rise from the floor and encase him, as he had encased animal specimens in wrof. Inside his helmet a voice growled, calmer than the Ged in the room, and in human: 'You are being protected. Do not struggle.'

Protected!

Grax slipped from between the fingers that would not tighten, and the other two Ged seized him. Growling they dragged him toward the door, and through it. The stasis shield began to release Dahar.

But it did so slowly, from the neck down, oozing with

its own time-altered rhythms back down into the floor. His upraised hands, with which he would have killed Grax, melted free a full minute before his legs would let him turn to where Ayrys lay dead on the floor behind him. Ayrys dead, R'Frow dying, Jela lost, and the science that had shone like every promise of the double helix fulfilled had instead led to this death, this destruction . . . There was nothing left but death and destruction, and he had caused it, he had caused Ayrys's death through his own blindness. She had been coming through the Wall for him, Dahar, brother-warrior . . . *brother-warrior* . . .

When the stasis freed his hands, Dahar grabbed into the wrof pockets Grax had helped him make and yanked out his weapons. He fired both pellet tube and heat gun at the door through which Grax had vanished. Incandescent glow blossomed at the muzzle of the heat gun. Pellets from the tube struck the door, ricocheted, and hit Dahar. Those that struck his helmet and upper body ricocheted again and filled the room with flying metal. Those that entered the receding stasis field suddenly moved slowly forward and slowly down, weird, distorted trajectories as if through melting glass.

Again and again, until the gun was empty, Dahar fired at the closed door. In the communications helmet that cut him off from all but Lahab, there was no sound but the tearing ones he made himself.

78

'. . . End applicable equations,' said the Library-Mind.

'Answer to the Central Paradox: In a species without morality or solidarity, violence aids technology by making possible the shifting of loyalties. Violence aids change.

'Change in turn brings together and makes possible the "temporary solidarity" of the most intelligent minds . . .'

79

When Jehane had seen Talot launch herself at Kelovar, a sharp thrill of pure joy sang through her: Talot was alive! But there was no time for joy. Kelovar, bigger and stronger, had straddled Jehane and raised his knife high above his head. The moment he had crashed into her, she had hurled away both pellet tube and heat gun; with his advantage in strength, he could have easily taken either away from her. Her knife was still at her waist, but Kelovar had pinned her left wrist across her body and she could not reach it. The best she could do was twist desperately to the right and fling up her left arm to take the downward slash of the blade in the forearm rather than the chest. But the blade never reached her.

Talot's kick caught Kelovar on the left side of the neck. His blade smashed into the wrof floor centimeters from Jehane's ear. She heard the sharp crack as the tip broke and the handle was wrenched from Kelovar's hand. He had not carried a Ged blade but a human one.

Jehane felt the sudden clean surge of honorable battle, as she had not felt it since she entered R'Frow. Kelovar's bulk still pinned her and his left hand still gripped her left wrist across her chest, blocking access to her knife. He fumbled for it with his right hand, and Jehane brought up her own right hand, fingers forked, and dove at his eyes.

He was too quick. He jerked to the side as Talot's hands closed around his neck from behind. But Talot was unarmed, and Kelovar grabbed her naked body and threw her forward, over his shoulder, on top of Jehane. Talot's body should have crashed into Jehane's hand as it came up for a second attempt at Kelovar's neck or chest, this time with the shattered knife tip she had had time to seize from the floor beside them. But Jehane had not attempted to slice upward. Knowing what Kelovar would do – knowing it without thought, in tendon and nerve – Jehane had instead swung her right arm low and wide along the floor. She drove the broken tip into his leg where it straddled her, into the clump of pain nerves taught to all training cadres by the warrior-priests of the double helix.

Kelovar stiffened and faltered, his face contorted by pain. He recovered fast – but not fast enough. Talot had hit the floor rolling after his over-the-body throw, and come up with Jehane's pellet tube in her hand. Before she had even stopped moving, she fired.

The pellet caught Kelovar in the forehead. He jerked convulsively and loosened his grip on Jehane, and she threw him off. But there was a moment, a brief shard of time, when he could still speak, and Jehane was not enough free of him to avoid hearing what he gasped.

'Ayrys . . .'

Fury, unrelated to simple danger, tore through Jehane. No just battles after all. There never would be again. She seized the pellet tube from Talot and killed him.

'Jehane,' Talot said, 'Jehane . . . don't, not again. He's dead.'

'I know,' Jehane said, with such force that Talot stepped back a pace. Jehane lunged forward and caught Talot in her arms, but Talot said in a strangled voice, *'The wall – '*

The wall behind what had been Talot's cage had a hole in it, and the hole was closing like some obscene metal mouth. In a last glimpse before it closed, Jehane saw Ayrys's wounded leg. In front of the wall lay the dark box the Delysian had used to get them to Talot.

'Spitslug whorish Gedshit *city*!' Jehane yelled. She grabbed Talot's hand and ran with her across the room, to the outer Wall. Delysian and Jelite, released from their pens, fought and raced and wailed over the shrieking from the walls. A mob of them held down a Ged, invulnerable in his armor but unable to escape their combined weight. Only his helmeted head was visible.

Jehane jerked to a stop, pointed the black box at the Ged's helmet, and pressed all over it as Ayrys had. She wanted to see the Ged helmet – and his head – open in boiling holes like the Wall. But nothing happened; whatever the dark box did, it didn't do it to Ged armor.

The cloudy Ged eyes stared back at her calmly.

Cursing, Jehane whirled to face the Wall and gripped the dark box with all her strength. The Wall boiled and puckered. More alarms began to shriek, the clamor became deafening, there was no sound but the Wall's blasting wails – as if, Jehane thought wildly, *it* were dying instead of Kelovar and R'Frow and Ayrys –

Ayrys. Jehane thrust her mouth close to Talot's ear and screamed, 'Go! Out the Wall! Wait for me!' She thrust Talot toward the hole she had just torn in the Wall. Others had seen it as well and scrambled toward freedom, their open mouths shouting wordlessly in the din from the alarms. Jehane raced back toward the cage from which Talot had been freed by Ayrys.

By Ayrys.

Enemy, whore, Delysian slug . . .

Jehane pointed the black box close to the floor; that was where she had seen the other hole, the one Ayrys must have made and dragged herself through, dropping the box on this side of the wall. Why? What was on the other side that Ayrys had been trying so desperately to reach?

The wrof dissolved. Jehane dropped to her knees and crawled forward. Bad air filled her lungs and reeked in her nostrils. She gasped, choked, and kept going. The wrof screened some of the clamor on the other side, enough for her to hear that someone was firing a pellet tube beyond the wall.

Enemy, whore, Delysian citizen . . .

Ayrys's body lay on the floor just beyond the wall. Jehane grabbed her ankles and pulled. As she did so, a pellet ricocheted past her ear. She could see the room clearly, and not even the Ged alarms exploded quite so noisily inside her head. The traitor Dahar stood with his back to her and his shoulders set and hunched, firing at a closed door as if he would never stop . . .

Dahar. It was for Dahar that Ayrys had come through the Wall. For a Jelite first lieutenant.

Jehane burst into a string of oaths, heard by nobody. She yanked Ayrys into the larger chamber, and kept yanking until she, Jehane, could breathe real air. Ayrys's face was white as bone. Jehane struck her in the chest, much harder than necessary to expel the bad air, until Ayrys began to sputter and gag. Then Jehane heaved Ayrys over her shoulder and started at a run for the far Wall.

The Wall had closed itself.

Naked men and women pounded on it, and it still shrieked. Jehane shifted Ayrys to point the dark box. Talot, against Jehane's orders, had appeared beside her; Talot held a knife, forced from who knew where, to cover Jehane while Jehane carried Ayrys. But Jehane would not risk Talot, not again, not so soon after losing her.

Jehane glanced behind her; a stocky Jelite citizen had just crawled from the hole behind Talot's pen, which was closing behind him. Light glinted from his head and hands – and he was wearing Ged armor. Then Dahar must have been, too, or he would have been as sick from the bad air as Ayrys. Pretend Ged, all of them – Jehane grimaced in disgust, and thrust Ayrys toward Talot. Talot took her, and Jehane screamed, 'Get the slug *out*!' If Talot had Ayrys to carry out, she would actually go herself. Jehane pointed the dark box and again opened the Wall. People leaning on it fell crazily forward.

But she, Jehane, was the crazy one.

No honorable battles. No honor, not in this shit-souled place. No honor in the first lieutenant, no honor in the Delysian soldier who had dropped Ayrys, no honor in the citizens who had killed Belazir. Then why was she doing this?

If not this – then what?

Ayrys had given her back Talot. Ayrys had gone through the Wall for Dahar. Of all the stupid and bewildering kreeshit things that had happened in this stupid and bewildering place lately, only those two – at this moment – made any sense.

Enemy, whore, Delysian slug . . .

Sister.

Shit!

Jehane ran back across the wailing room, the only one racing *away* from the outer Wall.

80

'- sis is killing us,' the old man finished. He peered from his sunken, rheumy eyes at the Ged probe. The faded star and crescent on his shoulder wrinkled as he raised his weak fist. 'Do you understand, probe? What are you? I don't even begin to understand the engineering. I who was . . . We've been in stasis Allah knows how many centuries, cut off, buried alive . . .'

He caught his breath, held it, warded off a fit of coughing. He spoke more quietly.

'Buried in stasis. Tell them *that*.'

The probe had finished its scan; it moved toward the door. The way was blocked by a woman, thin and weary. 'Ali – ' She shrank back and put her fist to her mouth.

'Tell them that,' the old man repeated. 'Stasis kills.'

81

The Library-Mind repeated its answer to the Central Paradox in changed configurations, searching for a grammar that did not exist: 'In a species without solidarity, the shifting of loyalties makes possible the "temporary solidarity" of the most intelligent minds. The "temporary solidarity" advances technological progress. Thus, in a violent species, violence aids collective intelligence.'

Silence fell. After a long while the Library-Mind – created by Ged, patterned by Ged, given the configurations of Ged poetry – said quietly, 'Violence aids intelligence.

'It poisons the pheromones of the universe.

'But it is so.'

VII
ISLAND OF THE DEAD

He makes the night seep into the day,
and the day seep into the night.
                                    —The Koran

82

Lastlight.

Ayrys opened her eyes and gasped. She lay outside R'Frow, her spine pressed to rocky ground. Above her the sky arched deep purple shot with silver. Purple – not gray but hard, rich purple that seemed to stretch away forever, without end. Two moons washed the veld with white light, and the Marker shone high and cold – impossibly high, impossibly cold. On the wind came the living smell of muddy water.

Ayrys whimpered.

'You're safe,' a voice said from behind her, and she squeezed her eyes shut against the rush of relief, of gratitude and wonder. Dahar. Alive.

When she struggled to sit, the fresh cold air slapped her like water. At the first sight of land falling away below the hillside – vast, unwalled – panic clenched in her stomach. Too much land, too much sky . . . Her fingers wound in a tuft of grass and held on.

The veld stretched to a distant horizon still faintly red with the setting sun. Above that bloody line curved the purple sky, flecked with the first stars. Below it curved hard gloom flecked with campfires, broken by hills and ravines, sliced by the winding river, silver in the moonlight. The land closest to her heaved and crawled, a great gray-green roiling as kemburi closed for Lastlight, as thornbushes quivered with spawning, as green, waxy,

half-remembered vegetable orifices rose and gaped . . .
Ayrys's skin crawled.

Another scent blew toward her: ripe dahafruit and
animal dung and the rich, subtle smell of decaying wood.
A kreedog howled.

Ayrys groped behind her with one hand until her fingers
met Dahar's. She whispered, 'How?'

'Jehane,' he said, so harshly that she turned. But the
harshness was not for her, nor for Jehane.

He sat with knees drawn to his chest, his black eyes
craters in the moonlight. Behind him burned a campfire.
SuSu crouched beside it with her back to Ayrys, a small
white stillness. Gladness flooded Ayrys. Beyond the fire
Lahab moved stolidly; beyond Lahab, not close, rose the
dark walls of R'Frow, blotting out the sky. The fire
crackled and snapped, a smokeless hot glow in the dusk.

Ayrys turned herself to face Dahar, although the movement made her leg throb. Just out of reach she saw a
kemburi closing for the night. Thick hairy coils snaked
over the ground. Ayrys looked away, at Dahar.

'Jehane . . . opened the Wall?'

'Yes.'

'Dahar – '

'I stand with her on the blade of honor for my life. And
yours,' he said formally, and Ayrys had the sudden fear
that he was going to put formality between them, and
make of it yet another wall.

She said deliberately, 'The blade of honor is for warriors. Not for you.'

But he didn't even flinch, and she saw that he had
already arrived at that ground, and gone past it to that
place where not even mockery was left. She knew that
place; she had been there.

'What we learned of Ged science,' she said as steadily
as she could, 'we still know.' Even as she growled the
Ged word, she had to fight off dizziness: *science*, here on
this crawling veld darkening into night . . .

Dahar said, 'And what we learned of Ged treachery, we still know.'

She said nothing. The distant fires brightened and a new one, much closer than the rest, flared beside a jagged outcropping of rock to her left.

'And what you learned of Jelite treachery you won't forget either, will you, Ayrys? I chose between the Ged and you, and I chose the Ged. As you did not. Why did you come after me?'

'I chose to,' she said, and this time her voice was as harsh as his. She moved to drag herself closer to him, and pain stabbed through her leg.

Instantly he was beside her. 'Don't move – don't jolt the bone. Does that hurt?'

'Only a little.'

He ran both hands over her leg, probing and she remembered that first night when he had set the bone, slipping into her room with a Ged thumblock, mistaken for Kelovar.

She saw that he, too, remembered. His hands stopped moving. 'Kelovar is dead.'

Her mouth went dry. 'You?'

'Jehane.'

'I'm glad it wasn't . . . wasn't you.'

'No. The only one I tried to kill was Grax.'

Ayrys shivered. The cold ground pressed against the backs of her legs. A redfly lit on her arm, bit, stung. Her fingers tightened on Dahar's.

SuSu turned her head but did not leave the fire. In the purple gloom Ayrys couldn't read the girl's expression. SuSu turned back, and Ayrys saw that she stared at the walls of R'Frow.

'Don't look at it,' Dahar said, and at the tone of his voice she shivered again. 'Not yet.'

'Not what yet?'

'The sister-warrior wants to talk to you alone.'

A figure had started from the new fire toward Ayrys:

Jehane. Dahar released her hand. She clutched at him, suddenly afraid he would not come back.

Dahar stiffened under her clutching. 'I love you,' he said angrily. In the anger she heard pain, not that she should doubt him but that she was justified in doing so. He strode out of earshot and stood with his back to R'Frow, staring at the fires scattered across that dizzying rush of land roiling toward the bloody sky.

'We are quit now, Delysian,' Jehane said. She stood above Ayrys, legs braced belligerently apart, but her voice was quiet, without rancor. 'You helped me get Talot out of R'Frow, and I helped you get . . . *him.*'

'Dahar,' Ayrys said. But Jehane did not want to fight. She squatted beside Ayrys, who thought how much her face had changed from that young sister-warrior traveling across the veld a scant year ago.

'Tell me what happened, Jehane. Everything.'

Jehane did, briefly and factually, without emotion. When she was done, Ayrys said, 'You could have left me in R'Frow. Dahar, too. He was sealed in the perimeter, he was a disgraced brother-warrior.'

Jehane did not answer. But she looked at Ayrys, a long look neither broke. Finally Ayrys said softly, 'I think there are other humans, Jehane. Out there in the sky where the Ged starboats go.'

Jehane considered, then shrugged. 'So what? They aren't here.' After a moment she added, 'I didn't get him for you. For me.'

'I know,' Ayrys said, surprised to find that in some way, some wordless glimpse through the labyrinthine walls of Jelite honor, she did.

Jehane stood, dusting off her hands.

'Talot still has the itching disease,' Ayrys said.

'Yes. But he says it will go away when Firstmorning comes. In the sunshine.'

'Where will you and Talot go?'

'Back to Jela.'

'Jela and Delysia will soon be at war again.'

'Yes.'

'You will be made leader of a cadre.'

'Yes,' Jehane said, almost angrily. And then. 'I didn't make this war.'

'But you will fight it.'

'I'm a sister-warrior. And so is Talot. Good-bye, Ayrys.'

'Good-bye, Jehane.'

Jehane strode toward her fire. After a few paces, she stopped to speak without turning, over her shoulder. 'Don't let Dahar take you near the war. Go somewhere else.'

'Where else?'

'*Anywhere* else!' Jehane snapped. 'If you can figure out who lives up in the sky, you can figure out somewhere to go down here!'

She stalked toward her fire. Ayrys found herself smiling.

It seemed a long time before Dahar returned to where Ayrys sat. SuSu, too, sat unmoving, staring at R'Frow with eerie intensity. Ayrys grew cold and hungry. It was Lahab who brought her something to drink, kemwood-leaf tea heated over the fire in a large clear bowl, which she would also have to use as a drinking cup. Lahab's face was stolid, the same broad, impassive look she had seen him wear daily in the Hall of Teaching.

The bowl was a Ged helmet.

The stars came out, cold and sharp on clear black. Ayrys stared at them, craning her neck, and her throat grew thick. How had she forgotten? . . . The familiar constellations mocked her: the Scimitar; Kufa; the Ship with its glowing red star. Spheres of exploding gases; souls from the Island of the Dead. Frost tipped the grasses beside her. She couldn't stop shivering.

Dahar returned to carry Ayrys closer to the fire, his

face strained with expectations she did not understand. SuSu didn't glance at either of them.

'Dahar, what is it, what are you and SuSu waiting for?'

'You're cold. I should have thought . . . You don't have to be cold. Look.' On his hand he held a small flat plate of wrof.

Ayrys touched it with one finger.

'We have no burnous,' Dahar said, too steadily. 'You can't move around much yet, and you've grown used to warmth. Lie still, Ayrys.'

He showed her how to put on the Ged armor. She had a moment of panic when it closed around her, but then she felt neither the damp ground nor the cold. She was as warm as she had been in R'Frow.

'Lahab has one, too. He can share it with SuSu.'

Ayrys looked more closely; the faint shimmer of wrof already glinted around SuSu.

Dahar suddenly raised his head. A low rumbling trembled on the air, coming from R'Frow. Dahar had set her down facing R'Frow; watching Ayrys, he faced away from the city.

The rumbling grew louder, and began to rise in pitch. At the top edge of R'Frow, light appeared. Dahar clenched his fists. Ayrys saw him not turning to look behind him, and that the not turning was taking all the strength he had.

In that rising glow, SuSu suddenly appeared in front of Dahar, her small body taut and her black eyes opaque as polished stone. But her voice was firmer than Ayrys had ever heard it.

'I claim the blade of honor. I brought Ayrys the . . . the thing she needed to open the Wall for you. What is freely given must be freely returned.'

Lahab turned his head to stare at the Jelite whore.

SuSu did not waver. In the unnatural brightness shining from R'Frow, her tiny face looked carved in white rock. To Ayrys, sitting on the ground below SuSu and Dahar, the very air looked white, spun from glass as fragile as the blue and red double helix spiraling from city council hands off into exile. What spiraled between Dahar and SuSu was also, for a brother-warrior and a Jelite whore, a kind of exile.

Ayrys gripped her right hand with her left.

SuSu repeated, 'What is freely given must be freely returned.'

Dahar stood. The light at the top of R'Frow suddenly brightened to a brilliant white, turning the veld bright as day. At the other fire, Talot cried out. Still Dahar did not turn. His back rigidly to R'Frow, he said to SuSu, 'What is freely given must be freely returned.'

Ayrys groped with her wrof-clad hand toward his boot; he didn't notice.

The rumbling scaled sharply to a high whine. The white light arced slowly upward across the sky. As it rose, all of R'Frow suddenly bloomed into a brilliance that forced Ayrys to close her eyes and cover them with her hand.

The ground beneath her jolted, a deep, sudden shifting that seemed to come from the heart of Qom. Ayrys was flung to the ground. She saw a tree dip and crack and then the ground shook again, even harder. From all across the veld rose a terrified wail, not animal, topped by the sudden sharp scream of kemburi. The coals of the fire shook apart, flying red stars. One landed on the frosty grass beside Ayrys and smoked.

Then it was over. The ground stayed still, and nothing blocked the stars where R'Frow had stood.

Into the silence after noise, SuSu said clearly, 'I want to go where *he* came from. The white giant. I want you to take me there. You and Ayrys. What is given must be returned.'

SuSu faced the empty hill where R'Frow had been. She continued to look at Dahar, and in the flat black eyes Ayrys saw nothing of the jolt that had just torn the earth, nothing of the Ged city's destruction. Had she seen so much that was incomprehensible, thought Ayrys dazedly, that nothing now could make her wonder, or make her afraid? If that was so, Ayrys did not know which she felt: pity or envy. But SuSu needed neither.

Lahab methodically began to rebuild the scattered fire. Dahar said, 'Which way is the giant's city? Did he tell you?' At the tone in his voice, Ayrys tightened her grip on his boot.

SuSu pointed her fingers and bent her hand upward at the wrist. The fingers rose in a high, clean arc.

Dahar looked at Ayrys, who shook her head. 'I don't know. The giant did that when he was dying. He seemed to be trying to tell us something. I don't know what.'

Dahar said wearily, 'I can't take you to the giant's city if I don't know in which direction it lies.'

'That direction.' She pointed toward the veld below. Campfires scattered by the earthquake – if that's what it had been – blossomed again. Once more Ayrys felt the black swoop of vertigo at the vast darkness, the huge unwalled stretch of open wildness.

'That way lie Jela and Delysia,' Dahar said. 'If they still stand.'

SuSu said, 'Beyond.'

'Beyond is only the sea.'

'There is the Island of the Dead,' said Lahab from his fire, laborer and citizen and the only lens scientist in the world.

This world.

Ayrys felt the rigidity in Dahar's body, every muscle taut with the terrible pointless tension of hopelessness. He said. 'There is no way to reach the Island of the Dead. The giant could not have come from there. There is nowhere to go. Lahab, you at least should return to Jela.'

'No,' Lahab said. He glanced sideways from hooded eyes at SuSu.

Ayrys saw how it would be: the four of them moving aimlessly over the veld, along the river, traveling roughly on foot, competing for food with kreedogs and kemburi, going nowhere. While somewhere out there in the stars, other humans . . . they would walk from Firstmorning through Lastlight, covering as much ground as they could in Qom's long, unnatural day, sleeping as much as they could through Qom's long, unnatural night. Cold and hungry and aimless. Exiles.

She struggled to stand, pulling herself up with Dahar's hand. Her leg in its wrof lifesuit throbbed less than before. Dahar put his arm around her, and at that touch and support, comfort in the alien night, the knot in her throat eased a little.

Over the veld, a star flew toward them.

Lahab sank to his knees. The star grew to a powerful white light, traveling at immense speed. As it flew overhead Ayrys gaped at an underside of battered metal, painted with a crescent moon and three stars thrown into sharp relief by the bright light. Dahar drew a jagged breath. Then the flying metal had passed overhead and again become a single intense receding light.

It slowed, hovered, and descended into the black place that had been R'Frow.

Lahab stumbled to his feet and moved closer to Dahar. 'Ged?'

Dahar didn't answer. He leaned forward, taut as stretched wire, burning with electricity. Ayrys stood stricken, unable to speak. Only SuSu remained unmoved, her black eyes opaque as stones.

In the distance the light rose again and flew back toward their fire, the blaze closest to R'Frow. The metal starboat stopped forty lengths away, hovered, and began to fall. There was no noise when it touched ground. The bright light was joined by another, feebler light as an unseen door slid open.

Two men emerged. Men . . . *humans*. They walked forward slowly, carrying weapons Ayrys had never seen, but not raising them. She tightened her hand on Dahar's shoulder. He drew neither pellet tube nor knife.

As the two men approached, Ayrys saw by the powerful strange light that one had a huge, hairless head wobbling on a neck too small to hold it steady. On his left shoulder, beside the head, grew a mass of deeply wrinkled and purplish skin like a second, battered head. Her gorge rose. The other man looked both normal and hairy, his long dark hair plaited in dozens of tiny separate braids.

SuSu made a small sound.

The two men stopped ten lengths away. The one with the wobbly head said clearly, 'We come from the island. From the ship *Star of Mecca*. And in peace.'

A deep shudder ran through Dahar, like a current released. He picked up Ayrys and signaled to Lahab. Lahab took SuSu's hand, and the four of them walked forward to meet the other humans through the alien night.

A Selection of Legend Titles

☐ Eon	Greg Bear	£3.50
☐ Forge of God	Greg Bear	£3.99
☐ Falcons of Narabedla	Marion Zimmer Bradley	£2.50
☐ The Influence	Ramsey Campbell	£3.50
☐ Wyrms	Orson Scott Card	£3.50
☐ Speaker for the Dead	Orson Scott Card	£2.95
☐ Seventh Son	Orson Scott Card	£3.50
☐ Wolf in Shadow	David Gemmell	£3.50
☐ Last Sword of Power	David Gemmell	£3.50
☐ This is the Way the World Ends	James Morrow	£4.99
☐ Unquenchable Fire	Rachel Pollack	£3.99
☐ Golden Sunlands	Christopher Rowley	£3.50
☐ The Misplaced Legion	Harry Turtledove	£2.99
☐ An Emperor for the Legion	Harry Turtledove	£2.99

Prices and other details are liable to change

Bestselling SF/Horror

☐ Forge of God	Greg Bear	£3.99
☐ Eon	Greg Bear	£3.50
☐ The Hungry Moon	Ramsey Campbell	£3.50
☐ The Influence	Ramsey Campbell	£3.50
☐ Seventh Son	Orson Scott Card	£3.50
☐ Bones of the Moon	Jonathan Carroll	£2.50
☐ Nighthunter: The Hexing		
& The Labyrinth	Robert Faulcon	£3.50
☐ Pin	Andrew Neiderman	£1.50
☐ The Island	Guy N. Smith	£2.50
☐ Malleus Maleficarum	Montague Summers	£4.50

Prices and other details are liable to change

Bestselling Thriller/Suspense

☐ Skydancer	Geoffrey Archer	£3.50
☐ Hooligan	Colin Dunne	£2.99
☐ See Charlie Run	Brian Freemantle	£2.99
☐ Hell is Always Today	Jack Higgins	£2.50
☐ The Proteus Operation	James P Hogan	£3.50
☐ Winter Palace	Dennis Jones	£3.50
☐ Dragonfire	Andrew Kaplan	£2.99
☐ The Hour of the Lily	John Kruse	£3.50
☐ Fletch, Too	Geoffrey McDonald	£2.50
☐ Brought in Dead	Harry Patterson	£2.50
☐ The Albatross Run	Douglas Scott	£2.99

Prices and other details are liable to change